Street's of Hope

Book Three
'The Lizzie Series'

J. Robert Whittle

By J. Robert Whittle

The Lizzie Series

Lizzie: Lethal Innocence
Lizzie's Secret Angels
Streets of Hope

*

Victoria Chronicles

Bound by Loyalty
Loyalty's Reward (2003)

*

By J. Robert Whittle and
Joyce Sandilands

Leprechaun Magic

Street's of Hope

ଈଔଔଈ

J. Robert Whittle

If you are unable to obtain a copy of this book in your local bookstore, please contact Whitlands Publishing.

Whitlands Publishing Ltd.
4444 Tremblay Dr.,
Victoria, BC V8N 4W5
Tel: 250-477-0192

www.whitlands.com or www.jrobertwhittle.com
email: info@whitlands.com or robert@jrobertwhittle.com

Original cover artwork by Barbara Porter
Cover design by Jim Bisakowski.
Back cover photo of Mr. Whittle by Terry Seney

National Library of Canada Cataloguing in Publication Data

Whittle, J. Robert (John Robert), 1933-
  Streets of hope / J. Robert Whittle.

  (The Lizzie series ; 3)
  ISBN 0-9685061-5-1

  I. Title. II. Series.
PS8595.H4985S77 2002   C813'.54   C2002-911127-7
PR9199.3.W458S77 2002

--

Printed and bound in Canada by
Friesens Printing, Altona, MB

iv

To Shayla,
a special granddaughter
whose vibrant personality
reminds me of Lizzie, and
sparkling approach to life,
keeps me young.

Acknowledgements

The past four years have been a fascinating, albeit unexpected literary journey, enabling my wife, Joyce, and I to meet thousands of delightful people from all walks of life and dozens of countries. Whether they have heard of J. Robert Whittle and his books did not often seem to matter, they were impressed with our undertaking and wanted to provide their moral and/or financial support.

We are exceedingly grateful for our many thousands of readers who come from the far reaches of Canada, each of the United States, and over 30 other countries. We are now delighted to inform our fans that you have made *Lizzie: Lethal Innocence* a Canadian Bestseller!

Thanks also to those who tell me I must continue to write; our families and friends for their understanding; and the growing number of teachers, home-schoolers, and families who love to read together, for choosing our titles; your encouraging words press us ever onward.

Thanks to our team of professionals who are always nearby when we most need them: Barbara Porter, for capturing the flavour of Lizzie's dockland in her awe-inspiring cover; our graphic designer, Jim Bisakowski, for his year-round assistance and advice, and for transforming Barbara's original art into another magical cover; Deborah Wright, our proofreader with the magic pen; and Carey Pallister, once again for her honest critique.

When Joyce and I began this journey 4 years ago, we printed 500 copies of *Lizzie: Lethal Innocence* and wondered how long we would be warehousing them in our basement. We had no concept of what was in store for us as our arduous schedule was yet to begin. It is often said that true reward only comes through hard work ... it's genuinely remarkable when one can admit that their hard work has also been a heap of fun, thanks to the love and support of so many.

Sadly, our dearest fan, supporter, and oft companion, Joyce's mother, Dorothy, passed away suddenly this summer leaving a large void in our lives. In April, Dorothy accompanied us to the UK on a research trip for *Streets of Hope* and future Lizzie volumes—her eager enthusiasm, and energetic spirit, will always be with us, especially as we remember that happy journey.

J. Robert 'Bob' Whittle, November 2002
robert@jrobertwhittle.com

Main Characters (in order of appearance)

Lizzie Short – a Londoner, partner in TLS Co.
Quon Lee – Lizzie's friend; partner in TLS Co.
Joe Todd – Lizzie and Quon's adopted father; partner in TLS Co.
Martha Johnson – Joe's Yorkshire housekeeper and cook
Ada Mason – TLS bookkeeper; mother of 5-year-old Willie
Mick O'Rourke –TLS yard foreman
Captain Johann Davis – captain of government excise ship, *Falcon*
One-Eyed Jack – first mate on government excise ship, *Falcon*
Clem Radcliff – baker
Richard Dixon – corn miller
Bill and Connie Johnson – Yorkshire baker and his wife
Billy, Tom Day, Olivera O'Mara – bakery delivery lads
Angus McClain – Scottish brewery manager
John Watson – master maltster
Margaret Sutton – daughter of Lord and Lady Sutton
Nathan Goldman – Jewish businessman, cousin to Abe Kratze
Dan and Wick – gypsy drivers/bodyguards to Nathan Goldman
Charley Mason – TLS engineer, Ada's brother-in-law
Grey and Green Grim – twins who work for TLS and Charley Mason
Jeb Dark – local gypsy leader
Lady Penelope Sutton – wife of the late, Lord John Sutton
James Sutton – businessman
Abe Kratze – Jewish tailor and teacher
Tom Legg (Pegleg) – retired mariner
Captain Benjamin Thorn – captain working for government & TLS
Joshua Thorn – cousin of Ben, clerk at Crowther Shipping
Ned Cabin – office clerk with TLS
Sam West – stagecoach driver
Chew Fong Lim and Fung Won Chow – Chinese Doctors
Jessy Jones – school teacher

Main Characters (cont'd)

Jacob Tide – Bishop of Chester
Jonas Crowther – corn merchant and councillor
Captain Gabriel Flood – army officer and banker's son
Clara Spencer – dressmaker
Frank Firth – flour miller
Sidney Sweeney – butcher
Walter Groves – wine cellarman at the Bishop's Palace
Cuthbert Dunbar – printer
Frederick Monk – printer
Sir David Walton – Admiralty officer
Admiral Joseph – Admiralty officer and councillor
Joel Ridley – highwayman
Patch Morse – highwayman
Slink Ridley – highwayman
Wallace Dawson – grain shipper
Minnie Harris – Wallace Dawson's sister
Alexander Harris – son of Minnie Harris
Josiah Cambourne – printing magnate
Simon Cambourne – son of Josiah Cambourne
Captain Elijah Harmon – grain merchant
Judge Aurelius Harvey – judge and councillor
Albert Potter – artist and councillor
Arthur Miller – wool merchant and councillor
Patrick Sandilands – Scottish rag merchant

Streets of Hope

Chapter 1 - 1808

"You're awfully quiet this morning, young lady. What's wrong, Liz?" asked Ada, looking over at the beautiful, auburn-haired young woman staring off into space.

"Oh no, nothing is wrong, Ada. I was just thinking ... thinking about the day you and Mick got wed."

"My goodness that seems like a lifetime ago, doesn't it?" returned Ada, sighing deeply. "So much has happened in those ... good gracious, almost two years! What a wonderful surprise you gave us. And that Captain Davis, we barely knew him back then ... he can be quite the gentleman when he wants to impress!"

"I remember he looked awfully handsome in his blue uniform," Martha, the housekeeper, chuckled.

"Yer managed to tame that rough sea captain didn't yer, luv," added Joe from his chair by the hearth, "and he's the better for it, too!"

"It was amazing where you and Quon found all those people ... such a shock when Mick and I saw them all lined up on the dock, wasn't it dear?" she mused, patting her husband's hand as a faraway look came into her eyes. "And that party ... the gypsy music was simply marvelous. I didn't think my head would ever stop spinning from all the dancing!"

For a long minute there was absolute silence in the cottage as if everyone was remembering that day when Ada and Mick returned from their three-day wedding cruise aboard the government ship *Falcon*. The surprise party had begun on the dock where their many friends and acquaintances had gathered to welcome the newlyweds home. Nathan Goldman and Abe Kratze, the Jewish cousins, had dressed in their finest attire, and the lowly bread delivery lads were spit-polished in their new, second-hand clothes raided from the rag shed with Quon's help.

Present also were many ex-mariners who had been integrated into the TLS Company in some invented capacity in order to give them back their self respect. They were proud and eager to be earning a modest living, despite their missing limbs or grotesque war injuries, and many a hardened sailor cast a silent tear in gratitude that day.

During those two years, the TLS Company's dockland empire continued to flourish. The once-street waifs who had adopted Joe Todd so many years ago had become his partners ... and his life. Lizzie Short, now nearing the age of 18, and Quon Lee, 17, as near as anyone could guess, were becoming quite well known, a situation Quon was not comfortable with at all. If rumours could be believed, there was a growing resentment building among the less scrupulous who ran businesses in the area.

Although now married, the O'Rourkes remain part of Joe's closely knit family which also includes Martha, their cook and housekeeper. Ada's son, Willie, whose father, a navy lieutenant, was mortally wounded in a sea battle against Napoleon's navy when he was a mere baby, is now a robust five-year-old. Martha's youngest charge, Willie keeps her company during the day while his parents work at the TLS offices nearby. They often take meals at Joe's cottage arriving early to feast on one of Martha's famous breakfasts.

Ada, a former schoolteacher before her earlier marriage, had long ago begun teaching the boy the rudiments of education. He was a happy little lad, growing in leaps and bounds as children tend to do, enjoying the carefree life in and around the cottage with its many animals and diverse businesses nearby. However, he still loved to spend time at the cottage with his idol, the only grandfather he would ever know, and often slept over when his parents worked late.

Today was one of those occasions and Willie had woken up to find himself at granddad's. As he came tearing into the room looking for Joe, the old man was pretending to look for him behind a chair.

"Granddad, I'm here!" he giggled, running by just beyond Joe's reach.

Martha turned her huge frame, picked up a wooden spoon and set off toward the boy, waving it menacingly as Joe sought his chair.

"Save me, Granddad! Save me!" Willie screamed, leaping into Joe's arms sending his chair rocking wildly.

The housekeeper came closer, then stopped and lay down her spoon going over to tickle the pair which caused Willie's screams to turn into uncontrolled laughter. Wriggling wildly, Joe set him down on the floor and he finally managed to escape Martha's unrelenting fingers.

Quon Lee's hand talk spoke a silent message to Lizzie as she scooped up the giggling youngster and hugged him tightly.

"Yer right, dumplin, his laughter *is* worth all the gold in England."

A few minutes later, Ada and Mick arrived and the wedding became the topic of conversation.

"Sure and don't forget it was the first time we saw our Liz all dressed up in her new dress," chuckled Mick, breaking into everyone's thoughts. "Remember, Ada luv, we didn't even recognize Quon Lee!"

Everyone laughed and Quon's face went red as a beet-root as he remembered the silly clothes he had been forced to wear by Abe Kratze's friend, Emma Burton.

"Something I'll always remember," Ada added, "was Jeb's comment that his people were being domesticated by Lizzie and liking it! I wonder what we would do without them now. Those gypsies have become an integral part of our lives."

"Sure and begorra, that is mighty true," agreed Mick, in his lilting Irish brogue, as each of them savoured their own memories.

Lizzie's thoughts were perhaps the most profound, spinning quickly through the almost eight years since she had found Joe lying on the street battered and bleeding from a carriage accident.

In the beginning, the gypsies had become involved in their lives by supplying stock for the slaughterhouse, but since the formation of the TLS Company (an abbreviation of Todd, Lee and Short) the gypsies had made themselves indispensable as guardian angels to the young partners.

In the past two years, Jeb and his men had been called upon several times—to escort the young partners out to their Hertfordshire farm—the purpose, other than as a holiday, was unknown to the rest of the family although several harboured their own suspicions. Here they spent some of the happiest days of their young lives visiting the orphanage children—the nine secret angels Lizzie and Quon had rescued and called their own. Being able to see how the once frail, mistreated little orphans had grown strong and happy under the loving care and attention of their teacher, Jessy Jones, and the gypsies, made Quon and Lizzie exceedingly happy.

Suddenly, Lizzie jumped to her feet and headed for the door pulling her coat off its hook.

Quon, taken by surprise, scrambled to follow.

"Look out, Willie!" Joe called. "Ther off, lad."

Springing off the old man's knee, the boy tore around the table.

"Wait for me, I need hugs!" he screamed, grabbing Quon's legs.

Laughing, the Chinese lad picked him up and threw him into the air. As the giggling youngster returned to his arms, Quon hugged him quickly then set him back down. "Willie getting too heavy for Quon!" he groaned playfully, pretending to be hurt, then wacking the boy's behind affectionately.

In the doorway, Lizzie knelt on the floor waiting. When the boy turned toward her, she opened her arms and he rushed into them.

"Oh Willie!" she whispered. A tear escaped from her eye and she quickly wiped it on the shoulder of his shirt, as thoughts of her angels came to mind. Then she steered him into Martha's waiting arms and quietly closed the door.

It was the last week in February and Lizzie and Quon followed their usual pattern going down Water Lane toward the Thames docks. Church bells calling the faithful to worship announced it was Sunday in dockland and shops were closed. Although there was less traffic to be dodged there were plenty of people about enjoying the unusually warm winter day as they went to and fro to worship or made family outings. As they walked, they found themselves often exchanging greetings with those they passed.

Even from a block away, they could see there was a full contingent of ships in dock, many having arrived since their last visit late yesterday afternoon. Trying to count their masts, the new arrivals included a three-masted barque, two brigs, a schooner, and farther down at the government wharf were two small frigates. Dodging a lumbering, dust-covered coach, they crossed Dock Street and made their way onto the wharf, moving amongst tall stacks of cargo.

They were surprised to find Charley Mason's horseless cart empty. Neither he nor the Grim brothers were anywhere to be seen. Concern tugged at Lizzie's mind and she quickened her pace, but Quon had already noticed her concern.

"Dare!" he exclaimed, pointing down the row of ships to the deck of the *Falcon* where Charley and Captain Davis could be seen deep in conversation.

Creeping slowly forward, their thoughts of surprising the men were quickly dispelled when the booming voice of One-Eyed Jack rang over the quay.

"Visitors comin aboard, captain!"

Looking up, Lizzie saw Jack waving from the upper deck.

"Come aboard, lass," Davis growled from the rail, pulling his hat down further to shade his eyes against the rising sun.

At the top of the gangway Lizzie stopped. "Are you working today, Charley?

"No lass, just talking. An idea I have ... I wanted to talk to a man of the sea about it."

Lizzie's brow wrinkled from squinting, as she often did when thinking. "Is it to do with us ... and ships?" she asked, abruptly.

Captain Davis' booming laughter interrupted them. "May as well tell her, lad. She won't stop 'till she knows!"

Charley rolled his eyes. "Well, a week ago a ship came in loaded with grain from Hull. The captain informed me that grain in the area was very cheap as all the local markets were swamped with it; exporting by sea was out of the question as the cost of bagging and loading made the process too slow and expensive." He stopped, watching their reaction.

"Is it the right stuff for making whisky?" she asked.

"Yes ...," said Charley, scratching his head, wondering if she had heard a word he said. "But the labour costs are too high," he repeated.

Quon's hands went wild. Lizzie nodded and grinned.

"Well, what did he say?" asked the engineer.

"Oh, he just answered yer question for ya," she giggled coyly, dropping back into the rough street talk of her youth. "He reckons yer the engineer, Mister Mason ... and if yer any good at what ya do, yer'll solve it yerself!"

Captain Davis burst out laughing and Charley threw one of his walking sticks at Quon who caught it deftly and handed it back.

Lizzie jumped to her feet and strode toward the gangway with Quon right behind. Over her shoulder, she threw a challenge to Charley. "Better solve it, lad. It's business we need so don't take too long!"

The words had no sooner left her lips when a loud bang rent the air followed by the sound of hissing steam. The alarmed shouts from the nearby Kings Dock drew their attention to a plume of smoke rising into the still morning air.

Lizzie and Quon moved along the dock joining the group of onlookers. Some minutes later, another loud boom reverberated against the buildings, this time like an explosion. A shout from behind alerted them to the arrival of Charley and his boys as they pushed their way through the crowd.

"What happened?" asked Charley, from atop his cart as Captain Davis pushed past them.

Lizzie and Quon climbed up behind Charley to get a better view. When the disinterested crowd began to move away, they could see Davis conversing with another man. He beckoned them to come closer. Warily, the Grim boys edged the cart past the last of the onlookers coming to a halt beside the captain and a man they recognized only slightly.

"Bloody hell! It's a steam engine!" exclaimed Charley, impatiently banging his stick on the side of his cart.

The Grims rushed to his side and lifted him down. As soon as his feet touched the ground, he could hardly contain himself and quickly wobbled over to examine the equipment. Charley's fingers gently caressed the now-useless engine.

Lizzie and Quon, remaining in the background, looked at each other and raised their eyebrows. Davis and the stranger watched in fascination. Finally, the captain interrupted the engineer's thoughts.

"Charley, I want you to meet Clem Radcliff, the owner of this ill-fated machine."

Turning remarkably quickly for a man on sticks, Charley threw a beaming smile at the crestfallen owner. Glancing over at the young partners, he winked, then stuck out his hand.

Radcliff apparently didn't share his enthusiasm and his hand remained at his side. An average, working man in most respects, Clem Radcliff was middle-aged and clean-shaven; his solemn face now deeply portrayed his thoughts even before he spoke.

"Lost it all ah av, an just when ah thought ah were winnin," he muttered, sadly tipping his flat cap back further on his head.

"Will it repair, lad?" Lizzie asked quietly.

Radcliff's eyes glazed over and his voice whimpered slightly. "'Av no funds, girl. No, 'am done fer."

Charley interrupted with a barrage of questions snapping them out so quickly he didn't even give the poor man time to answer. "So what made it blow up?" he repeated, impatiently.

"Too much pressure, ah guess," Radcliff replied, slowly.

Excitement now completely overtook Charley's caution. "Want to sell it for scrap? I'll find you a buyer and you can walk away."

Clem raised his head, his face a study in misery.

Quon Lee's hands began to move slowly then pick up speed as Lizzie watched.

"You want it do you, Charley?" she asked. Receiving a smile in acknowledgement, she continued, "Then let's see what can be done."

Clem Radcliff looked startled, his eyes opening wide as he struggled for words. "I'm not dealing with a woman, much less a young lass!"

Taking a step closer, Lizzie whispered, "Are ya afraid, Mister Radcliff? Why man, you've nothin to sell." Moving back to Charley's side, she spoke quietly so no one else could hear, "Can it be repaired, Charley?

The engineer pensively rubbed his hand back and forth over his chin and began to circle the engine again coming to stand behind the young partners.

"It needs a blow hole with weights but then it'll never blow up again," he replied, quietly. If my idea works, it'll save the labour of 20 men and empty a grain ship in half a day!"

Lizzie glanced sideways at her partner. Their eyes met and held. Quon's hands began to move but stopped as they were interrupted by two passing soldiers.

Noticing the torn end of the boiler, one of them laughed. "Damned new-fangled machines, should ban 'em all I say!"

His partner agreed and they continued on their way.

"Now!" said Lizzie, in an irritated manner. Turning back to Clem Radcliff, she continued. "I've wasted enough time on yer, lad. A guinea for yer scrap iron ... yes or no?"

"But, but ...," Radcliff wailed.

Charley hid his amusement by turning away.

"Yes or no?" the girl repeated, flicking a gold coin toward Quon.

Nodding his head as though in a trance, Clem shuffled his feet uneasily. Davis, who had been quietly watching the whole procedure, glowered, then sprang into action.

"Damn it, Radcliff," he said impatiently, "save yourself some pain. That's Lizzie Short you're talking to. It's a fair deal and you know it."

Clem's head came up sharply and his eyes flickered between Davis and Lizzie. Quon glanced over at his partner again. She nodded and he dropped the golden guinea into Davis' waiting palm.

Davis turned back to Radcliff and, taking the man's hand, slapped the gold coin into it. "Deal done!" he snarled. "Now listen to her, lad, 'cause there's more to her tale yet, I'll be bound."

Charley chuckled.

"W-w-what am I-I ta do n-n-now?" Radcliff asked, barely able to summon the words.

Charley waved his stick to call the Grim boys. As they assisted him into his seat, Davis continued his assault on Radcliff.

"Mark my words, you'll do right to listen to what this girl has to say." Turning to Lizzie, he tipped his hat slightly, gave her a wink and walked away.

Waiting until Charley's cart had also moved off, Lizzie took a step closer to Radcliff.

"Gor a family, lad?" she asked gently.

An affirmative nod sent Quon's hands into motion. Puzzled, Clem watched their silent exchange. His eyes asked a thousand questions but his mouth seemed unable to utter a sound.

"Want a job?" the girl asked quietly, observing him closely.

He nodded again and his face brightened slightly. He began to relax and she got him talking. Self-consciously he told how he had thought his plans for the steam engine would make him his fortune.

Casually, Lizzie eased the information she needed out of him.

Then, turning to face him, she looked him squarely in the eye and ordered in a gentle tone, "Report to Angus McClain at the cider brewery on Corn Street at thirty minutes past six tomorra morning." Then nodding slightly to Quon, they moved off toward the entrance of the dock, leaving him alone with his broken engine.

Watching the young pair leave, Clem Radcliff had the distinct feeling he had been in the company of someone important to his future. *Who did that captain say she was? Lizzie Short? Have I heard that name before? She seemed to make all the decisions but how could that be? Who was she?* Shaking his head, he took one last look at the engine that had been his heart and soul for so many years, then turned and walked away.

Rounding the corner into Corn Street, Lizzie and Quon were surprised to see old Mister Dixon on the street outside his mill. He was actually standing right in the middle of the street just staring up at his old building. Traffic was cautiously moving around him—the old corn miller had finally surfaced after an unexplained absence.

His strange behaviour, eccentric ways and sudden disappearances had caused long delays in finalizing the purchase of his mill. Now the waiting was over for Ada had told them last night that Dixon was being paid out this week.

Quon's hands began to gyrate as they approached. Lizzie snapped impatiently. "Stop it, Quon. I don't know what he's doing!"

Slowly, they moved closer not wanting to surprise the old man and cause further harm. They were sure he must have seen them by this time and was paying them no mind.

"What yer doin, Mister Dixon?" Lizzie asked. "Are you all right? Just then she heard Quon's excited voice. "Wook wizzy, wook!"

Spinning around, she saw a fire in the yard, blazing furiously. They moved toward it.

"LEAVE IT!" Dixon boomed in a stern voice, then as if all the fight had suddenly gone out of him, he continued in a weary voice. "Leave it, let it burn."

They could see clearly now that it was only a small bonfire, there was nothing to save and it had almost burned itself out. Quietly watching until the blaze reduced to a glowing red ember, Lizzie walked back to the old man.

"Whatever were you burning?" she asked.

Without turning his head, in a voice crackling with emotion he replied, "Memories, lass, memories ... all mine and nobody to pass them on to."

She could feel the old man's pain as he performed his last act of defiance and hoped she was in no way to blame. With no surviving kinfolk, he was the last of the line, Abe Kratze had told them. He had no doubt already suffered the fate of loneliness. She had sensed it in their earlier meeting three years ago, prior to the decision to purchase his building.

Watching him slowly shuffle back through the yard gates, she felt sorry for the old man. Slipping her arm around Quon's waist and pulling him closer, she whispered, "Sadly, m'lad, that's progress. Damned if I want to be on that end of it, though."

Quon put his arm over her shoulder giving her a squeeze as they watched Richard Dixon disappear into the building. It was the last time they would ever see him.

Continuing up the street, they suddenly heard the rattle of familiar iron wheels.

"Bled cart!" exclaimed Quon.

Quickening their pace they arrived at the bakery to find Billy, Tom and Oly, the bakery delivery lads, parking their cart. Bill Johnson, the baker, was unstrapping one of the empty cider barrels. The lads yelled their greetings as they gathered armloads of bread to refill their empty cart.

"Busy day, Bill? It's Sunday you know."

Bill nodded, but his mind was on his job and he didn't reply. His wife, Connie, came out of the house with a tin tray of fruit bread and small tankards of cider. When she saw Lizzie and Quon, her eyes lit up and she rushed over to envelop them in one of her big hugs. The young partners grinned helplessly and the other boys giggled as they watched.

They sat down at the table and were soon joined by Bill and the others. As the delivery lads chattered excitedly, unnoticed Quon's fingers tapped out a message on Lizzie's hand.

"Rush orders, Bill?" she asked.

Bill had just taken a large bite of fruit bread and was unable to answer, so young Billy took up the conversation. "Two ships leavin at noon, miss. New order from Gamble's dock."

"Tell Miss Lizzie about that ship blowin up on King's Dock," added Tom, Billy's partner and the older of the two. He emphasized his statement with fearful eyes and hand gestures.

"We heard a big bang, Miss Lizzie!" added Olivera, the Portuguese lad, who was the newest member of the team.

"No, no," Lizzie laughed, "it wasn't a ship at all, it was a new-fangled steam engine!"

"Ee, wor it really?" the baker asked, reverently. "They say them things are dangerous. I don't want one of them anywhere near me!"

They all laughed, not quite believing that such a big man could be afraid of anything. They finished eating and the three boys left the table ready to be off again. Olivera ran over to Lizzie and waited patiently until she noticed him.

"My goodness, but you are growing tall, Oly," she said, patting the still-small boy on the head.

"Oly get big to look after Miss Lizzie, just like Quon do!"

Quon stood up and ruffled the boy's hair. "No need, Oly, Wizzy mine. Quon protect Wizzy forever."

Spinning around, Lizzie belted her partner across the arm, to the amusement of the others.

Leaping off his seat to escape the mock beating, he yelled at the lads. "Better go now, Wizzy mad!"

Bill Johnson laughed as he watched Quon run backward across the yard until he tripped and fell in a heap. Lizzie stood with her hands on her hips as Quon jumped to his feet and helped to push the bread cart out of the yard.

"Have you need for an extra man, Bill?" she called.

"Yes, he does, lass, but only five days ... not a full week," Connie's voice rang out across the yard. "Then perhaps he'll take a Sunday off for a change!"

Lizzie waved her acknowledgement as she met Quon at the gate and they headed for the brewery to find Angus.

Chapter 2

Since taking on the job as brewery manager six years before, Angus had been a model of reliability. With the assistance of old Joe and John Watson, the Master Malster, they now had the business running at almost maximum production and efficiency. With the purchase of Richard Dixon's property, to be settled at last, the whisky making division would be able to finally expand.

Entering the big wooden gates, Lizzie and Quon heard the distinct sound of hammers and saws at work. Coming to a storage bay, they found a man tapping on barrels and stopped to watch. He was listening carefully to the sounds they produced and didn't hear them come up beside him.

"Where's Angus?" asked Lizzie.

The man started slightly but, recognizing the voice of his young boss, turned and pointed to another building. They threaded their way through the rows of stacked barrels to the building's side door. The construction noise was obviously coming from this building and now they could hear the sound of men's voices.

Opening the door to peek in, Lizzie couldn't believe her eyes. The room was swarming with workmen. Some were packing wood from a large stack in the centre of the floor to another group who were measuring and cutting. Still other men were erecting new walls and hammering them into place. As the workmen noticed the young partners, many called out their greetings.

Quon pushed inquisitively past her.

John Watson's voice boomed over the noise. "COME IN, COME IN, YOUNGSTERS, BUT WATCH WHERE YOU WALK!"

Quon pointed to the other side of the building where Joe stood talking with John and Angus. Carefully making their way through the maze of activity, Lizzie shook her head and tried to look stern when she caught some of the good-natured banter. She could tell from his confused expression and speechless hands that Quon thankfully didn't understand most of what was being said.

"Surprised yer didn't we, young'uns?" Joe chuckled, welcoming them each with a hug.

The whisky maker held up a drawing of the room before laying it down on a makeshift table behind them. "Look at this, Liz. Let me show you what we are doing here."

Lizzie and Quon watched as he explained the lines on the floor plan, his finger tracing the details. All three of the men were obviously proud of their accomplishment.

"This place will be ready for running by the end of next week!" Watson exclaimed, loud enough for many of the workmen to hear. Then looking at the girl, he continued, "These men are receiving no pay today. They just want to say thanks to you three and TLS." He sighed audibly. "You know, lass, when we first met you had me a wee bit worried. I just couldn't imagine myself taking orders from a girl, it seemed unthinkable!" He paused, his eyes never wavering from her face. "Well, a lot has happened since then and now I understand."

Lizzie raised an eyebrow. "Care to elaborate, Mister Watson?" she asked, quietly.

"You give a man pride, lass. Pride in himself, pride in his job, pride in the company … an most of all, you make these men proud to be your friend. That blasted Scot, Patrick Sandilands, was telling no lies when he told me about you, though I doubted him fiercely."

Angus and Joe stood back, grinning silently as they listened to the conversation. They knew their friend would feel better now that he had declared himself.

Lizzie suddenly realized that the building had gone quiet. Quon's hands moved, stopping instantly when she nodded to him.

"WELL NOW YER DONE YER TALKIN, LET'S GET ON WITH THE WORK, LADS!" she shouted. Then turning, she laid her arm on Quon's shoulder and they began to walk toward the door. Almost reaching it, she remembered why they had come. She walked back toward Angus. "You've a new man coming in the morning named Clem Radcliff. Give him a job would you, Angus, or send him over to the bakery. Bill Johnson told us he can use a man."

Angus touched his hat and smiled. It was becoming quite commonplace. *You can always trrrust ourrr Lizzie to find someone who needs a helpin hand*, he thought.

Outside, Lizzie's expression indicated she was in deep thought. Quon stood back, quietly watching her.

"Big ploblem, Wizzy?"

"No, dumplin. I was just thinkin how much I wanted to see the children again. We haven't been to the farm since last September. They'll be growing so fast we won't recognize them!" She kicked fiercely at some stones as they walked. At the cottage gate, she hesitated. "I've got it, lad. I've a feeling we're going to be needed around here soon, so let's go with Jeb when he takes supplies this month. Come on, let's go tell him."

They were almost at the camp when they spotted three riders coming across the paddock behind the slaughterhouse. They were dressed in fancy riding clothes so they knew they weren't gypsies. They carried on up the lane to take a look.

Climbing onto the paddock fence, Lizzie realized one of the riders was a girl in her early twenties. She was well-dressed and riding side saddle on a high-spirited thoroughbred. Her companions, dressed in fancy riding breeches and black jackets with white shirts, were young men also about the same age. The seemed to be giving her some trouble as she looked most unhappy.

"Stop your whimpering!" snarled one of the men, hitting the girl's horse on the rump with his riding crop.

The horse jumped into the air bucking so hard it threw the girl to the ground where she landed in an unmoving heap. Lizzie and Quon leapt off the fence and ran to her assistance.

The other man raced over cutting them off and raising his riding crop above his head. "GET AWAY TRASH, BEFORE I HAVE A MIND TO WHIP YOU! THIS IS NONE OF YOUR CONCERN."

Lizzie jumped aside but Quon lunged forward grabbing the horse's tail and pulling sideways with all his might. Unaware of Quon's actions, the rider tried to turn, unbalancing his mount even more. Staggering sideways, the horse flopped over onto the grass but the rider rolled off expertly landing on his feet. Now aware of Quon's action, his face contorted with anger as he came toward the lad.

The girl, seemingly unhurt, was now sitting on the ground with her skirts and petticoats askew about her, no doubt having cushioned her fall. As she pulled back her long blonde hair and retied her bonnet, she watched the scene unfold around her.

Lizzie, aware of Quon's danger, bent to pick something off the ground. She hurled it at the advancing horseman hitting him high on the chest. A large brown stain appeared on his white shirt. He stopped, recoiling in horror as he looked down and saw his horse-dung-splattered clothes.

The girl burst into laughter further infuriating her companion who turned toward her again, slapping his riding crop angrily against his breeches.

"RUN, LADY, RUN!" Lizzie screamed.

Scrambling to her feet, the girl scooped up her skirts and ran toward them as Quon advanced on the angry man once again.

Suddenly, the sound of a galloping horse interrupted them as it came skidding to a halt beside Quon.

The familiar voice of Jeb Dark, the gypsy leader, cracked through the air. "MAKE YER LAST WISH, DANDY!" he declared, moving his horse forward. "Catch her horse, lad, while I deal with this dog," he ordered Quon.

Whimpering, the dandy turned and began running, followed by his riding partner who had been standing back and watching.

"NO JEB, LEAVE IT BE!" Lizzie cried, as they watched the rider pull his friend up behind him.

Coming to a sudden stop, the gypsy slowly turned his horse, a wisp of a smile crossing his lips as he dismounted. "What the hell was that all about?"

The girl stepped forward. "I thank you profusely for your timely intervention, sir," she replied, in a cultured tone. "My whole-hearted thanks and admiration go out to these people for coming to my rescue." She pointed her delicate, gloved hand toward Lizzie and Quon. "Your friends are terribly brave, sir."

Jeb burst out laughing.

Intervening, Lizzie scolded the gypsy for his rudeness as she watched her partner's hands.

"Is he dumb? Can he not talk?" asked the girl.

Again Jeb laughed aloud. "Who are you, young lady?"

All three waited expectantly for the girl's answer. Seeming to suddenly become aware of her disheveled appearance, she looked down at her clothes and began to brush the dust from her dress. Then, lifting her head, she stood up proudly and smiled.

"I am Margaret, the daughter of Lord Sutton. Those pompous rogues are my cousins, Humphry Pellam and Clarence Sutton, both in the military and home on leave."

"I think we had better talk," said Lizzie, moving toward the paddock gate.

Margaret looked curiously at the girl who seemed a bit younger than herself. She got a sense that she was used to giving orders—and being obeyed. Even the gypsy was dismounting. She also noted that the Chinese lad was staying very close to this girl and was now at her elbow as they left the paddock and moved toward several upturned barrels. Lizzie sat down and motioned the girl to join her. Margaret did so, straightening her dress over her knees and brushing off some dust. The creaking of leather and accompanying grunt told them Jeb had sat on his heels behind them.

"My name is Lizzie and these are my friends, Quon Lee and Jeb Dark," she said, indicating each in turn. Now, first tell us where you live and how you come to be in our paddock?"

"My father owns a house over in the vale," Margaret replied, pointing out across the pastures. Hesitating, she added sadly, "He passed away two years ago."

"I'm sorry, but why were your cousins so angry with you?"

"They were angry because I wouldn't ride faster," she said, as concern clouded her face. "I'm afraid they'll be waiting for me when I return home."

"Then don't go," said Lizzie.

"That is impossible," she retorted, her shoulders slumping forward. "Mother will be worried sick when I don't come home."

Quon's hands went into action.

"I merely meant, you don't have to rush home, you could stay with us for a day or two," Lizzie suggested. "We'll get a message to your mother and I think we might be able to arrange something which will discourage your cousins from bothering you again!"

Margaret's doubtful eyes searched their faces.

Jeb grunted, interceding calmly, "Don't worry, miss. Our Lizzie knows how to deal with such matters."

Although Jeb had meant to be reassuring, it seemed to have the opposite effect and Margaret looked from one to the other with a look of helplessness.

"Dammit girl, just say yes or no!" insisted Lizzie, coming to her feet. "Don't worry, we'll make it right. Come, we don't have time to waste."

Finally, with a wane smile, Margaret, the daughter of Lord Sutton, agreed to be the guest of Lizzie Short, former waif of London's waterfront.

Jeb was already rounding up the other two horses. "If you get her some clothes from the rag yard, I'll get one of the boys to teach her ta ride like a gypsy." Lizzie waved her hand for him to be quiet, but to no avail. "Dress her in lad's clothes, like gypsies do when we want to hide a girl!"

Lizzie stopped, deep in thought. "Go and find Mick, Jeb. Tell him I need Nathan as soon as possible. He might need the help of your men."

Handing the reins of the two horses to Quon, the gypsy set his own mount in motion. One hand on the saddle, he bounced twice on the turf and mounted at a gallop.

"My gracious, what a horseman!" gasped Margaret.

An hour later, the three young people were coming out of the rag shed as the sound of galloping horses caught their attention. Nathan's buggy came to a halt in front of the nearby TLS office. He was accompanied by a group of about ten gypsy horsemen. His excited, shrill voice was easily heard as they drew closer.

Mick was coming out of the stableyard but ignored Nathan as he came quickly toward Lizzie, grinning broadly. "Now what be yer problem me darlin, an who's this young lad?"

"Inside!" she growled, walking past the men and entering the office, followed by the others including the now-sulking Nathan. Sitting on the edge of Ada's desk, she began to explain. "I need you," she said pointing at Nathan, "to deliver a message to Lady Sutton."

"To whom?" asked the trader.

"My mother … we live at Sutton House in the vale," Margaret purred, lifting her cap and letting her long blonde hair fall about her shoulders.

Mick couldn't believe his eyes. "Yer a lass!" he exclaimed.

Nathan, struck amazingly speechless, just stared at the girl.

Mick turned to Lizzie and winked. "Who's yer friend, Liz?"

Lizzie chuckled, her eyes flicking to Margaret who was smiling with curious interest at Mick.

Feet hurrying down the stairs from the house above, alerted them that Ada was on her way. As soon as she entered the room, she went to sit at her desk not showing the least bit of interest in the visitors.

Ignoring Mick's question, Lizzie introduced them to Margaret, explaining briefly about the incident with Margaret's cousins.

"Miss Sutton," said Ada, after considering the girl's options, "you are most welcome to stay here with us for a day or two, if that is necessary. However, we'll send Mister Goldman to take a message to your mother." Turning back to Lizzie, she added with a twinkle in her eye, "Wick and Dan should be able to convince those cousins to behave."

Lizzie grinned, and they all silently agreed that Nathan's burly gypsy drivers could easily deal with this situation.

"We won't be at the cottage tonight," said Ada.

"See you tomorrow then," replied Lizzie, opening the door for their guest.

It was late in the afternoon when Lizzie, Quon and their guest headed over to the cottage. Margaret's eyes darted about trying to absorb her new surroundings and she realized she was quite enjoying herself. Quon giggled as her nose twitched, picking up the smell of the slaughterhouse.

"Pray, what is that dreadful aroma?" she asked, holding her nose.

Lizzie's eyes twinkled. "That ain't no aroma, lass, that's a good old-fashioned stink!"

"Is this your house?" asked Margaret, as they stopped at the gate. "Oh, how quaint!"

Martha greeted them with surprise, wiping her hands on her apron as she suspiciously cast her eyes over their guest. "Now who ye brought with ye, Lizzie? Is't a laddie or a lass?"

"What did she say?" Margaret giggled, eyes darting about the room.

"Martha's from Yorkshire and although she talks a bit funny she has a heart of gold," Lizzie explained. "She's also a wonderful cook, as you'll see for yourself."

Joe arrived at the door and, hearing the sound of laughter on the lane, announced, "Charley's comin."

They all heard the sound of iron wheels as they stopped nearby. Loud laughter followed and soon footsteps were coming up the path as the Grim brothers arrived with their human load. Setting Charley down in the doorway, Grey Grim announced, "We'll be back for him at nine, Miss Lizzie," and they were off again.

Charley struggled to the table on his sticks. Joe moved to help but the engineer waved him away. "That wind came up really bitter cold this afternoon, Joe. Gets right into my bones is all."

"It's still winter, lad. Don't let that sun fool yer," said Joe, stopping in his tracks when he saw the girl. "A friend of yer's Lizzie?"

Margaret smiled, but she was watching Charley's every move.

Charley sat down and wiped the sweat from his brow. At last, he noticed the visitor. "Well, hello," he said pleasantly. "I'm Charles Mason, who are you?"

Another round of introductions followed before Martha started banging plates and passing dishes full of steaming food onto the table. Following their lead, Margaret filled her plate. A tap on the door caused heads to turn and Jeb stepped inside, cap in hand.

"Come eat, lad," Joe invited, waving for him to enter.

"No, no," Jeb replied, struggling with himself for refusing one of Martha's meals. "I've just called to tell Miss Lizzie that everything at Sutton House has been attended to successfully and the two men have decided to leave ... permanently. I'll be taking some men and supplies out to the Hertfordshire farm, leaving at first light. Then, moving in behind Margaret, he placed his calloused brown hands on her shoulders and whispered, "You'll be safe now; just you listen to our Lizzie." And turning, he departed without another word.

Disappointment was obvious on Lizzie's face as she glanced quickly at Quon. "Damn!" she muttered, not quite under her breath.

"What's the troub...?" Joe asked

Lizzie stopped him by raising her hand as she paid attention to Quon's fingers tapping out a message on her arm.

Nodding almost imperceptibly, she realized she now had an explanation to make. Keeping her eyes averted, she chose her words carefully. "We had been talking about going up to the farm, before we got too busy, but didn't know Jeb was leaving so quickly."

Everyone's cutlery stopped for a moment but Martha quickly changed the subject knowing Lizzie was secretive about these trips. "Eat up while it's hot! I didn't slave over this fire all day cookin yer all roast pork and applesauce just to see yer eat it cold!"

Margaret wondered why everyone seemed so uncomfortable with Lizzie's comment but she soon forgot about it and her troubles, tucking into a generous helping. One by one, they finished and the cutlery stopped rattling. Joe moved to his overstuffed rocker by the fire, a new chair purchased by Lizzie and Quon for his birthday the year before. He filled his pipe with fresh tobacco while Martha hovered nearby, a splinter of wood in hand.

As the others cleaned up the dishes, Charley asked for some chalk and a slate so he could show them the steam engine's problem. Quon went off returning with the items, laying them on the table in front of him. Charley began to draw as the others watched.

"That won't do," he muttered in frustration, pushing the slate away and sitting back in his chair.

Lizzie went over and reached for the slate. "What is it, Charley?"

"A steam valve," he replied, as Margaret and Quon came closer.

"But what are you tryin to do?" asked Lizzie.

"I want to know," he began sharply, his frustration obvious, "when the boiler has 40 pounds of pressure, and how to keep it there." He paused, noticing their blank expressions. "Oh, it's easy to make a safety valve but how to regulate it is the problem."

Margaret, sitting next to him, moved the slate closer and began to study the drawing. Reaching for the chalk, she began to draw. Charley watched in amazement. Skillfully, their visitor adjusted the drawing by rubbing bits out and adding bits on until she was finally satisfied with the result.

His mouth dropped open in surprise when he suddenly realized what she had drawn. "How do you regulate it?" he asked, cautiously.

"By adding or subtracting the weights on that rod," she explained, pointing to it on the drawing as a slight smile twitched at the corners of her perfectly shaped lips.

Charley scratched his head. "Did you just dream that thing up?"

"No!" Margaret laughed. "When I visited Cambridge University with my father a few years back, I remember a drawing by a man named Leonardo Da Vinci that fascinated me. He invented something very similar."

"Can we get him to help us, Margaret?" asked Lizzie.

Margaret smiled. "That would be difficult, Lizzie. He's been dead for about 300 years, but he was a wonderful inventor."

A knock sounded on the door.

"Come in," Martha called, wiping her hands on her apron.

Nathan Goldman stepped inside, lightly holding the arm of a diminutive, well-dressed woman who timidly stood in the doorway.

"MOTHER!" cried Margaret in surprise, going over to hug her.

Martha hurried over, pulling out a chair for Lady Sutton and persuading her to sit down. Margaret sat down next to her.

"Oh Daisy, what has happened to you now?" the woman gasped, looking her daughter over from head to toe. Removing a neatly folded linen handkerchief from a small, black velvet purse, she dabbed at her nose. "I was so worried when you and the boys did not return. Mister Goldman has been most kind."

"Can ah get yer a cup of tea, luv?" the housekeeper asked.

"That would be most welcome, thank you," replied Lady Sutton, looking around at the faces watching her curiously.

Margaret began to explain the events of the afternoon, reassuring her mother that they were amongst friends, and she began to relax.

Nathan coughed loudly to draw their attention. "Lady Sutton, I believe it is time to introduce you to these people who came to your daughter's aid." Moving toward the hearth, he introduced Joe first. "This is Joe Todd, father-figure to these two young rascals ... Lizzie and Quon, who found your daughter in a compromising situation and offered their assistance." His arm swept around to indicate the young partners. "The man on your right is Charley Mason, dockmaster for the TLS Company and a first-class engineer, and this is Martha, their housekeeper, and mother to all."

Lady Sutton smiled politely, obviously a bit bewildered.

But Nathan hadn't finished yet. Slowly walking over to stand behind Lizzie's chair, he placed his hands on her shoulders. "And this young lady, is our Lizzie Short, the brains behind the TLS Company!" he announced, rather proudly. Then satisfied with his introductions, he found a chair and sat down at the end of the table.

Lady Sutton's eyes met her daughter's then moved onto Lizzie. Her eyebrows shot up and she murmured, "But you are only a girl, my dear, how can this be?"

Quon Lee took matters into his own hands jumping to his feet and punching his fist into the air. "My Wizzy damned smart!"

Taken by surprise, Joe almost choked on his tobacco smoke and many in the room began to snicker, watching Lady Sutton's reaction.

Martha picked up her wooden spoon and leaned over the table to wave it menacingly at Quon. "Ye'd better behave yerself, m'lad!"

Quon tucked in closer to his idol, pretending to be afraid.

Lady Sutton finally relaxed and began to laugh with the others. Then, patting her daughter's hand, she stood up. "Time to go, my darling," she sighed, looking around at the faces watching her. "I owe you all such a debt of gratitude and Mister Goldman has been most gracious in bringing me here to meet you all and collect Margaret. This visit has been most refreshing."

Martha suddenly leapt up from the table and bustled out of the room. Margaret also rose and Nathan quickly moved toward the door.

"Whatever are you wearing, Daisy? My, you do look a frightful sight!" her mother sighed, noticing her trousers for the first time.

Lizzie pushed back her chair and stood up before the girl could answer. With just a trace of a smile, she said softly. "We'll come visit you soon, Margaret. Keep the clothes, you may need them again!

"I almost forgot, Miss Margaret. Here are yer clothes," gasped Martha, bustling back into the room carrying a large package wrapped in a piece of white cloth. I was going to wash 'em up for yer but ther wasn't time, luv."

"Thank you, Martha. You are so kind," said Margaret, taking the parcel from the housekeeper and giving her a little hug.

Quon tapped on Lizzie's arm.

"Quon says, your horse will be delivered home to you by one of the gypsies. Make him welcome, he's a friend. And, if you're lucky and you ask him nicely, he'll teach you to ride gypsy-style which is much easier than the way you ride! You'll be safe at Sutton House now, I guarantee it."

Lady Sutton smiled, eyes now twinkling although she still looked a bit confused. Before Nathan could open the door, she turned to Lizzie.

"Young lady," she said, "you give me an impulsive belief that we have found the friends we have needed for sometime. I am no business woman," she apologized, her voice breaking slightly, "but I am the daughter of a general and you talk with the same confident authority he once did. If you could find it in your heart to help us with a difficulty we are having, one that appears beyond the control of our limited resources, we would be forever grateful."

Without waiting for an answer, Lady Sutton went outside and her daughter followed through the open door. After it had closed behind them, there was complete silence as everyone just stood for a moment. Then they heard the sound of the trader's buggy moving off.

"Yer goin ta help 'em, luv, in't yer?" asked Martha.

Joe, who had been taken aback by the presence of Lady Sutton in his humble cottage, finally spoke, "'Am ah dreaming, lass, or is she fer real?'"

Laughing, Lizzie watched her partner's hands. "He's right you know, Dad," she chuckled. "Dumplin says they're only people, just like us."

"But what are you going to do?" asked Charley.

"I'm going to tell you to forget all you've seen and heard here tonight," she replied. "We've got a steam engine to repair."

"I can manage that now," said Charley, listening to the familiar rattle of more iron-rimmed wheels in the lane. Quick footsteps sounded on the garden path, followed by a knock on the door and one of the Grim's heads appeared.

"We've come for Charley, Miss Lizzie. Is he ready?"

Martha hurried to the door, prodding the boys inside as Charley climbed shakily to his feet. The boys locked hands to make a seat and easily lifted him into position. Then, quick as a flash they were gone.

"Them are good lads," Martha muttered. "Ah've never ever heard a grumble out of 'em and they sure look after Charley. You lot need some sleep, so get out of here an go ta yer beds."

Quon's hands sent a sudden sharp message on Lizzie's arm.

Nodding quickly, she leapt from the table. "Be back in a minute!" she called over her shoulder as she and Quon disappeared out of the door.

Martha shook her head, throwing her hands into the air. "Good gracious, where are those young'uns off to at this time of night?"

Racing up the lane and into the gypsy camp, dogs howled a

warning as they approached the campfire where a group of men sat talking.

"Is Jeb here?" Lizzie asked.

"I'm here!" said a familiar voice and the gypsy leader and several other men were suddenly beside them.

Quon gripped Lizzie's arm, stepping past her to place himself between her and danger.

Jeb grinned, spreading his arms in a gesture of surrender, now well used to the gentle lad's protective nature. As the others took their places around the campfire, he continued. "What's yer problem, missy?"

"Yer leaving for the farm in the morning, we want to go with you," she said, looking at him intently.

"We're takin a wagon and it'll take many more days than normal to travel," he ventured, cocking his head and looking at them doubtfully. "We've work to do and cattle to bring back. That's at least another two weeks. You'd be better waitin, missy." Slowly, the gypsy leader convinced Lizzie he was right although he knew how desperately she wanted to see the children again. "We'll go again soon," he promised, as he walked them back toward the lane.

Chapter 3

Over the next three days there was little time to even think about Margaret Sutton. They sent her horse back with Jeb's nephew, Ben, a particularly handsome lad who was a superb horseman. Jeb had been a day late leaving for the farm, having undertaken the responsibility of setting gypsy guards around the Sutton estate. He left orders for them to report to Mick if the need arose.

On Thursday morning Lizzie and Quon went to visit Ada at the office. They were discussing Charley's steam engine when Nathan called with some urgent orders, Everything seemed to be urgent with Nathan. During the course of the conversation, he mentioned that his next stop was at the Sutton's and Lizzie jerked to attention.

"We'll go with you!"

Showing no surprise, Nathan laughed. "Aye, I thought you might." Putting his papers away, the trader prepared to leave.

Ada laid down her pen and turned to face Lizzie. "Don't you go get yourself into something you can't handle, young lady. Those people live in a different world to us and you're not accustomed to their ways."

Lizzie listened attentively but Ada already knew full well that nothing she said would sway the girl from her plan to help her new friends.

Leaving the office a few minutes later, Lizzie and Quon joined Nathan in his carriage. Wick closed the door behind them then, joined Dan up on the driver's seat. They were soon cantering off toward the vale and Sutton House. Soon realizing they were going through an unfamiliar district of London, their eager faces were full of expectation as they looked around them. Nathan explained that this area was called Bloomsbury.

The youngsters gazed in wonderment at the huge stone buildings, many of them white and so clean looking with their decorative embellishments and so many statues. They rarely had the opportunity or need to leave dockland, except the few times they had gone to the

Bishop's Palace in Westminster. But they were younger then and hadn't really noticed such things. Large buildings were to be found all over London and had became commonplace to the youngsters, but today these buildings were different. Nathan explained that very wealthy people lived in the long row houses and large estates half-hidden behind groves of trees.

"Look at that one, dumplin. I wonder if people live up in those tall turrets, they could see forever!"

"Too big, much big house. Quon get lost. I wike Joe's cottage better!" exclaimed Quon, grinning at Nathan whose mouth had dropped open, not used to hearing him speak.

"But it is so beautiful. Look at all the lovely parks and wonderful lawns and gardens." Lizzie rambled on relentlessly, ignoring them both as they passed several more large homes behind tall wrought-iron gates and decorative iron fences.

Nathan pointed out two estates that he knew by name, explaining that they belonged to shipping and coal merchants.

Arriving at the stone-arched iron gates of Sutton House, Wick jumped down and proceeded to open them, quickly closing them again as the buggy proceeded through. A short ride and they were pulling into the stable block, to be met by a pleasant old man who turned out to be one of the Sutton's grooms.

"Mornin, Mister Goldman, sir," he greeted them warmly as they stepped from the buggy. "Madam is in, sir. She's had no visitors for the last day or two and will be pleased to see you, I'm sure."

Nathan nodded, thanking the old horseman before he led the horse away. Suddenly, a long, shrill whistle rang through the air, followed by two shorter blasts. Quon's hands reacted and he glanced at his partner. Her eyebrows shot up and she was about to reply when Wick answered with his own short, sharp whistle.

Gypsy guards! She looked around even though she knew their presence would not be obvious. Meanwhile, Dan had gone to the front door and was banging the brass doorknocker. Lizzie grasped Quon's arm and they joined the others as they made their way up the stone steps, arriving just as the huge oak door swung open. A man of doubtful age, tall, thin and displaying an extremely sour expression, glowered at the gypsy then swung his eyes onto Nathan.

"Madam's not home, sir," announced the butler officiously,

stepping hurriedly back inside. He attempted to close the door but Dan overpowered him. Voicing loud objections, the alarmed butler soon wilted under the gypsy's strength and menacing glare.

"She's in!" Nathan snapped. "Now tell her we're here!"

Lizzie giggled behind her hand and the butler scurried away. Nathan was obviously in charge of the situation and enjoying himself. This was the first time she had seen the little man in action with his gypsy servants and she was impressed. *A formidable trio,* she thought, winking at Quon.

Re-appearing, the embarrassed butler bowed low and humbly begged their pardon for the mistake he had made. Showing them down a short, wide hallway they entered a sumptuous drawing room where they were greeted warmly by Lady Sutton and Margaret. Nathan, being used to visiting stately houses, quickly chose a straight-backed chair with arms, near the window. Lizzie selected a chair facing Margaret and Quon went to stand behind his partner.

Lady Sutton smiled at the partners' antics and pulled a decorative chord hanging from the wall. Within a few seconds, a young woman dressed completely in black, except for a heavily starched white apron, appeared.

"Yes, mum," she said pleasantly, standing just inside the door.

"Our guests will be joining us for tea, Sarah."

The young maid curtsied and left the room, returning within minutes carrying a tray of teacups and a plate of small cakes. As she moved about the room serving their guests, Sarah seemed surprised when Lizzie shook her head refusing the cup of tea.

"You'll find our tea most refreshing, miss."

Lizzie wrinkled her nose. Never having tried tea before, she was quite confident she wouldn't like it.

Quon's hands began talking on Lizzie's shoulder and Lady Sutton watched spellbound.

"Look Daisy, he's doing it just like you told me!" she exclaimed.

Lizzie looked up and chuckled. "He says we should try your tea," Lizzie said with a groan. Nathan looked over at her and frowned disapprovingly. She took the offered teacup and was bringing it to her lips when she stopped. "Missus Sutton, why do you call your daughter, Daisy, when her name is Margaret?"

Nathan again frowned at her but Lizzie wasn't looking in his direction.

"Oh dear, let me explain," Lady Sutton chuckled. "When my daughter was a little girl, she was forever collecting daisies and presenting them to me and her father. In the summer we had little vases of daisies everywhere, so we called her, our little daisy."

Blushing, Margaret giggled as she took a teacup from Sarah.

"I must beg your understanding, m'lady," Nathan announced, coming to his feet. "I must be on my way."

"I fully understand, Mister Goldman," replied Lady Sutton producing a piece of paper that appeared to contain a list, from the table beside her. "Here is my next order and thank you so much for your delivery," she said, handing it to the trader.

His eyes scanned it quickly. "I will see to this immediately," he answered, taking Lady Sutton's proffered hand. Turning to Lizzie, he continued in an extraordinarily polite manner. "I'll escort you home on my way, Miss Lizzie."

"You go do yer business, lad," she replied. "We'll walk home when we're ready. We can find the way and it's still early."

"But I must insist ... for your own safety," Nathan replied sharply.

Lizzie moved as if to rise but Quon held her down, quickly tapping a message on her shoulder. She glanced up at him and smiled. "Mister Goldman, I give the orders. Now, please go!"

Nathan's face turned crimson and looked like it was going to burst. He bowed to the Suttons, then strutted from the room. Margaret began to giggle only to be stopped immediately by her mother's sharp expression.

"Don't you think you should have gone with him, my dear?" asked Lady Sutton with a concerned frown. "Mister Goldman seemed to think you could be in danger."

"Missus Sutton," Lizzie began, again forgetting to address the high-born lady with her title. "I am no stranger to danger but there is no danger here. One whistle would bring ten men into this room, ready to tear someone's heart out," she exaggerated.

Lady Sutton gasped. With wide eyes, she glanced furtively around the room. Margaret chuckled, reaching out to pat her mother's arm.

"It's the gypsies, Mother. They're Lizzie and Quon's friends. They're here to keep us safe and I'm sure they will escort them home if they feel the need."

Quon's eyes narrowed as he tapped out another message to Lizzie.

She patted his hand in return. "It was Ben who told her, dumplin. Perhaps he taught her to ride while he was here, too!"

Margaret giggled as her mother glanced from one to the other trying to make some sense of the conversation. A slight tap on the door was heard and the sour-faced butler re-entered.

"Shall I show these people out now, ma'am?" he asked, scowling at the young people.

"No, you shall not!" Margaret intervened. "Now go away until you are called."

"Margaret!" her mother gasped, as the servant quickly withdrew. Quon's fingers transmitted a quick message to Lizzie which the girl appeared not to notice.

"How long have you had that butler, Lady Sutton?" Lizzie asked, standing up and moving to the back of the room.

Margaret glanced at her mother. "Only since Daddy died, about two years."

The thought struck both the partners at the same time and their eyes locked for a moment.

"Who picked him?" Lizzie asked. "What other servants have changed in the last two years?"

The Sutton women looked at each other, puzzled by the request.

"The butler, one maid and a head stableman, in the last two years," said Margaret, quietly. "Uncle James arranged it. He's done everything since Daddy died."

Lady Sutton noticed a smile creep across Lizzie's face, and saw Quon's elbow nudge her slightly.

"Go on, luv, tell us the problem … or shall I tell you?" Lizzie whispered.

Margaret wasn't sure what Lizzie was getting at but the look of sadness on her mother's face made her feel uncomfortable. Suddenly, Lady Sutton slumped back in her chair.

"Mother, are you all right?" asked Margaret, turning to assist her.

Waving her daughter away, Lady Sutton visibly took a deep breath and looked up at Lizzie. She was not used to explaining her troubles to a stranger and now tortured by embarrassment she nervously dabbed at her mouth with a silk handkerchief.

"Will you tell them, Daisy? I simply can't bear it."

"Well, it's simple enough," Margaret began. "We are being ruined and Uncle James is doing his best to stop it."

"Explain ... how?" Lizzie persuaded gently, watching the older woman's torment and beginning to understand.

"My father had a long-term financial arrangement with a shipping house," Margaret continued. "He bought the cargo and took half of the profit." She lowered her eyes, her voice growing softer. "But since his death, the last three cargos have been stolen at sea by privateers or brigands and we have lost all our investment."

Quon Lee startled the Suttons by spinning around to face Lizzie, arms waving wildly.

Lizzie grinned, putting a hand on his arm. "Who is the shipping agent?" she inquired. "And what is your uncle's full name?"

Margaret looked at her mother for confirmation. "William Crowther is the agent. He is located on Dock Street near the Lancaster Dock. My uncle's name is James Sutton. He's my father's younger brother." As she mentioned her uncle's name, her expression had changed to one of total disdain.

She doesn't like her uncle very much, thought Lizzie.

"Now, now, Daisy," scolded her mother. "James is doing his best. He has no control over what happens at sea."

The partner's eyes locked for a moment remembering how Crowther's shipping agents had been trying to cheat the import tax by using Portuguese vessels running from French ports into the south coast of England. They had fortunately been caught by Captain Davis and stripped of all cargo which, in turn, landed in the TLS warehouse ... earning their company a sizeable profit. Lizzie couldn't help but wonder if those ships hadn't been financed with Sutton money.

"Were your goods being imported or exported?" she asked cautiously, feeling a slight pang of guilt.

"Exported, mainly wool or cloth," Lady Sutton replied, looking at her daughter. "That's right, Daisy, isn't it?"

"Yes, Mother, that was written on the contract Uncle James showed us last year."

Lizzie let out a silent sigh of relief and went back to sit down. She finally reached for her teacup, desperately in need of a drink. Quon watched as she gingerly tipped the cup and swallowed a mouthful of the cold liquid. Her face went into contortions showing pure revulsion as she swallowed the bitter liquid.

"Oohh, that's awful stuff!" she spluttered, causing everyone to laugh.

"No, no, my dear," exclaimed Lady Sutton, "you should add milk and a little sugar. That will make it much more palatable."

Lizzie shook her head. "No, I believe I've had quite enough, thank you, Lady Sutton. Can we look around?" she asked, suddenly. "If you don't mind. We have never been in such a nice ... or large house."

Margaret sprang to her feet as her mother nodded her consent. They were almost at the door when the butler knocked and entered.

"James Sutton has arrived, madam."

"That's odd," murmured Margaret. "Uncle James didn't tell us he would be back so soon."

Lizzie looked at Quon and raised an eyebrow.

The man who entered was of approximate middle age and short stature. He seemed to be in a hurry and his forced smile was as ludicrous as his garish attire. Breezing into the room, James Sutton expressed a half-hearted greeting to Margaret and strutted over to stand in front of his sister-in-law. Lizzie and Quon moved closer to the wall hiding their smiles, although he was taking little notice of them.

With an exaggerated flourish he withdrew a paper from his inside coat pocket and declared, haughtily, "Sign these papers and I shall be on my way."

Lady Sutton looked quite bewildered but he was obviously on a mission and thrust the paper into her hand. Her eyes desperately sought out her daughter and Margaret returned to her mother's side.

DON'T SIGN THOSE PAPERS, Lady Sutton!" Lizzie's voice cracked like a whip.

Spinning on his heel, James Sutton glared menacingly at the girl. Quon moved quickly to the centre of the room standing between Sutton and his Lizzie, and glared back.

"Who the hell are you? BUTLER!" Sutton snarled, and the butler who had been standing just outside the door, entered quickly. "Throw these two unwelcome guests out of here, immediately."

Lizzie sent a piercing whistle ringing through the air. Lady Sutton slumped back in her chair and Margaret went to her aid. The butler stopped, appearing confused as he looked from James Sutton to this young stranger.

Suddenly, through another door, rushed two rather large gypsies, obviously ready for action.

"Yer need us, Miss Lizzie?" one of the men demanded.

James Sutton nodded quickly to the butler and they both moved toward the door. Remembering why he had come, Sutton turned back and grabbed the paper still clutched in his sister-in-law's hand.

Margaret gasped, though her mother seemed quite oblivious to what was happening.

"Oh no you don't!" Lizzie cried, motioning to one of the gypsies who quickly moved toward Sutton, intercepting him and grabbing the paper from his hand. The gypsy handed it over to Lizzie. James Sutton hesitated for one brief moment then ran whimpering out of the door after the butler. In a few minutes, shouting was heard outside, the crack of a whip, and then the sound of hooves and carriage wheels as Sutton's conveyance thundered away.

A motion of Lizzie's hand and the gypsies disappeared as quickly as they had come. Lady Sutton tried to regain her composure but her fingers were noticeably white as she gripped her daughter's hand. She looked up at Lizzie with misty eyes and then her head sunk onto Margaret's shoulder and her body began to shake.

Lizzie handed the paper to Quon who folded it and slipped it into his inside pocket. Lizzie looked sympathetically at the women. She had certainly not expected to confront the Sutton problem so abruptly but at least they now had some idea of what they were dealing with.

Moving in behind the two women on the sofa, Lizzie put her arms around them. "Come on now, try to be strong," she whispered.

Lady Sutton sat up and squared her shoulders. She blotted her eyes with her handkerchief and turned to face Lizzie. "Are you telling us that James has been using our money for his own use?" Receiving a nod in reply, she continued, "Mister Goldman was right; you are a force to be reckoned with, my dear. Oh my, and I trusted him so!"

"Oh Lizzie," said Margaret, clutching her mother's arm, "it makes so much sense now, but how would we ever have found out? I suppose we should thank you but what are we to do?"

Quon moved forward. "You wisten to Wizzy, she fix. You see!"

"If you have any trouble, Margaret, I want you to whistle, loudly. The gypsies will continue to be on guard in case you need them. And don't sign anymore papers without talking to us, Lady Sutton."

"She won't, but I can't whistle," Margaret confessed in dismay, as she showed them to the door.

"Ask the old groom to teach you, he was whistling when we arrived today," Lizzie laughed, watching her partner pucker up his mouth. "We'll be back soon. Give us a week or so, but come visit us at any time or if you need anything."

As they walked toward the gate, they looked for the gypsy guards, to no avail, they were totally invisible. The only person they saw was a gardener at the other side of the house. At the gate, one of the gypsies suddenly appeared to open it. As it swung shut, they turned to say goodbye but he was nowhere to be seen.

About half a mile down the road, they stopped at the top of a small hill and looked back at the beautiful scene in the vale. Sutton House estate was clearly visible with its circular driveway and large copse of trees bordering the paddocks. From their vantage point, they could see many other large estates, some set so neatly amongst the trees that only their roofs and high chimneys could be seen.

Turning away, Lizzie sighed. "One day, dumplin, we shall live down there."

"Why Wizzy want to do that, she not happy in Joe's cottage?"

Lizzie merely shrugged her shoulders and started off down the hill.

It was late in the afternoon when they realized they weren't far from home as they saw a wisp of smoke and recognized the gypsy camp up ahead.

"Me big hungly, Wizzy."

Laughing, his partner poked him in the ribs. "You've got enough meat on yer bones to last you 'till next winter!

A dog barked furiously, alerting the camp and two horses shot out from between the wagons. Two young boys riding bareback came toward them to investigate but recognizing them, they quickly turned back. Climbing the wall into Drover's Lane, they walked on toward home arriving at the same time as Joe and Charley.

"Coming for dinner, Charley?" she asked, giving Joe a hug as the Grim boys helped the engineer down to the ground.

Charley nodded and waving the boys away set out on his own, struggling up the garden path on his sticks. Martha was busy with dinner and greeted them as if they were her first visitors all day.

A squeal of delight sounded as Willie tore into the room, leaping onto Joe's knee almost before he sat down. Martha swung around with a rustle of skirts and petticoats, wagging her finger at the boy.

"I'm hungry, Grandma," he pleaded.

Martha's expression softened as she handed the boy a crust of bread.

"By God, he's got you wrapped around his finger, lass!" Joe declared, frowning.

Martha looked lovingly at her two charges, the young one and Joe. "Aye, tha right. Perhaps yer should take a look at the'self! One's allowed when it's a grandchild!"

Dinner was already half over when Ada and Mick finally arrived and went to give Willie a hug before sitting down. Martha got up and filled their plates, mumbling to herself, "Ah wondered where ye'd got ta."

Quon stuffed himself to capacity then continued with the apple pie, liberally covering it with cream from the earthenware pitcher. Lizzie jabbed him in the ribs and glared at him.

"What yer been doing with him this afternoon, Liz? That boy has a hollow leg!" teased Martha.

When the men retired to the fireplace and lit their pipes, Ada, who was clearing the table, looked over at her brother-in-law. "Have you had a problem today, Charley? You've got that worried look on your face tonight."

"Sort of ... well, not really," he began. "I've been thinking that I'd like to talk to that girl again."

"Girl?" asked Ada, not having been at dinner the night before.

Charley squirmed a little under the bookkeeper's gaze, muttering so quietly no one but Ada and Lizzie heard his answer. "Margaret Sutton."

Coming over to stand behind him, Ada put her hands on his shoulders. "Oh yes, I remember her, she had a problem with her bullying cousins. Goodness, do we have a romance blooming here?"

Lizzie quickly intervened when she noticed the redness creeping up Charley's neck. "No, no, you've got it all wrong, Ada. This girl knows about steam valves, that's all he means."

Ada and Mick glanced at each other, smiles crinkling their faces.

"Ah sure yer a wild one, lad, dreamin of a Colleen an her steam valves! Begorra yer should be ashamed of yerself!" Mick chuckled, winking at Lizzie.

The bookkeeper smacked her husband across the shoulder, as everyone began to laugh, including Charley.

As quiet again descended on the cottage, Lizzie's expression turned serious and she held out her hand to Quon. He withdrew the Sutton paper from his pocket and placed it in her open hand. Unfolding it carefully, she silently spread it out on the table and began to read. Every eye was on her ... but she read it silently.

When she was finished, she pushed the paper across the table to Ada and Mick. Her face was drawn into a tight frown but she made no comment. Ada drew it toward her, eyes growing wide as her gaze proceeded down the page. Mick, being a much slower reader, pulled the paper even closer. As he read, he began to mumble, scowling so hard his eyes were almost shut. When he finished, he lifted his head and looked up at the girl.

"Give it to Charley," she said softly.

Charley glanced around the table at the serious faces then drew the paper toward him. Being an educated man, he quickly read it and handed it back to Lizzie, who was now smiling wickedly.

"Your thoughts, please," she stated, evenly.

"What fool would allow somebody to draw £30,000 out of their bank?" Charley began.

The young partners grinned ruefully. Lizzie turned to Ada, her eyes inviting comment.

Ada sighed. "That is a document designed at deceit. I can feel it," she paused, her eyes fixed on Lizzie, across the table. "James Sutton. Who the devil is this rogue that dares such a ploy?"

Mick nodded his agreement, knowing his wife had a better under-standing of documents and business practices than himself. Then he frowned. "Sure darlin, hoy be knowin this ain't the first time the scoundrel's done somethin like this." Lizzie's eyes flicked up, but he continued. "It's blatant, loyk he never expected being questioned."

Lizzie watched as Ada's hand affectionately rubbed Mick's arm.

"You're *all* right," she announced. "Let's just take the points one at a time. James Sutton is Margaret Sutton's uncle, a relative, and trusted. Yes, it's a document done in a hurry and full of deceit ... and not the first time, I agree. You're no doubt correct, Mick, he certainly wanted it signed in a hurry. We were there and saw him!"

Joe's pipe tapped on the fire grate. All eyes turned his way but both he and Martha remained quiet, interested but not fully understanding the situation.

Suddenly, Charley sat back in his chair and tapped his stick on the floor in anger. "I still say they must be fools to have trusted him ...."

Lizzie held up her hand for him to stop They did not often see her so quietly agitated, but several noticed that she had clenched her fist and was holding it so tightly her fingers had turned white. "So Mister Engineer," she began, "you think it's foolish to trust someone even if it's a person you know and care for ... like a family member?"

Ada, feeling defensive toward the young man she cared for like a brother, whispered to Lizzie, "He didn't mean it that way, love."

"I trust *you*, Charley Mason!" Lizzie snapped, her eyes burning like coal. "Does that make me a fool, too?" Charley was stunned and obviously embarrassed. She reached across the table and took one of his hands. "Trust is something a person must give freely, Charley," her voice now so soft everyone was straining to hear. "It's only when somebody betrays your trust that it turns bad. Tell me, lad, would you betray my trust?"

"Oh no, I would never let you down, Liz," he retorted. Hanging his head, he tried to pull his hand away but she held it too tightly and would not take her eyes off his face.

Joe cleared his throat then tapped his pipe on the fire grate, as he looked around the room. "Trust is what makes us a family ... she gives it to all of us," he growled, pausing to ruffle the hair of the squirming little boy on his lap. "You want trust? Why it's sat right here on me knee."

Mick looked over the table at the girl he had grown to love as a sister. He watched his wife wipe away a silent tear and realized they probably all had similar thoughts. Their Lizzie had often given them demonstrations of fairness, love and understanding, but never one as poignant as this one. She wanted to get a point across and she was certainly succeeding.

Slipping an arm over Ada's shoulder, he turned toward Lizzie. "Ah sure an begorra you know the lot of us would do anything that's necessary to help each other."

"I know, Mick, and I think there is something we can do but it will take some planning. Here's what I think …."

Sometime later, the group finalized their course of action and delegated Charley to check with his contacts and see if William Crowther had ever actually shipped out cargo for the Suttons.

"Ned's been around this area a long time. He might know something or somebody," Ada suggested. "We'll ask him."

Joe puffed contentedly on a new charge of tobacco. "Go see Tom Legg, luv; if there's anythin to be known he'll be able to rout it out."

A knock sounded on the door. The Grims had arrived to take Charley home.

Before he stood up, Lizzie went over and gave the engineer a special hug, whispering into his ear, "One big happy family, lad."

"Sorry, love," he muttered sheepishly, struggling to his feet.

Willie yawned from his seat on Quon's lap where they played with some wooden toys. His mother announced it was time for them to go home and Willie gave Quon a hug and leaned toward Lizzie.

"Goodnight, little man," she said. "See you tomorra."

Giving out goodnight hugs to everyone, the tired little boy finally went over to see Martha sitting in her chair by the fire. Holding out his arms, he said softly, "Night, Grandma."

Martha picked up the child and held him tightly for a minute before Mick took him. She planted one last kiss on the boy's nose.

Chapter 4

Next morning Lizzie and Quon went to visit their old teacher, Abe Kratze, at his tailor's shop on Water Lane. Lizzie showed their learned friend the document taken from James Sutton. The old man's eyes narrowed and his fingers twitched nervously as he slowly digested its contents and their implications.

"Bad," he muttered, passing the paper back to the girl. "How do you know this person, my dear?"

Lizzie grinned impishly. "Do yer know of a man named James Sutton, Mister Kratze?"

The tailor rubbed his bony chin, thinking hard, but he shook his head. Quon's hands suddenly flew into action.

Lizzie began to smile. "He's a dandy. High-class stuff, probably has an expensive tailor," she said, winking at Quon. "Put out the word, Mister Kratze, I want him found. I need to know more about him."

Abe shook his head and they hurried out of the shop. Abe was a bit bewildered by the request but knew full well that Lizzie would have her reasons.

Dodging through traffic, they narrowly missed being trampled, raising the anger of several drivers

Lizzie yelled over the noise. "BILL'S ... FOR SOME PIE!"

"NOT HUNGLY," Quon yelled back, pushing her to safety.

Reaching the other side, Lizzie spun around to face him. "What did you say? Are you all right?"

The boy's eyes sparkled as he pulled up short of knocking her over. "Wizzy worried!" he exclaimed, making a face like he was sick. Dodging her slap, he ducked nimbly under her arm and tore off down the lane toward Bill's. "ME FIRST!" he called over his shoulder.

Bill Johnson looked startled as Quon raced into the yard with Lizzie, skirts flying, on his heels screaming abuse at him.

"Na then, na then, what's amiss with you two?"

"You crafty little turd ... you slimy son of a frog!" she cried.

Quon did not often laugh out loud, as he was doing now, and Bill rarely saw these busy young people having such childish fun. He assumed that Lizzie had been the brunt of one of her friend's jokes. *Aye, it's nice to see 'em havin some fun. Those young'uns have grown up so fast and so many people depending on 'em,* he thought. *"Sometimes we forget ther barely more than children."*

Seeing the stack of small barrels Bill was setting out, Lizzie commented, "You must be waiting for the lads, Bill?"

Laughter, and iron wheels on the cobblestones, answered her question as the bread cart swung up to the gate, which Quon was already opening. With Billy pulling, Tom riding and Olivera running behind the empty, bouncing contraption, they pulled up beside the barrels.

Connie Johnson came hurrying across the yard balancing a tray of freshly baked pies. Behind her was one of her younger boys struggling with two jugs of cream.

"Here we are lads ... and Lizzie, of course!" she said, setting her tray on a table. "That's a good boy, Bobby," she praised her son, quickly rescuing the sloshing cream jugs.

Quon reached for the first piece of pie as his giggling partner tried to beat him off with her hat. He set it onto a metal plate and poured cream over it until it was swimming. Lizzie did the same. Oly and Billy arrived at the table but just as they reached for a piece of pie, Tom's voice of authority rose over the commotion.

"WE LOAD UP FIRST, LADS!"

The boys groaned, but grinned and ran to help. Bill stepped in to join them. He quickly released the empty vinegar and cider barrels and soon had the full ones into their place, as the boys loaded the bread. The whole operation took no longer than ten minutes and they were all sitting down together.

Tom picked up the empty pie plate. "Who et this one already?"

Lizzie pointed at Quon, trying to hold back her smile then grabbing her hat to hit him again.

Little Olivera jumped off his seat and ran to protect Quon. "Please don't hurt him, Lizzie. He my friend!"

Lizzie grinned mischievously at the Portuguese boy. "Will you look at that, you little turd, you've got a protector!" Then turning to Olivera, she said just loud enough for Quon to hear. "I wouldn't hurt

39

him, Oly lad. I've had him since he were a baby." Then winking, she stood up and quickly got out of Quon's way as he took chase.

The fun was on and the boys loved it. One of them was always getting in trouble and it was usually Quon.

They were all leaving when suddenly Bill turned and called to Lizzie from the bake house doorway, "AH HAD A VISIT FROM ANGUS LAST NIGHT, LASS." She walked partway back until she could hear him. "He brought a new man ta see me, said he wants ta be a baker. Nice sort, ah think his name wor Clem Radcliff. He starts on Monday." Then expecting no answer, he turned and disappeared into the building.

Lizzie and Quon's eyes met. They were opening the gate for the boys when Quon's fingers quickly tapped out a message on his own arm causing Lizzie to laugh aloud.

"From steam engine to loaf maker, that is quite a jump!"

"Miss Lizzie, we've somethin to ask yer," said Tom, hesitating at the gate, but now having the partners' attention.

"It's like this, miss," continued Billy, taking up the story. "Ther's an empty shop over on Long Lane just off Chandler by *Swans*. We wondered if we could start our own bake shop?" He paused as he sought the right words. "It needs cleanin, but we've a lot of customers around there an it would save us time cos they could come an get ther own. We've talked ta Bill about it an he would still supply us." He added with a hopeful smile. "He thinks it's a grand idea."

Lizzie and Quon looked at each other remembering their own start in business. They had been wondering when something like this would happen and admired the boys' spirit.

"If Bill's got the address we'll tek a look," she said, and the boys happily got back to their task and began to move the cart forward. "HOLD UP," she cried, "we want you to do something for us."

The boys set the cart on its legs, exchanging curious glances.

"We want you to ask around if anybody knows a man named James Sutton. Can you remember that? Do it quietly and be very careful. We don't want to make him suspicious. When you find him, come an tell us."

All three nodded gravely.

"What's he done, Miss Lizzie …?" asked Billy, but he was interrupted by Tom who gave the younger lad a quick, hard look.

"Sorry miss, he's nosey, wants ta know everythin. He's a real ferret."

"It's all right, Tom," Lizzie chuckled. "Maybe he'll find James Sutton for us. Go on now, ger off with yer."

As the boys and cart disappeared out of the yard, Bill returned with a piece of paper in his hand. "I heard the lads tell you about the shop. Here's the address, lass. Av been an seen't shop, it's in a right good spot but it needs some repairs an what with expandin here ah just can't afford it. I'd help them lads though by givin 'em credit, just like ah did for you," Bill chuckled, reaching out and patting Quon's back. "Ther good lads an that Tom has a good head on him for business. They tripled my output a long time ago!"

Lizzie nodded silently and they followed the lads through the gate.

The stableyard at *The Robin*, was overflowing with people as they made their way around to the front of the busy coaching house. The sound of Tom Legg's roguish laughter reached them long before they saw the barrel-sitting old sailor and his two toothless, grinning friends.

Banging his shepherd's crook hard on the ground, his ale sloshing over the side of his tankard, he flung up his arms in an exaggerated gesture of welcome when he saw them. "Greetings lass, what brings you to my door today?"

Quon eased forward, his eyes watching closely for the first sign of trouble. He had never liked this man.

Lizzie deliberately rubbed two pennies between her fingers attracting Tom's eyes like magnets. Slowly, he lowered his tankard.

"Who would yer be wantin watchin this time, young lady?" he rasped in an ale-laden voice.

"James Sutton, a high-bred dandy," Lizzie said quietly. She dropped the pennies into her pocket and watched a look of dismay cross the old mariner's face.

"Don't recall havin heard of that one. Anythin more you can tell me?" he muttered, stroking his beard.

Quon's hands flashed and Lizzie nodded imperceptibly.

"Try watching Crowther's ships or their office. Sutton does business with them we're told." They turned away.

Tom came off his barrel and began to whine pitifully, "A coin, miss … just a coin … ta help us through the day."

She winked at Quon and spinning around she flicked a penny at the pegleg. He caught it deftly, balancing precariously on his one leg, and tipping his head slightly, winked at her saucily.

Moving across the busy street they set out to find Charley amongst the usual turmoil of the London docks. As soon as they reached the first warehouse, they heard a strange sound coming from farther down the jetty. Straining to see around huge stacks of cargo and dodging the array of snorting horses and drays, they located the engineer sitting high on his cart. He was waving his stick and shouting orders to someone they couldn't see.

Unnoticed, they peered around the corner as the hissing and clanking noise grew louder. There, totally unattended, was the steam engine. Its firebox glowed as it chugged away contentedly through the mist of an occasional blast of scalding hot steam.

"My word, dumplin! He's got it workin already."

Quon kept his distance from the fizzing monster then jumped back as a larger blast of steam shot forth without warning. Charley looked up and saw them, quickly banging his stick on the side of the cart. The Grim boys appeared out of nowhere, lifted him down and then disappeared again.

As he wobbled over to them, he was grinning broadly. "It's worked like a dream," he chuckled, obviously pleased with himself. "That Da Vinci fella must have been a smart one!"

Quon's eyes were fixed on the steam engine, yet his hands moved quickly.

"He wants to know how I got it fixed so quickly, doesn't he?" asked Charley. Not waiting for an answer, he continued, "Well, I talked one of the gunsmiths down at the Navy yard into working all night. It's been running all day without a moment's trouble."

Lizzie scowled. Charley knew she was puzzled about something and waited patiently for her question, which he knew would come when she was ready. Suddenly, another loud blast of steam made Quon jump behind her. This seemed to break her concentration.

"But what does it do?" she asked.

"What does it do?" he laughed, staggering back to his cart. Banging his stick on the side again, the Grims appeared and hoisted him into his seat. "Oh you just wait an see lass, yer in for a shock any day now!" Turning away, Charley began calling out orders to nearby workmen once again.

Lizzie shrugged her shoulders in answer to Quon's puzzled expression. They had been dismissed.

As the afternoon drew to a close, they wandered toward home, a feeling of not having accomplished very much hanging heavy on their minds. Knowing they were too early for dinner, they decided to go up to the gypsy camp. Halfway up Drover's Lane, they heard the noise of galloping horses and loud, excited voices. Not being able to see past the slaughterhouse buildings, they quickened their step.

"Wonder what's going on, dumplin? The camp must be havin some visitors."

From the noisy barking of dogs intermingled with children's happy screams, something was definitely going on. They hurried toward the throng gathered around the new arrival who was just stepping out of a fancy carriage.

"Wook Wizzy," Quon exclaimed, "it Wady Sutton!"

Stopping dead in their tracks, they watched as the lady alighted and was enveloped by the crowd. A shout from one of two riders galloping by attracted their attention momentarily, but they were more interested in why the lady was here. The crowd parted to let them through and they found Lady Sutton sitting prim and proper on a log near the fire talking to the Romany grandmother.

"Well, I'll be damned!" Lizzie hissed under her breath.

As they reached the high-born lady, she smiled amiably, greeting them happily in her well-cultured voice. "Lizzie ... Quon, it's so nice to see you, my dears."

Before Lizzie could reply, the two riders returned stopping at the edge of the crowd. Sliding easily from the horses' bare backs, they dismounted and two young boys led the mounts away. The smaller of the riders turned around and began to walk quickly toward them, grinning broadly.

"Margaret?" gasped Lizzie. "What are you doing here?" Then realizing who her companion was, she continued, "Hello Ben, giving a riding lesson today, are you?"

Jeb Dark's nephew, smiled broadly, quickly removing his hat.

"Margaret's mother came on my invitation … to meet my family." Then he paused, biting his lip. "That's not strictly true, miss," he admitted, more softly. "We didn't want her left on her own at Sutton House."

Quon touched her arm, his hands moving rapidly.

Lizzie nodded.

"What did he say?" asked Margaret, her eyes sparkling. "Oh, do tell me please, Lizzie?"

"He says Ben is your guardian angel," said Lizzie. "Now what do you think to that, Margaret Sutton? Not many people can say they have a gypsy for an angel!"

Twiddling his cap nervously, Ben lowered his eyes as a pink flush crept up his neck. Margaret, moving toward her mother, didn't notice.

Lady Sutton was obviously enjoying her conversation with the Romany woman even though it was mostly one-sided as the kindly woman spoke nor understood little English.

"Margaret!" her mother greeted her gaily. "Remember your manner, please. Come and meet these delightful people."

Lizzie indicated to Quon it was time to head for home; they said their goodbyes and waved from the gate. Lizzie couldn't help wondering what was going through Lady Sutton's mind. She was truly getting an introduction to the real world of ordinary working people. She had to admit, the woman certainly seemed to be enjoying herself and Lizzie was beginning to like her immensely.

Dinner was a quiet affair as everyone seemed unusually restrained after their busy day. Willie lay on the floor playing contentedly with his blocks, having eaten earlier. Martha was moving somewhat slower and the sound of clanking dishes was abnormally subdued. It wasn't long before Ada and Mick decided to leave, helping Willie put his blocks into the wooden box and safely stashing it under his bed.

Martha finally seemed to get a renewed burst of energy and was soon humming one of her favourite tunes. Dishes and pans clanked together once again as she cleaned up and prepared the kitchen for the next meal. Joe escaped to his chair and sat puffing on his pipe as his eyelids began to droop.

Lizzie and Quon finished drying the dishes and went over to sit on the floor at the old man's feet. With their backs leaning gently against his legs, they stared into the roaring fire soaking up the warmth.

Joe's gnarled hands reached out and ruffled their hair. In a gruff, tired voice, he whispered, "God knows how much ah loves thee. 'Am so proud of yer both."

Martha glanced up, catching her breath sharply as she watched the touching scene. She was so glad to be part of this odd family but she often wondered where this exceptional girl, who was fast becoming a beautiful young woman, would lead them next.

Turning back to her chores, her mind strayed back to when these two young adults had been no more than children. They had always displayed their affection openly for each other, and for Joe, the grateful old man they had so willingly adopted. Theirs was a family like no other she had ever known and she was mighty glad to be a part of it.

Chapter 5

Captain Ben Thorn turned up at the cottage early the following Monday morning, the *London Queen* having arrived on the evening tide. Greeting him warmly, Martha soon had him eating a huge breakfast and amusing everyone with his latest tales of the sea.

He shook his head vigorously when Martha offered him a fourth egg and an extra rasher of ham. "Easy Martha, yer goin ta ruin me figure!"

Joe laughed, reaching for his cap and coat from behind the door. "Too late for that, lad!" Turning in the doorway, the old man looked back with a thoughtful expression. "John Watson wants to get his first load of malting barley in, lass. So, we could do with getting Dixon's corn mill cleaned out."

Quon's hands began to move as the sound of Joe's boots faded on the path. Ben smiled, but having seen the Chinese boy's actions many times before, he just waited.

"Bit dangerous comin in at night in't it, captain?" asked Martha, picking up Ben's empty plate.

"Full moon helped," he replied.

"Know a man named James Sutton, Ben?" Lizzie asked, eager to get her friend's reaction. "He's an investor ... ships with Crowther, I'm told."

"Not personally," he replied, thoughtfully, "but I know somebody who will, if he ships with Crowther's."

Lizzie jerked to attention. "Who?" she demanded, feeling Quon's fingers on her arm.

Ben grinned. Watching these two when their minds were at work fascinated him. "Why, my cousin Joshua works in their office."

"Can we meet him?" she asked, excitedly. "Why don't you bring him here for dinner ... tonight!"

"No, I think it would be better if I went up to see him," he replied.

"When?" she asked.

The suddenness of the request startled Ben. "I don't ...," he began, interrupted by the sound of a buggy horse as it trotted briskly by taking Lizzie's attention.

She flew to the window. "Nathan!" she announced. "He can take you." A flick of her hand sent Quon tearing out of the door. Ben took a puff on his pipe, trying to work out what they were up to.

"Come on, lad, let's go find yer ride," she urged, opening the door and beckoning to him.

Ben thanked Martha and dutifully followed. Keeping up to her was not an easy feat for a man of his later years. They found Quon standing beside Nathan's empty buggy waiting for them outside the office. Entering, they received a cheery greeting from Ada and Mick while Ned Cabin, their clerk, nodded politely from behind his desk. Then she noticed Nathan pacing impatiently in the corner.

"STOP IT!" cried Lizzie, making Ben jump but having the desired effect on Nathan. "I want you to ride Ben down to Crowther's."

"Crowther's?" the trader echoed, tapping his silver-topped cane on the floor as his temper rose. He took a step closer to Lizzie.

Quon jumped forward, eyes blazing.

Nathan stopped, took a deep breath and then relaxed again, a smile spreading across his face. He turned to Ada, bowing with an exaggerated flourish. "Good day to you, ladies and gentlemen. Come along, Ben; let me take you for a ride."

Ada, with eyes dancing, glanced up at her husband. Mick winked. He reached for the order sheet Ned was holding out to him and moved toward the door reading it.

"Sure hoy be admirin that, Nathan. Look at these orders he brings in." With a quick wave, he stepped outside and was gone.

Ada watched him through the window and sighed audibly before turning back to Lizzie. "Did you find him?" she asked, sharply. "James Sutton, I mean."

"No, but we will," Lizzie promised, with an obvious air of confidence. "That's where Ben's gone now."

The partners headed for the door but Ned's voice droned from the back of the room causing them to stop and listen.

"Joshua Thorn ... could that be Ben's brother? Josh has worked fer Crowther's fer many a year," Ned asked, turning to the girl who was now smiling in the doorway.

"Cousin, actually," she offered.

"So," said Ada, "that's why you sent Ben there in such a hurry."

Closing the door, Lizzie and Quon walked slowly back down the track to Slaughter Lane. Her arm rested lightly across his shoulder as they silently entertained their own thoughts.

A church clock began striking and when it had reached nine, Quon said abruptly, "Bled shop!"

"Too early, you can't be hungry already?"

"No, bled shop for boys!" he exclaimed.

Realizing he was referring to the new enterprise, they turned into Wozer Street then down several back alleys until they found Chandler. It was an old area with rows of soot-blackened stone buildings in ill repair. Stained black from centuries of exposure to open fires and coal-spewing chimneys, this area was home to the multitude of London's poor people. Living and working here, sometimes for their entire lives, they formed their own community within dockland. This morning several small groups stood around small coal fires warming themselves as they smoked and talked. Children played nearby, running about to keep warm and getting in everyone's way.

Standing back a good distance and keeping to the far side of the narrow street, they watched a coach pass by and disappear into a yard down near the river. Nearing *Swans* ale house, they noted the unusual number of people milling about across the street and crossed over. Pushing through the throng of residents and shoppers, they turned onto Long Lane and found the address Bill had supplied.

Another smart coach passed by more slowly, its driver furtively looking about before entering the same yard as the first. Watching more carefully now, the street-wise girl jabbed Quon silently in the ribs and pointed as another coach appeared coming from the opposite direction. It too, turned into the same yard.

Moving toward the grimy, cobweb-loaded window of the vacant shop, they peered in. Noticing a ray of light coming through a hole in the roof Lizzie grimaced and turned to Quon but he had moved off and was already checking the other shops in the street.

Turning her attention back to the shop, she became aware of the steady stream of customers entering and leaving the butcher shop next door. Curious, she stepped into the street to get a better view. To the left of the boy's shop was a tiny little corner store. Everything about it was small, unusually small, yet its neat and tidy little window held a sign which said, CANDLE MAKER AND OIL LAMP REPAIR.

As she walked back to the empty shop, a little child ran into her, falling at her feet. She stooped to help the youngster who was so dirty she couldn't tell if it was a boy or girl. A rough-looking young woman, no doubt its mother, appeared in close attendance.

"Is it always so busy around here, marm?" Lizzie asked.

"Folks av ter buy their vitals!" the woman snapped, eyeing Lizzie scornfully, as she pulled the child toward her. "We're poor folk an money's scarce."

Quon arrived back at her side and they watched the woman hurry away with the child desperately hanging onto her skirt as it tried to keep up. His hands began to gyrate, causing passers-by to look at them with distrustful eyes before scurrying away.

"We'll ask the butcher," she whispered.

Entering the butcher's store, they found the proprietor chopping meat while a woman, no doubt his wife, was wrapping up some meat for a customer. He was a tall, yet plump, red-faced man wearing a red-and-white striped apron and a straw hat. He had a massive growth of graying mutton-chop whiskers. Looking up from his work, he rested his blood-stained axe on his shoulder and came to the counter.

"Well, what can ah do fer yer?" he inquired, loudly.

"Who owns the derelict shop next door?" Lizzie asked.

Laying his axe down, he came across the sawdust-strewn floor toward them and looked them over curiously. "It ain't worth a damn. Roof leaks an it needs work inside. Crowther owns it."

A lady customer interrupted their conversation and the butcher turned back to his work. Taking her order, he unhooked a large piece of meat hanging from the ceiling. Swinging his axe, they heard it crunch through meat and bone. Shuddering, they quickly backed out of the shop amusing three young street urchins who had been watching.

"Food miss? Food for the hungry," said the scrawny lad of about eight, putting on his most doleful expression.

"Wait here," Lizzie snapped. Walking back into the butcher's shop she gave the woman her order. "Three meat pies, please marm."

Making sure she got the money first, the woman wrapped the pies and handed them to her.

Outside, Lizzie sat down on the curb and opened the parcel. "Sit down the'selves, lads," she ordered.

Realizing she was not going to part with the pies until they did as they were told, they reluctantly obeyed.

"Eat 'eartily, lads," she said, then lowering her voice added, "Then ah want somethin from yer."

Although unsure of what was to follow, they hungrily gobbled down their pies. As the last crumb was gleaned from their grubby palms, they stood up but Lizzie held up her hand.

"Whot's in the yard down ther?" she asked, pointing to where the coaches had gone. "Is ther a way in?"

With a serious expression, the first lad put his hand to his mouth and whispered secretively, "Gentry, miss. Ther drinkin an gamin. You don't want to go ther. Them'll kill yer if they catch yer!"

Lizzie bit her lip. Quon's arms began flailing about, startling the street lads. Shaking her head, Lizzie merely smiled, inquisitiveness was getting the better of her.

"Show us how yer ger in," she demanded, coming to her feet.

A glance passed between the boys and the taller lad stepped forward. Pulling himself up to his full height, he stuck out his chest and said confidently, "We'll do it fer free farvins, miss!"

Lizzie nodded her agreement, appreciating the style and audacity of these street rascals. The other boys took up their friend's lead, running ahead and beckoning Lizzie and Quon to follow. Darting down the nearest alley, they twisted and turned through several archways finding a narrow snicket which took them to a little-used yard. They went straight to a wall up against which stood a rickety ladder. Without hesitation, the boys began climbing the ladder which took them to the roof. Stepping out onto the flat surface they again beckoned Lizzie and Quon to follow.

Motioning them to be quiet, the boys waited until they were all together. With the stealth of cats, they moved across the narrow expanse in single file until they reached the next building. With the buildings so close together, in no time they had crossed several roofs. The lad up ahead stopped, appearing to bend over and lift something.

All of a sudden, he dropped out of sight, then the other two as well. Arriving at the spot where the boys had last been seen, Lizzie and Quon discovered a small open door under which they found a set of stairs. One of the lads was waiting at the bottom. Climbing down, they let their eyes adjust to the darkness.

"Careful, miss," one of the boys hissed near Lizzie's ear. "Watch yer feet!"

Suddenly, they realized they could hear the sound of men's voices coming from below. They moved slowly forward an inch at a time, feeling their way in the dark, at the same time listening intently.

"Hell, if it wasn't for bad luck; I wouldn't have no luck at all!" came a loud but muffled voice from below.

One of the street lads roughly grabbed her arm and turned her toward a small hole in the floor a few feet in front of them. Light was shining through it so it was easily seen but it was only large enough for one person to look through at a time.

She went down onto her knees and inched closer, being very careful not to make a sound. She braced herself between the wooden beams and bent over to look through the hole.

Beneath them she could see the hands and tops of the heads of five men around a table. She could see parts of other men but had no idea how many more were in the room. They were playing some kind of game with dice and a pile of golden guineas lay in the middle of the table. As each man took his turn with the dice, he threw another coin into the pile, which was getting quite large.

Seeing no benefit from her observations, she crawled back along the beam and they retreated the way they had come. Once back in the street, she paid the boys their three farthings.

"What is that place?" she asked.

"They call it *The Pit*, miss," one of them called over his shoulder as they scampered away.

Trying to follow, Lizzie and Quon looked to see which direction the boys had gone but they had quickly disappeared. Finding their way back to the shops, they took one last look at the empty store. Lizzie began to visualize it as the delivery boys had no doubt seen it in their minds. Her memory turned back to the time she was the bread delivery girl and Joe collected rags. *Happy times,* she thought, *and so long ago. So much has happened since the day I met Joe ... and Quon.* Feeling his hand on her arm, she surprised him by grabbing it. Silently she set off toward the river pulling him along beside her.

They cut down onto the riverfront road then grabbed a ride by hanging onto the back of a coach that took them right by *The Robin*.

Not surprisingly, they found Tom and his cronies in their usual spot. A shout from the peg-legged sailor quickly brought the partners over. Quon's hands began moving, though never taking his eyes off the man on the barrel.

"No! Yer jesting?" Lizzie said, grinning impishly at her partner. She walked over and peered down at Tom's legs ... that is, at Tom's one leg.

"What 'appened to yer leg, Tom, av yer misplaced it?" she asked, trying not to laugh.

Banging his crook on the cobblestones, the ex-mariner scowled fiercely. "That ornery hound went an et it, chewed it all to bits!"

"What hound?" she snickered, hearing Quon giggling behind her.

Tom was not in any mood for explanations. "That damned hound at Crowther's shipping office, an you sent me there!" he snarled.

"What?" retorted Lizzie, giggling behind her hand. "They set the dog on yer? Well thank goodness it didn't pick the one with meat on it!" she cried, now laughing so hard she had to sit down, which didn't do anything to appease Tom's bad temper.

He hobbled toward her using his shepherd's crook, but Quon pulled her back to a safe distance. In his drunken state, he couldn't manage to keep his balance and almost fell over flopping onto a nearby barrel and glowering at his mates who were snickering behind their tankards.

"Oh, I'll get ya a new one, stop yer whinin," she chortled, as Quon pulled her toward the street. "Go down to Brown's Yard and see Lumpy. He'll fix yer up. Just tell him to send the bill to TLS."

They were still laughing as they reached the tailor's shop. Sat at the sewing table, Abe peered over his glasses at them as Lizzie slid into the chair opposite.

"Any news for me?" she asked quietly, staring at him. She could feel Quon's fingers begin to move on her shoulder and she reached up and lightly touched his hand. It stopped immediately.

"Dixon's gone, been paid out. We have the keys and all," he said, sounding distantly relieved. "All the papers you wanted are here."

"Good, any news of James Sutton?"

The question seemed to give the old man a jolt and he dropped his needle and thread. "Good gracious girl, don't you ever stop pushing," he said in frustration.

Lizzie felt the pressure of Quon's fingers on her shoulder, sending a warning.

"Never, old friend, never," she replied gently. She stood up and they moved toward the door leaving their old teacher cradling his head in his hands and moaning softly.

Moving outside into the late winter sunlight, they threaded their way through the afternoon crowds. They were headed for their favourite eating spot, having now realized they had completely missed lunch. Not expecting to meet the delivery boys so late in the day, it was a surprise to find them in the yard loaded and getting prepared to leave.

"Late aren't you, Tom?" she asked.

Hearing her voice, Bill came out of the bake house mopping his brow on a large cloth.

"Watch them loaves, Clem, not too brown now," he called over his shoulder.

"'Ar ship's leavin late, miss. It's all one order!" Tom explained, obviously pleased with himself but eager to be off. "Did yer see that shop, miss? Can we ger it?"

Bill looked from one to the other. Clem called from the bake house causing the baker to swing around but, before he went inside, he looked back at Lizzie. "Well, what do yer think of it, luv?"

"Yes, we'll do it, but it's going to take a little time to get organized," she replied, watching the elation on the boys' faces.

Olivera ran around the cart wrapping his arms around Quon's waist and giving him a squeeze. Quon patted the still-small boy on the top of his head then he ran to catch up with the boys.

Clem stuck his head out of the bake house door and waved.

"LIKE YER NEW JOB, CLEM?" Lizzie shouted, as her partner nudged her arm and pointed toward the house.

Connie was on her way across the yard with a plateful of sandwiches and several tankards of cider on a large tray. Moving toward the table, they waited for Clem's answer.

"AYE LASS, CERTAINLY DO," he shouted back.

While eating, they listened as Missus Johnson voiced her concern about the new bakery shop. Bill had told her about the broken-down place the boys had their sights set on.

"I can't help wonder if the boys might be trying to take on too much," she said, in a worried tone.

Lizzie reached over and patted the good-hearted lady's hand. "Missus Johnson, you're a luv. You already have six children of your own but them lads are like kin to you, aren't they?" She noticed the damp sheen glistening in the lady's eyes. "Well, I think they've worked hard for us for a long time and now they want the chance to have something of their own. They deserve to have that chance."

"Yer an angel, Lizzie," she said softly, picking up the soiled dishes and brushing the crumbs off the table. "And yer right too."

Out in the street, Quon suddenly began flailing his arms about. "Blewely men will help," he said aloud.

"Yes, let's go talk to Angus, dumplin; he'll get that shop cleaned up for us real fast."

They had almost reached the brewery gates when Quon stopped dead in his tracks. Lizzie stopped, too, eying him suspiciously.

"Now what?"

Watching his hands, she began to understand his concern. She turned and pointed back the way they had come. "Abe, it's Abe we need to negotiate on that shop. We're going too fast on this one."

Quickening their pace they were back at the tailor's shop in less than five minutes. Bursting through the door, they startled the poor man who tried to remain calm as he followed them to the rear of the shop. He knew better than to question the girl before she was ready.

"Slate and chalk, Mister Kratze," she demanded. "Crowther owns it an I want it dirt cheap. Steal it if you have to!"

Abe shuffled around looking for his chalk. His head was in a whirl, but that was usual when Lizzie was around. He handed her the two items. "Slow down, slow down, girl. What is it?"

Chalking the address on the slate, she pushed it across the table toward him. Reading it, he grinned. "I know this place, but you don't really want this old building."

"Yes, I do, and quickly," she retorted, leaping off her chair and headed for the door. "Do it, old friend," she yelled over her shoulder.

Chapter 6

As Ben Thorn climbed down from Nathan's buggy at the entrance to William Crowther's shipping office, he found himself in the path of two high-spirited hackney trotting horses being driven in a wild and reckless manner. Jumping back to safety, he caught a brief look at a lace-festooned dandy as the skittish horses and shiny black carriage with a large emblem on its door, careened by.

He caught Nathan's look of alarm and noticed Wick had stood up and was waving his big knotted club menacingly after them. Ben let out his breath. *Now there's a man I wouldn't want to meet when he's really mad!*

Jumping down from the buggy seat, Wick landed beside him. Touching his cap, he asked, "Shall I stay, sir?"

Captain Thorn was astounded. This was the first time in his adult life that anyone had offered to take care of him, least of all a gypsy. He remembered the event several years ago when he had spent some time with Jeb—the night Lizzie had stolen the Bishop's gunship in an effort to save Captain Davis and the crew of the *Falcon* from disaster. His attitude was changing toward these once wandering Romanies.

"No, lad, I'll be fine," he replied. "You go with Mister Goldman, but I'm grateful for the offer."

He watched Nathan's buggy until it went out of sight, then he turned and looked up at the massive, four-storied stone building he had not visited for some years. It was even more oppressive looking than he remembered. Moving toward the high iron gate with its impressive gilded crest on top of a high steel arch, he moved into the yard. It looked deserted but he forged ahead climbing the wide stone stairway toward the great oak door. The only sounds he could hear were his own footsteps and a ship's bell in the distance.

He banged the door knocker and waited. It was almost a minute before the door swung partially open. A deep voice inquired from the gloom within, "Who shall I say is calling, sir?"

Ben drew himself up to his full height. "Captain Benjamin to see

Joshua Thorn ... and quickly if you please," he announced.

The door closed and he drew a sigh of relief, having deliberately not given his last name. A few long minutes went by before the door opened again.

"Come in, sir," the voice announced, closing the door quickly behind him. "Follow me, sir. Mister Thorn will see you now."

Ben followed the doorman across the dark expanse of the stone-floored hallway, entering a long passageway. Their shoes pounded loudly on the polished wooden floor. It was much quieter than he remembered from visiting a few years before. Surprisingly, there seemed to be no one about. The doorman turned a corner into a narrower hall and led Ben to a door in the dark corner. He opened it slowly and it creaked softly. An unexpected brilliant ray of sunshine shining through the small window caused him to shade his eyes, brightening the gloomy room and his mood.

Stepping into the room, Ben saw a man with long, but sparse, white hair bent over his books at a high desk. A tall stool supported his light frame that was wrapped in a long back overcoat. The door snapped shut behind him and he turned slightly to assure himself they were alone.

"Joshua?" he asked, moving closer.

Slowly, the old man straightened, wincing slightly with pain. He adjusted his glasses that were perched precariously on his small nose, and peered over them, his hand shaking a little.

"Ben, is it really you?" Joshua croaked, his mouth twitching into a slight smile. "What are you doing here?"

"Looking for information about a certain young dandy called James Sutton," Ben explained, moving closer so he could keep his voice down.

Reaching out to shake his cousin's hand, Joshua slowly lowered himself back onto his stool. Pulling a ledger from the bookshelf in front of him, he re-adjusted his glasses and studied the list of entries. Turning over several pages, his finger ran jerkily down the column of names.

"No Sutton here now," he muttered, "used to be though. I believe he died a couple of years back." His finger, still running down a page, stopped suddenly. "There," he pointed. "Like I said, only a John Sutton, over two years ago."

Ben thanked his cousin profusely, then answered Joshua's query about several long-unseen family members.

"Haven't seen any of them for years, but I'd heard my youngest brother, Harold, couldn't wait to join the Navy and went off to fight Napoleon." Then, changing the subject, he added, "Is old man Crowther still around?"

The effect of these words on his cousin was dramatic. He hurled his quill at the wall and came off his stool so quickly Ben moved closer lest he fall. Joshua raised his fist, his eyes blazing fire. "No dammit, he's not! That young popinjay he calls a son runs this place now an we're going to the dogs, fast," he snarled. Then staggering back to his stool, he wearily slumped against the desk resting his head in his hands. "He just left before you arrived. He's always looking for money for drink and gambling."

"A shame," Ben lied, remembering what a tyrant William Crowther used to be, hard as nails to his workers and so bad-tempered men detested doing business with him. *So his son was his downfall. Well, you reap what you sow,* he thought scornfully. "So you've never heard the name James Sutton, Joshua?" Ben asked again, watching his cousin's face.

"Didn't say that," Joshua snapped. "Hear it all the time from that young fool ... they're friends of a sort."

"What sort?" Ben inquired, trying not to appear to eager.

Peering over his glasses, the old man frowned as his fingers drummed angrily on the desk. Obviously giving some consideration to his next words, he took an audible breath. "Gambling, and living wild ... up to no good, I'll be bound," he growled. Then pushing his glasses back on his nose again, he took another deep breath. "You know, lad," he whispered, leaning closer and grasping Ben's sleeve. "I've worked here over 30 years and never enjoyed a single minute of it."

The doorman's deep voice interrupted their conversation as he knocked and entered. "Someone to see you, sir."

Joshua nodded and stood up, extending a hand to his cousin as the door closed again. Their visit was over. As they shared a warm handshake, Ben knew he had learned all that was possible.

The doorman was waiting to usher him out so he never saw Joshua's visitor. Stepping outside, he listened to the echo as the big door banged shut behind him. Ben stood for a moment and pondered his mission. He'd been a seaman most of his life and knew every ship's officer that sailed from the Thames. He quickly went down the stone steps knowing his mind was already formulating a plan. His feet turned automatically to the river.

As he crossed the street to the docks, he counted six ships at the Lancaster and Queen Anne jetties. Of various sizes, they were almost all merchant cargo vessels, except for the sloop converted for carrying coal. At the King's Dock were two barques, but there was little activity going on in the vicinity.

When his gaze strayed down toward the TLS dock, however, even from this distance he could feel the energy, something he had noticed many times before.

Striding westward, he scanned the familiar jetty. Yes, there was Charley. It was his incomparable and unfailing enthusiasm that went a long way in making this company successful. *Apart from Lizzie, of course!* he thought with a smile. *Oh, to be 20 years younger.*

The sound of carriage wheels broke into his thoughts and, for the second time that day, he leaped to safety as iron-shod hooves crashed onto the cobblestones behind him and turned down to the dock.

Ben recognized the driver and the carriage emblem, realizing it was the same one he had escaped from earlier. Quickening his pace, he tried to gain a look at the passenger who had already left the carriage and was strutting along the dock toward one of the offices. The wind was rustling the silly frills of his silk shirt cuffs and neckline. *My Lord, another dandy!* thought Ben, his attention rivetted on the man.

"What yer doin here, Ben?" growled a voice in his ear, making him jump. Turning, he grasped the offered hand of Arthur Strickland, an old friend.

"Who's that popinjay strutting around down yonder?" Ben asked.

"That's James Sutton," Tom muttered. "One of young Crowther's clan."

Grim lines deepened on Ben's face. "Had any trouble with privateers lately, Tom?"

His friend chuckled sarcastically, a twinkle of devilment in his eye. "No privateers, not for ten years, lad. Mighty quiet around here these days except for the illegal cargo the tax ship keeps takin, you know ... Davis and his mate, what's his name? Oh aye, ah remember, Ben Thorn ain't it!"

The men laughed heartily without a trace of bitterness. Offspring of ancient seafaring families, whether Ben worked for the government or for TLS they were essentially on opposite sides, yet still regarded the other with great esteem.

Leaving the docks, Ben walked over to *The Robin,* suddenly feeling the need for food. He hadn't been in this public house for some months. Ordering a beef and pickle sandwich with a flagon of ale, he decided to sit outside and took a table facing the river. Turning up his collar against the cool breeze of the river, he sat back to watch noting the unusual number of drays coming and going from the TLS area. His order arrived and, as he ate, he became even more curious.

Suddenly, he heard loud puffing and hissing followed by some strange clanking sounds. Then a cheer erupted from an unseen group of men down on the dock.

"What's going on over there?" Ben inquired of the man at the next table.

"They've got some kind of new-fangled machine down there, been messing with it all week," replied the stranger.

Ben drank the last of his ale, threw some coins on the table, and climbed to his feet.

Anticipating his actions, the stranger called to him. "Won't let you near, captain, no good tryin. Top secret is the word on the docks."

Smiling, Ben touched his hat and left the table in the direction of the noise. He cursed under his breath, noting the increasing traffic with frustrated drivers trying to get through the busy intersection. Not being quite as nimble as he used to be, Ben carefully negotiated the mad throng.

At the entrance to the TLS dock area, the noise became more obvious. Two sailors stood guard just as the stranger had said. They saluted and allowed him to pass without question. Farther up the dock, Ben could see Charley on his cart concentrating on something and totally unaware that he was approaching. Keeping back a distance, he looked around to see what was going on.

Ben could hardly believe his eyes. A broad belt-like apparatus reached from the dock across the open space to the deck of a ship.

Sacks were being transported from the ship and being deposited onto a large dray. Ben watched fascinated, yet still keeping his distance from the hissing monster. The two men stacking the heavy sacks onto the dray were having difficulty keeping pace, although being loudly urged on by Charley's encouragement. It was not long before the dray was full and the empty belt ground to a halt.

A great cheer rang out from Charley and the men on the ship, although the two men stacking the sacks collapsed on the ground panting for breath. Charley checked his watch and wrote something on his slate. The driver of the dray climbed aboard and began to move the heavy load forward. Soon the six snorting shires had the groaning dray moving off toward the city.

"THIRTY-ONE MINUTES, LADS!" Charley whooped, then noticing Ben nearby, he waved him over. "Did you see that, Ben?" he asked excitedly. "We loaded that dray in 31 minutes." He paused, scratching some calculations on his slate. "That means we can ship grain in sacks from Hull, unloading it in one day."

"Fifty to eighty ton in one day?" gasped Ben.

"Easy," Charley boasted. "I'll tell Lizzie at dinner, she'll be a mite thrilled."

Captain Ben cocked an eyebrow. "Now she'll want all the grain trade. My God, lad, where will it end!"

It was a quarter of six when Ben arrived at the partly open cottage door. Tapping lightly, he heard Martha's greeting and entered. Joe was sitting in his armchair, puffing contentedly on his pipe and watching the smoke rings slowly rise to the ceiling.

"Something sure smells good, Martha!" he exclaimed, moving toward the chair she indicated. Then, remembering why he had come, he asked, "Where's Lizzie?"

Joe looked up, sliding the pipe from between his lips. "Gone for a minute to see Mick an Ada ... took Willie with her." He had hardly finished saying it when Willie burst through the door. Seeing the not-too-familiar figure of Captain Ben, he shyly ran by and jumped onto Joe's knee.

Martha smiled and continued fussing over her cooking at the open fire. Lizzie's voice was heard chattering to someone as she came up the garden path; and Mick and Ada came through the door first with the youngsters following closely behind.

Greeting Ben, they all took their places around the table. The group talked noisily until Martha banged two pan lids together and called for peace and quiet. Plates were filled in silence except for a sigh or two when they saw the large roast and Yorkshire puddings.

"That's better," Martha chuckled, "yer a noisy lot tonight!"

The sound of wheels outside announced that Charley was also arriving.

"Did he tell you?" he asked breathlessly, his voice rising with excitement as he made his entrance.

"Charles Mason," Ada scolded, "come and eat, we can talk business later."

"But I did it, Ada, I did it!" he exclaimed, his voice rising with each word as he made his way painfully to the table.

Quon's fingers went unnoticed under the table, but Lizzie smiled as she shoveled another mouthful in, watching Charley out of the corner of her eye.

Ben's fork hadn't stopped moving as he lit into his food with enthusiasm. Suffering the lack of good home-cooked meals for many days, he tried to support Charley but received a menacing look from Ada for talking with his mouth full.

Martha chuckled in the background, finally joining them at the table. Then all went quiet and only the click of cutlery and the occasional slurp was heard as people cleaned their plates and sat back with contented sighs.

"Did you make a pie, Martha?" Ben asked.

"When av yer ever eaten here Ben Thorn when ther's been no pie!" she retorted.

Laughing, the rest of the group watched the captain retreat, trying in vain to voice an apology.

Martha continued on with her ranting. "By gum, lad, yer like an eating machine," she scolded, rising from the table. "I've used the last of the cellar apples for this pie, so be grateful lad, it may be yer last! Perhaps ah shouldn't give you any, yer cheeky devil."

"Go on give it to him, Martha," Ada encouraged. "We can't bear to see a grown man cry!"

Willie jumped off Joe's knee and ran over to Martha just as she picked up two pies from the kitchen counter. He wrapped his arms around the stout housekeeper's legs and looked up at her.

"Grandma, please don't be cross with Captain Ben," he cried.

Martha's temper melted like butter under the boy's big brown eyes. Putting the pies down, she scooped him into her arms and hugged him close for a moment.

"Yer getting too big for Grandma to pick up anymore, Willie. I guess I'm just feedin ya too well!"

Willie ran off and she picked up the pies again. Quon got up to bring the large jug of custard to the table.

"I suppose you want a bigger piece for helpin!" she teased. "Yer another one who's growin too much ... too much pie, I dare say."

Quon quickly sat down, head hung to hide his red cheeks.

Martha began to dish out the pie. She poured a generous portion of custard over the first large serving, passing it to Ben as a slight smile crinkled her face. Then she repeated the action with a slightly smaller piece passing it to Quon.

Quon looked over at Lizzie and grinned sheepishly.

She patted his leg. "Eat yer pie, dumplin."

When they all sat back commenting on how full they felt, Ada noticed Charley's frustrated expression.

"I think we've kept Charley waiting long enough. Give us a few minutes to clear this table, lad, and you can tell us this news of yours."

Getting up, she was joined by Martha, Lizzie and Quon and soon the table was cleared in record time. Charley was now fidgeting with his pipe, as he waited none too patiently. Finally they were all seated again and everyone turned to face him.

"As I said ... today, I got the machine working ... the steam engine, I mean." He looked around the table. "You saw it, Ben, we unloaded four ton of grain from a ship and onto a dray in 31 minutes."

"Thirty-one minutes for four ton!" gasped Joe.

Ben nodded. "Aye, and nearly killed the poor men loading the drays!" Then he leaned back and took a big puff on his pipe in silence.

Mick's eyes narrowed, his brow creasing into a frown. "Ah sure, it sounds to be awful fast, if it's true!"

"Oh, its true," Charley assured him. "It's that steam engine that does it, works faster than ten men and never needs a rest."

Quon's fingers burst into action on the table top.

Lizzie smiled, looking sideways at Ada. "That means you've solved us the grain problem, lad. Well done!"

Quon's fingers drummed the tabletop again, only to be interrupted by Ada making her calculations out loud.

"Thirty-one minutes for four tons ... let's say ten minutes a ton, and a load of fifty ton of grain," she said solemnly, looking over at Lizzie. "Why it would all be unloaded in under ten hours, even with a lunch break! Is that the best you can do, Charley?" she added, winking at Lizzie.

Lizzie giggled and Mick almost choked on his smoke.

"Right!" Lizzie announced. "We can buy that grain in Hull then, if it's cheap."

"Wait, wait!" cried Charley. "It has to be bagged before we receive it."

They nodded in unison.

Ada cocked her head in their direction. "Customers," she reminded them, "we're going to need some new ones now!"

Again Quon's fingers talked to Lizzie and she pushed her chair back. Rising, she faced the group while still watching Quon. She smiled coyly but made no effort to answer Ada's comment.

"First, we send Ben to Hull to pick up that grain. You can write him a contract for supply, Ada." She paused, watching the bookkeeper nod. "Next job is yours, Mister Mick," said Lizzie. "The Dixon corn merchant's buildings are in need of some cleaning and fixing up."

"But hoy don't be havin any men spare," Mick grumbled, taking his pipe from his mouth.

Joe tapped the table with his pipe stem. "I do, lad, we'll talk about it later."

"Thanks, Dad," Lizzie murmured. "Is Mister Watson ready for a load of grain?"

"Been talkin about it fer days," said Joe, wiping the back of his hand across his mouth. "Told him ye'd take care of it though." Satisfied with his input, he leaned back in his chair again.

No one spoke for awhile and Ada raised her eyebrows inviting Lizzie to carry on.

"Now for your news, Captain Thorn. You've been off all day. Can you report any success?" she demanded, sitting down again.

Ben described the events of his visit to Crowther's, relating the information his cousin Joshua had provided. Lizzie's fingers drummed on the table and her eyes squeezed into narrow slits as her thoughts grew more intense.

Ada watched Quon's hand slowly reach out and rest on his partner's forearm.

"So, no doubt we should be expecting trouble from Mister Sutton," said Lizzie thoughtfully.

"Ah sure, these are the big boys, Colleen," Mick interceded, a note of concern in his voice. "Men with influence and money, they spit on little people like us."

Ada lowered her head and turned toward Mick hissing, "Now you've done it!"

Lizzie's hand came crashing onto the table. Ada's head came up instantly and Lizzie jumped to her feet, almost knocking her chair over backwards.

"Spit on us, will he?" she snapped. "Well that's what Long John Stroud thought, and the Bishop, and the Spanish at Zarauz, but we beat the lot of 'em didn't we?"

Ben began to laugh, turning to Mick who was rolling his eyes. "Slow learner, lad!" he chuckled. "My money's on Lizzie."

Ada smiled at her husband, slipping her hand into his. "It's all right, love, you don't have to worry. She'll work it out and God help them!"

"She's right, Mick," agreed Ben. "We've a secret weapon out there," pointing a finger into the air haphazardly.

Lizzie giggled as she watched the interplay between her friends and Mick's blank expression. Quon's fingers tapped on her arm. "It's Captain Davis, Mick," she laughed, winking at Ada. "And you're just a big lovable Irishman, though daft as a brush. Take him home, Ada, the poor lad's tired!"

Mick's face went beet-root red but his wife nudged him and pointed at Willie, fast asleep on Joe's lap. In a few minutes, they had said their goodnights and were heading for the door.

Closing the door behind them, Lizzie turned to Charley. "Your lads should be here soon."

"They're already here," he replied, "heard them ten minutes ago. They're just waiting for me to call them."

"Then do it," she coaxed, through a big yawn. "I'm going to bed."

"Wait a minute, Liz," Ben cried. "When do I leave for Hull?"

"As soon as Charley has a ship ready and Ada has the contract. I want you to work with Charley but first find out when *Falcon*'s due back."

Ben nodded, relieved that he now knew what was expected of him. Pushing his chair back, he rose and went to find his jacket from behind the door. When he pulled on the latch and opened the door, Charley winked at Lizzie, curled his lip back and whistled loudly. Joe stirred in his chair. Ben shook his head as he left, closing the door behind him. A few seconds later, a knock was heard and Grey Grim's head appeared in the doorway.

Chapter 7

A few days later, Lizzie and Quon decide to visit Dixon's old corn mill. Inside the yard they find two burly strangers loading a dray with rubbish. Quon opened the gate and they entered walking over toward the men.

The first man to notice, stopped work, and resting a badly scarred arm on the end of his shovel, looking up curiously. "Somethin ah can help yer with, miss?"

Quon's hands went wild for a moment and Lizzie noticed the frown on the man's face as he watched suspiciously.

"Know who we are, mister?" she asked.

His reply was lost in a shout from the street as Lefty came running toward them.

"Found yer, Miss Lizzie!" he panted with obvious relief, mopping his brow as he settled down on one knee.

With a concerned frown, she was at his side in an instant. "What's the matter, Lefty?"

"There's a call out for yer. Maybe yer can't hear the cottage bell from here," he gasped. "Ada needs yer urgent."

Even before his last word was spoken she and Quon were off at a run. Crossing Mast Lane, they met the delivery boys.

"MISS LIZZIE, YER NEEDED AT HOME!" Tom shouted.

Quon stopped just long enough to signal to him.

Bursting through the office door it crashed out of control against the wall, startling both Ada and Ned.

"It's Jeb, love ... says it's the children," said the bookkeeper with a puzzled look. "He needs to see you right away."

"Oh no!" Lizzie cried, turning quickly and bumping into Quon.

He hurried after her almost running Mick down as the foreman walked toward the back door. Mick grabbed Quon to steady him and noticed the uncharacteristic show of emotion on his face.

"What? What?" Mick asked, but Quon pulled away.

Entering the office, Mick looked at Ned and he merely shrugged.

Ada turned from the window. "Don't ask, love, we don't know exactly. Something to do with some children," she said, in a voice strained by concern. "I knew it! she said, under her breath.

"Come on, Mick, we've work to do, lad," Ned urged. He was always the cool one despite his gruff, old-fashioned ways. "Lizzie will tell us about it when she's ready."

"WHERE'S JEB," Lizzie gasped as they entered the gypsy camp and saw a group of the men gathered around a wagon. Jeb came out from behind another wagon and shouted orders in Romany. The strangely silent group moved off quickly into different directions and the gypsy leader hurried toward the young people.

"Everybody up at the farm including the children and the village has come down with a strange fever," Jeb exclaimed, the words tumbling out of his mouth in a manner quite uncharacteristic for the usually unemotional gypsy. "Two of the old folk in the village have died. Everyone's sick!"

Lizzie's mouth dropped open and her face went suddenly pale. She turned toward Quon, covering her mouth with her hands. Her knees began to buckle and he reached out to catch her just in time. Jeb moved to help but Quon shook his head. Putting his arms around her he held her until she indicated she was all right. Then he took a half step backward and, taking both her hands in his, he looked deeply into her eyes.

Jeb watched as their eyes met and held, the intensity so strong it seemed as if time was standing still.

Suddenly, Lizzie pulled her hands away. "Go quickly," she pleaded, barely able to speak.

"A horse!" the boy snapped and Jeb immediately whistled.

"I'm coming with you, let's go," Jeb growled, already on the run.

When the horses arrived, Jeb helped Quon mount, then jumped astride his own.

"Fowo me, Jeb. No talk!" Quon yelled over his shoulder, digging his heels into the horse's side. By the time they reached the wall at Drover's Lane, they were almost at full gallop. Sailing over it they quickly disappeared behind the slaughterhouse.

Lizzie walked to the gate and opened it. As she went toward home, her legs suddenly felt like jelly and she sunk down onto the grass covering her face with her hands. *My angels, my children*, she sobbed, as images of them flashed across her mind. Hearing a carriage coming toward her, she quickly stood up and composed herself. The carriage passed but she was left with a burning need to see Ada and set out at a run for the TLS office.

Ada saw her coming from the window and knew at once the girl's fears had been realized. She went quickly to the back door and opened it. Lizzie quickened her pace and, reaching Ada's arms, melted into them and began to sob. Ada realized she was mumbling something about angels and she held the girl tenderly.

"What on earth has happened? It's the orphans, isn't it, dear ... I should have known," she said, softly. She had heard Lizzie mention angels once before and now it was all coming together. This was a totally different Lizzie she was seeing, and she liked it. "Come in and tell me about it, love."

At that moment, Nathan's buggy came thundering up the lane and Lizzie quickly dried her eyes on her sleeve.

"That news caught me right where it hurts, Ada," she admitted softly, wiping her eyes. "Quon and Jeb have gone for help," she said, looking out of the window. "Oh no, Nathan looks to be in an awful hurry, we'd better go see what he wants."

Nathan's coach had pulled up in a cloud of dust and he had hardly waited for it to stop before trying to alight. Pushing past Dan, he sailed into the office just as the women were coming through the inside door. It was obvious to everyone that he was annoyed at something, or someone.

"Now look here, young lady," he snapped, waving his silver-tipped cane at Lizzie. "What the devil is my cousin talking about?" He suddenly stopped and looked at Lizzie, noticing her red eyes and the lack of Quon's presence. A worried frown came onto his face. "Where is he? Is something wrong?"

"Yes," Lizzie snapped, "something *is* wrong, but what is your problem?"

Nathan looked a bit confused and his eyes flicked between the women. "Not Mister Quon, I hope," he said, turning to Ada.

The bookkeeper shook her head.

With no more information being offered, he continued, "Abraham says I shall be selling grain soon! All I want to know is, is it true?"

"Yes, it is. I'll get you a list of Dixon's old customers," said Ada.

"No need," he replied, curtly. "I know them all." He paused to stroke his chin and a faraway look came into his eyes. "Crowther's has the business now."

"What? Crowther services the mills?" Lizzie exclaimed, her eyes beginning to show their old fire as Nathan impatiently tapped the floor with his walking stick.

"Malting barley and milling wheat, first grade," he muttered, his eyes beginning to twinkle as his level of excitement rose. "When can we deliver?" Not waiting for an answer, he began to stride back and forth talking to himself as he rubbed the silver handle of his stick. "Six-week delivery ... ten-ton lots ... today's price base for a year plus any increase at the source after that." A smile came onto his lips. "And a ten-year contract for stability," he added gleefully, finally looking up and going red in the face as he realized he'd been talking out loud. "Well, give me the terms and I'll be off ... six-week delivery you said?"

The women looked at each other and burst out laughing.

"Whatever you think is fair, Mister Goldman," Ada replied.

As Nathan left the office, banging the door behind him, Ned tittered with amusement.

Lizzie shook her head. "It's quite amazing who and what that man knows."

"Everybody and all their business, too!" Ned growled.

Ada slipped her arm over the girl's shoulder. "Come sit down and tell me about the children. Worrying won't help, love, but if I know you, you'll find a way to solve the problem no matter what it is."

During the next half hour, Lizzie talked to Ada about the children, only briefly mentioning Quon and Jeb's quick departure. Then she remembered the store Abe was going to negotiate on for the delivery lads, explaining to her about its rundown state and how the repairs should be handled.

Ada cocked an eyebrow when Lizzie told her that the lads had to be involved in the work.

"So they feel part of it," she explained, misinterpreting Ada's silent comment. With a rueful smile, she added. "Nobody gets a free ride around here."

Ada nodded in agreement.

Suddenly, hearing galloping hooves, Lizzie leapt from her chair and ran to the window. "Ther back!" she yelped, running to the door.

Thundering up the slaughterhouse track, the men saw Lizzie at the door and the two steaming, sweat-stained horses skidded to a stop. Quon slid from his saddle handing his reins to the gypsy who continued toward the camp. Quon came toward the women but stopped several paces away sheepishly grinning.

"Look at you! Oh my Lord, what a stench!" exclaimed Lizzie, gaping at Quon who was literally covered in stinking river mud. Then remembering his mission, she shrieked, "Did you get it!"

"Get what? Where on earth have you been?" Ada gasped, holding her nose and backing up to stand in the doorway.

"Does he know what to do with it?" Lizzie inquired, ignoring her.

Quon's hands began moving wildly, only stopping when Lizzie threw up her own in frustration. "All right, all right, but first we've got to get you cleaned up."

Without a word of explanation to Ada, they hurried off toward the slaughterhouse. Going inside, they found the hog-dipping shed empty but knew they would find hot water there. Selecting a clean trough, they proceeded to fill it with warm water and soap.

"You wash up and I'll get some clean clothes for you and hurry up about it!" she called as she headed out the door.

Quon slowly climbed into the trough, clothes and all. He put his head back, resting it against the edge, knowing he could easily go to sleep. Then remembering Lizzie would be back soon, he began to rub himself fiercely. Soon the water was so dirty he couldn't see himself. He removed his clothes, throwing them over the side onto the dirt floor. Then he waited. The hot water felt mighty good!

In less than ten minutes a breathless Lizzie returned, unceremoniously dumping his clean clothes nearby and placing a soft sackcloth towel into his outstretched hand. She quickly turned to leave again, flinging three words back at him. "Gypsy camp ... hurry!"

Quon knew Jeb would tell Lizzie about their trip to Tower Bridge, but he'd better not be far behind her. He stood up and began to towel himself dry and the roughness of the cloth brought him back to life.

Walking quickly toward the camp, Lizzie was aware of frantic activity around one of two horses being saddled and loaded down with supplies. Jeb was shouting orders between spoonfuls of lunch from a bowl in his hand. The scene was quite obviously one of urgency.

Threading her way through the group, she tugged on his sleeve. "Jeb, do you know how to use the medicine?"

The grim-faced gypsy leader handed his empty tankard to one of his men. Taking Lizzie by the arm, he moved away from the group "I ain't got much time," he growled. "Don't talk, just listen. Quon told me what to do and that big Chinese Tong-man from under Tower Bridge is sending two doctors to help us."

"How did Quon get so dirty?"

A smile crinkled Jeb's lips and his eyes brightened as he remembered. "Told me not to help him, he did. All I could do was watch! That little devil fought them guards like a wildcat, but he couldn't win. They dragged him through the mud and under the bridge. I was helpless, Liz. I lost sight of him for awhile and was so worried what they would do. But Quon had warned me this was the only way to meet the Tong-man." Jeb went suddenly quiet.

"Well, go on man, tell me the rest!" she snapped, impatiently.

"Aye, I will," Jeb growled. "A strange thing happened next. Two of them oddly dressed guards came rushing out from under the bridge, carrying four stone jugs and brought them to me. Gave me quite a turn it did, I could hear 'em talkin in their language but it made no sense at all to me. Then out comes the lad, damn it if he even turned and waved to 'em all friendly-like, but he was quite a sight covered head to toe in mud."

"Hmm, I'll agree with that, awful smelly, too! So how do you know about the doctors and how to administer the medicine?"

Jeb laughed. "Quon told me. He talks you know."

"Of course I know," she snapped, "but could you understand him?"

"With difficulty lass, with difficulty," Jeb chuckled.

Just then one of the men shouted for him.

"I have to go, I need as much daylight as possible," he said, his tone indicating his deep concern. Nonetheless, he moved closer and wagged a finger menacingly under her nose. "And nobody comes up to the farm, you hear me, girl? Nobody ... 'til we've dealt with this sickness."

"Take care of my children, please Jeb," she begged softly, grabbing his arm and looking deeply into his eyes.

He took her small hand and, holding it briefly in his, he looked into her sad, but lovely face, and slowly nodded. Moving quickly now, he strode toward the group of men, speaking to them briefly. Then he mounted his horse, gathered up the lead rope of the packhorse and began to move away.

A shrill whistle rang across the paddock and Jeb turned to see Quon racing toward them. He shouted a farewell as his horse gathered speed. Quon joined the silent, solemn-faced group; they were all well aware of his mission and the danger it posed. Slipping his arm through Lizzie's, Quon drew her attention away from the fast-disappearing rider and led her away.

She tried to speak but the words stuck in her throat and she just dropped her head onto his shoulder and sighed.

"Wizzy not worry. Quon here now," he said softly, wrapping his arm reassuringly around her.

As they walked away, she realized the camp was quickly returning to normal. *These gentle folk have interesting ways of dealing with sadness and disaster*, she thought. They turned toward the stables and, as a feeling of extreme tiredness washed over her, she stumbled on the uneven ground. Quon caught her, looking at her with a worried frown.

Later that afternoon, Lizzie and Quon were passing the blacksmith's shop when they noticed Nathan's white carriage horse tied to a ring outside. It appeared to be having some work done to its feet and clouds of smoke were rising from the hot shoes and burning hooves. Neither Nathan, Dan nor Wick were anywhere to be seen.

Lizzie watched for a moment then looked up at the sun. "What time is it, dumplin?"

"Ten past five," he replied, returning his timepiece to his pocket.

Lizzie stopped in mid-stride and scowled at him. "Are you sure?"

"All day gone, me big empty!" He shrugged his shoulders and grinned, like he used to do when he was younger, but it had no affect on her this day and she turned abruptly and walked away.

Mick was standing at his desk sorting orders for the next day's deliveries when Nathan passed through on his way to the main office. Without speaking, he stopped before he reached Ada's desk and sat down on a nearby chair not daring to interrupt her. For the next few minutes, an occasional, unconscious grunt of frustration escaped his lips.

Lizzie and Quon entered, throwing a noisy greeting at Mick, causing Ada to look up and see Nathan.

"What can I do for you, Mister Goldman?"

"Threw a shoe," he mumbled, tapping his cane nervously on the floor.

Mick stuck his head around the corner. "Threw a shoe, Nathan? Who'd yer throw it at?"

"My mare, not me!" he snapped. "Oh it's been another one of those days! I see you found him, lass," he said, turning to Lizzie and pointing his stick at Quon.

"Never lost him," she said, "but yer right, it's been one of those days."

Ned suddenly announced he was going home, handing Mick another pile of papers. A knock sounded on the door and Dan's head came around the corner.

"Ready, sir? We can be off now," he said to the trader, who readily jumped to his feet.

When they had gone, Ada slowly spun her chair around to face the obviously exhausted youngsters who had collapsed into chairs. Mick, not wanting to miss anything, came to sit on the edge of his wife's desk.

"What did Nathan want?" he asked.

"Didn't seem to be anything, nothing urgent at any rate," replied Ada. "Now, you two sneaky little devils, it's time you told us what is going on. It's been a long time since this began but we know you have those orphans hidden away somewhere. Now something has happened. We want to help, if you'll let us." A frown creased her brow for a moment as she searched the partner's faces.

Lizzie and Quon looked at each other with barely an expression passing between them. For a moment there was absolute silence in the room.

"Angels velly bad sick," Quon blurted out. "Tong-man give Quon medicine water."

"Angels?" asked Mick.

"Our secret angels, that's what we call them, Mick," said Lizzie.

"They're the orphans who went missing from that orphanage. Remember, dear?" Ada reminded her husband. "The authorities launched quite a search for them but never found anything to explain their whereabouts. Word was that the couple looking after them had kidnapped them. It was all very mysterious. We thought at the time you two may have had something to do with it, but you wouldn't tell us a thing about that night."

"Ah sure, they must be growin up now, the poor little buggers. How long ago was that, Lizzie m'girl?"

"Almost three years isn't it? Jeb helped you, didn't he?" said Ada. "That man is very loyal to you two. Mind you, he's had more than one demonstration of your fairness. But it's more than that I realize, and today he's done something to help you again." She smiled sympathetically at Lizzie and her voice became a whisper. "When you reacted to Jeb's news today, it was just like any mother would have reacted, and it got me thinking. That's why you've gone to visit the farm so often, isn't it? You must have them hidden somewhere out of London. I only just worked it out this afternoon."

Quon's arm crept around his partner's shoulder. Lizzie gently patted his hand as a tear balanced on the edge of her eye.

"You're right, Ada," said Lizzie, swallowing hard. We took 'em with the help of Jeb and his gypsies and some of the boys, but they're ours now and we need to look after them. They were so frightened that day. They desperately needed us," she said, looking up at Quon as a faraway look passed across her face. "Now, they've become the most precious things possible!"

Then, changing the subject, she grabbed Quon's arm, pulling him toward the door. "Come on, let's go eat," she exclaimed. "I could eat a horse! We'll tell you the rest after dinner."

Mick eagerly jumped off the desk. "Hoy, I'm all for that," he exclaimed, also wanting to change the mood that had descended on the room. "Come, my dear," he said reaching for his wife's arm. But she held up her hand to stop him.

"You two go ahead, I've got to finish this contract for Ben, so he can leave for Hull tomorrow. We'll be along shortly."

Later, as dinner dishes were being cleared away, Ada kept giving Lizzie questioning looks and the girl knew she was bursting to hear the rest of the story about the children.

Finally, Lizzie sat down and leaned back in her chair looking around the table. Martha, realizing that something was afoot, left her work and sat down also.

"You all know," Lizzie began, "that Quon and I have visited a gypsy farm north of here with Jeb ... three times actually. But I have been so worried about information getting to the wrong people, we decided to keep it a secret. We have been surprised, and pleased, with your patience," she added, looking around the room at the serious faces. Then, beginning with that day almost three years ago, she told how Billy and Tom had brought them news of the nine little waifs who had been locked up and virtually forgotten in the old warehouse that served as a church orphanage.

Everyone listened with rapt attention. Other than the occasional sound of Martha's clucking and a sigh or two from Ada, there was barely a sound in the room. When she got to the part where the Johnsons had helped bathe the children and they discovered the youngest ones were covered with bruises, the family's horror was obvious. Lizzie's eyes misted over and they all knew she was having a rough time speaking of it.

Clearing her throat, she told how Jeb's men had played an integral part in the rescue, quickly and secretively transporting them out of London to their new home in Hertfordshire just north of Epping Forest. Here, some of his most trusted gypsy friends had been looking after the children with the help of Jessy Jones as their teacher.

But now they were sick and Quon had visited the Tong-men again this very afternoon and been given some of their medicine water. At this very minute, Jeb was on his way to the farm with the precious medicine.

Joe stood up, going over to the fireplace and tapping his pipe out on the hearth. He wiped his mouth on the back of his hand returning to the table. He reached for his tobacco tin and cleared his throat.

"All right, we've all heard it, now forget it!" he said gruffly. "Them two can deal with it." He applied a burning splinter to the fresh tobacco and sucked hard on the pipe stem. "They've done very nicely up to now."

"But if we can help ...?" Ada began, looking toward Lizzie who was looking down at the table.

Mick reached over and patted his wife's hand. "Leave it be, luv," he whispered. "She'll be telling us if she needs our help."

Small footsteps and the sound of a whimper sent Martha hurrying to Willie's bedroom. She returned with the boy half asleep on her shoulder and handed him to Joe.

"Don't wake him, Joe, we're going home," Ada whispered, quickly moving about the room to gather their belongings.

Chapter 8

It was almost dark as Jeb neared The Red Lion Inn at Leytonstone, his first stop since leaving home that afternoon. His route north had taken him first to the outskirts of Clerkenwell, a popular holiday resort destination for wealthy Londoners now becoming an industrial area. Farther on, the main road traversed the lush farming country adjacent to the River Lea.

As always, he had left the main northern highway as quickly as possible. He preferred the little-known and much less frequented country lanes and byways of the drover's route which meandered through hamlets and villages in its own haphazard way. Gypsies, like the drovers who herded cattle over the moors, knew shortcuts through forests and across wild moorland and heath.

Jeb made steady progress on the open road that day despite a light spring rain that fell intermittently. He knew the distance to the next inn friendly to gypsies was still several miles away and he desperately needed to change horses. He had travelled this portion of the road many times before, and always when driving livestock from Bishop Stortford and Harlow to the TLS slaughterhouse.

Coaches, too, were often a menace to travellers thundering by with little or no regard for others. Several times he had even found himself lending aid to a stranded driver in need of a helping hand on a dark and lonely road. Some innkeepers were visibly grateful for the business Jeb brought to their door, but still others were harsh and distrustful of the Romanies and their wandering ways. Despite this, Jeb often made the most unlikely friends.

But tonight Jeb was making no detour. The route planned out in his mind was almost as direct as an arrow's path to the village of Blackrock and then to their farm just north of Much Hadham. He had anticipated the journey would take four to five days, if the weather was kind.

Around midnight, he pulled his weary mount into the yard of The Royal Pheasant Inn just inside the southern edge of Waltham Forest. Waking a stableman, he quickly acquired a change of horses, a meat sandwich and a glass of ale, walking as he ate to relieve his numb limbs. He could feel the tiredness overtaking him but knew he must go on as long as he had enough light.

Back on the road again, he was thankful for brief glimpses of moonlight as he slumped low in the saddle urging the horses forward as they picked their way over the rutted road. Two hours travel brought him to the crest of a familiar hill where he reined in the horses and dismounted. Peering out across the dark countryside, he searched for the outline of familiar landmarks. Suddenly, he caught the flash of a light below. *That was no illusion,* he thought.

Remounting, he rode carefully down the hillside to investigate. Again seeing the flash of a light, he could now make out the outline of a coach and heard the snorting horses. Hearing a voice, he stopped and listened, then smiled. Dismounting, he moved cautiously forward in the dark listening as the coachman cursed his bad luck as he walked around the coach swinging his lantern. Jeb was almost beside him when the coachman realized he was not alone.

"Bloody hell, where in tarnation have ye come from Jeb?" he asked, shining the light into his face.

"You have a wheel off, Sam," said the gypsy. "Is it broken?"

Sam West handed Jeb the light and disappeared around the side of the coach, returning with one of the front wheels.

"No, it ain't! You think we can get it back on?" he asked hopefully, removing his coat.

An hour later, after much muscle-wrenching heaving and lifting, they finally secured the wheel back onto its axle. Collapsing on the ground, the two men gathered their breath.

"Where you headin fer, Jeb?"

"Direction of Bishop's Stortford."

A few minutes later, Sam went to get his horses and hooked them up to the coach. When he finished, he took Jeb's horses and tied them behind the coach, waving the tired man inside.

"You rest now. I'll be stopping at Waltham Abbey before I turn westward, that's on yer way."

Jeb smiled tiredly, greatly relieved his friend had taken matters in hand. He stepped up into the coach and collapsed gratefully onto the seat. The coach door banged shut behind him. In a minute he heard the crack of a whip and Sam shouting to his team.

Not used to the luxury of riding in a coach, Jeb was only too aware of its squeaks, groans and wild heaving from side to side as it encountered uneven road. Finally, the motion lulled him to sleep and his tired body became totally oblivious to the discomfort.

Clouds drifting across the moon made it difficult to see in the two hours that were left before dawn, but Sam was an experienced coach driver and knew the road well. He kept the team moving knowing the land was relatively flat offering few surprises.

At daybreak, the sun's warming glow pushed away the cold chill of the night and the coach picked up speed. Sam shrugged off his heavy nightcoat working the reins along the horses' now steaming backs.

It wasn't long before he was pulling into an inn where they would find a change of horses and a much-needed meal. Sam opened the door and gave Jeb a shake. Jeb shook his head and stepped groggily down the two steps to the ground, stumbling sleepily as he crossed the yard.

Leaving Sam to tend to the horses, he located the outhouse and then headed inside knowing he would find a warm, and most welcome, meal. The large room was noisy despite being half empty, and the rough-looking men in attendance appeared to be consuming their morning meal. *Drovers and coachmen*, he thought to himself. Selecting a table, he pulled up a crudely built wooden chair and sat down heavily, briskly rubbing his hands over his face.

"Come on, lad, ye've gotta eat," Sam growled, pulling out the chair beside Jeb and sitting down.

The innkeeper brought them each a bowl of stew with a thick slice of heavy brown bread. Jeb gratefully ate the meal, slowly returning to his senses as Sam talked with acquaintances at nearby tables. When they finished eating, Sam caught Jeb's eye and they headed back outside. Before he could protest, Sam had ushered him once again into the coach and slammed the door.

Grateful for Sam's kindness but realizing sleep was now useless, he sat up and squinted through the sunlight at the bouncing landscape. Deciding Sam's company would be much preferable to this, he looked about him. Finding what he was searching for, he opened the canvas flap behind him and crawled through the small opening that led to the roof of the swaying coach. Feeling slightly dizzy, he lay there for a moment before scrambling up onto the driver's box. `

"FEEL BETTER DO YE, LAD?" the older man yelled above the noise. "BE AT WALTHAM ABBEY IN A LITTLE OVER TWO HOURS. I'LL TAKE A BED THERE FOR AWHILE," he said, looking sideways and grinning. "POTTER'S BAR IS MY NEXT MAIN STOP, BE BACK IN LONDON IN A WEEK."

This was the first time Jeb had ridden topside on a coach and its violent rocking motion was even worse up here. He almost wished he'd stayed below ... he certainly didn't envy Sam his job. As they drove through a less dense section of Epping Forest beside the river, he vowed it would be his last coach ride ... if he had any say in it.

True to Sam's word, the village of Waltham Abbey soon came into sight with the familiar square spire of the old Abbey Church, the highest building around. Sam swung the coach into the courtyard of the *King's Head* and they jumped down.

"You'll want to be on your way I expect, Jeb. Which way yer headin ... Stanstead or Harlow?"

"Stanstead ... thanks for yer kindness, Sam," returned Jeb, taking Sam's hand.

Jeb shook it warmly and went to tend to his horses. Checking the precious stone jugs on the packhorse while they indulged in some food and water, he assured himself the bottles were safely packed, then mounted up. He looked up at the sun and turned west. Pulling his hat down over his eyes, he dug his heels lightly into the horse's flank.

By the time he had passed over the bridge and through the village of Waltham Cross, with its ancient and intricately carved monument standing starkly in the market square, he had settled into a comfortable canter.

Away from the noise of the rattling coach, Jeb felt more comfortable than he had in the past 24 hours. This was the area he loved and in the quiet of the lush green, gently rolling countryside beside the River Lea, he felt comfortably at ease again. But now an urgency gripped him and he knew he couldn't waste time enjoying himself.

Finding himself in a sudden rainstorm an hour later, he stopped to rest his horse and take a short nap under the trees. Half an hour later, the sun reappeared waking him and he got on his way again needing to make good use of the light before sunset. He climbed the highest hill for miles and searched the flatlands. He knew he had made good time and Stanstead Abbots should only be about two miles away. Here he'd change horses for the last leg of his journey.

However, seeing a cluster of buildings about a half mile distant, he decided to stop instead at Royston where he knew the proprietor of The White Hart ale house. Before he left his vantage point, he noticed that the smoke from nearby chimneys was rising in a straight line to the sky. It had turned into a perfect night, despite the leftover clouds from the little storm. He should have the benefit of at least partial moonlight for the remainder of his journey.

Arriving at the little hamlet, he made his way to the ale house and entered the yard. He handed over the reins of his horses to the stableman, then carefully removed the jugs from the packhorse. He stored them safely then allowed the stableman to unsaddle them. It was growing cool outside and, entering the coaching house, he was greeted warmly by both his friend and the familiar, large roaring fire on the hearth. He found an empty table within range of its heat and sat down gratefully. He purchased a flagon of ale from the barmaid, drinking it down thirstily, then ordered another ... as well as their specialty, lamb stew.

Thirty minutes later he was mounted on fresh horses with his precious cargo safely loaded and they set off into the twilight. Now on the main road the going would be easier for he was well familiar with the area. Here the land was almost flat and although having to be cautious, in no time he had passed through the sleeping village of Hadham Cross. The moon appeared again and he urged his mount forward.

Less than a mile beyond, the large, shadowy house known to area resident's as the Bishop's Summer Palace, told him he had reached Much Hadham. The degree of darkness indicated it was still too early in the season for the bishop to be in residence or else they had all gone to bed early this night.

Another hour is all, he thought hopefully, patting his horse and encouraging him on. Hearing voices, he realized he was close to the

Rob Roy Inn, a favourite of the local farmers. "Closing time," he grunted under his breath.

Even the horse was feeling his exhilaration as he scoured the darkness for the familiar large sycamore tree that marked the crossroad. Seeing the tall dark shape against the moonlit sky, he swung off the main road onto the lesser-used track.

Suddenly a feeling of trepidation washed over him—would he be in time?

A dog barked as he opened the farm's wooden gate and a lantern flashed from the door of the house. A familiar voice called for him to identify himself.

"IT'S JEB," he shouted. "BRING THE LANTERN, GEORGE. AN EXTRA PAIR OF HANDS WOULD BE USEFUL."

The gypsy's stiff fingers fumbled with the ropes holding the bags on the packhorse. As the light approached, he carefully extracted the stone jugs.

"What yer got there?" George asked from the darkness behind the lantern, but he took the jug Jeb held out to him and letting Jeb go ahead of him, they proceeded toward the house.

Almost to the farmhouse door, it opened suddenly revealing two gypsy women in night clothes also holding a lantern. Greeting the women by name, Jeb moved inside, putting his jugs on the table. The women fussed around him offering food and drink. He declined the food and pulled up a chair, sitting down with a heavy sigh.

"How many more cases of sickness since we were here?" he asked, sipping gratefully on his tankard of cider.

"Only five more and none very serious," said Erma, the elder of the two women.

"That's a relief, but Quon got us some special medicine from the Tong-men. It's to be administered immediately and exactly as I tell you," he began. Then he gave the instructions just as Quon had told him. When he finished, he made very sure they understood, then he came slowly to his feet. "Wake me if there's any trouble," he said wearily, moving toward the bedroom he had used many times before. Shutting the door, he quickly removed his shoes and outer clothing, and collapsed on the bed.

With the dawn, the farm came alive with activity. Jeb rose, feeling thankfully refreshed and was informed that his orders had been carried out precisely. The farm workers had obtained the help of two gypsy women who had not succumbed to the fever, and together, even before daylight, they had silently moved about the village. Knocking on every door, they had administered Jeb's medicine to the willing occupants.

By the time breakfast was ready, every single person on the farm and in the village had been dosed with the clear water-like substance. Jenny Jones and the children had been dosed twice.

The chatter around the table sent Jeb outside into the quiet to smoke his first pipe of the day. The sound of a fast-galloping horse was heard in the distance and soon a rider approached. Going out to meet him, Jeb recognized one of the local gypsy sheepherders.

"JEB, LIGHT DRAY HEADIN THIS WAY," called the rider in alarm, reining in his horse. He paused to catch his breath. "Ther's two pig-tailed chinamen in it!"

"Lead 'em in," Jeb ordered. "I'm expectin 'em."

Puffing extra hard on his pipe, Jeb waited, never having really expected the Tong-man to keep his word. *Now we'll beat this*, he thought gratefully, suddenly feeling a newfound respect for these foreigners.

ᚠᚢᚠ

Fog hung low over the Thames and there was a heaviness in the air as Lizzie and Quon ran down Water Lane. Stopping at Abe's, they found the door locked so they sat down on the step to wait.

Strange, thought the girl, shivering with the damp. Then Quon pointed into the fog. Coming through the mist toward them was a familiar shuffling figure.

Spotting the pair, Abe growled, "Dammed long walk!" Producing his key and unlocking the door, he entered quickly and made straight for his little stove. Taking the poker from the hook on the wall, he stirred the dying embers into a flame. He added a few bits of coal, checked that there was water in the kettle and then held his hands over the heat, rubbing them together slowly.

"Fog gets into me old bones these days ... miserable cold morning," he croaked, a visible shiver running through his frail-looking body.

Lizzie took the bottle of clear syrup off the shelf above them and reached for Abe's china cup. Pouring in a small amount of his special peppermint syrup, she purred, "Soon have you nice and warm again, old lad."

He sat down and Lizzie silently stirred the fire once more. She knew he would tell them his news when he was ready.

"Blasted Crowther whelp," he finally rasped from between tightened lips, "made me buy the whole broken-down row!" He paused, looking up at the girl and a wicked grin displayed his smoke-blackened teeth. "But I smelt he needed money and bought 'em for a pittance ... the fool!"

Steam began puffing from the kettle and Lizzie quickly grabbed a cloth. Carefully lifting it over to the table, she poured the boiling water into the peppermint syrup and slid it in front of Abe. With both of his bony hands wrapped around the hot cup, the old tailor gratefully took a tentative sip.

"So you bought 'em," she exclaimed eagerly. "Got the papers signed, too?"

"Easy, easy girl," Abe protested, his drink dribbling down his chin. "They're yours all right. I wrote out a note and got it witnessed by Joshua Thorn, their office man."

Abe reached into the pocket of his coat, producing a folded paper. Lizzie moved over to the worktable, laying the paper out under the light and studying it. Quon came to stand beside her.

"Chalkboard," she muttered, never taking her eyes off the document and her partner scurried off to get it.

"Know what rent those three shops pay, Mister Kratze? There's five in that row, ain't there?" she asked, as she began to write with squeaking strokes.

"Isn't there," he corrected. "Yes, five."

Quon's hands flew into action. Lizzie watched him with obvious interest, then smiled and began writing again. Then she stopped and glanced over at Quon again. He pointed to some words on the paper and she nodded, continuing to write.

"There," she said proudly, setting down her chalk and beaming.

Abe's mood seemed to brighten and he was watching his pupils with gathering interest.

"According to the price you've agreed to pay and the return on the rents, we should recover our capital in three years," she announced, glancing at her old friend who now nodded in agreement. "Add into that the renovations for the two empty shops and their extra rent and we should be free and clear in ...." The girl stopped, noticing the surprised look on the old man's face.

"In-in forty-two months!" he spluttered.

"No," Lizzie whispered, watching Quon's hands. "In a mere two years and eight months, gentlemen!"

"Less than three years ... can't be, yer wrong. That cannot be right," Abe protested, shaking his head slowly from side to side.

"Listen," she began, patiently. "We're going to add 40 percent more rent with the two extra shops. The property will be more valuable with all the shops full. It'll bring more people to shop there, so now we can raise the rent!"

Lizzie's last words fell like a cannonball. Abe's head jerked up as he realized Lizzie had bested him again. His eyes shone with pride.

"Bless you, girl," he muttered. "An yer right, too."

The young people burst out laughing at Abe's reaction. Lizzie picked up the contract and slipped it into her pocket, starting for the door.

"We'll give this to Ada," she assured him, then just before the door closed, she poked her head back in. "Thanks, Mister Kratze!"

"Second load, Tom?" Lizzie called as they watched the boy's cart being loaded with baked goods.

Bill came toward them carrying two barrels of cider on his shoulders, groaning in mock pain at the weight.

"These boys will be the death of me, lass," he exclaimed, winking.

"Third, Miss Lizzie!" Tom replied, depositing his load of loaves on the cart and turning back quickly for more, almost bumping into Clem who had his apron piled high with bread. Olivera ran over to Quon dragging him toward the table where a fresh pie sat cooling.

In a few minutes, they all gathered around the table.

"Where's Billy, not sick I hope," commented Lizzie.

"No, miss, just busy," Tom laughed, shooting crumbs over everyone. "We've set up a table an he's sellin bread outside that new shop." He paused to take another quick bite of pie, chewing hurriedly and emptying his small tankard as they stood up to leave. Noting the question on Lizzie's face, he added, "We're doin real good and it gets people used to us bein there, too."

"Now that's smart," Bill chuckled, before Lizzie could make a comment. Just then Clem came back into the yard. Lowering his voice, Bill said confidentially, "By gum, lass, he's a good man that Clem, couldn't manage without him now. Ah hope you'll not be wantin him back."

"He's yours to keep, Bill," Lizzie assured him. "And yer right about Tom and the lads, they're smart and thinkers, too." She suddenly smacked Quon's hand as he reached for the last piece of pie. "Oh no, you don't, lad. That one's mine, you're getting much too fat!" she frowned, scooping it up herself. "I think Oly's beginning to grow a bit more, don't ya think, Bill?" she commented, as the lads called their goodbyes.

"That little lad is a true joy to have around. Aye, I do believe he has grown a bit … certainly a wee bit rounder!" Bill laughed. He took a mouthful of cider and looked up at the girl with questioning eyes. "Ye've had a problem haven't yer, lass?" he asked, quickly adding, "it was Lefty that told me. He called yesterday."

Lizzie's eyes flicked up to the big Yorkshireman's gentle face. Hearing the concern in his voice, she reached out to pat his hand. "It's all right, luv, we've fixed it."

"It-its just that I'd like to help if I can," he offered, a bit embarrassed, then realizing what she had said, he added, "oh, you have, that's good, luv." There was an uncomfortable quiet for a moment then he collected his thoughts. "Did you ever find that Sutton fella yer were lookin fer?"

Lizzie laughed, watching as Quon's fingers gave her answer.

"Dumplin says that Mister Sutton is due for a fall. Somehow we're going to have to teach him a lesson he won't easily forget."

The girl's words had an ominous ring to them sending a little shudder down the baker's broad back. He had already been party to several of Lizzie's little escapades and knew full well just what this young lady was capable of.

Leaving the bakery with full stomachs, they made their way back toward the river. They spotted the back of Nathan's buggy as it left the TLS dock, disappearing quickly into the thick midday traffic.

They again passed *The Robin* where several mud-splashed coaches had spilled their passengers. They milled about in the yard, no doubt easing travel-worn bodies before they moved on.

Above the noise they heard Tom and his cronies' loud laughter. Glancing over at her, Quon pushed his way through the crowd then stood aside to allow Lizzie to boldly approach the ex-mariner.

Seeing them, he suddenly turned and extended his crook motioning them closer. Quon eyed him suspiciously, moving slightly in front of Lizzie, which caused the pegleg some frustration and he flung his crook onto the ground.

"Dammit, he still doesn't trust me," the pegleg cried, wobbling precariously on his barrel. "I've news for yer, young lady, but first I want to thank ye kindly for me new leg."

"That's all right, Tom. Now, out with yer news, man, we haven't all day to waste."

"Some young'un has set up a bake shop, over that way," he said, pointing an unsteady finger. "Could be trouble for yer friend, the baker. The lad's doing a good business already."

Lizzie giggled. "Mister Tom, just what do you think you can do about it?"

"Why we could rough 'em up for yer, Miss Lizzie!" he exclaimed, proudly. "Rough 'em up and send 'em packin!"

Quon's hands moved quickly and he stepped up closer to the pegleg. Tom drew back in fear.

"Stop him, lass, stop him!"

Quon stopped as soon as Lizzie reached for his arm.

"He's trying to tell yer," Lizzie snapped, her eyes blazing, "that if yer so much as touch those lads, I'll have yer dropped in the river with an anchor tied around that neck of yers!" Winking at Quon, she spun on her heel and marched away.

A mad dash took them across to the TLS dock where they found Charley's empty cart, but no Charley.

"Where Charwy?" Quon asked, hurrying along behind her, his eyes searching the dock area.

Suddenly, he pointed up ahead to where two large barques were tied. Sure enough, there on the jetty was the engineer in deep conversation with Ben Thorn.

Lizzie whistled, drawing the men's attention as they ran up the jetty toward them. "Going soon, Ben?" the girl panted. "Did you find out when the *Falcon* gets back?"

"Be off in half an hour," Ben replied, squinting up at the sun. "*Falcon* will be back any day now. They're late. I imagine they're around at Sheppey unloading."

Charley balanced carefully on his sticks and looked up at the youngsters, throwing Ben a smirk.

"Have I to tell 'em, captain?" he asked.

Ben nodded.

"We just had a visit from Nathan with a rush order. One of Crowther's customers wants some sheep taken to Hull."

"Sheep!" Lizzie gasped.

Just then the sound of bleating sheep and barking dogs filled the air. Looking in the direction of the noise, they saw a mass of white bodies unloading from a dray and bounding toward them.

Captain Ben quickly picked Charley up in his arms and sat him on top of some crates. "Can you manage from there, lad?" he asked. Receiving the right reply, he turned to the youngsters. "We had better get up …," he began, but they were already on their way and he scrambled up behind them.

Nearby, curiosity had got the better of some workmen and they had lined up along the dock to watch the odd sight. Although this made a lane for the sheep to follow, the four dogs accompanying them seemed to have it well in hand. Meanwhile, at the ship, everything was ready and their handlers soon had the small herd of woolly creatures loaded without too much fuss.

"Time to go," Captain Thorn announced, jumping down and lending Lizzie a hand. "Perfect weather for sailing, lass!"

"What about food for the sheep, Ben?" she asked, giggling at the thought, as she watched Ben lift Charley to the ground.

"It's all onboard, Liz, and extra water, too. Now don't you go worrying about those mangy animals," he assured her. "There's more to it though, you ask Charley," he called over his shoulder, as he strode up the gangway to the *London Queen*.

Once on board, he shouted orders to his crew and bodies began moving into action aboard the massive vessel. The gangway was quickly pulled in, lines turned loose, and with jib sails fluttering, the barque slipped gently away from its moorings. With men clambering quickly aloft and finding their positions in the rigging, it was a sight to behold and Lizzie and Quon never seemed to tire of it. The *Queen* slowly rounded the mouth of the dock and as the sailors prepared to drop more sail, it eased out to the centre of the mighty river, causing smaller ships to jockey for position.

Lizzie and Quon stood shoulder to shoulder watching as Ben's ship rounded the corner and soon moved out of sight.

"We go on ship again, Wizzy?" asked Quon.

"You think we should go for another ride do you, dumplin? I would have thought our little trip to Zaurez ...."

"LIZ, I'LL BE COMING FOR DINNER. I'VE SOMETHING TO TELL YOU," Charley yelled as the Grims settled him on his cart.

The young people waved as they headed for home.

Chapter 9

It had warmed up in the past few days and Lizzie and Quon found the cottage door open and Joe at the table when they came home for a late lunch one afternoon. Willie came charging across the room to meet them.

Martha turned from the fireplace, blowing an annoying wisp of hair from her face. "Nathan called," she announced, "Mick wants to talk to you, luv, but have yer soup first." Sliding two steaming bowls onto the table, she wagged a finger at Willie who had scrambled onto Quon's knee obviously intent on sharing.

"Has Ben gone, lass?" Joe asked, leaving the table and going to the fire to light his pipe.

She looked up and nodded as Joe went to find his cap behind the door. Puffing away, he waved before heading back to work.

"That man certainly enjoys his job at the brewery, thanks to you two," Martha commented. "When I came to work for you young'uns, I thought Joe was an old man, but he doesn't act it anymore!"

Quon pushed his empty soup bowl away, slid Willie off his knee and tapped out a message on the table. Martha decided not to ask.

Lizzie pushed her chair back, tapped her bowl twice with her spoon and headed for the door. "Good soup, Martha," she said, giving Willie a quick hug before grabbing her light jumper from behind the door.

Two minutes later, they were entering the office.

"You wanted to talk to us?" Lizzie asked, peering around the corner into Mick's empty room.

"Early this morning Nathan had the chance to take on one of Crowther's shipping customers," Ada began.

Quon's hands went wild and Lizzie giggled.

"Sheep ... we saw 'em!" she gasped.

"It's not just the sheep, the man who shipped them is from Whitby," Ada continued, now having their complete attention. "He's the owner of a coal mine and apparently is in need of ships ... lots of them, to bring coal down to London! He's fed up with Crowther's because they wouldn't take his sheep."

Lizzie made a face, her suspicions aroused. "Sounds too easy. Who is he?"

"Samuel Beaumont," replied Ada, a twinkle in her eye, "son-in-law of the Earl of Durham."

"You're jesting?" said Lizzie. "Why would somebody like that come to us or, it's a trap."

"Oh no, it isn't," Ada assured her. "Lady Sutton introduced him to Nathan at Sutton House."

The partners glanced quickly at each other and grinned. Just then Mick came banging in the back door, singing loudly. He poked his head around the corner.

"Ah sure it's me favourite Colleen and her whoyte knight come ter visit me!"

Ada wagged a finger at him. "Sit down you noisy devil," she scolded. "We're having a serious discussion."

"And we don't need that singin either," Ned wailed. "You sound like an axle without grease!"

As the laughter subsided, a dejected-looking Mick turned back to his office closing the door behind him, but leaving it open a crack.

"Samuel Beaumont," Ada continued, "told me that if we sent cash with Captain Ben, we would get an even better price on top-quality malting barley." She paused. "Those farmers are really hurting, nobody has cash."

Quon's hands began to move but Lizzie grabbed them.

So what did you do?" she asked, eagerly. "You should have given Ben the money, he's trustworthy."

"I did," Ada replied. "But there's more yet. Mister Beaumont has used Crowther Shipping for a long time and, just recently, over the last year and a half, they've been mysteriously losing ships and cargo."

"Hmm, same problem Lady Sutton had," said Lizzie, looking over at Quon. "Sounds like young Mister Crowther needed some free money."

Quon's hands moved again and this time both women watched carefully, nodding in unison.

"Know what he said?" giggled Lizzie.

"Don't have a clue!" replied Ada.

Lizzie winked at her partner. "My dumplin said Captain Davis and the *Falcon* are due back and he'll know the right of it." She looked at Ada and whispered, "I'll bet Crowther's been telling him lies, too!"

Nodding thoughtfully, Ada looked down at the work on her desk.

Lizzie remembered Abe's contract in her pocket and, pulling it out, laid it on top of Ada's papers. It didn't take her long to read the document and when she was finished she sat back in her chair and looked up at them.

"Pay it?" she asked.

"No, I have other plans for Mister Crowther," replied the girl, her brain in deep thought. "Get Nathan to make you an official-looking receipt from the Government Inspector of Shipping ... and then send Lefty around to Crowther's office with it."

"Oh, dear me," Ada gasped, "we'll all be in big trouble if I do that."

"I don't think so. I believe they'll assume the game is up."

"But-but," the bookkeeper stammered, nervously covering her mouth with her hand.

Lizzie laughed but Ada seemed not to notice, so Lizzie continued, "And if young Mister Sutton comes here looking for his money, you tell him the government man took it."

"Oh, I couldn't, love," Ada cried. "I couldn't tell a lie like that."

"No lass, you couldn't," said Ned, but his serious tone turned to delight. "But I can ... and for you, I will, Miss Lizzie!"

"Thanks Ned," Lizzie murmured, looking over at the clerk as she went towards the door. "Yer one of us now."

Once outside, the partners agreed that they were surprised at the sudden turn of events, then ducking into an alleyway they went up the back to Billy's new shop.

Approaching it slowly, they noticed more people around the shops on the corner than any other place. Then, they heard their friend's voice and saw the amazing sight of Billy, the shopkeeper. He was standing on a small barrel yelling his head off, advertising himself in a most professional way. Several nearby shopkeepers stood in their doorways and watched, obviously enjoying themselves.

"BILL JOHNSON'S HIGH-CLASS BAKED GOODS," the lad yelled, "SO CHEAP YOU'D THINK WE STOLE 'EM!"

Down from the barrel he jumped when he saw he had a customer, his money bag bouncing on his slim waist. As quickly as he finished, he returned to his perch and waited for the next round of customers. He was doing a roaring business.

The rattle of approaching wheels caused everyone to momentarily scatter making way for Tom and Olivera with new supplies. Oly was hanging onto the back dragging his feet as they came down the little hill.

"Oly must go through a lot of shoes," Lizzie commented to her partner. "I wonder where he gets them?"

"Rag yard," said Quon, causing Lizzie to look at him in surprise.

The boys unloaded most of the bread and the butcher stepped forward to heave their barrels up in place onto a specially made block of wood. Then, just as quickly, he hoisted the empties onto the cart.

"What an operation," Lizzie whispered in admiration. "Let's go talk to that butcher."

They threaded their way through the throng of shoppers as the bread cart disappeared up the street. Billy spotted them and waved them over but he had so many customers lined up they didn't want to bother him so they merely waved back.

"A grand lad is that one," said a deep voice behind them, "just what we needed around here."

Turning, Lizzie found herself looking into the ruddy face of the butcher. "Who is he?" she inquired. "Where did he come from?"

"He's one of 'em delivery lads with Johnson's bread cart. Says he works for the TLS company, but that can't be, I get my meat from them and that lad doesn't even know them." Scratching his head, the butcher pushed past the crowd and returned to his shop.

Quon tugged on Lizzie's arm, making signs that they'd seen enough. Lizzie nodded and they went back to look through the dirty window of the empty shop.

"You know, dumplin," she said, quietly. "I think what this shop needs is farm produce ... we'll have to see about it."

Entering the brewery yard late that afternoon, they were seen by one of the yard men who, without a word, pointed up the stairs. As they neared the top, they could hear Joe's voice. Tapping lightly on the door, they walked in.

"Time for home, Dad?" she asked, noticing the three men.

"Ach yerr just in time, lassie," Angus greeted them cheerfully. "We need yerr thoughts tae help settle our whisky maker's mind."

Joe tapped the chair arm with his pipe stem. "Just a minute, lads, ah'll do the askin."

Lizzie waited, aware that there was some tension in the air as John Watson shuffled his feet uncomfortably.

Joe took another puff on his pipe almost like he wanted to make John squirm a bit longer. "He'd like more space to set his barley off," said Joe, pointing his pipe stem at the whisky maker. "But we haven't any ...."

"We do! We've all of Dixon's mill space just down the lane ... when you get off yer rear ends an get it cleaned up!"

John let out a sigh of relief and Joe began to chuckle.

Angus' mouth dropped open in surprise and he grabbed his pipe before it slipped from between his teeth. "Nobody told me," he grumbled.

Lizzie and Quon began to laugh, too.

"Blame him," she chuckled, pointing her finger at Joe. "He should have told you."

"Good Lord," exclaimed Joe. "Ah've been so busy ah'd completely forgotten to tell 'em!"

"No matter," said Lizzie. "I want four of yer builders from tamorra morning. I need them for a month. Tell 'em to be at Mick's office at six-thirty." She winked at Joe. "Ready to go now, lad?"

"Ah'll be along shortly, luv, you young'uns go ahead."

As Lizzie pushed him out of Joe's office, Quon's hands started moving. Ignoring him, she took off down the stairs and it wasn't until they were out in the lane that she stopped and pointed up to the open window. Even from their position, they could hear the two managers arguing with Joe.

"Oh, they'll quieten down, don't worry about 'em," she giggled, setting off again.

Turning the last corner before the cottage, she stopped to wait for him. "Where would we get vegetables and farm produce?"

Quon's hands began to gyrate but Lizzie turned to glower at him, hands on her hips. "No! Talk to me," she said impatiently, moving toward the gate.

94

"Wizzy talk to gypsies," he said, struggling with the words. "They travel all places ... but still winter, too early for vegebles."

She nodded, going through the gate and heading up the path. "That's right, probably too early. We'll ask 'em later."

Hoofbeats coming fast down the slaughterhouse track, caused Quon to peer around the shrubs. "Naten," he exclaimed, as the grey swept around the corner, sliding to a stop in front of them.

"Young lady," the trader exclaimed, pointing officiously with his cane through the window. "If you think I'm going to make that false document ...!" He got no further before Lizzie was under his nose.

"Oh yes, you are!" she snapped.

Startled by her reaction, Nathan flinched, sliding away from her on the buggy seat and dropping his cane.

The girl grabbed the top of the buggy door with both hands. "YES YOU WILL ... AND DAMNED QUICK. I WANT IT BY NINE IN THE MORNING OR DON'T EVER COME BACK!"

Nathan Goldman squirmed under her tirade, imagining his numerous commissions evaporating. He'd known many strong-willed people in his time but none could compare with Lizzie Short.

"Y-yes, my dear. I-I was only going to ask when you needed it," he whined, trying to reach his cane that was rolling about on the floor. Finally recovering it, he reached outside and tapped his grinning driver on the back. "DRIVE ON," he commanded.

Watching the buggy disappear, they noticed Joe and called to him. Suddenly, the cottage door opened and Willie ran outside.

"Can't hold the bairn when he hears his granddad," chuckled Martha, from the doorway.

"What's for dinner?" asked Lizzie, sniffing the air as they entered.

"You'll find out soon enough, young lady," the older woman retorted. "Don't just stand there, the table needs settin."

After dinner, Joe moved to his chair, filled his pipe and settled back. "Well, lass, ah got yer men for mornin," he announced. "They'll be at Mick's at six-thirty."

Both Mick and his wife looked up sharply.

"And for sure just what would hoy be wantin with them?" Mick inquired, looking across at Lizzie.

Ada quickly intervened, telling her husband the location of the newly acquired mill and the row of shops, including the delivery boys' new bake shop.

"Yer going to need a light dray and ya better use the back lane," Lizzie instructed. "I want the shop for the boys cleaned up and the roof fixed, counters put in and bread shelves, then painted." She paused. "The two end ones need cleanin, too, they're both empty. Then I need you to finish up at Dixon's old mill."

Mick's mouth dropped open. "If yer think I've toym for all that, yer crackers!"

"No, no, silly," Lizzie laughed, shaking her head. "Just organize it. I've got yer four men to do the work."

"Aye, she has, lad," Joe grouched. "Pinched 'em from us, she did."

At last a smile began to creep over the Irishman's face. "Mother o' Murphy, lass. Yer a wonder! Is there no end to it?"

Joe sat bolt upright in his chair. "Yer right, lad," he growled. "She's a wonder all right ... makes yer wonder what's comin next!"

Lizzie winked affectionately at old Joe and pushed her chair back. "All right, just so you can all stop yer complaining, here's what's happening. The delivery lads who took over our bakery delivery about five years ago are hard workers and want to expand. We can see that they're ready to run their own operation now. That's how Quon and I got started and we want to help them. It will improve Bill Johnson's sales, too."

Ada gave the girl an inquiring glance. "And what's in it for us, love?"

Quon's hands went wild.

"He says, increased property value, control of fixed retail outlets and ...," she paused, "and I say, more friends and influence in an area where the poor people can be helped when times are rough."

Martha sighed deeply. "Oh my! Ah can't keep track of what's goin on here anymore."

"Sure and begorra, sounds good to me, Colleen. Come on now, Willie," Mick called, rising and pushing his chair back under the table. "Granddad needs some rest ... as do we all!"

Climbing off Joe's knee, the boy quickly ran away, crawling under the table and scrambling up onto Quon's lap. "Save me, save me, Quon," he cried, grasping Quon about the neck.

Quon, wrapped his arms protectively around Willie and smiled at him. "Quon your big flend ... for evely time, Willie."

Mick stopped and the only noise in the room was the crackling fire.

Ada, halfway out of her chair, whispered, "What did he say, Lizzie?"

"He said ...," she began, going over to hug both Willie and Quon. "He said he would protect Willie all his life."

"That's what I thought he said," Ada murmured, swallowing hard.

Joe coughed and a pan banged on the counter.

Mick playfully wrestled the boy from Quon's grasp, then hurried outside as Ada walked slowly toward the open door.

"Goodnight, you beautiful people," she whispered, pulling the door quietly closed behind her.

Chapter 10

Jeb held the farmhouse gate open as the sheepherder directed the slow-moving dray toward the outer gate.

The wagon, pulled by two magnificent shires, was controlled by a very small Chinaman dressed in odd-looking black clothes. His hat was a squat, multi-coloured lid with short sides, a tassel dangled from the top; a stiff-plaited pigtail hung from the back of his head. His coat was quilted and had wide, floppy sleeves but no collar; it covered him from neck to toe. Beside him sat another equally small, strangely dressed Chinaman. Coming closer, one of the lads held the horses and the diminutive driver stood up to get their attention.

"We shall need an open space to erect our clinic," he announced in almost perfect English.

"To erect yer what?" Jeb retorted, watching a smile spread across the Chinaman's face. "We've no time for building, m'lad. There's sick folk here."

The back tailgate of the dray crashed open as the second man released the catches and rolled a large white parcel out onto the ground.

"What the devil is that?" Jeb asked, moving to the back of the dray to take a look as several of the farm workers came to stare.

The first man calmly held up his hands for silence as he patiently waited for all conversation to stop.

"I am Doctor Chew Fong Lim," he announced, slowly and deliberately. "You call me Chew." He indicated his companion. "This is Doctor Fung Won Chow. You call him Fung."

A ripple ran through the watchers but Doctor Chew quickly began talking again, a more urgent note creeping into his voice. "Please to carry roll of cloth to open space. We will require three 10 foot poles for tent."

"Do it!" Jeb instructed, motioning to two of the men. "I'll get the poles."

Following the doctor's simple instructions, a 20-foot tent quickly rose on the ground near the house. The sides were made secure with ropes and pegs. By this time, they had also unloaded several barrels and four flimsy chairs and a table.

The gypsies stood back in amazement, viewing and touching the large tent. This was something they had never seen before.

Again Doctor Chew held up his hands for silence and pointed at Jeb. "You will now show me the Lady Lizzie's children," he instructed. "Doctor Fung will visit the most serious cases of sickness in your esteemed establishment and in the village. Please arrange a guide for him." Picking up a small leather bag, he strode purposefully toward Jeb who delivered him into the house and introduced him to Jessy and Myra who would assist him.

Once inside the farmhouse, the doctor wasted no time. Dealing with the children and Jessy first, he then turned to the rest of the household. Two hours later, he asked one of the women to get Jeb.

"I find everyone except one young lad and one old lady very fine," Doctor Chew reported. "I'm sending them to clinic. Keep isolated for a few days. Lad is strong and will be velly fine. I believe lady will survive also." The doctor snapped his bag shut and moved toward the door. "Tell me, Mister Jeb" he asked, quietly, "who has visited your establishment in the past three weeks, perhaps a stranger?"

Jeb had no answer but vowed to find out. Chew bowed and moved off toward the clinic tent.

By the time dusk came creeping over the moorland farm and the candles and oil lamps flickered into life, the gypsy leader had his answer. So weary he could barely put one foot in front of the other, Jeb went to visit the doctors. They were still attending to their patients ... six village folk, the lad, and the gypsy woman. Chew stepped outside and in the low light studied the gypsy's face.

"You found the stranger. He was a sailor, back from the South Seas, was he not?"

"Yes, Missus Thomson's nephew apparently died here," said Jeb, resignedly. "He was a sailor."

I knew it," Chew exclaimed, in a voice slightly laced with emotion. "Everyone will get better now. I promise you, my friend, three more days and all will be well."

"Have either of you eaten?" Jeb asked, feeling his own pangs of hunger.

J. Robert Whittle

Calling in Chinese to Doctor Fung, the other little man came outside to join them. Smiling, both doctors began chattering in their native tongue.

"Come, we show you," said Chew, beckoning him to follow. "We bring own food."

They led him around to the back of the tent where a campfire was burning. A gypsy woman was attending a cast iron stew pot swinging on a chain over the flames.

"What is it?" Jeb asked, sniffing the strong aroma and making a face as he looked into the pot.

The doctors giggled behind their hands.

"Rice and Chinese herbs," Fung announced. "Velly good!"

"You seem to have it all under control, but if you don't mind, I'll go have some meat!" Jeb muttered, walking away leaving them both laughing behind him.

80C3

How are the boys doing, Bill?" asked Lizzie, watching as the baker wiped the beads of sweat from his face with the corner of his apron.

"Doin a roarin business," the Yorkshireman boasted. "Yer know that young Billy's taking orders from ships now. He gets 'em ta pay up front, too. Ah think we've turned a monster loose, Liz. That lad's a natural salesman."

Quon's hands spoke and his partner winked back at him.

"We sent some men over to clean the shop up," said Lizzie.

"Ah know," Bill smiled. "Mick was over there real early, lads told me on their second trip."

Hearing Clem calling him, they bade Bill goodbye as he hurried across the yard.

It was only a short walk around to Dixon's where they found the iron gates standing wide open. Inside, two drays were being heaped with what could only be described as garbage. Several men were moving about the yard as they put shoulders to their task.

Standing in the middle of the huge cobblestoned yard, looking up at the two storied smoke-blackened buildings, Lizzie cast a quick glance at Quon and smiled. *If John Watson needs space, now he's got it!* she thought, feeling Quon's hand on her elbow.

"Over dere," he said, pointing to a doorway half-hidden behind a dray. Joe was backing out of the building carrying one end of a pile of lumber. They moved quickly to help but were too late as Joe dropped his end, cursing softly.

"Dammit, that's heavy," he groaned, rubbing his hands, still unaware of the visitors.

"Dad ...," Lizzie said softly, trying not to startle him yet causing the old man to turn quickly. "If I ever catch you lifting anything like that again ...," but she couldn't finish the sentence, so she merely wrapped her arms around him. When she released him, she wagged her finger good-naturedly under his nose.

"Ah were only tryin to help, luv," he said, grinning sheepishly as Lizzie directed one of the men to pick up his load.

Two days later, the *Falcon* sailed up the Thames and into her berth. Lizzie was at the office talking to Ada about the children when Lefty arrived with the news, retreating just as quickly.

"You've done all you can, love. Try not to worry about them. They're being looked after by caring people," Ada assured her gently. Then her eyes caught some movement outside as a buggy pulled up.

"Who's that?" Lizzie asked.

"Your Mister Sutton, I believe!" she replied. "At any rate, he's quite the dandy and he appears to be on a mission!"

"HOLD THE HORSE, STUPID MAN!" James Sutton screamed at a passing stableworker as he leapt from the conveyance. Turning, he stormed into the office shouting even before he entered.

"I DEMAND MY DAMNED MONEY, NOW!" he bellowed.

Ned smiled inwardly. *I'm going to enjoy this.* His fingers reached for the official-looking paper Nathan had written. At the top in bold heading, the words TAX OFFICE SEIZURE glared from the sheet.

"Sorry, lad," Ned grunted. "Tax man beat yer to it. Says he'd like to meet you at his office to discuss matters further."

Sutton's face grew a shade redder, if that were possible. He snatched the paper from the clerk's hand, his eyes wincing as they lingered on the heading.

"Bloody hell," he hissed under his breath. Hands shaking, he screwed up the document flinging it violently into the fire. "YOU HAD NO RIGHT ...," he shouted, stopping abruptly when he saw the large mass of Mick O'Reilly appear in the other doorway. Eyes filled with hatred, he glanced furtively about the room then stomped out of the office.

"Mission accomplished!" Lizzie said, quietly. "Lesson Number One, Mister Sutton."

"We could still be in trouble if he goes to the tax office," said Ada, with a frown.

The rare sound of laughter came from the direction of Ned's desk. "That dandy only read one word … tax," he chortled, "and that scared him half to death! That black-hearted robber got what he deserved but I guarantee it won't be the last we see of him."

At dinner that evening, Ada related the story to the others. Davis sat back and glowered from under bushy eyebrows. When Lizzie questioned him on the recent activities of pirates and privateers, and also coal ships from Whitby becoming lost in the stormy seas of the English Channel, his irritability grew.

"Seems there are no pirates left since we took care of John Stroud," he growled. "I ain't heard of any colliers from Whitby going down either."

"I told you, Ada," Lizzie chuckled. "It's all lies."

Davis' dark eyes scanned the faces around the table. Unseen, Quon tapped out a message on Lizzie's arm, receiving a slight nod in reply.

"Well," Davis muttered. "Who are we talking about?"

"Crowther's ships," said Lizzie, winking at Ada.

"Oh, they're finished," he chuckled, ominously. "I've just confiscated another of their illegal cargoes. We left most of it on Sheppey for your ships to bring in."

Joe tapped the table with his pipe. Willie took this moment to climb up onto his knee and with tired fingers began to fiddle with the buttons on his waistcoat.

"We need barley, lass," announced Joe, settling the sleepy boy in his arms. "The new warehouse will be ready soon and John is eager to get started."

"Ben's bringing a load back with him, Dad," Lizzie murmured.

"That's a fool's enterprise," Davis grunted. "Takes too much time unloading."

"No, it doesn't!" objected Charley. "I've got that stream engine running and it can unload a ton in less than ten minutes."

"Wait, wait, before you get onto that," Mick interrupted. "That shop for the bread lads, sure it'll be ready in a week if we can keep them out of it that long. Now we're goin home, but let me tell yer Davis, Charley's right, av seen his engine workin."

"Impossible!"

Mick picked Willie out of Joe's arms and strode toward the open door, as Ada said goodnight to everyone. After the door closed, Charley quickly began his explanation of the workings of his unloading machine, eventually convincing the captain of its validity.

"How are the bakery lads, luv?" asked Joe. "They must be lookin forward to getting their own shop."

"Shop? What shop?" demanded Davis. "Mick mentioned a shop. Is my Oly involved? He's much too young."

"Yes, he's involved with Tom and Billy," Lizzie replied, understanding the captain's concern. "They're a good team."

"Does he need money?" Davis asked, pulling his purse out and dropping it onto the table. An unusual moment of softness passed across the rough sea captain's face. "He's mine, I'll provide what he needs," he mumbled, self-consciously.

Martha turned from the fire and Joe's eyes flicked open. Here was a side of the bad-tempered captain none of them had ever seen before. Lizzie reached for his hand but Davis quickly withdrew it.

"Yer a good man under all them whiskers, Captain Davis," she remarked softly.

During the next week, Lizzie and Quon ventured to the gypsy camp at least twice, hoping for news from the farm. Jeb had been gone for two weeks now and although they were always able to keep themselves busy, the time was dragging by especially as they had received no word as to how the children were doing.

They knew spring was coming when they saw a TLS gardener and another at *The Robin* pushing wheelbarrows full of foul-smelling dung obviously from their stables.

"Let's go to Bill's. Me big hungly," he said, pulling her along.

"I'll race you!" she cried, picking up her skirts.

It would not be much of a race and they both knew it. Quon was well used to his friend's tactics and although he tried valiantly, her long strides and lean body were a hard act to follow.

Three minutes later, they were just opening the gate when they heard the rattle of the bread cart hurtling down the lane toward them. They waited until it came into sight.

"MISS LIZZIE, QUON ... WE'RE OPEN!" Tom called, more excited than usual as the cart swung into the yard "You should see Billy, he's a shopkeeper now."

The partners helped with the pushing and in no time they had the cart turned around and were beginning to unload the empty barrels. A quarter of an hour later, it was reloaded and they were all sitting at the table eating. At first only the sound of clinking forks on metal plates broke the silence. Suddenly, Quon became alert and banged the table with his fist, holding up his hands for silence.

In the distance, they could faintly hear the sound of Martha's wagon-hoop bell urgently calling them home. Dropping their forks, the partners leapt from the table and raced out of the yard.

"Jeb's back!" Martha shouted from the window as they arrived at the cottage gate. "He's down at the office."

They carried on with a new eagerness and by the time they burst through the office door, they were both gasping. Urgent questions flashed from Lizzie's eyes bringing the dusty, road-weary gypsy to his feet, uncharacteristically taking the anxious girl in his arms.

"Slow down," he murmured, gently. "The danger's past, everybody is fine."

"Even the children?" Lizzie panted, hands clutching his shirt as she waited for his nod.

Mick arrived and they all listened silently as the gypsy unfolded the story. A note of admiration crept into his voice when he told of the efforts of the Chinese doctors and the strange canvas building they had erected.

Quon grinned, waving his arms about.

Lizzie giggled. "He wants to know if you sampled their Chinese food?"

"Hell no!" Jeb grimaced. "Rice pudding with bits of black stuff in it ... yuuk ... not for me!"

Ned cocked an eyebrow and picked up his pen, tapping it impatiently on his desk.

"What is it, Ned?" asked Ada.

"Them doctors," he frowned. "Where did they come from? What happens if we need 'em again?"

"He called them," Jeb replied, pointing at Quon, "but they told me how to get them if we need 'em again."

"How?" Lizzie and Ada chorused.

"Using a special flag," Jeb chuckled, digging into his bulging pocket. Bringing out a bright red silk flag, he unfurled it and they saw that it had a large white circle in the middle. "Put it on a pole near the office and someone will come, they said. We have one at the farm, too." Folding it carefully, he handed it to Ada. "There'll be a shipment of cattle and hogs arriving later this week, Ada. The drovers were leaving two days behind me." Looking over at Lizzie, he changed the subject. "You can come with us on our next trip, Liz."

"When will that be, Jeb?" she asked, hoping it would be soon.

"Sometime in April."

A smile lit up her face momentarily. *Hopefully sooner, rather than later,* she thought, then turning to Quon, her mood became serious again. "Time to go, m'lad." Waving to their friend, they turned and strode away.

Martha was expecting them and already had sandwiches and cider on the table.

"Is everything all right, luvy?"

Biting hungrily into her cheese sandwich, Lizzie nodded.

"Where's Willie, Marta?" asked Quon.

"Gone with his granddad to see Charley at the docks. He loves to watch the big ships and Charley allows him to climb on his cart. I suspect yer dad will show the lad off to some of his old shipmates, too. They'll be gone all afternoon and be fair exhausted when they return!"

Chapter 11

The little church, with its grim, blackened gravestones looked less than inviting and Quon shuddered noticeably taking her by the arm and pulling her along. They hesitated when they noticed the minister and Bishop Tide in deep conversation by the gate and quickly turned down Long Street to avoid confrontation.

They were almost to Chandler when the sounds of Billy's banter wafted past them on the breeze. Nearing the corner, they decided to stay back and watch. He seemed to be continually on the move bounding from curb to barrel making change as he shouted his wares to the people passing by.

"Yer right, dumplin, they'll do well," she said.

Suddenly, a carriage pulled around the corner and thundered uncaring through the street scattering the shoppers who leapt for safety. Quon recognized the occupants and looked to see if Lizzie had noticed. As they watched, the carriage turned down Cooper's Lane and into the yard of the warehouse that housed the secret gambling establishment.

"Let's go take a look," she whispered, pulling Quon's arm.

Moving across the street, they headed toward the warehouse. Taking the same route the street urchins had shown them, they found the ladder and retraced their steps to the hidden stairway and down into the building. Cautiously easing their way across the rafters, they found the hole in the ceiling. Lizzie could hear muffled voices but looking through the hole she could only clearly see two men.

She was surprised when she recognized James Sutton and Jonas Crowther. Several other players came into view and, all of a sudden, a cheer went up and the pile of coins was swept aside by two hands.

"YOU CHEATING SCOUNDREL!" Sutton screamed, coming to his feet and shouting across the table.

Crowther came to his feet upending his chair as he tried to restrain his friend, angering Sutton even more. The room went deathly quiet.

"It's to be like that is it? All right ... all or nothing, Sutton!"

growled the supposed winner, his hand returning the pile of coins to the middle of the table.

Hearing the commotion, Lizzie concentrated on the conversation below. Quon, having experienced a feeling of foreboding ever since they arrived, desperately wanted to leave. However, she ignored his urgent tapping on her arm. She wanted to tell him what was going on but there was no opportunity, it was imperative that she didn't miss anything. He looked nervously over her shoulder.

"But I'm broke," Sutton cried, returning to his chair.

"No matter—I'll take the Deed for that house of your aunt's you've been telling us about—as collateral," said the calm voice.

Quon again tugged on Lizzie's sleeve but she continued to ignore him.

James Sutton's face twisted in rage and he turned to his friend, his eyes begging for help.

"Not my problem, James," Crowther was saying as he stepped back from the table. "It seems this is between you and Flood."

"ROBBER!" Sutton growled contemptuously. Then, putting his hand into his vest pocket, he extracted the precious Deed he'd tricked his aunt into signing. He slammed it onto the table then picked up the dice and shaker.

"One throw takes all," the voice of Flood said calmly.

Sutton shook the container violently then allowed the dice to trickle out onto the table.

"Two fives!" gasped a deep voice.

"Beat that, you dog!" Sutton snarled with elation, his chair scraping on the floor as he leapt to his feet again.

Gabriel Flood slowly picked up the dice. No matter which way they fell, he wouldn't really suffer. This was merely a game to him— he didn't need the money. Of late, a Captain in the Lancers, and the youngest son of a rich banking family from Oxford, he was enjoying himself immensely, having attended as a guest of his cousin, young Lord Astor. As he calmly shook the dice he looked over at his cousin and winked. Astor grinned back.

Lizzie could see more heads as they gathered closer to the table. Flood continued to shake the dice adding to the suspense. Lizzie lay mesmerized. Having heard enough of the men's conversation, she knew it was her friends that had everything at stake now.

One die tumbled from the holder ... falling almost silently to the table surface. A six-spot shone in the light. The second die slowly followed but Flood added a slight flourish this time and, as everyone held their breath, it rolled across the tabletop ... landing in front of James Sutton ... a five!

Realization struck hard in Sutton's pounding chest. He'd lost it all. Even cheating could not help this time.

Laughing, Flood scooped up the paper. Sutton collapsed back into his chair, moaning piteously as the others whispered amongst themselves.

Suddenly, a loud cracking sound rent the air. Heads turned upward as large pieces of plaster began to rain onto the table. Pandemonium struck as men leapt to their feet falling over chairs and each other as the ceiling began to cave inward.

Suspiciously, Gabriel Flood kept his eyes averted as he pushed his chair back to escape the haze of dust and falling plaster. Thus, he was the first to see the frantic look of terror on the girl's face as the hole widened and she tumbled screaming through the air.

Lizzie had only seconds to act and soon realized it wouldn't be enough as she frantically reached out in the dark for something ... anything that would stop the inevitable.

The men moved back, spellbound, as flailing limbs and petticoats flying, she landed with a bone-jarring thud upon the large table. Gabriel had instinctively moved forward wanting to help yet realizing it was already useless. As she landed several of the men move angrily toward her as if regaining their senses and needing to halt her escape, if such a thing was possible.

Quon, meanwhile, clung desperately to the broken beams but hearing the frightening thud he regained his senses and began to move toward the door. He knew he had no time to waste and must find help immediately, appropriate help.

As fast as he dared, he inched backwards to the stairway knowing it would take precious minutes to get off the roof. Wild thoughts careened through his mind. *Poor Wizzy! Wizzy hurt, must find help! Bad men be velly angry now, what will they do to my Wizzy. Must find help qlick!*

Held fast by strong hands, Lizzie opened her eyes slightly,

feigning unconsciousness. She wasn't sure how badly hurt she was … if she was hurt at all. She couldn't move, they had seen to that, but aside from being a bit dizzy and sore, she felt no real pain. Recognizing her plight and realizing Quon had not fallen with her, she began to whimper and cough, hoping to cover any noise he made as he escaped. Who knew how these men could react to being spied upon.

"Unhand the girl, you jackals!" barked Gabriel Flood. A handsome man with a strong, square jaw, he possessed the cold, unforgiving eyes of a soldier who'd seen the many horrors of war. It was Lizzie's fortune that he still held a high regard for chivalry and harboured a bold urge for adventure.

Heavy hands released their grip allowing Lizzie to cautiously raise herself on one arm. At first, her mind was a whirl of confusion but as she lay there, her nimble brain was beginning to settle on a plan. Many years before, in a moment of bravado, old Abe had told her his method of dealing with argumentative customers. *This may be a good time to try it,* she thought.

"Who the hell are you? Why were you up there?" one of her captors growled, staring at the dust-covered girl.

"Up there?" Lizzie repeated, concentrating on Abe's story, then rubbing her eyes with one hand and trying to look both confused and dazed. She now realized she was unhurt, albeit bruised and the men had relaxed their hold but were still gathered around watching her closely. Slowly, she came to an upright position.

"Yes, girl!" another voice joined in, pointing through the dust at the hole in the ceiling. "What were you doing up there?"

"Up there?" she repeated, also glancing upwards.

Questions came faster as more of the men got in on the act but Lizzie continued her charade.

Climbing down off the roof, Quon Lee looked around desperately. Seeing no one he knew, he set out toward home where he could find Mick and some men. Nearing the new bake shop, he was relieved to see Nathan's buggy blocking the road as the curious trader watched Billy.

"What's wrong lad, where's Lizzie?" Nathan asked, seeing the look of panic on Quon's face.

"Get Mister Mick. Wizzy twouble with bad men ... need help velly qlick!"

Wick leapt into action even before Quon had finished. Taking his cudgel from under the seat, he landed cat-like on the cobblestones beside the boy.

"Show me," he rasped, as Dan took up the reins and the buggy tore off up the lane toward the TLS office.

Rushing down the hill, Quon tried to explain to Wick what had happened. By the time they reached the warehouse the gypsy realized he might need more help but Lizzie was in too much danger to wait. They started toward the building but, Wick suddenly stopped, gripping Quon's shoulder.

"You wait at road for others," he hissed, then hearing loud voices he hurried inside the old building.

Meanwhile, Lizzie's foolish answers were quickly driving the gamblers to a point of screaming frustration. Gabriel Flood stood back and listened to the strange conversation between his friends and this unknown girl. His trained senses told him there was more to this girl than met the eye and he began to laugh. The men turned and stared at him. Their incredulous expressions told him they were not as aware of the situation as he was.

"She's only an idiot peasant, Gabriel," one ranted.

"No, my friend," Gabriel chuckled, "I believe we're going to discover very shortly that it is ourselves who are the idiots. If I'm right, his lass has been playing for time and we're the ones who are in danger!"

With that Wick stepped boldly into the room, swinging his cudgel. "THE GAME'S OVER GENTS, LET HER GO!" he cried.

"ONE STEP MORE AND I'LL ...," screamed Sutton, trying to sound convincing as he moved toward Lizzie grabbing her arms from behind.

But she was too quick for him, sinking her teeth into his arm.

"AAGGG!! YOU LITTLE WITCH!" he cried in pain, releasing his vise-like grip on one of her arms.

She elbowed him in the chest and managed to squirm off the table even though he kept his hold on her other arm. Twisting violently, she managed to finally pull herself loose falling to the floor at

Gabriel Flood's feet.

But Sutton moved in on her, grabbing her again, however, he hadn't counted on Flood's intervention ... receiving a crack across the wrist before being pushed violently aside.

In true cavalier fashion, Gabriel Flood smiled broadly and offered Lizzie his hand. The others stood back and waited with bated breath. She took the hand cautiously, still not sure of this man named Flood who seemed to be different from the others.

As he pulled her to her feet, he brought her overly close and hissed in her ear, "Now go!" pushing her toward the door.

Lizzie only had time to take three quick strides toward Wick when Jeb and six of his men burst into the room. Cudgels waving, they were making such blood-curdling sounds as to frighten the most stalwart soldier. Bringing up the rear was a now panic-stricken Quon screaming his beloved partner's name.

Flood, realizing his gallant act had come too late, watched calmly as the gypsies surrounded them. Sutton and the others looked helplessly from one to the other.

Quon moved boldly forward, embracing Lizzie.

"What do you want done with these dogs, Miss Lizzie?" Jeb snarled.

The gamblers looked from one to the other, hearing her name for the first time.

"Let them go," she said tersely. "Except for that one named Sutton," she said disdainfully, pointing him out. "And him!" she continued, looking over at Gabriel Flood.

Four gypsies moved quickly toward the two men grasping their arms. The rest were escorted from the building scurrying for their carriages with barely a backward glance.

James Sutton cringed from his captors and tried to pull free but they held him tightly. *Who is this girl?* he pondered. *Something about her is vaguely familiar, but why? What are they going to do?*

The immediate thought passing through Gabriel Flood's mind was, *Serves the devil right.* But when he realized Lizzie was pointing at him also and the gypsies were swooping down on him, he had to force himself to remain calm. Arms pinned to his side, he waited. *Who are these people? Who is this girl they seem so devoted to and why her interest in James Sutton ... and me?* He had also noticed the young Chinese lad and his grave concern for the girl. *An interesting combination.* Now, they were deep in conversation; ignoring Sutton, they were coming toward him—her expression one of pure business.

"You can unhand this one now. The Deed to Sutton House, if you please, sir," she demanded, holding out her child-like hand.

Gabriel wanted to laugh or, at least, to smile. This was inconceivable. This girl was hardly more than a child. "I won it fairly, young lady," he retorted, but seeing the look on the gypsies' faces, he removed the document from his waistcoat pocket and handed it to her.

"I'm going to pay you for it," she explained, a wry smile playing on her lips. "How much was it covering, Mister ..., I believe the name is Flood, is it not, sir?"

A puzzled expression crept across his face. "Captain Gabriel Flood at your service ...," he replied, "and 200 guineas was the amount, young lady."

"Quon, I need 200 guineas and some tatty men's clothes from the rag shed."

Quon nodded, turned on his heel and left the building.

Gabriel watched the chemistry between the young people with fascination. Just then, two more people entered the room and made straight for the girl.

"Take what you need, we've just seen Quon outside," said the short, well-dressed man offering his purse to the girl. Despite previous clashes with Lizzie, Nathan Goldman had been desperately worried for her safety.

"YOU AGAIN!" Sutton screamed at the trader, pulling against his captors and interrupting Gabriel's thoughts. "DO YOU KNOW THIS GIRL? WHO THE HELL IS SHE?"

Nathan cringed from the man but realized the gypsies had him well in hand. Wick stepped in, brandishing his cudgel and Sutton soon quieted down again.

Lizzie turned her back on the group, opened Nathan's purse and slowly counted out 200 guineas placing them on the table. "That's yours, Captain Flood. You are free to go now but I could use your help if you would stay."

Gabriel Flood looked from the girl to the money. His brow

wrinkled into a deep frown but he moved toward the table. As he picked up his money he tried to imagine what help he could possibly be to this fascinating girl, but he was damn sure he was willing to find out. He hadn't been much older when he had joined the army and learned to think for himself. They had been hard lessons to learn and he'd been kicked around a bit, but he had remained strong and determined, just like this one ... but she was a girl!

Putting the last of the coins safely in his own purse, he was about to say something when the sound of a carriage was heard and all eyes turned to the door. Quon burst into the room carrying a sack which he dumped unceremoniously onto the floor in front of Lizzie. She nodded and he emptied them out onto the floor. They appeared to be dirty rags and Flood remembered she had sent him to the rag shed.

Now what? Gabriel wondered, noticing the girl's slight smile.

"I want Sutton in those rags," she snapped, the smile gone as she turned to Jeb.

Grim-faced, Jeb gave an order in Romany and the gypsies fell to their task.

"WHAT ARE YOU DOING?" Sutton cried, panic taking hold of him for the first time, as his captors stripped him to his undergarments. "How dare you treat me this way," he wailed, continuing to fight against their actions.

The gypsies performed their task well receiving no help from their subject. Choosing clothes that made him look like a seaman, they soon had him dressed and left whimpering pathetically on the floor.

Having virtually ignored Sutton during this process, Lizzie now turned again to Jeb. "I want him aboard a ship bound for Australia," she commanded, her eyes flashing and a look of utter hatred on her face. "I think a press gang would be a fit punishment for what this scoundrel has done to his family!"

A stunned silence descended on the room.

"Australia ... the penal colony? Good Lord, you can't do this to me. How can this be happening?" cried Sutton tiredly, as his wrists were tied behind his back. "I demand ...."

Before the prisoner could say another word, Jeb grabbed a sock from the pile of clothes and stuffed it into his mouth. Sutton dropped to his knees, his will to fight suddenly gone. Caught by his guards before his exhausted body collapsed on the floor, he turned his head toward Lizzie his eyes pleading for mercy. Jeb's men picked him up and carried him from the room.

Gabriel watched in shock and amazement knowing there was nothing he could do to help his friend even if he wanted to. *Does Sutton really deserve this*? he wondered. *Would he ever manage to return?* He did not know who this Lizzie was but he certainly planned to find out ... and it couldn't be soon enough. He ascertained she must be about 18 years of age. Dressed as she was in working-class clothes that were covered in plaster dust and cobwebs, it was hard to be sure. She was certainly a beauty ... and that name, he couldn't get it from his mind, he had heard it before.

She was handing the trader his purse and obviously surprised him when she asked, "Mister Goldman, could I borrow Wick's services for an hour?"

Fumbling for words, Nathan nodded. "B-by all means, my dear. I'll be waiting at your office when you return." And with that, he turned and was gone.

Lizzie went over to Wick. "Thank you for your timely arrival, Wick. Now, if you can find two more men, we'll be ready in a few minutes."

Gabriel's mind was racing. *Her office...she needs two men ...*! Finding himself quite entranced by Lizzie's confident handling of this unusual situation, he wondered why a girl would be involved in any of Sutton's ill-doing.

Looking about the room, he now realized he was alone with these two young people ... that is, except for the vigilant gypsy and the two men waiting outside. *She seems to trust me,* he thought, turning toward the door.

"And you, sir," she snapped, stopping him in his tracks, "were out of place with these popinjays. You can tell me your story as you drive us to Lady Sutton's."

"Lady Sutton?" Gabriel repeated incredulously, as the young people moved toward him, indicating the open door. "I seem to have no choice in the matter," he mumbled. *This is turning out to be a bloody interesting day*!

Outside, two gypsies were already aboard the Sutton coach, the only remaining coach in the yard save for the one with the Flood family crest emblazoned on the door.

Gabriel climbed up to the driver's seat of his own coach and took the reins. Wick opened the door and waited.

"Mister Flood!" came the girl's voice interrupting his thoughts as she and the Chinese boy climbed up beside him. "I should introduce you to our gypsy friend. This is Wick. Listen to him closely."

Gabriel nodded, trying not to let his curiosity appear too obvious, and looked down at the gypsy.

"I'll be ridin inside yer coach, if yer don't mind, sir," announced Wick, then indicating the others, he continued, "just follow the other coach."

Gabriel fully understood the gypsy's warning. *These people work together as if they are used to each other*, he thought. More confused fragments rushed through his head as he waited until Wick closed the door. He turned to Lizzie and was surprised to find it was the Chinese lad who was sitting beside him. The young man grunted and with a brisk hand movement, indicated it was time to leave as the other coach pulled ahead of them.

Smiling wryly, Gabriel flicked his wrist and the horses obediently moved forward.

∞∞

"Australia, you say," Charley Mason muttered, after hearing Jeb's brief description of the day's events. *Lizzie means business*, he thought, looking over at the wagon but unable to see anyone besides gypsies.

He signaled for the Grim boys. "Take Jeb to Captain Williams on Royal Dock," he ordered. "The *Ocean Queen* sails for Australia tonight and he's searching for crew. Tell him I sent you."

Jeb motioned for the wagon to follow the Grims who had set out on foot and they arrived at the gangway of the *Ocean Queen* some minutes later. They found Captain Williams at the rail talking to one of his men.

"WHAT YOU GOT THERE, MATEY?" he growled, peering down at them as they brought their now unbound, bedraggled-looking prisoner from the wagon.

"THE DOCKMASTER SAYS YER LOOKIN FOR CREW?"

"HOW MANY?"

"JUST ONE!"

Scowling, the captain nodded, but the scar on his cheek twitched violently. Calling for two of his sailors, he directed them to collect the new crewman. Sutton uttered one last, hopeless cry as Jeb's men handed him over to the sailors, who grabbed him roughly by the arms and urged him up the gangway.

"One-way passage!" Jeb called after them.

"Aye, if he survives!" came the captain's snarled reply.

Chapter 12

Leaving the city, they soon found themselves on the less-travelled road that took them past the estates of upper-class Londoners. Having no idea how far they were going and, finding the scenery quite commonplace, Gabriel settled comfortably back in his seat and watched the road.

Soon overcome with a burning desire to engage this mysterious girl into a conversation, he began to speak, in a casual manner. "I'm the third of three sons," he said, speaking loudly so she could hear, "no title nor chance of the family business, only the army and a lifelong subsistence allowance." He looked sideways at the girl. "Now I'm through with the army and need a purpose in life. I'd give anything to have friends as loyal as the ones you seem to have, young lady." His gaze settled on Quon whom he noticed was holding tightly to Lizzie's arm. "May I ask your name, miss?"

"My Wizzy damn smart," said Quon quietly.

"Did he say Wizzy?" Gabriel chuckled.

"Quiet, Quon," Lizzie chided him. "He means Lizzie. My name is Lizzie Short. Joe Todd of the TLS Company is my father. Do you know Lady Sutton?" she asked, abruptly changing the subject.

"Only Sutton I know is the one you apparently just sent to Australia!" he said, with a tinge of dismay in his voice. "Although, I have a nagging feeling you meant every word you uttered!"

"Oh, I did!" Lizzie assured him. Their conversation continued until the other coach pulled off the road allowing them to pass. "Turn in here," she commanded.

Gabriel, looking in the direction of her outstretched hand, saw a great walled house set behind tall iron gates. *That's unusual,* he thought, noticing the two dark-skinned men behind the gate. *Those men are gypsies.* The girl waved to the men at the gate and it instantly swung open. Even before the carriage stopped in front of the house, Wick was offering Lizzie his hand. She was the first to reach the massive doorway set between two marble pillars and, taking the doorknocker in her hand, she tapped twice.

The door opened to reveal an unfamiliar gentleman dressed in butler's clothes.

"Can I help you, sir?" the new butler asked pleasantly, looking up at Gabriel and smiling from behind grey mutton-chop whiskers. Gabriel's eyes flicked onto the girl and the butler followed his gaze looking in surprise at the waif-like girl. A slight smile passed across his face as he remembered his ladyship's stern instructions about a beautiful red-haired young woman and her companion. Although this person did appear to fit the description, he would have liked to put both she and her clothes into a bath before presenting them to the lady of the house.

"You must be Miss Lizzie," he said, hesitantly. Receiving a sweet smile from the girl, he swung the door open. "Do come in, miss. Lady Sutton and Margaret are in the parlour."

Gabriel followed them as the butler led them down a wide, dark passageway lit by small gas lamps. About halfway, he stopped in front of a pair of French doors upon which he knocked lightly... twice. Quickly opening it, as if hearing an agitated request for speed, he entered and announced their arrival, standing aside to allow the guests to enter.

Lady Sutton and her daughter were sitting in a large, bright room with many windows. They were talking quietly when the door opened and they couldn't restrain their pleasure at seeing their young friends again.

"Lizzie and Quon! What a pleasant surprise," Margaret cried with obvious delight. "What brings you here? My goodness, Lizzie, did you have a fight with a bag of flour?" she giggled, taking her friend's arm. "Let's go get you dusted off, then you can tell me all about this handsome visitor you've brought us!"

They disappeared briefly and re-entered laughing.

"There, that's a bit better, now you simply have to introduce us to this handsome man, Lizzie!" Margaret declared.

"Daisy," her mother laughed, also looking curiously at their visitor. "Where are your manners? Where did you find this young man, Lizzie, dear?"

"Captain Gabriel Flood, these are my dear friends, Lady Sutton and her daughter, Margaret," introduced Lizzie.

Gabriel moved forward to take Lady Sutton's hand and, bowing low, he brushed her fingers with his lips. "My pleasure, Lady Sutton," he said softly, looking into her eyes.

"Thank you, captain," she replied, blushing slightly as she returned her hand to her lap.

Margaret cleared her throat rather loudly.

"Miss Sutton," said Gabriel, bowing slightly, his eyes lingering on her lovely blonde hair for a moment.

"He is a true rascal as you can see for yourselves," Lizzie exclaimed. "I just met him earlier this day. He's here to help me right a terrible wrong."

Quon's hands began talking rapidly to Lizzie as Gabriel watched in obvious fascination.

"No, you do it, Quon," said Lizzie, lightly. Quickly reaching into her pocket, she handed the document over to Quon Lee. Blushing through his naturally dark skin, he stepped forward helped on by his partner's nudging hand.

"Pwees accept this gift, Wady Sutton, from Wizzy and me," he said, handing her the paper.

As Gabriel watched, the colour drained from his face as he realized the enormous act of goodwill Lizzie was offering to her friends. He felt suddenly very humble.

Lady Sutton's lip quivered and she dropped her head. Touching her handkerchief to each eye she looked up at Lizzie as the Deed fluttered to the floor.

"What is it, Mother?" Margaret whispered, picking up the fallen document and reading the title. "Why, it's the Deed to Sutton House! How on earth did you get it, Liz?"

"If you don't mind my saying it, Miss Short, I think you should all be aware that this is the second thing this young woman has done to help you today," offered Gabriel, taking the seat indicated by Margaret.

"And the first was?" Margaret asked quickly, glancing curiously from Captain Flood to her friends.

"Well," Lizzie hesitated, "we arranged a passage to Australia for your Uncle James. He won't be able to harm you anymore."

"He's g-gone?" Lady Sutton gasped, watching Lizzie nod. Her hand flew to her mouth then dropped limply to her side.

J. Robert Whittle

Gabriel rushed to Lady Sutton's side. Going down on his knee, he took her hands and spoke softly to her, "James Sutton was once my friend but more recently he had become quite simply, a scoundrel, but I had no idea he had stolen the Deed to your home, dear lady. If there is anything I can do to help you, please tell me."

Lizzie watched silently, then leaning closer to Quon, she whispered, "I think we've found the Suttons a protector, dumplin."

Gabriel stood up and turned abruptly to face Lizzie. "Who in the name of heaven are *you*, Lizzie Short?" he demanded. Feeling the touch of Margaret's hand as it fell gently on his arm, his mood softened slightly and their eyes met, locking intensely for what seemed like an eternity.

"*She* is the TLS Company, Captain Flood. Just be thankful she's made you one of her friends," said Margaret.

"We have a proposition for you, Captain Flood," Lizzie announced. All eyes turned her way. "On the drive here, you said you needed a purpose in life and friends that care about you. Well, here's your chance. Lady Sutton and Margaret need a friend who cares about their welfare; would you like to be that friend?"

"B-but I'm not really domesticated and I-I've no knowledge of estate matters," he stammered, his face going a light shade of crimson before he began to pace the floor.

The Sutton women glanced at each other, raising their eyebrows.

"Who fired that sour old butler of yours?" asked Lizzie.

"Why, Mister Goldman," said Margaret. "He also fired the maid and the stableman Uncle James had employed."

"On whose authority?" Lizzie demanded.

"He said you would have wanted it done," said Lady Sutton, "and he has brought in very satisfactory replacements."

"Now it's easy, Gabriel," Lizzie chuckled. "All you have to do is rebuild the Sutton fortune. You're from a banking family, ask for their advice. Do you live far from here, captain?"

"I'm recently returned from the army and have not found a permanent residence as yet."

"We have plenty of room, you will stay here with us, dear boy," announced Lady Sutton, in a voice that demanded no argument.

"That's terribly kind, Lady Sutton, but ...," Gabriel began.

"There's no room for argument, Captain Flood," interrupted

Lizzie. "It will be the perfect arrangement until they have their affairs in order with no more worries about people taking advantage of them."

"It's settled then," Margaret announced, coyly. "Welcome to Sutton House, Captain Flood. I'm sure you'll find our home is up to your standards."

"Ma'am, after the army ...," he began, surprising even himself by accepting this unusual offer.

A shrill, piercing whistle from the garden interrupted their conversation as Ben Dark's face appeared at the window.

Jumping happily to her feet, Margaret quickly kissed her mother on the cheek. "Ben's here for my riding lesson, Mother. It was delightful to meet you, Captain Flood. I suppose we will be meeting again rather soon. Goodbye everyone!" she called over her shoulder.

Lizzie grinned. Gabriel, shook his head and chuckled, moving to take the chair Margaret had vacated.

"My goodness, sometimes that girl has such poor manners," Lady Sutton complained.

Gabriel was too busy with his own thoughts to notice. He really didn't understand what had come over him in the last four hours. Gone was his devil-may-care attitude as he warmed to his new task accepting a challenge from this unusual young woman from dockland.

He'd seen her courage when she fell though the ceiling, watched the cunning as she played her charade, and her power when she disposed of James Sutton. However, he had also viewed firsthand her sense of fair play by returning the Sutton's Deed to its rightful owner. Now he was totally amazed at how she had managed to persuade him to completely change his plans. This was one woman he would not desire for an enemy.

Gabriel announced he was going to drive Lizzie and Quon back to dockland before he carried on into London to gather his belongings. He chuckled as they got a whiff of the slaughterhouse, remembering their earlier conversation. As Lizzie directed him toward the TLS office, Ada heard the carriage and looked out.

"My word, look here! I wonder what our girl has been up to now?" she exclaimed, causing Mick and Ned to hurry to the window.

"I wonder what the "F" stands for?" asked Ned, reading the emblem on the carriage door.

At that moment, Lizzie and Quon entered, followed by a tall, handsome stranger. Lizzie made the introductions before giving a very sketchy account of the afternoon's events and the reason for Gabriel's presence. When she had finished, the rather embarrassed captain looked over at Mick.

"May I ask, sir, who is the owner of this establishment?"

"Joe Todd ... and them two!" Mick growled, nodding toward Lizzie and Quon. "Why?"

"But, they're so young," Gabriel muttered.

Ned's pen scratched monotonously in his books as he grinned to himself. He knew the thoughts running through the captain's head; he'd had them himself when he first met Lizzie. He lay down his pen and took his pipe from his mouth.

"Yer head's in a whirl ain't it, lad?" he grunted. "Somethin else has 'appened today, ah can see it in yer faces ...."

Ned never finished his statement as the sound of another conveyance stopping outside caused Ada to return to the window.

"Nathan's here and he looks agitated about something."

"Indeed!" the trader snapped, appearing at the door. "Will you please tell Charley Mason, I'm not his errand boy!" Then seeing Gabriel, he stopped abruptly. "What, you again?"

"Do you two know each other?" Ada frowned.

"I'll say we do," Nathan eyed the newcomer. "He's caused me enough trouble for one day, thank you."

"Stop yer grumbling," Lizzie snapped. "What did Charley want?"

"*Falcon*'s on her way in, and you owe me 200 guineas!"

"No, she doesn't," interrupted Gabriel. "I do!" Opening his moneybag, he counted 200 guineas onto Ada's desk.

The others watched in surprised silence as the coins were laid down and Nathan immediately went to pick them up. Eyes glowing, his fingers seemed to caress each piece as he put them into his purse. When he finished, half-smiling, he looked up and backed toward the door, muttering to himself something about lost time and Wick.

"So that was Mister Goldman," Gabriel laughed. "Well folks, if you'll excuse me, I'll beg my leave." Bowing to Lizzie, he continued, "You know where you can find me if needed."

As the door closed behind him, Ada looked at Lizzie and frowned. "Now, young lady, what was all that about, especially the part about the 200 guineas?"

Lizzie glanced at Quon whose hands were sending a quick message. She sighed, nodding her head in obvious resignation.

"He says I should tell you," she muttered, going to sit down. So she began at the beginning, this time telling of her fall through the ceiling and capture by the gamblers. Ada's face went dreadfully pale but she made no comment. Then Lizzie told of how she had discovered the Deed to Sutton House, forcing Gabriel Flood to sell it to her after winning it from James Sutton.

"I'll kill James Sutton if I ever see the man again," declared Mick.

Lizzie and Quon began to giggle.

"That's going to be difficult, lad," she explained. "He was dressed in rags and pressed into service on a ship bound for Australia."

They were interrupted by the patter of small feet outside and they all waited expectantly as Willie's fingers fiddled with the latch.

"Daddy?" he called, just before the door flew open. Racing into the room, the boy leapt into Mick's arms. "Grandma says it's dinner time."

Joe and Charley had already started eating when they arrived. Martha eyed Lizzie and Quon with a look of utter annoyance, chuntering loudly as she served up their meals.

"Where the devil have you two been, it's late and we've been mighty worried ... and look at your dirty clothes, Lizzie! I saw Nathan's coach race up the lane this afternoon with only his driver ... I was sure I saw Quon inside. Not five minutes later they were back, going in the opposite direction!" By now Martha's voice was becoming quite shrill with anxiety and she had to stop to catch her breath.

Not garnering a response from anyone, least of all Lizzie, she took another deep breath and continued, "Not much earlier, Jeb rushed away with a wagonload of gypsies, going in the same direction. They were in a frightful hurry!" Her face red, she dropped into a chair and again paused to look about the room. Still no explanation was forthcoming so she looked helplessly over at Joe.

"Well, what *was* goin on?" Joe growled, searching their faces as the uncomfortable silence continued.

"I didn't send for 'em," said Lizzie, almost too casually.

Quon's eyes remained glued to his plate as his fingers tapped out a message on Lizzie's hand under the table.

"I believe it was something to do with the Suttons," Ada murmured, cautiously.

"It was," Charley intervened quickly, "they came and asked me to arrange a trip for one of their party."

Joe looked sideways at Lizzie again. *I know there's more to it but she obviously doesn't want us to know*, he thought.

Resigned to this lack of information, the afternoon was soon forgotten as other business came into the discussion including the fact that John Watson was eagerly waiting for Ben's grain ship.

Willie fell asleep on Joe's lap and it wasn't long before their eventful day finally drew to a close.

Chapter 13

An unusually cold spring breeze was blowing up Water Lane as the young partners ventured out the next morning intent on checking the dock for the *Falcon*. They found Abe huddled on the doorstep smoking his pipe. They heard him coughing and noting his pallor, encouraged him inside.

Lizzie stirred the fire back into life making him a hot drink, liberally laced with peppermint syrup. "Have you eaten today?" she asked.

"No, love," he wheezed, in an unusually tired voice. "I just couldn't be bothered."

Quon's hands made a sign. She nodded and he turned quickly and ran out the door.

Running across the street to the nearest ale house, he headed straight for the kitchen. Once his order was given, it took but a few minutes and he was on his way back with a towel-wrapped plate of ham, eggs and sausage swimming in fat. Tucked carefully under his arm was a small loaf of bread.

When he placed the meal in front of the tailor, he noticed that some colour had already returned to the old man's cheeks. Together they coaxed him to take one mouthful and then another. More colour returned to his face and he began to eat without prodding.

"We'll be back later to check up on you," Lizzie announced.

Out on the street, Quon's hands began to gyrate.

"Stop," Lizzie snapped. "Talk properly to me, we're on our own."

"Him not wook after himself. Abe need mother!"

"Yes, you're right. He does need a woman to look after him, but where are we going to find one?"

Dodging the morning traffic, they soon found themselves at the docks. The first person they saw was Charley standing beside his cart watching one of their ships slip away from the quayside. With the assistance of the wind and tide it was quickly being pulled out into the swollen river as men clambered about in the rigging readying the sails. Lizzie loved to watch as the small sails filled with wind pulling the ship along.

"Where they going?" Lizzie asked.

"Plymouth, with a load of sailcloth, then on to Cornwall for china clay ... that goes to the Bristol Channel for the potters where they load up with fine bone china for Liverpool. He'll be back in eight weeks with cloth from the cotton mills in Lancashire bound for the tailors of London. That's what we call back-loading, lass, we're paid every foot of the way. No sailing empty." He banged on the side of his cart and the Grim boys appeared lifting the cart and moving off.

"When's *Falcon* due?" Lizzie called after them.

"Three o'clock."

As they walked back past the TLS dock, they noticed the new steam engine was wrapped in oilcloth to protect it from the weather and, no doubt, the prying eyes of their competitors. Heading across the busy road toward *The Robin,* they jumped for safety, turning to look when they heard an angry coachman's voice. The sudden yelping of a dog explained the situation and they watched it quickly limp away up a nearby alleyway. From the other direction, a mud-splattered coach swept into *The Robin*'s stableyard right in front of their noses.

Following it, they found Tom and a group of his cronies, sack-cloths wrapped around their shoulders as they huddled together.

"I got news," the pegleg hiccupped, banging his tankard on the roughly hewn table, "but it'll cost yer a penny."

"Don't want to know," Lizzie grunted, moving away but feeling Quon's fingers on her arm.

"A ha'penny will do," Tom shouted, moving too quickly in his eagerness and throwing his balance off.

"Well, tell me then," she said, still showing little interest.

"One of Crowther's crews walked off their ship this morning. Haven't been paid for three months," he announced.

"Means nothin to me, old man," she muttered, turning away. *Most likely brought on by the owner's wild drinking and gambling,* she thought, glancing at Quon.

He turned and flicked a shiny ha'penny piece at the ex-mariner.

Going across the street to Abe's, the bell above the door rang a warning as they entered. They found him at his worktable.

"You know this lady, I presume," he growled, nodding to indicate a woman they had never seen before, sitting beside him at the worktable. "Missus Spencer is a seamstress, sister of Missus Robinson across the road. She tells me she needs a job so she's going to sew ladies' dresses for me two days a week."

Clara Spencer looked up shyly. "Hello," she murmured.

"Hello," Lizzie answered, feeling her partner's fingers tapping a message on her hand. "What brings you to this district?"

"A bereavement," Clara whispered, so softly Lizzie moved forward a step to hear her next words. "My husband passed away."

"Oh!" replied Lizzie, taken slightly aback, "and your children?"

"We were never blessed with any children," Clara sighed, her sad eyes lifting to face the girl.

Lizzie smiled kindly at the woman as a myriad of thoughts went running through her mind. *Perfect!* she thought as she went to stand beside the sad little woman. Putting her hand on her shoulder, she said aloud, "Tell you what, luv, if you'll look after Mister Kratze, do his washing and make sure he's fed, he'll double your wages."

"Oh Lizzie," he objected. "I can't afford such wanton expense."

Blushing, Clara looked down to the table, but Lizzie's next statement brought her eyes up quickly.

"I'll double your business in ladies' wear!" Lizzie coaxed.

Sighing, the tailor dropped his needle and thread on the table and began rubbing his hands together. "We'll try it," he said, with a heavy sigh. "Now get out of here, we've work to do."

Giggling triumphantly, Lizzie wagged her finger at Clara Spencer. "I want you to check on him every day," she said softly, knowing the old tailor could hear her.

"One less worry for us, dumplin," she muttered when the heavy wooden door banged shut behind them.

Clara Spencer was confused and it was obvious to Abe Kratze, as he waited for her question. When it didn't come, he looked over at her.

"Well, what is the matter?" he growled.

"Is-is she your daughter, sir?"

Abe shook his head.

"Then who is she?"

"Don't ask so many questions," the old man shot back

impatiently. "Just do as she says."

"But when do I start, sir?"

"Now!" Abe snapped, "and your first job is making two workday dresses for her and some pants for the lad."

"I'll just pop across the road and tell me sister 'am startin work today," she murmured, rising from her chair.

"Don't be long," Abe snorted. "I'm not paying for time you're not here."

Clara, a short, slim-framed woman of middle age, with hair graying at the temples and a tightly wound bun, shuddered at the thought of working for the grumpy old tailor, but needed a job much too desperately to complain. Her training had been in a high-class ladies' dress shop in the heart of London's fashion district. After marriage to Albert Spencer, she had moved on to the Grand Hotel in the Strand where he worked as head porter and she as a seamstress doing dress alterations for fine ladies. Albert's sudden death the month before had caused enough anxiety, but then she discovered that hotel policy only employed married couples. She found herself immediately homeless and out of a job.

Crossing the street between drays and carefully stepping over fresh piles of steaming horse droppings, she opened her sister's door.

"I have to start right away, Lena," she called, pausing to listen as she heard the sound of her sister's footsteps coming toward her. "Do yer know a girl named Lizzie? She's 'bout seventeen years old, dresses a mite poorly but extremely handsome, and cheeky as the devil himself!"

"Was ther a Chinese lad with her?" Lena asked. Seeing her sister's nod, she smiled, "Yer just met our Lizzie ... Lizzie Short."

"Who's Lizzie Short?" Clara asked, turning to leave.

"Best thing that ever 'appened to this part of dockland," Lena admitted, her eyes shining. "Men say she runs the TLS Company with Joe Todd and that Chinese lad. They live in that cottage up by the slaughterhouse."

Now, even more puzzled, Clara waved to her sister and quickly headed back to work.

It was almost lunch time when Lizzie and Quon turned into the bakery yard. They found Tom and Oly just leaving as they struggled with their overloaded bread cart. Rushing over to help, they pushed the two-wheeled contraption up Baker Lane, stopping at the junction where Water Lane meets Chandler, all gasping for breath.

"Big woad," Quon observed, as Lizzie went around to the front.

"You need a larger cart, lads!" she panted.

"Aye and a bigger horse!" Tom quipped, rubbing his bad leg.

Quon's hands spun wildly and Lizzie's eyebrows went up. "He wants to know how many loads you took to your new shop yesterday?"

"Four," Olivera chimed in wearily as he sat perched on the back of the cart.

"I know, I know," Lizzie snapped as Quon's arms began moving again. "We'll get you a cart with a pony, just for the shop," she said, waiting for Tom's reaction.

"Don't know, miss," he began, cautiously. "Depends how much it cost … hard work in't hurtin us any." Then his voice softened. "But Oly gets mighty tired."

"Tell you what, lad," she said smiling, "if you do a few deliveries for Mick and also for Angus at the brewery it might even pay you a profit."

"Could we deliver big loads to ships with it, too?" Tom asked.

"Of course you could."

"Then we'll do it," he retorted, happily, gripping the bars again. "Thanks, Mister Quon, for thinkin of us."

"You good flends, Tom. You work hard," Quon muttered, but his voice was drowned out by noise. "Me big empty," he added, changing the subject.

"Me too, let's go back and see Bill."

The baker's yard was strangely quiet when they entered. Only the crackle of the huge fire could be heard through the open doors. Looking inside they found Clem talking to Connie.

"Where's Bill?"

"Eh lass, ah never heard yer comin," the startled woman declared as Clem nodded a subdued greeting. "Can I get yer sumthin ta eat?"

"Yes, you can, but where's Bill?" Lizzie repeated.

"We're waitin for a flour delivery and the mill's broken down," Clem moaned. "Oh, here comes Bill here now. He'll tell you."

"Nice ta see yer, luv," the baker grinned. "Is the missus feedin yer?"

"Bill," said Lizzie, as Connie slid plates of hot meat pies onto the table. "What's this problem with flour?"

"Ah bless yer lass, but it's a bit outa yer scope. Ah needs five ton of flour ta last us through next two weeks but we've only two days' supply left."

Bill could tell she was thinking hard because she continued to eat although her eyes never left Quon's face. He'd seen this happen many times before.

"Let's go, dumplin," she muttered, taking a quick drink. "Five ton you say, Bill? That's an awful lot of flour."

"It keeps us going for only two weeks," said Bill. "Business is growin, lass, we use eight bags a day yer know."

"Buy it somewhere else then," she retorted, reaching the door.

"Aye lass, but ther in't any. I've tried all't millers, seems ther's a shortage," he replied in an anguished voice.

Outside in the yard, she stopped. "There's got to be flour somewhere," she mumbled.

Setting off, they reached the lane and turned in the direction of the brewery. Quon hurried along beside her. Her brain was obviously working on the problem and he knew better than to interrupt. At the bottom of Goat Hill, they saw Joe.

"What's the matter?" he frowned.

"Bill Johnson needs five ton of flour, urgent," declared Lizzie.

"We don't have flour, yer know that, or he could have it," said Joe, taking his pipe from his mouth and scratching his head with it.

Quon's hand began to move.

"Maybe," she muttered.

"Maybe what?" asked Joe.

"Have you a list of the millers we got from Dixon?"

"John Watson has it."

"Then let's go get it," said Lizzie, taking the old man's hand.

"He's gone home," said Joe, stopping in his tracks. "We all left early tonight."

"Do you know where he would keep it?" she asked.

"Yes."

"Then let's go get it," she repeated. "I need to deal with this now."

It took them half an hour to walk back to the brewery and find the list. Lizzie took Joe into his office and she sat down with the paper and scoured it carefully.

"Anybody on here that buys a lot of liquor, Joe?"

"They all do," he chuckled.

"Five ton to a dray," Lizzie calculated, her mind on the flour.

Joe nodded. "Better go see Mick, he does all the hauling."

Lizzie's heart was pounding as she rose to the challenge. She set off at a run for Mick's office, not even looking back for Quon who had decided to walk with Joe.

"Call Mick on yer bell, Ned," she gasped, as she entered.

"Now what's happening?" Ada asked, as the sharp clang of the bell rang in their ears.

When Quon came through the door, he had an unusual air of confidence. Striding over to the bookkeeper, he reached for her hand.

"Hello, my dear!" he said slowly, before turning to the order clerk whose mouth had dropped open. "Good afternoon, Mister Cabin!"

"Well done, dumplin ...," Lizzie shrieked, "but you sure could have picked a better time!"

When Mick arrived he could hardly believe his eyes. Ned, totally out of character, was roaring with laughter and muttering over and over to himself, "Well I'll be dammed!"

Ada stood hugging Quon Lee in front of her desk and Lizzie stood watching, obviously trying hard not to laugh herself.

"Can you tell me why it is you needed me in such a hurry?" Mick asked, "that is, if you can stop the party long enough to tell me."

"It's all right, love," soothed Ada, "we'll explain."

"Bill Johnson needs five tons of flour. He's only two days' supply left and the mill has broken down," said Lizzie.

"We don't have flour, luv," the Irishman replied, frowning. "Bill has a problem. If the other mills find out, they'll up their price and be wary who they sell to."

"Oh, they'll sell to us," Lizzie predicted, smiling wickedly. "We'll trade 'em for French brandy."

"She's right," Ned chuckled, "and I know just who to see."

Ada did a quick calculation as Mick dashed outside and into the lane stopping one of the delivery drays returning empty to the yard.

"YOU'LL NEED TWO—10 GALLON HOGS' HEADS OF NUMBER ONE BRANDY," Ada called after him.

"WAIT!" Lizzie shouted. "We're going, too." She grabbed the piece of paper Ned held out for her and she and Quon raced out the side door. Leaping into the dray, whose driver had already received instructions from Mick, they turned and waved to him as he watched, shaking his head.

At the brewery, Joe smiled when he heard her plan, quickly ordering the loading of the brandy before they were off again.

A clock struck two as the dray pulled into Frank Firth's yard.

"Where's the owner?" their driver called to a passing workman.

"Over yonder," he replied, pointing at a pipe-smoking, white dust-covered figure standing in a doorway.

"What do you want here, girl?" asked Frank, glowering as he watched her approach. "I don't do business with lasses!" Removing his pipe, he spit a stream of tobacco juice onto the cobbles.

"It's not business," Lizzie retorted. "Joe Todd from the TLS brewery said you'd like a hog's head of brandy, but I guess he was wrong." She turned on her heel and began to walk away.

Frank rubbed hard on his bright red nose, his mind conjuring up a glorious taste. His pipe began to totter in his mouth and he grabbed it before it fell. Moving after her, he now felt some sense of urgency.

"Hold on a minute, girl. Joe Todd you say?"

Lizzie stopped and turned slowly. Quon leapt from the dray to stand by her side. The miller strode toward them, flour dust billowing from his clothes.

"It's a trade," she snapped, "best Number One French Brandy for a load of flour."

Frank stopped, his eyes narrowing as his face twisted into a frown. "You're Lizzie, Joe's lass, ain't ya?"

Lizzie looked up at the man and gave him her best smile. "Joe said you could taste it—if ya want," she purred. "Bring a hammer and a tap and try it."

The offer swept all Frank's caution away. It was almost too good to be true—a free tankard of Number One French Brandy. Dashing across the yard, he returned quickly to remove the barrel bung and hammered in the tap. Putting his tankard under the tap he gave it a single turn. The ruby red liquid spilled slowly into his tankard. His lips quivered as they held back the saliva that threatened to escape from his mouth. Half filling the tankard, he turned off the tap and raised the vessel to the light. As if in a dream his eyes closed as he felt the anticipated ecstasy. He brought the tankard to his lips and let some of the precious liquid trickle slowly down his throat.

Lizzie and Quon exchanged glances. Lizzie winked. Frank was definitely enjoying himself and there was no need to rush the man.

After what seemed like several minutes, he took the tankard away from his lips and opened his eyes. "That's the good stuff all right!" he said softly, licking his lips.

"You'd better make sure, Mister Firth," she suggested.

The miller happily nodded his agreement draining the vessel, this time without the ritual. He set the tankard down and began to walk toward them. Staggering a little, he quickly sat on a nearby barrel.

Gathering his composure, he slurred, "Ithh's all yersh, young lassie! I'll give ye f-five ton of flour for the whole barrel!" Taste buds screaming and brain only working at half speed, Frank yelled to his men to fill the dray with flour.

In less than an hour they were rumbling out of the yard loaded with Bill's flour, still having one barrel left in the dray.

It was nearly four o'clock when they rumbled into the baker's yard. Bill hurried out to see what was going on and they giggled when they saw his expression of surprise.

"Where'd yer get it from?" he asked incredulously, craning his neck to read the inkstamp on the sacks. "Frank Firth wouldn't sell it to *me*. How on earth did you talk him into it?"

"Oh, Frank weren't no trouble, Bill," she laughed. "It just needed some bait on the line and brandy served the purpose."

"Bait?" asked Bill, heaving two heavy sacks onto his own back with one deft movement. "The lads were just here," he grunted, adjusting the load, "said the *Falcon*'s in dock. They were inquirin about that pony and cart you promised 'em."

"Blow me down, I clean forgot!" she exclaimed, watching Quon's arms wave frantically. "All right, all right! We'll do it right now."

Watching them disappear, Bill muttered, "Brandy? What the dickens has brandy to do with flour?"

Chapter 14

Ada's eyes asked the unspoken question when Lizzie and Quon burst though the cottage door. Lizzie indicated her reply by her smile and took her place at the table.

"How's my lad?" Davis growled, his mouth full of food.

"Yer lad?" Lizzie exclaimed, reaching across the table for her plate of food. Her eyes danced with fire as Quon's fingers tapped on the table.

Martha, looking up from the kitchen, waited with interest for the rest of Lizzie's reply which came with stunning simplicity.

"What about Tom and Billy?" she asked quietly, her knife and fork hovering over her food.

The comment was totally unexpected and the captain dropped his fork noisily on his plate and frowned. The thought of he, a bachelor all his life, accepting responsibility for three lads scared him more than a sea battle.

Ada's voice cut through the sudden silence. "They are almost like brothers, sir.

"Hold on a minute," commented Joe, pushing his empty plate away. "The captain is only tryin to help. I were over ther yesterday an them lads are doin well."

"I know he is, Dad," Lizzie sighed, "but they are a family just like we are and Mister Davis doesn't understand that yet."

"Understand what?" Davis's voice thundered.

Lizzie turned to face him, a smile dancing on her lips as Willie came to sit on her knee. "Olivera needs you," she explained, "but so do the other two. You're a giant figure to them, captain. I know you care but they all need someone like you to help and protect them ... not just Oly." She paused, winking impishly at him as she so often did when she was trying to break him down. "Don't stop now, captain. You've come this far."

Quon's fingers again tapped on the table. Everyone could tell Davis was struggling with himself as Lizzie's gentle logic tugged at his heart.

"Damn you, Lizzie Short," he declared, his deep voice rumbling ominously.

Martha smiled to herself and went back to stirring tomorrow's stew. The silence seemed endless.

Joe pushed his tobacco container into the centre of the table.

"Baccy anyone?" he asked.

Davis reached over and pulled the can closer, slowly stuffing his pipe as the silence lengthened. Finally, sitting back in his chair, he took a long puff, letting the smoke dissipate toward the ceiling. "We caught one of Crowther's ships out in the channel a few days back ... fully loaded with contraband French liquor. Two Frenchmen were on board."

"Spies!" Joe spluttered.

Davis glowered at the old man and shook his head. "We arrested the captain, mate and them two Frenchies, put One-Eyed-Jack on board with a few of our men and sailed her into the government wharf."

"And its cargo of liquor?" Lizzie asked.

"Most of it's on our dock," offered Charlie. "We've discovered that Crowther Shipping is also in big trouble with the military." Then Charlie, with the help of the captain, filled them in on the new developments. For the next 20 minutes they all took turns voicing their opinions on the impounding of Crowther's ships and the possible results of an investigation.

"The government will have no mercy," predicted Davis, pushing back his chair. "Crowther is finished." He stood up and made for the door. Almost there, he stopped and turned. "Where is that shop the lads are running?"

Ada and Lizzie exchanged a quick glance and the bookkeeper gave him the directions. He nodded his goodbye and, after banging the door shut behind him, they listened as the sound of his footsteps grew faint.

"Hoy be thinkin ye've got to that old sea dog tonight, girl," Mick chuckled, peering over the table at his son, fast asleep on the girl's shoulder.

Quon's fingers drummed on the table top.

Lizzie nodded and turned to Mick. "Tom Day wants a pony and a larger cart, Mick," she said, as Ada scooped up the boy from her lap.

"But there's no stable at that shop," Mick retorted, his eyes pinched in thought.

"Yes, there is," said Joe. "There's a communal stable in the alley behind. It's empty, nobody uses it anymore."

"Right then," said Mick, standing up and taking the child from Ada. Holding him low for Martha to kiss, he slung the boy over his shoulder. "We've a pretty little black-and-white Shetland that will be just right for them. I think I can find them a cart, too. Sure hoy'll have it ready at six-thirty in the morning."

Soft falling rain greeted them early the next morning as they walked through the fog toward the stables. The office glowed dimly with lantern light and they could see Ned through the window talking to a driver.

"Dirty mornin, Miss Lizzie," David Jones shouted from the stableyard. He had the piebald Shetland pony by the halter rope, its shiny black harness gleaming even in the dull light. Behind him was a gaily painted cart.

"Oh, how grand, the boys will be pleased," cried Lizzie.

"Me drive, Wizzy," said Quon, hopping onto the corner of the cart like he'd seen the rag collectors do. Accepting the reins from the stableman, he clucked his tongue and the pony moved off deceptively quickly almost causing him to lose his balance.

"Don't leave me, dumplin!" Lizzie squealed, running to catch up. Leaping onto the low cart, she grabbed Quon's seat and pulled herself aboard, skirts flying around her as she held on for dear life.

David Jones stood watching and one of the other stablehands came up to join him. "Well, that's not a position we see our boss in often!" David laughed.

"Aye, we tend to forgit ther still young'uns no matter how you look at it!"

Trotting freely, head high, the intelligent little pony took them quickly down Goat Hill into Baker Lane and on to the Johnson Bakery. Bill's voice barked loudly when he saw them arrive informing the delivery boys they had a visitor. The lads left their half-filled handcart to gather around the newcomers. Olivera squealed happily as the pony nuzzled him and Tom and Billy excitedly inspected their new acquisition.

"Is it really for us, Miss Lizzie?" asked Tom. Without waiting for an answer, he continued, "Blimey, look at the size of it Billy, we can get two loads on at the same time!"

"Yer going to need feed for the pony and a stable," the baker reminded them.

"Joe mentioned there was an unused stable behind the butcher's. Have you seen it, Tom?"

"Yes, miss," said Billy. "Mister Sweeney, showed it to us already. We cleaned it out last night.

With the men's help, the new cart was soon set up for holding their barrels, loaded up with bread, and the boys were happily on their way. Bill stood with his hands on his hips watching them go.

"Ther good lads, them boys. Yer must be awful proud of them."

Lizzie smiled as she slipped her arm over Quon's shoulder and led him toward the gate. "Yer a good lad, Mister Lee, and 'am proud of you, too, but I'm fair famished. Let's go have some breakfast." Giving him a push, she waved to the men and leapt into the lead.

Captain Davis was also up early this day, having left the *Falcon* just before dawn. Unable to sleep, he dressed in civilian clothes and strode purposefully up Pump Street quickly travelling the several blocks toward the new bake shop. Head down against the heavy fog that was producing a misty shower, he glowered fiercely at the cobblestones. Lizzie's comments still coursed through his brain.

"What the devil do I want with three youngsters?" he muttered.

Almost at the corner of Chandler and Long Lane, a light in the butcher's shop alerted him that he was near the boy's unmarked bake shop. Hanging back, he pulled his hat down over his eyes and crossing the street he stepped into a dark doorway to watch.

A short while later, the young man he thought was Billy appeared from the dimly lit shop carrying Olivera on his back. He unceremoniously dumped the squealing youngster on the hand cart standing ready at the curb and went to stand between the shafts.

A sigh escaped the hardened sea captain's lips while deep in his pocket his fingers fiddled nervously with a loose coin. He heard another voice and an older lad with a limp appeared. He took up a position behind the cart and ruffling Oly's hair, pulled the little lad down beside him.

That must be Tom Day, he thought. *He's the only one who still looks about the same as the first time I met them. He must be about 24-years-old by now. They seem to be happy lads ... yes, just like a family.* Davis smiled unconsciously as a strange sense of longing swept over him. He wanted to call out to the boys, yet he didn't know what he would say. Was he ready for this yet? Groaning, he held on precariously to his emotions, stifling the sound of Lizzie's words ringing in his brain. Then, it was too late, for the boys had moved the bread cart out into the street and disappeared into the fog.

A moment later, a subtle movement farther down the street caught his eye jerking him back to reality as two hazy figures materialized. As they came through the fog, he noticed they were stopping every so often. Watching with more interest, he soon realized they were trying the doors of each house and business as they moved stealthily along the street. Reaching the bake shop, they peered into the window before trying the door. Finding the door unlocked, they looked about furtively, then slipped quickly inside.

A mixture of anxiety and rage gripped the captain. Throwing caution to the wind, he hurriedly crossed the street to the butcher's shop. Hesitating for only a second, he rapped urgently on the window. The butcher came cautiously to the door and looked out. He eyed the captain suspiciously, never having seen the man before. His blood-stained apron, together with a meat axe in his hand, portrayed an ominous picture as his eyes fastened on the stranger.

"There are robbers in the lad's bake shop," Davis growled, keeping his voice as low as possible, despite his fury.

As if proof was needed, at that moment, the two men emerged and Davis and the butcher moved silently, but with purpose, toward them. Seeing the butcher's blood-stained axe and a raging stranger coming at them, the younger men turned to run but Davis clamped a hand on each of them. No match for the two larger men, the would-be robbers fell to the sidewalk, begging for mercy. A while later, Davis and the butcher stood back admiring their handiwork ... their prisoners sitting on the cobbles trussed up like chickens ready for the oven.

"I believe it would be proper to introduce ourselves, sir. My name is Sidney Sweeney," chuckled the butcher, wiping his hand on the cleanest part of his apron before extending it.

"Davis ... uncle to the lads in the bake shop," the captain replied without thinking, extending his hand. "I am grateful for your assistance, Mister Sweeney."

Sidney Sweeney looked curiously at the other man. "Well then, I would think you can deal with this matter yourself from here on, Mister Davis. I have work to attend to." With that, he turned and went back to his shop.

The sound of wheels and tiny metal shoes striking sharply on the cobbles drew the captain's gaze and he realized the fog had lifted. Trotting briskly toward him was a black-and-white Shetland pony pulling a cart. The laughter he heard sounded familiar but he was too busy with his prisoners to take much notice.

Olivera was the first to recognize the familiar figure standing beside the two men on the curb. Shrieking excitedly, he ran over and flung himself at his benefactor.

Davis, taken aback initially, laughed when he realized it was Oly and joyfully returned the boy's hug. An uncharacteristic lump in his throat prevented him from speaking as the Portuguese boy wrapped his arms around his neck.

"You ain't takin him away agin, are yer mister?" Billy protested.

"No, lad, I'm not," Davis chuckled. "I want to talk to you boys."

"Wor is it?" asked Tom. Then noticing the two men sitting on the ground, he continued, "Who are them two?"

"Oh, them two are scum, lads, but we'll soon be rid of them," Davis growled, having noticed two soldiers rounding the corner. "HEY, SOLDIER BOYS," he shouted, the tone of his voice bringing them immediately to his side. "Take care of these two for me. I caught them trying to rob this store. I'm Captain Davis from the government ship, *Falcon*."

"Yes, sir," replied the soldiers in unison, saluting the officer, then going to take a look at the belligerent looking prisoners. Cutting the strings that bound their legs, they pulled the two men roughly to their feet. As they were led away, David heard a string of curses being thrown his way before the soldiers put a quick stop to their tirade.

"Now," began Davis, turning his attention back to the boys. He knew he must push on. Lizzie was right, these boys did need him. "Boys, I-I-I want to be your friend if ...."

"You my friend now," said Olivera.

"Yes, yes, of course I am Oly. I mean, I would like to be a special friend ... to Tom and Billy ... as well."

Tom and Billy moved closer together, their heads almost touching as they whispered secretively, not taking their eyes off this man that they hardly knew. Then Billy took a step forward.

"If we say yes, will you protect us, too?"

"Yes, of course I will," Davis replied, feeling slightly agitated, yet somehow relieved. "Haven't I already proved that to you? I'd also like to help you expand your business."

"Then I vote, yes," announced Tom, almost too eagerly.

"Me too!" laughed Billy. "Uh, what shall we call you, sir?"

"I call you Uncle Captain!" blurted out the young lad.

"No, no," Davis laughed, relief now spreading through his body. "My real name is ...," he stopped as a red blush began to creep up his neck, "is Johann Straus Davis. Alas, my mother wanted a musician ... why don't you call me Uncle Johann?"

Martha had breakfast waiting for Lizzie and Quon when they returned from delivering the horse and cart. Willie sat quietly at the table practising letters on his slateboard. With her back to them, Martha listened intently, not daring to move as Quon spoke to Lizzie.

"You make arrangements with Jeb," he said, forming the words carefully. "We need to see our children."

"You're right, luv," Lizzie replied. "We'll do it straight after breakfast."

"By gum, yer talkin better and better, Quon!" Martha gasped. Then clasping her hand over her mouth, she gasped. "Ee 'am sorry, luv, but ah forgot to tell ye, Mick says the gypsies want to see you as soon as yer able."

"Jeb's ready," Lizzie mumbled through a mouthful, turning back to Quon as she pushed her plate away with disinterest. Martha noticed the eager sparkle in her eyes.

Quon continued to eat hungrily but his other hand reached over in front of the girl to tap a short message on the table.

"You eat your breakfast first, young lady," admonished the housekeeper. "What did he say?"

"Same thing you did," Lizzie giggled, "only nastier!" Pulling her half-finished breakfast back in front of her, she playfully tweaked Quon's ear, then picked up her fork.

As she finished, Willie came to stand quietly by her chair. She turned to say something and realized he was holding a broken toy in his hand. He looked up at her and his sweet little mouth curled into such a sad expression that her heart melted. As she pulled him onto her lap, a tear ran silently down his flushed cheek.

"Oh Willie, it's all right, luv," she soothed, wiping his tear away with her finger. "Lizzie will fix it for you."

Quon reached over to stroke the boy's head and Willie stopped crying.

Martha held her breath and felt a tear in her eye, too. *My, how the years have gone by*, she thought. *They are so good with that child.* She couldn't help but wonder what the future would hold for this lovely girl she thought of as her own and so quickly becoming a woman. Her compassion and confident business ability continue to shatter the minds of all who knew her, but still Martha worried.

As the youngsters left the cottage awhile later, Martha and Willie stood waving in the doorway. The older woman felt a shiver run through the child's body and her grip on the boy's shoulders increased.

"It's not spring yet, young Willie. Let's get us something warm to drink and we'll play in front of the fire for awhile."

It began to drizzle as they slowly made their way up Drover's Lane toward the gypsy camp. Stopping momentarily at the warehouse yard to watch a dray being loaded, Mick noticed them just as they were turning to leave.

"HOLD ON A MINUTE, hoy've a message for yer," he called.

"Martha told us," Lizzie replied, as he came up beside them.

"No, she never," he panted. "It's Walter Groves, wants ta see yer. Urgent, said the driver." He paused, turning his back on the wind to light his pipe. "Sure it were the gypsies hoy told Martha about ... when might Patrick be back, we can use some more cheese?" he demanded, all in one breath.

"I don't know!" she snapped, not wanting to think about how long it had been since she last saw her friend. She missed the big, burly Scotsman a great deal but he had his own family in Aberdeen and unless business brought him to London they didn't see much of him. "You'd better ask Charley. We should be off, dumplin, seems we're in demand today."

A loud call took Mick's attention and he stroke off in the opposite direction. Quon, frowning, turned to his partner but said nothing.

"What is it?" she asked, as they continued toward the gypsy camp. "Are you worried about Walter?"

"Wong time since we saw him," he commented as they heard the gypsy dogs bark. A rider came galloping toward them but recognizing them waved, and retreated.

Over their fire, the gypsies had suspended a large piece of sailcloth between several trees and a pole. It afforded shelter and partially protected the fire from the rain. A group had gathered and one old man was playing a mournful song on a squeeze box.

Jeb rose to meet them, sending a shower of sparks shooting upward as he spit a stream of tobacco juice into the flames. A man of few words, he came straight to the point.

"Can't go to the farm 'til the middle of next month or perhaps later, Liz," he muttered, his black eyes noticing the look of disappointment on the girl's face.

"Why?" she demanded, softly.

"Hogs to bring in and we've a baby comin soon."

"A baby?" Lizzie asked awestruck, suddenly forgetting her disappointment. "A new baby?"

Spinning around to face her partner she grabbed his hands, holding them tight as she stared into his eyes. "A new baby, dumplin," she said, excitedly and the gypsy knew exactly what was coming next. "We want to be there when it's born, Jeb! When?"

"*You* can," Jeb growled, taking a lighted splinter from the fire and applying it to his pipe, "but *he* stays outside."

"Wizzy?" Quon pleaded, his hands spinning.

"No, dumplin," Lizzie said, gently. "This is women's business, you stay with the men."

Smiling inwardly, Jeb was not at all surprised with the girl's reaction. He had watched her with interest over the years and his respect for this girl, who was fast becoming a woman, knew no bounds. She was the one person he trusted over all others in this strange world of city folk.

One of the women who had been sitting at the fire got up and came toward them. She smiled at Lizzie before she leaned over and whispered into Jeb's ear. He, too, smiled and removing his pipe blew the smoke into the air.

"This is Marla, Miss Lizzie. She wants to make you a special dress," he announced, looking slightly uncomfortable. "One that's traditional to wear at the birth of a gypsy baby."

"Of course she may. I'd like that."

Marla produced a length of string from the pocket of her ankle-length, beautifully embroidered skirt. As she silently took Lizzie's measurements, her quick fingers tied knots here and there along its length.

Quon frowned suspiciously, his eyes following the fascinating performance. After a moment, he shook his head and made a sign to his partner.

"Mind yer own business," she said, in an unusually soft voice, her thoughts on babies and the children she called her own.

Chapter 15

A sudden ray of sunshine broke through the clouds as if attempting to chase the rain and accompanying haze away as the young partners made their way through the slick, cobblestoned streets of dockland toward the Bishop's Palace.

They were surprised to find themselves being greeted by residents and shopkeepers who knew who they were. Word travelled quickly in a close-knit area like dockland, but crossing into the area known as Westminster, they were many blocks from home.

Half an hour later the rain stopped, but now shivering and wet through, they picked up their pace as the thought of Walter's warm fire became more appealing.

"It will be nice to see Walter again, dumplin. I wonder what's happening over at the Bishop's Palace."

"Many months since we've seen Walter. Bishop Tide much nicer bossman for him!" chuckled Quon.

Their thoughts went back a few years to the previous bishop who had dropped dead suddenly, saving them and many others a heap of grief.

With the bishop's large house in sight, they went around to the rear entrance. Entering the yard, they were struck by the absence of guards. This worried them slightly but they knew the way to Walter's underground apartment so they found the service tunnel and entered the labyrinth.

Proceeding cautiously, they listened for any unfamiliar sounds as they moved through the damp, dimly lit interior of the eerie subterranean passageway. It wasn't long before they saw a bright shaft of light up ahead which told them they were almost there.

"Welcome friends," came Walter's voice echoing along the tunnel walls.

Startled, Quon clutched at Lizzie's arm then they saw their friend's silhouette a few yards away in the shadows.

"Hello Walter," she whispered, pushing Quon forward.

"Go on in," the voice prodded. "I'm right behind you."

Well-lit and warmed by its huge fire, they entered the familiar room of rock that was Walter's home. His dark eyes shone brightly as he stepped into the light and he looked his friends over with keen interest.

"It's been a long time. You've both grown taller," the young man laughed. "Oh my, you're wet, come closer to the fire. How's Jessy doin?"

"Very well, she really enjoys being a teacher," said Lizzie, always cautious not to give out too much information.

Walter sighed and a sad look flicked across his face as he thought of the girl who had once been his special friend. Several years ago they had both worked upstairs in the main house. One day Jessy had been mistreated by a staff member and Walter had gone to her aid. With Lizzie's help, she left her job, finally taking a teaching position. Walter was banished to the tunnels.

He indicated a rough bench near the fire and pulled his own seat closer, a small barrel he had fashioned into a chair. "I'm glad," he whispered. "Jessy deserves the best ... but that's not why I called you."

"Is something wrong?" asked Lizzie, moving closer to the fire.

"I don't know," he said, frowning. "I overheard a conversation on the speaking tubes which might concern you."

"Tell us," interjected Quon.

"One of the old Bishop's men had a visitor the other day," said Walter, referring to their nemesis, the deceased bishop. He paused, struggling with his memory. "Crowther, I believe was the name. He wanted the church to loan him money to save his business. I could only hear portions of it but they kept mentioning the TLS company and a man named Charley Mason.

"What about Charley?" Lizzie coaxed.

Looking puzzled, Walter shook his head and peered into the fire. "I remember!" he said, after a full minute had passed. "They're going to report him for contraband running to Captain Davis on that government ship."

Quon's fingers tapped out a message on Lizzie's shoulder. She translated it into a question.

"Bishop Tide in on this?"

145

"No, he ain't," Walter assured them. "He's been out of town. Bishop Tide is a good man, not at all like the other one."

Thanking Walter profusely Lizzie changed the subject back to Jessy. Realizing from past experience, Walter was totally honourable and would never repeat anything they told him in confidence, she decided to tell him that Jessy was teaching a group of children at the farm where she lived. Walter's face lit up at the thought of his friend working with children, something she had talked about often.

A few minutes later, he led them out of the damp tunnel and into the yard. Waving goodbye, they hurried through the big iron gates, always relieved to be leaving this dark and depressing place.

Winchester was always one of the busiest areas of London and today was no exception. If Tom hadn't spoken they wouldn't even have noticed the diminutive pegleg in the crowd.

"HOLD UP THER, ME HEARTIES," the familiar voice greeted them as he and his cronies passed on their way to the coaching house. "Av news ... ah'll give it to yer for a penny."

Quon watched Tom closely, willing him to stay back. With hands balled into fists, his black eyes appeared to shoot menacing bolts of fire at the old drunkard.

"Keep him away from me lass, ah mean yer no harm."

"Then tell us yer information," coaxed Lizzie. "We'll judge what it's worth."

"Crowther's ship, it's goin up for sale next week."

Glancing at each other, the partners grinned. A wink from the girl sent Quon's hand into his pocket and a penny went spinning through the air.

The afternoon was quickly passing as Lizzie and Quon made their way back along the waterfront toward home. They were on the outskirts of dockland when they saw a young lad handing out sheets of paper to passers-by. He was yelling at the top of his little voice.

"GOVERNMENT SALE ... READ ALL ABOUT THE COMIN GOVERNMENT SALE!"

"What's it all about?" Lizzie asked a young woman holding a child in her arms.

"Debt collectors must be selling some poor soul's possessions, I declare," she sighed sadly and hurried off.

Interest drew Lizzie closer to the boy, taking the paper he offered. Reading only the large print, a thought flashed through her mind. "We can use this idea, too," she muttered, pulling on Quon's arm.

They were eating meat pies at Bill's when they heard Olivera's voice shouting to them as he opened the gate for his pony.

"Are you on yer own, Oly?" asked Lizzie, a concerned note in her voice.

"That he is, lass," Bill shouted. "By gum, he's a regular little drayman. No need to rush, Liz. Me an Clem'll load Oly's cart."

Oly came to join them but kept glancing over his shoulder, watching Bill and Clem.

"What Oly wooking at?" asked Quon.

"Counting," replied the boy. "Billy needs 200 loaves."

"Two hundred loaves ... my goodness, you boys are doing some business! You think Mister Johnson would cheat you?"

"No, no, Miss Lizzie, he cheat himself, give too many!"

"RIGHT, OLY LAD, OFF YER GO," Bill's voice rang across the yard. "And ah know av given yer ten extra loaves. Now be careful crossing the lane."

Taking the halter rope, with a click of his tongue he led the pony toward the gate. Talking to the animal over his shoulder, he giggled when it affectionately nuzzled his back.

As Bill came toward them, he watched as Quon's hands went spinning wildly.

"That hand talk fair mystifies me," Bill growled, taking a swig from his tankard.

"Bread ready, boss," Clem called from a doorway.

Fascinated by the sight of so many loaves coming out of the large oven, Lizzie and Quon followed Bill. Clem swung the heavy iron doors wide revealing tray after tray of golden brown bread. The released heat swept across the room.

"Time to go, dumplin," Lizzie gasped, as the heat hit their faces.

Unnoticed, they went outside. They were a block away when slipping her hand into her pocket, she found the newssheet she'd meant to show Bill. *Blast it*, she silently chided herself.

After dinner Captain Davis was noticeably missing and Charley offered some puzzling information by way of an explanation.

"*Falcon*'s not leaving until after the sale of Crowther's ship, I know that much," he said, with a frown. "I heard he's been visiting neighbouring docks talking to all the captains." He paused, his voice dropping to a whisper. "Don't know why though."

Heavy footsteps sounded on the garden path then a knock on the door brought Martha's welcoming, "Come in."

Captain Davis stepped into the room.

"Yer late," she snapped, continuing to clear the table.

"I've eaten already," he muttered, finding a chair then swinging his dark eyes around the room settling on Lizzie.

Quon's fingers sent a warning on his partner's arm. Winking at him, Lizzie left her seat. Ignoring the captain's eyes, she recovered the paper from the pocket of her coat hanging behind the door. Slowly unfolding it, she handed it to Ada.

"What makes these papers?" she asked, returning to her seat.

"I don't know, love," answered the bookkeeper. "Why do you ask?"

Mick took the paper out of his wife's hand. "Sure and begorra, ther selling Crowther's ship!" he gabbled excitedly.

"That's what I came to tell you," said Davis. "And I have orders to watch the TLS ships very closely from now on."

"Then do it," Lizzie snapped. "Ben Thorn's on his way in with a load of grain from Hull. Go check him out," she laughed. "I'm sure Charley will give you a list of the cargoes we're carrying. Pick them carefully, Mister Davis!" Lizzie wagged her finger. "And the informant will look awfully stupid, don't you think?"

"You knew all about it, didn't you?" Davis thundered, banging the table with his fist.

"Calm down, sir," admonished Ada. "We only know what's written right here on this paper. Where did you get this, Lizzie?"

"A boy in the street was handing them out ... but I want to know how they get to look like that?" Lizzie insisted.

Charley and the captain passed the paper between them but they were interrupted by a noise outside. Someone tapped on the door and Nathan hurried inside, slamming the door behind him.

"Can't you be a bit quieter, man!" Joe snapped from between half-closed eyes, looking down at Willie curled up on his lap. "The lad's almost asleep."

"Sorry," the trader muttered, sticking a sheaf of papers close to Mick's face. "These are urgent, I need them delivered tomorrow," he demanded, standing over the yard foreman.

Nathan's fierce concentration suddenly broke when Quon leaped up from the table and ran over to Joe whose eyelids had fluttered shut and his still-smoking pipe was slipping from between his lips. They watched silently as Quon caught the pipe and put it safely onto Joe's pipe stand, then he eased Willie's arm into a more comfortable position and kissed the lad's head before returning to the table.

Ada gripped Mick's hand as they gazed at the old man and the child sleeping so contentedly together. She glanced at Captain Davis and noticed that his eyes seemed to hold a softness she'd never seen before. *There's a change coming over this man,* she thought. *Lizzie's logic is working on that stubborn captain's brain.*

Coughing, the ignored trader drew their attention back to his problem. "So I can be assured you will comply, sir?"

"One of these days, me boyo," Mick growled, "hoy'll be stuffin yer orders ...."

"Mick!" Ada snapped, slapping his hand.

Nathan turned for the door, his hand dropping from the latch when he heard Lizzie's voice.

"Don't go yet, Mister Goldman."

Reaching for the printed sale notice on the table in front of Charley, she handed it to the trader.

"What makes these?" she asked.

"A printer does."

"What's a printer?"

Everyone fell silent, waiting for the trader's explanation as he carefully selected his words.

"It's a man who prints paper with words and ink. They call them printing presses. There's one in a dirty little shop at the corner of an alleyway on Chandler across from Brown's. Go look for yourselves." Glancing around at their puzzled, silent faces, Nathan sighed. "They make books and newspapers, too." Still seeing blank expressions, he threw up his arms in frustration. "It's messy and very time-consuming, lass. You don't want anything to do with it."

Quon's fingers began drumming out an excited message on the

tabletop, grinning when Lizzie wagged her finger at him.

"What did he say?" asked the trader, again reaching for the latch.

"Nothing you'd want to hear," Lizzie laughed. "Off you go."

Willie stirred in Joe's arms when the door banged, causing his mother to leap from her chair. Taking the warm blanket Martha had been warming on a chair by the fire, she wrapped it around her son then picked him up off Joe's knee. Handing him over to Mick, she slipped into her coat.

"Let's go home, love," she murmured, opening the door. "Thanks for dinner, Martha. Goodnight everyone," she called, as she followed Mick outside.

As they walked up the slaughterhouse track to their apartment above the TLS office, Mick broke the silence. "What would yer be thinking she's up to, Ada m'luv?"

"I'm not even thinking about it, sweetheart. We'll get to know soon enough."

Inside the cottage, Davis was scowling at the youngsters, while Charley, sitting beside him, grinned impishly.

"Are you bidding for the Crowther ship?" snapped Davis.

"We don't have that kind of money," retorted Lizzie.

"Oh yes, you do," he shot back, his eyes narrowing. "You still have Stroud's treasure ... don't you?"

An uncomfortable silence settled over the room as Quon pushed back his chair, scraping it noisily as he stood up and moved in behind Lizzie. Davis had seen this protective stance many times since that day some five years ago when these two had entered his cabin on the *Falcon*. They were just starting out then and had shown quite an aptitude for business.

Quon's fingers pressed out a message on her shoulder. She gave him a slight nod, then turned her attention squarely on the captain. Davis could see that her lips were drawn tightly together in a show of anger and he braced himself. *Looks like I've done it again,* he thought.

Suddenly alert and sensing danger, Joe sat bolt upright in his chair. His eyes open, he reached for his pipe, his own protective instincts alert. Martha offered a flaming splinter with dithering hands, her body quaking inside at the expected confrontation.

"You got yer share, didn't you?" Lizzie whispered.

Davis nodded. This young woman was no more the mere slip of a girl he had once faced across his desk. He had always been beaten by her fearless logic and he feared nothing had changed. A thought struck him. *Has she got other plans for the auction and I'm interfering?* Suddenly self-conscious and deflated he looked up at the young partners. "Sorry, lass, that was none of my business."

Charley could hardly believe his ears. *Davis apologizing, indeed!*

A swift hiss of air left Martha's lips as she stood stirring tomorrow's pot of stew hanging over the fire.

Joe's pipe rapped sharply on the table. "Whistle for yer lads, Charley," he growled. "Enough business for this day."

Chapter 16

"MORNIN, MISTER KRATZE," Lizzie called when she saw Abe standing on his doorstep.

Abe swung his gaze up the hill and smiled. Lizzie, still much taller than her more-rounded companion who had not yet reached full height, definitely was getting the shape of a full-bodied woman. She was slim and one could feel her energy despite her tatty appearance and dirty old dress. Her crumpled straw hat, perched at a jaunty angle on a head of long, flowing auburn hair, screamed confidence at the Jewish tailor as he listened to the laughter passing between them.

Abe's eyes next roamed over Quon Lee. Yes, he was still half a head shorter than Lizzie but his body had grown thicker in the past year, aptly earning his dockland title as Lizzie's guardian angel. His devotion to the girl he'd grown up with was unquestioned by all who knew them. *That lad's got some growing to do yet*, he thought. Outloud, he muttered, "What a pair!" Then he shuffled back into his store to await their arrival.

As expected, she threw out her first question as she came through the door. "I want to know," she began, causing the tailor to wince. "How does a person get to use a ship somebody else owns?"

"They lease it." Abe sighed, relieved at the simplicity of her question. "Why, who's going to do that?"

Ignoring his question, she posed another. "How much will Crowther's ship fetch at auction?"

"How on earth would I know?"

"Because you know everything!"

"Twenty-eight to thirty thousand … it's in bad repair I'm told."

He was saved from further questions by the tinkling of the doorbell as Clara arrived with his breakfast.

"Beg pardon, miss," she said, so meekly they could barely hear her as she slid the tray in front of the tailor. "Please eat, sir. You hardly touched it yesterday."

"Stop fussing woman, you've work to do," Abe growled irritably, taking a quick bite of the crispy, dry bread.

Clara Spencer bit her lip and moved quickly into the back corner. Quon's fingers lightly tapped on Lizzie's shoulder.

"Blast you, Mister Misery," Lizzie snarled, banging the table with her fist. "Can't you be civil to anyone?"

Clara flinched at the girl's outburst even though she was now more accustomed to the banter that went on between these two strong personalities. Peeking around a pile of half-finished garments, she asked timidly, "Can I do a fitting of your dress, miss?"

"What dress?" Lizzie asked.

"This one!" Clara held up the dress she was making and Lizzie came over eagerly to look. The dress was grey with shiny brass buttons on a bib and brace top, attractive but simple with its dark blue checkered bib and matching trim around the hem.

"Beautiful," Quon whispered, almost inaudibly.

"Please try it on, Miss Lizzie," the dressmaker urged.

Stepping behind the screen, the girl stripped off her ill-fitting tatty black dress, dropping it into a crumpled heap on the floor. Standing in her vest, bloomers and petticoats, she shivered, hugging herself.

"It's chilly in here!"

"White blouse first, then the dress, please miss."

Sun streamed through the side window as Lizzie stepped from behind the screen to view herself in the long mirror. Clara, her mouth full of pins, clutched frantically at the buttonless waistband.

"Is that the best you can do, woman?" Abe growled, peering over his spectacles.

"Oh be quiet and eat your breakfast," Lizzie giggled, turning to the dressmaker. "Don't take any notice of him, luv, his bark is much worse than his bite. How soon can you have this dress finished?"

"Ten minutes should be enough, it fits perfectly," Clara replied, with a hint of pleasure. "Keep it on, I just need to sew one button." Clara kneeled on the floor and, with supple fingers, she sent the needle flying through the cloth.

Lizzie noticed Quon's hands. "Stop it!" she commanded.

"Stop what?" Clara asked, peeking around from behind the girl.

"No, not you, him!" she giggled, pointing at Quon.

Quon's hands began moving again. This time Clara was watching, obviously trying to translate. Slowly, he reached for Lizzie's hand raising her fingertips to his lips.

"Is he dumb?"

"Definitely not!" she laughed.

"Then what did he say?"

"That dear lady," Lizzie whispered, coyly, "is strictly between him and me!"

The seamstress climbed to her feet as a pink tinge rose on her neck. The rattle of Abe's empty breakfast plate jerked her loose from her thoughts. Shaking her head, she noticed the fierce old tailor's eyes soften to a gentle glow as he gazed at Lizzie in her new dress.

"Suits you, my dear," he muttered.

"How much?" she asked.

Hands rubbing together, Abe heard the jingling coins in Quon's hand. Steeling himself against his natural instinct, the old tailor frowned. "Take it and begone, girl," he said, flicking his hand in dismissal. "We'll make you two more, they'll be sixpence each, same for his trousers."

Lizzie bent to pick up her old dress.

"Leave it!" Abe commanded, so sternly she dropped it at once.

Grinning, Quon walked to the door and opened it with a flourish, bowing low when Lizzie walked by him. As the door banged shut behind the laughing twosome, Clara picked up the old dress holding it between thumb and finger.

"And what shall I do with this?" she asked.

"Rags," Abe grunted, irritably. "Now, let's get on with our work."

As they neared the cottage, they could hear the housekeeper singing to herself as she beat the dust from the array of rugs hung over the garden wall.

"By gum, you're as pretty as a picture, luvy," Martha chuckled. "You'd better go show Ada."

Ada saw them coming. "Just look at this, Ned!" she exclaimed. "Lizzie's got a new dress."

Very little excited old Ned but this he had to see. Lizzie in a new dress could only mean one thing in his estimation; she was beginning to think like a woman.

"She gets more beautiful every day," he muttered, peering over

Ada's shoulder out of the window. "But look who else is comin," Ned chuckled, seeing Nathan's buggy turn into the track. "They'll land together and she won't stand for any nonsense this morning."

"You think she's changed because of a new dress?" asked Ada.

"No indeed, she won't change," Ned grunted, shuffling back to his desk. "But she's a woman now and she feels her destiny calling. You mark my words, we'll be seeing some changes very soon."

Arriving at the office door first, Quon pushed it open. Lizzie hesitated watching Nathan's actions and assessing the urgency of his visit as he impatiently tapped on the buggy door. Wick jumped down, winking at the girl as he pulled on the handle opening the carriage door and offering the trader his arm.

"New dress!" Nathan observed, hurrying past them. "Ring the bell for Mick, Mister Cabin. I need him right away!"

A smile strayed across the clerk's usually blank face as he tugged on the bell rope.

Ada ignored him, welcoming the youngsters and purring admiringly at Lizzie's new attire. As she did so, she noticed the girl's hands tighten into fists.

"Ever considered having some manners, Mister Goldman?" she asked tersely.

Whiskers bristling, Nathan's eyes shot fire at the young woman, his cane tapping irritably on the floor. "This is urgent business, young lady," he blustered. "I need to speak with Mick. It is imperative for me to find out if certain orders have been filled."

Mick's office door opened suddenly and the Irishman stepped in.

"Sure tis moyself that's here, m'darlin," he called. "What's yer problem? Ah, tis you agin, Mister Goldman. Are these women troublin you?" he asked, eyes full of devilment as he looked from one to the other. But it was Lizzie who now drew his total attention. "And who moyt this beautiful Colleen be, I ask yer?"

"Orders, I must know about the orders, man!" interrupted Nathan. "Enough of this nonsense, add a ten pound round of Cheshire cheese to Lady Sutton's order."

"Can't, order's gone," Mick replied, casually.

Ada put her hand to her mouth and smiled. Her husband's eyes had never wavered from Lizzie. He moved toward her and slowly walked completely around her looking her up and down. Everyone

155

waited, well aware that his gentle snub would infuriate the trader.

"Hmm ... well now ... what have we 'ere?" Mick murmured, giving the girl a saucy wink.

"Then send a rider!" Nathan snapped.

Quon tapped on his partner's arm. Looking at him , she grinned, then nodded. Quon turned quickly and went out the door.

"You can bring him the cheese, Mick," Lizzie purred. "He'll deliver it himself. We're going with him as soon as Quon gets back!"

Striding away, Mick called to Wick who was just inside the door. Having heard their conversation, the gypsy obediently followed, though not relishing his duty as he hated the smell of cheese.

Ada walked over to Lizzie and ran her fingers down the seams of the new dress. "Whoever has made this is an expert. Was it Abe?"

Nathan had not moved but he suddenly stopped pouting, his eyes darting from one to the other as he listened intently for Lizzie's answer. *Quality ladies' clothes made in this part of dockland?*

"Clara Spencer made it," replied Lizzie. "She's the new lady working for Mister Kratze."

Both Ada and Nathan made mental notes of the dressmaker's name, though for very different reasons.

The strong smell of cheese filled the buggy as they set out for the Sutton mansion. Nathan sat grimacing by the open window.

"Ever bought a ship, Mister Goldman?" Lizzie asked.

Her question seemed to have a dramatic effect on the trader. Swinging sharply to face her, his eyes became inquiring balls of interest almost leaping from his head.

"TLS wants to buy Crowther's ship at the auction," he surmised, then he seemed to become suddenly exasperated as he watched Quon tap out a message on her forearm. "That's most unnerving you know," he hissed. "Why can't he talk like the rest of us?"

"If it bothers you, don't look!" Lizzie snapped. "Now answer the question, sir."

Manufacturing a hurt expression, the trader turned and looked solemnly at her. "For a price I could represent you, young lady. I know the procedure."

Quon tapped on his partner's arm again and Nathan turned away in frustration. The buggy slowed as it made the turn at the front entrance of Sutton House. Dan shouted a greeting to his friends as they swept through the gates. Climbing down, they noticed a horse standing ready held by a stableman, obviously awaiting a rider.

"Bring the cheese," Nathan ordered, scrambling out of the buggy.

"Mister Goldman," said Lizzie, in a softly commanding tone. "Come back here."

Groaning, the trader stopped but did not turn around. Wick leapt to the ground and plucked the cheese from the seat of the coach, making a face.

"No, Wick," Lizzie said firmly. "This reward belongs solely to Mister Goldman!"

"Reward?" Nathan asked, frowning as he took the cheese Wick was pressing into his hands. "What reward?"

They were almost at the door when it opened, revealing Lady Sutton, her daughter and Gabriel Flood, looking even more handsome dressed in his riding attire.

"Hello, hello, how nice of you to visit us," cooed Lady Sutton. "Oh my, look! Mister Goldman has personally delivered the cheese cook ordered. What a wonderful man!"

"My pleasure indeed, madam," returned the glowing trader. "I'm always at your service, m'lady."

"Do come in," invited Margaret. "Gabriel is just leaving for Oxford."

"Don't go yet, Mister Flood, we need to speak with you."

Leading them down the hall and into the lounge, Lady Sutton indicated the chairs and ordered tea from the hovering butler.

Lizzie came straight to the point. "Mister Flood, Crowther's ship is going to auction and you will be wanting to make a bid on behalf of your employer. Your father's bank will give you a loan."

"Impossible," he groaned. "We haven't enough security."

Nathan's eyes flashed around the room, unsure why Lizzie was making him a party to this conversation. He noticed Quon had remained standing behind Lizzie as he often did, resting his hands on her shoulders. He had also noticed how carefully she had chosen her seat—immediately across the room from this man Flood. Turning his gaze briefly away from the partners, he didn't notice the slight movement of Quon's fingers and Lizzie's almost imperceptible nod.

One of Quon's hands slipped momentarily out of sight and

returned to lay a small leather bag into her now-waiting hand. In one quick motion Lizzie flipped it across the room toward Gabriel who instinctively reached up and caught it.

"Now you have!" she said, softly.

"What is it?" asked Margaret, moving forward in her chair.

"Daisy, sit still and listen," her mother scolded.

Looking first to Lizzie, who nodded slightly, Gabriel frowned and began to pull on the drawstring opening of the bag. Looking inside and seeing the contents, his shocked expression quickly turned his cheeks crimson and he looked up at Lizzie again.

"Show us, Mister Flood," she directed.

Gabriel turned the bag upside down onto his teatray as if it contained something too hot to touch.

Unable to contain themselves, Nathan and Margaret gasped as the precious gemstones spilled onto the table, sparkling in the light.

"Where in heaven's name ...?" asked Gabriel.

Lizzie, her eyes glowing, cut him short with an emphatic, "No! It's my sort of justice, lad," she said, almost in a whisper. "Shipping stole the Sutton fortune and shipping will give it back."

Nathan's palms began to sweat as a sudden thought came to him about some rumours which floated about London a few years ago. It had been said that a wealthy Scotsman was transporting a treasure of gemstones to London but the ship and all aboard had gone missing. If these were the same, how had Lizzie got them? *Nothing should surprise you about this girl anymore!* said a voice inside his head.

"But Lizzie, why would you do this?" Lady Sutton asked, her voice breaking slightly.

"It's not charity, m'lady," Lizzie grinned. "Mister Flood has access to a bank and I don't. A banker wouldn't listen to me, I'm only a woman." She paused to glance about at their faces, an ominous tone appearing in her voice. "Some day, they'll know who I am. Perhaps it will be Gabriel who makes it possible."

"My goodness," Nathan interrupted, mournfully. "Whatever are you planning now, girl?"

Quon's hand spun sharply as Lizzie glanced up at him. He tapped his nose, pointing at Nathan. Margaret giggled.

"He says ... ," Lizzie began.

"I know," said the trader irritably. "I'm to mind my own

business!"

With questioning eyes, Gabriel interrupted, "But how?"

"Let me explain," she said quietly, standing up and moving across the room to the window behind them. "I need you to conduct a business arrangement for me. After expenses, we should be able to split a tidy profit."

"It's a gift?" Gabriel murmured, turning so he could see her.

"Don't you believe it!" Nathan growled. "That's just her bait, wait until she tells you the rest."

"Is there more?" asked Gabriel, beginning to warm to this girl's highly calculating mind. This was a far cry from the type of adventure he was used to.

Lizzie nodded, wagging her finger at the trader as she came round to stand in front of them. "I'm going to use you to get the Crowther ship for TLS, Mister Flood. We'll be partners and Charley will use it on the grain run to Hull." Turning to face the Suttons, she continued, "Then, I want you and Margaret to learn the printing business," she said, watching their shocked expressions. "My intuition tells me there's going to be a future in it very soon."

Lady Sutton suddenly came to life, sitting bolt upright in her chair and clapping her hands jubilantly. "What a splendid idea! We'd love to be involved," she declared, her eyes bright with anticipation. "Women in business, that's what this country needs more of!"

Margaret however, was quite obviously shocked at Lizzie's suggestion. Her mother had never expressed such radical views before. "But Mother, you can't do this. You're not a business person, you're Lady Sutton!"

"Why not?" Lizzie enjoined. "It only takes brains and effort. I know you have the brains, if you want to recoup your fortune, you must work for it, girl!"

Always up to something that one, Nathan thought, listening to their conversation. W*omen in business—Lizzie would certainly give them their come-uppance!*

Lady Sutton giggled and Gabriel couldn't contain himself.

"I-I only thought it best ...," Margaret began, her cheeks flushing.

"Lead on, Miss Lizzie," her mother cried, enthusiastically. "You can be sure we will do our best."

"Looks like you have a deal, young lady," Gabriel chuckled,

scooping up the precious stones and putting them safely back into their bag and into his jacket pocket. "I'd best be off; it's a long ride to Oxford and back," he said bowing slightly to Lady Sutton.

"Now, where do we start, Lizzie?" Lady Sutton asked, as the door clicked shut.

"Just a moment, dear lady," interrupted Nathan, his eyes fastened on Lizzie. "I'd like to know why I've been allowed to hear all this."

"Why you're the brains of the whole plan, Mister Goldman," Lizzie chuckled. "Between you and Lady Sutton you must know everybody in London!"

"But what's that got to do with printing?" he asked, doubtfully.

Margaret Sutton and her mother waited in fascinated silence.

She's building up the poor man's ego, manoeuvring him into just the position she wants him, thought Lady Sutton, experiencing a new respect for the girl.

She was right, in Nathan's mind he could already feel his elevated importance and the commissions filling his pockets. Eagerly, he took the lady's outstretched hand and bowed regally over it.

"I have no doubt she already has a plan for us, Lady Sutton. You can rest assured I will assist you in every way possible. Thank you for your hospitality. Come," he murmured to his passengers, going to the door and opening it. "We can start planning as I drive you home."

"We're going to walk," said Lizzie, smiling disarmingly. "You may go; I know you're a busy man, Mister Goldman."

Taken aback, Nathan bowed slightly and left hurriedly, strutting down the long hallway with renewed energy, twirling his cane

"What should we do first?" asked Lady Sutton.

"Start with your friends," said Lizzie, "find out what their needs are for printing and what they would like to see in a regular newssheet. We'll meet again when Gabriel returns."

Chapter 17

The sound of playing children, mixed with the mournful bellowing of cattle, greeted them as they passed the gypsy camp about a week later.

Drovers must have returned, thought Lizzie, her mind turning to the new baby and wondering when it would arrive. *Soon,* was all Jeb had said. They passed the camp with its noticeable absence of menfolk and took a shortcut past the stables.

Rounding the corner, they were met with a very strange sight. One of the workmen was writing with chalk on a stable door while several of his fellow workmen sat watching. They stopped to watch, soon realizing he was teaching the men some schooling. Each of his aging pupils had a slate and they were labouriously copying the letters and numbers he had written on the door.

"Would you look, they're learning to read and write," she whispered.

"Yes, they are," said a familiar voice behind them, startling them. "Angus is doing it at the brewery, too."

"Who's that doing the teaching, Mick?"

"He's one of Ned's men, seems he's an ex-minister."

Quon's hands went wild.

"He wants to know how do you become an ex-minister?"

Shrugging, Mick walked away, muttering under his breath. "Damned if hoy know, that's his business now, ain't it."

Passing by the office, Ada called through the open window beckoning them to come in.

"*London Queen* is coming up the Thames heavily loaded with grain. Your dad and John Watson are hopping with excitement," she announced when they came through the door.

Lizzie's thoughts turned to Charley's new machine. If it worked, unloading would cause quite a stir in the next few days. Quon touched her elbow sending her a quick message.

"Who's the ex-minister Ned brought with him?" Lizzie asked.

"The one who is giving the men lessons on reading and writing."

Ada frowned then looked across at the order clerk. "Ned, was one of your men an ex-minister?"

"Minister?" the old man chuckled, removing his pipe. "We had a stableman called Frederick who used to be a monk, if that's who you mean. Fred's a very educated man."

Quick glances were exchanged between Lizzie and her partner, and his sign language urged her to ask more questions.

Frowning in concentration, she continued, "What was his job in the monastery?"

"Writer," Ned muttered grudgingly, never lifting his head.

"Could be he knows about printing," suggested Ada.

Could be, Lizzie thought to herself, moving toward the door as her mind pondered why an educated man would be working as a stablehand, when he obviously enjoyed teaching. *I wonder why he left the monastery.* "When will Ben ...?" she asked aloud, opening the door.

"Late tide," finished Ada, "they'll be unloading in the morning."

Banging the door behind them, they walked quickly toward the cottage.

"Ben will be in tonight," Martha called, as they entered.

Willie waved from the table where he was working on his own slateboard.

"You two had any lunch?" the housekeeper inquired, suspiciously.

"Not a morsel," Lizzie laughed, "and we're both starving!"

Wiping a wisp of graying hair from her brow, Martha began humming to herself as she filled two bowls to the brim with the stew that had been simmering all night. She carefully pushed them across the table and went to get spoons and a plate stacked with fresh bread.

Smiling at the boy who was now sitting on Quon's knee, she kept her hand behind her back and waited. Willie's big brown eyes turned upward, pleading.

"Grandma?"

"What is it, lad?"

"Spoon please, Grandma."

"Tease!" exclaimed Lizzie, winking at the housekeeper who opened her hand to reveal the boy's small spoon.

They had just finished when Joe walked in. He pulled his watch out and scratched his head when he saw the youngsters eating pie and custard.

"Eating early today?" he asked.

"More like late, I'd say," Martha exclaimed, pouring a warm cider for the old man.

"Yer home early today, Dad? Everything all right?" asked Lizzie, giving him a hug.

"Just thought I'd have a little shut-eye before tea," he replied, sitting down heavily.

"Well, we'll be off. See you at dinner," said Lizzie, and before either could question them, the youngsters had disappeared.

At six o'clock Lizzie and Quon had just finished washing up for dinner when they heard noises outside as Mick, Ada and Charley arrived. Willie raced to the door to meet them.

Wobbling precariously, Charley moved toward his seat at the table, gently poking at Lizzie with his stick as he passed. "Ben will be in dock later tonight, Liz," he grinned. "Tomorrow we'll be unloading!"

"Charley Mason!" Ada snapped, wagging her finger sternly. "We don't talk business until after we've eaten."

"Sorry, love," he whispered, winking at Lizzie and Quon.

The young partners waited patiently and when the last plate had been cleared from the table, Charley looked toward Ada with a comical, pleading expression.

"All right, Charley, now you can tell us," she said, resignedly.

"We can start at dawn," Charley bubbled, excitedly. "I'll guarantee that ship will be empty by nightfall."

Quon's fingers burst into life on Lizzie's arm and a flick of her eyebrows told him she understood.

"What about storage, Dad? Is Dixon's building ready?"

"We're ready," Joe growled. "Half goes to Dixon's and half to the warehouse at the brewery. John is waiting none too patiently." He paused to take a puff on his pipe. "We'll use four drays and fill Dixon's first."

"Ah sure," Mick interrupted, "and yer goin to kill them men if yer try ta shift eighty tons in ten hours."

Smiling, Martha looked up from the sink as the argument now

raged between the men. She noticed Ada was sitting very quietly, her eyes fixed on Lizzie and Quon who were talking in sign language.

"We need three extra men," said Lizzie, during a brief lull in the conversation.

"Don't have 'em," said Charley.

"Yes, we do," she retorted.

"Where?"

"The sailors on Ben's ship!"

Grinning, the engineer pounded his fist on the table as hurrying footsteps sounded on the garden path and an urgent knock was heard on the door.

"Come in," Martha called, as Willie scrambled onto Joe's knee, peering inquisitively toward the door.

"Jeb says to come quick, Miss Lizzie," gasped the familiar-looking gypsy boy.

Alarm spread over Ada's face as the girl leapt from her chair and raced off into the night without a word to the stunned group. She stared in disbelief at Quon who sat fidgeting in his chair, not making any attempt to follow.

"What's wrong?" she asked, her voice trembling with concern.

"Baby comin," Quon sighed, cradling his head in his hands. "Quon not welcome."

"Oh, my," chuckled a relieved Ada, "and I thought it was something serious."

The last of the daylight was quickly fading as Lizzie and the gypsy lad tore up Drover's Lane. By the light of the fire, she found Jeb standing silently with two older women. They were wearing the finest embroidered dresses Lizzie had ever seen.

"Dress her ... quickly!" Jeb snapped.

Taking Lizzie's arms, they hurried her away to one of the tents. Quickly they helped her undress, slipping a dress as fine as their own over her head. Gentle brown hands fastened buttons with amazing dexterity and speed.

"No talking, girl!" one of the women hissed as she opened the tent's flap and pulled her outside.

Leading her to the open space near a smaller fire, they found a group of women gathered about a heap of blankets laid on the ground. Lizzie's eyes were drawn to the naked woman lying atop the heap of blankets. She was covered only in a light blanket and it was very obvious her belly was swollen with child.

Lizzie could hardly recognize her—her face glistened with sweat and her hair hung in damp tresses about her head. She slightly raised a hand in welcome lifting her shoulders; then twisting in pain, she released a bone-chilling moan that sent shivers up and down Lizzie's spine. *Good thing Quon's not here!*

One of the women silently instructed her to sit down at the edge of the blankets. All night long, at more or less regular intervals, the moaning continued. Each time, several of the gypsies massaged the woman's body with warm oil brought from the fire. It had a distinctive smell, not altogether unpleasant. *It seems to help keep me awake,* was the thought passing through Lizzie's mind as she fought off droopy eyelids. The pregnant woman had been covered with several layers of blankets as the air grew colder. She seemed to sleep from time to time, though how she managed it puzzled the girl.

Having seen many animal births, Lizzie was not unfamiliar with the process. However, seeing a human give birth was decidedly different, she decided, and it was becoming quite disconcerting. She wondered how long the poor woman, and the rest of them, would have to endure this agony.

Then, just as dawn was breaking and amber streaks of colour covered the sky, one last scream of pain sent the older gypsies to her side. At last they heard the slap of a hand on bare flesh, and the first welcome cry of a child.

Lizzie was silently invited to sit in the place of honour beside the new mother. She moved closer and dropped to her knees. The first thing she knew, the tiny bundle wrapped in a warm blanket, was being handed to her. Taken by surprise, she took the bundle and looked down at the precious child. It was so tiny. She looked into its small red face, awestruck. Suddenly, silent tears welled in her eyes sweeping down her cheeks. The mother held out her arms and she lightly kissed the baby's forehead before handing the small bundle to its mother's waiting arms.

"Miss Lizzie ... you and Mister Quon be my son's godparents," she whispered, smiling tentatively. It was not really a question but a respectful statement. Lizzie gently touched the woman's hand and nodded gratefully, unable to speak.

A friendly hand grasped Lizzie's arm helping her to her feet then leading her back to the tent. The unknown woman helped her change and escorted her over to the campfire. Jeb was waiting. Hat pulled low, the gypsy leader's black eyes twinkled in the morning light.

"Now yer a gypsy, Miss Lizzie," he said, looking at her with unusually soft eyes.

"But why in the open? It was very cold."

"It's a tradition. We gypsies are born to the wide open spaces of land and sky." He pointed his pipe stem toward the lane and, for the first time, she noticed the familiar-looking form huddled at the foot of the gatepost.

"Yer better go talk to him, lass. He's been waitin all night."

The gypsy blanket slipped from Quon's shoulders when he heard the hurrying footsteps and he rose shakily to his feet. Holding his arms wide, Lizzie walked into them and he folded them protectively about her. She dropped her head onto his shoulder.

"Oh dumplin, my dumplin," she sobbed. "We're godparents to a precious gypsy boy!"

"Don't care," he whispered tiredly, tightening his grasp. "Wizzy always mine."

"Ben Thorn was here for breakfast," Martha informed them as they sat down at the table and she placed steaming bowls of porridge in front of them. "Charley was down at the dock before dawn. He has his steam engine running already."

"It was a boy," said Lizzie, tiredly. "And Quon and I are his godparents. He took such a long time coming!"

"Oh gracious, I'm sorry luv, in my eagerness to tell you the news I clean forgot that ye've been up all night and have thee own news," exclaimed the housekeeper. "Godparents are you, child, that is quite an honour. You'll be tired out, luv."

"A bit, but I'll be all right, Martha," she replied, suddenly shivering and realizing how cold she was. "Could I have some hot milk, please?"

"I have some right here from the porridge," said Martha, pouring out a steaming cupful. Then, picking up Joe's blanket from his chair, she laid it over Lizzie's shoulders. "This will make you feel better, luv."

Feeling the warmth of the blanket around her, she took a sip of the hot liquid but continued to toy with her breakfast. Slowly, she began to feel her body return to life. She looked over at Quon and realized he was watching her with sad eyes.

"You wouldn't have wanted to be there, dumplin. The baby is so tiny. We'll go visit tomorrow," she said haltingly. "Martha, I think you better bring Quon some hot milk, too."

He drank down his hot milk, finished his meal, and tapped the table looking over at Lizzie's half-eaten bowl. Their eyes met and he reached for her hand.

Martha noticed their interaction, sighed softly and went back to her dishes.

"Wizzy sleep," Quon whispered.

"No, dumplin, we've things to do, I'll feel better soon." She took two more spoonfuls as Quon patiently watched, willing her to eat more. Then she pushed her chair back. Quon got to the door first, handing Lizzie her coat before opening it.

"Thanks, Martha," said Lizzie, stepping outside.

"Tanks, Marta!"

The housekeeper looked up, smiling, but they were already gone.

More slowly than usual, they walked down Water Lane to Abe's shop. They found him standing on the doorstep talking to himself as he strained to see the docks.

"Tain't possible! Tain't possible!" he was muttering, shaking his head and checking his watch time and time again.

"What's happening, Mister Kratze?"

"They're loading drays in 30 minutes from that grain ship. I've been timing them!" he slobbered, excitedly. "It's the talk of the waterfront already. Look at all the carriages." Raising a bony finger, he pointed at the growing row of carriages lining Dock and Water Streets. "I'll wager they're all curious shipping agents!"

Thanking their old teacher, they moved off with renewed vigour. Reaching the crowd, they mingled unnoticed, casually moving amongst the onlookers and eavesdropping on their conversations.

"I shall buy one of those machines," one heavy-set man stated pompously. "Tell me, gentlemen, who makes them? Where is their factory?" When no one answered, he tapped his silver-topped cane on the cobblestones in frustration.

"I knows who makes 'em, yer 'oner, sir."

Lizzie and Quon recognized the unmistakable voice of Tom Legg and went toward it.

Stumbling forward on his pegleg and shepherd's crook, the aging mariner lurched drunkenly into view. The impeccably dressed shipping agents recoiled in horror as his ale-soaked body odour fouled their nostrils.

"Well, out with it, man," snapped the heavy-set man, keeping Tom at bay by raising his cane and applying it to the mariner's chest.

"Cost yer three pennies, yer 'oner," he slobbered.

With the three pennies clutched firmly in his hand, Tom was just about to speak when Lizzie stepped into his view, glaring darkly. Tom screamed, turning away quickly and stumbling as he did so. He yelled wildly, casting his stick about before him, parting the crowd.

"Damned madman!" one man observed, causing much laughter.

Lizzie and Quon slipped quietly away, heading toward the TLS dock. The noise here was deafening as the clanging reverberated amongst the buildings and several large ships nearby. As they reached the *London Queen* they watched in awe as the conveyer spewed grain sacks in a never-ending stream out onto the dock where two workmen grabbed them, passing them to more men on the dray.

Pacing the upper deck of the *Queen*, Captain Thorn beamed with satisfaction as he controlled the unloading, shouting orders to his men who were working alongside both sailors and dockworkers—the natural rivalry, legendary on London's docks, had seemingly been set aside this day.

Quon tugged on her sleeve, hands spinning, his thoughts apparently unaffected by the noise. She nodded and her eyes followed his pointing finger to where Charley sat high atop his cart organizing the loading of lumber onto a smaller ship nearby.

"Who's the man with the dockmaster?" Lizzie asked one of the workmen.

"Dutchman, I think, Miss Lizzie."

A quick, piercing whistle sounded through the noise as the engineer drew their attention, waving them over.

"This is Mister Van Horn, a shipbuilder from Holland, Miss

Lizzie," introduced Charley. "He was recommended to us by Patrick Sandilands. He wants to do a trade," said Charley, winking at the youngsters. "Cheese for the price of the shipping."

"Size of block, type and price?" Lizzie snapped back, to the astonishment of the Dutchman.

"Size and type are right," offered Charley.

"Then send Lefty to ask Ada about the price."

"I did. He should ...," Charley muttered, glancing up the dock. "Here he comes now."

Panting, Lefty hurried up to join them, handing the girl a paper, then tipping his hat and moving off. Quon's arms swung into instant action startling the shipbuilder as he watched with rapt attention.

"What did he say?" Charley asked, without thinking.

Ignoring the question, Lizzie nodded at Quon. Opening the folded paper, she recognized Ada's beautifully formed handwriting and a smile crept across her face. "You were right, dumplin," she whispered, before turning to the Dutchman. "Your price for the cheese, sir?"

Taken by surprise, the man stumbled for words. "Ten English shillings per block, b-but am I to do business with a woman?"

"Yes, you are!" Lizzie purred, her eyes glancing at the note in her hand which said nine shillings and eight pence a block from Patrick. "Don't play games with me, Mister Van Horn. I want your best price!" she said calmly, staring coldly at the continental businessman.

"How old are you, young lady?" Van Horn blustered, his face turning red.

"I'm a hundred and seventeen, a reincarnation of David ... and he's Goliath but he lost a few inches in the remaking!" she replied impatiently, hands on her hips. "Now do you want to do business with the TLS Company or pay cash for the shipping right here at the dockside?"

Reeling, the Dutchman grasped Charley's cart with one hand. "Nine shillings and eight pence is the best I can do."

"Nine shillings and four pence, or no trade!" Lizzie snapped back. "Stop the loading, Mister Mason, 'til we see his cash!"

Anxiety flashed in the Dutch shipbuilder's eyes as he glanced up at the engineer. Charley, trying not to smile, shrugged his shoulders.

Van Horn desperately needed the straight-grained oak lumber

which was stacked at the dockside. Trading for cheese had been a way of securing a sizeable discount on the lumber along with acquiring a large order for the family's cheese factory in Holland. Being beaten at the art of bargaining by a mere girl was something he had not counted on.

He slowly nodded his head in confirmation.

"Send Lefty up to the office for a contract, Charley," she ordered before turning back to face the despondent shipbuilder. "Tell me, sir?" she asked, so quietly he had to step closer to hear. "Would you have tried to cheat a man out of four pennies?" Before he had a chance to reply, she turned quickly on her heel and walked away.

Watching them, the businessman's mouth curled into a smile. He surprised even himself by feeling no animosity toward the girl. *That is a woman like none I've ever met before. It isn't often I am outdone in business but* .... "Start loading, Mister Mason," he called, looking up at the engineer who was watching him. "I've just changed my mind about women!"

"Hungry yet, dumplin?" she asked, as they left the jetty. "Let's call at the Johnson's but first let's see if we can find Mister Pegleg."

Pushing their way through the crowd, they ran between the traffic to *The Robin* searching for Tom. Tugging on her arm, Quon pointed to the corner of the stables. There sat the one-legged man on a wheelbarrow, tankard in hand.

"He's hiding from us," Quon muttered.

Unseen, they passed by, threading their way through the alley and along Mast Lane, turning toward the bakery.

"Look out, Oly, ther here!" Bill's voice boomed as they came through the gate.

Screaming a greeting, the lad raced across the cobblestone yard.

"Hello, you lot," Clem called, carrying a cider barrel on his shoulder.

Lizzie stared at the baker's helper as he lowered the small but heavy barrel onto the pony cart. "Yer puttin on weight, Clem," she said, admiring his bulging muscles.

"Aye lass, Bill feeds me now and then!"

"Feed him," the baker laughed, "the rascal never stops eatin!"

"It's quality control," Clem chuckled.

"Look, look," Bill whispered, nodding toward Olivera as the youngster walked across the yard, pie in hand. "The lad shares all his food with that pony of his."

Sure enough, Oly walked over to the pony and when it nuzzled him, he broke off a small piece of pie and fed it to him. Taking their own servings in hand, Lizzie and Quon followed the bread cart out of the yard. Shouting their goodbyes to the men, they waved to Oly before turning the corner.

Chapter 18

Locating the old printer's shop in the alleyway near Brown's carpentry yard was easy. Its dusty windows, thick with grime and cobwebs, easily fit Nathan's description. The door was slightly ajar so they peeked in finding a bespectacled old man bent over a workbench in the dimly-lit room. A large, strange-looking piece of equipment stood in the middle of the floor. Quon's knee accidentally bumped the door causing it to creak loudly.

"Come in," the old man called shakily, "be with you in a moment."

As they stepped inside, the pungent smell of ink filled their nostrils. Lizzie glanced around at the cobweb-hung walls and paper-littered floor. Large damp spots showed on the plastered ceiling and dust was obvious everywhere, even limiting the amount of light entering the sparsely furnished room. The printer wiped his black hands on an already ink-stained apron and adjusted his spectacles, leaving a thumbprint on one of the lens.

Bent from years of stooping, Cuthbert Dunbar moved with a peculiar shuffle, the thin bony structure of his face reflecting pain and frustration as he came to the counter and peered over his spectacles at them.

"What can I do for you?" he asked, suspiciously.

"Tell me, sir," Lizzie asked, "is there really a future in this printing business?"

A merry twinkle flashed in the old man's eyes. His voice squeaking with excitement, he began to talk about his dreams. "Someday," he cackled, "everyone will read. Books will be in every home and newspapers will be sold for a pittance on the street." Pausing, his expression suddenly changed, portraying his misery once again. "Sadly, I won't see it, I'm getting too old to work this two-bed press as it is." Cuthbert's shoulders sagged and he adjusted his spectacles. "No one will buy this place so I guess I'll be here 'till I die." Turning away, the old man shuffled back to his bench, unaware of the message Quon's hands were sending to his partner.

"Sir, will you sell it to us?" she asked. "We'll give you 50 guineas for the business and equipment and a further 10 if you stay and train the new owners."

"Yer jesting?" the printer squeaked, his tweezers falling from shaking hands and clattering to the floor. "I'd have to hear it from yer father before I could believe it."

"Then believe it now, sir," she said, walking toward him. Delving into her pocket, she jingled her bag of coins as enticement. Then removing it, she counted out 50 golden guineas, laying them on the bench in front of the old man.

Cuthbert's hands were now shaking uncontrollably and he stared at the money. "This is most irregular, most irregular."

Quon's hands formed a quick message, causing his partner to frown so he repeated it. Suddenly, she realized what he was trying to tell her and she quickly nodded. Quon hurried out of the shop and Lizzie picked up her coins, returning them to the bag.

Running hard, it took Quon barely five minutes to reach the TLS office, surprising Ada as he burst through the door.

"Wizzy need monk man," he panted, falling into a nearby chair.

"Lizzie needs who?" Mick growled, poking his head around the corner.

"He means Frederick, the stableman," Ned offered, not lifting his head.

"Don't stand there gawking, Mick, go get him!" Ada ordered.

Long strides of urgency took the Irishman quickly to the rag yard stables where he found his quarry cleaning out a stall. "Wash yer hands, me boyo. Then get down to the office as quick as yer can," he ordered.

Dropping the wheelbarrow, the stableman ran to the wash trough to clean his hands, wiping them on his overalls. Then he hurried down the track to the office, his mind a whirl of confusion as he pondered the reason for being called.

"He's coming," Ada advised, looking out the window.

"You come with me," said Quon, meeting Frederick outside. "Lizzie need you."

Without any more explanation, Quon hurried Frederick along. By the time they reached the printing shop, they were both gasping for air. Stepping inside, the stableman's eyes immediately settled on the Stanhope printing press and a broad smile appeared on his face.

Motioning him forward, Lizzie stood quietly and watched. His chest still heaving from the hurried journey, Frederick moved slowly toward the machine. Even in the dim light, she could tell his eyes were sparkling with anticipation. Standing over the press, his fingers caressed the great iron frame and slowly moved the levers.

For the first time, Lizzie noticed that, despite the dust in evidence everywhere else, the printing machine gleamed brightly as if it were cleaned and oiled regularly. *Mister Dunbar truly loves this machine.* She carefully watched the reaction of the old printer who peered suspiciously over his spectacles at the newcomer. Frederick pushed on the print bed, noting its smooth action as the second bed slipped into place.

"Mister Frederick," said Lizzie, after watching him for a few minutes. "Will you write out a Bill of Sale for this place ... lock, stock and barrel plus your training. The price is 60 golden guineas."

"I'll print you one, Miss Lizzie, if you give me half an hour!" he said, enthusiastically.

"No, just write it by hand."

Quill and inkpot were produced and the stableman wrote out the receipt in a beautiful hand, dusting the wet ink with drying powder before handing it to the girl.

"Sign it, if you please, sir," she instructed Cuthbert, who'd been watching over Frederick's shoulder. "Then I will pay you."

Eagerly scratching his name on the paper, the printer handed it back to her and held out his hand. Finally, his face broke into a toothless grin as she dropped the 60 guineas into his large, dirty hand, counting them aloud as she did so.

"The place is yours," he said tiredly, as if feeling a great weight had been lifted from his shoulders. Then, putting the money safely into his own moneybag, he went back to his seat and sat down.

Quon's hands began moving rapidly.

"Mister Frederick, do you really understand this printing stuff?"

"Yes miss, I was trained by the monks in Shrewsbury."

"But why did you leave the monastery?" Lizzie asked bluntly.

"They wouldn't allow me to work on the printing press any

longer," he replied, a faraway look in his eyes.

Lizzie was impressed by this soft-spoken man with comforting eyes. "Then I'll give you your wish ... from tomorrow you'll be working right here. But I want this place cleaned up first and ... what's your last name?"

Beaming, Frederick shrugged his shoulders.

"It's been Brother Frederick so long now, I've forgotten," he said, pondering for a moment. "You may call me Fred Monk if you like."

"Right then, it's settled. Now, Mister Cuthbert, Fred Monk will be here in the morning to begin work with you," she explained, reaching for the door latch. As the three of them went out on the street, Lizzie turned to Fred. "If you require any help with repairs, talk to Mick. He can find anything that's needed."

Fred nodded, then quickly turned and hurried off.

"Let's go home, dumplin. I think I'd like that rest now ... that was much easier than I anticipated. It will be dinner soon, too."

Ada and Martha were sitting at the table when they arrived.

"The menfolk are determined to unload that darned grain ship in one day," Ada groaned, adjusting the blanket covering Willie, fast asleep in his grandfather's chair.

"We'll not wait for them tonight," said Martha. "Come sit down, dinner is ready to eat."

As they ate, the three women talked quietly, conversation centering on Abe Kratze and his new dressmaker. No sooner had they finished eating when both Lizzie and Quon stifled a yawn.

"Bedtime for me," said the girl, pushing her plate away but not moving as the church clock in the distance struck seven.

"For us!" Quon added.

"We're for home, too," announced Ada, glancing at her sleeping son. "Help me lift him, Quon."

"Quon carry Willie home for you, Ada?" asked the boy.

"It's all right, thank you, Quon. If he gets much bigger, I'll be needing help very soon." Ada adjusted the boy on her shoulder as Martha planted a kiss on the boy's head and went to open the door.

When they had left, Martha closed the door and returning to the table, she looked questioningly at Lizzie who sat with her head on her arms.

"I'm so tired, mum!" she said, her voice hoarse with tiredness.

She stood up slowly and came to stand behind the housekeeper giving her a hug. "Thanks for being so understanding."

Martha's blood raced when she heard the word *mum* and felt the girl's arms enfold her. She had thought of this young woman as a daughter for so long but this was the first time Lizzie had indicated she felt the same. Turning around, Martha gently took the girl's head in her hands, kissed her forehead and held her close for a moment. "Go to bed, doy, dumplin's already asleep in his chair."

Lizzie went over and nudged Quon awake. The housekeeper watched them sleepily hug each other then disappear up the stairs. Hearing their doors close, the cottage was now quiet except for the crackle of the fire on the hearth. Sitting down heavily, she began to rock, listening to the unusual stillness.

Early morning fog swirled around the streets of dockland as Mick and Ada arrived, carrying Willie wrapped in Joe's blanket. Still in his night shirt, he scrambled onto Joe's knee to help him with his usual meal of sausage and rasher of ham and eggs.

Charley arrived next and then Ben and Captain Davis, the latter looking very sour and grumbling about the weather. After breakfast was devoured, the men remained for awhile. The conversation grew lively and centred on the triumph of the day before—the unloading of the grain ship. Charley blushed with embarrassment when Ben heaped loud praised on him.

"Eighty tons in one day," Davis glowered. "Can't be possible!"

"What time were you done?" Lizzie inquired.

"They wor all here and lookin for dinner at ten o'clock," said Martha, smugly thinking how she had even managed a little nap.

At almost half-seven, the men began looking at their pocket watches and talked about going to work.

Davis, who had been unusually quiet, slammed his fist down on the table. "With your eyes and ears around dockland, you must have heard the news ... seems I'm a landlubber now. The Admiralty took my command away yesterday."

"Why would they do that?" Ben hissed. "Who's taking over *Falcon*?"

"You are, damn yer!"

Every eye in the room turned toward Davis but he simply tugged on his beard and glowered.

"Truly, Davis, I didn't know," said Ben, looking over at Lizzie.

She broke the uncomfortable silence with a loud giggle, reading the message Quon was tapping on her leg.

"That's no problem, lad," she chuckled. "You can swap jobs with Ben and come work for us."

"But why has the Admiralty done this?" Ben asked.

"CROWTHER," Davis shouted at the ceiling. "There's a Crowther on the Admiralty Board."

"Oh, is there?" exclaimed Lizzie, smiling coyly.

"Well, I've got work to do," said Charley, beginning the movement toward the door.

In less than a minute, all the men had left except for Mick who stood by the door smiling smugly. "Now don't yer be gettin yerself into trouble now, young lady. Hoy seen the look in yer eyes when the captain mentioned the name Crowther."

"Who me?" she replied cheekily.

For half an hour they searched the government docks for the Admiralty offices, finally asking a passing sailor for directions. He turned and pointed to a seemingly unmarked, smoke-blackened stone building a few doors away across Dock Street.

"See the building those men are comin from," he said, pointing toward four uniformed officers coming down some nearby stairs. "There's the admiralty officers and that's the building yer want." He now lowered his voice as if fearful someone else would hear. "They'll be going to the coachin house for lunch. The first one is Sir David Walton, then behind him is old Admiral Jones. That last one, the big man ... is Jonas Crowther," he spat out venomously, beginning to walk away. "Don't you go near them girly, that Crowther's an animal!" he called, running to catch his mate.

Crossing the street, they followed the officers toward the coaching house. Quon grabbed her elbow, pointing to a TLS dray turning into the yard. It was loaded with cider and French liquor from their own brewery. Two street waifs, begging for coppers, intercepted their progress as they opened the back door.

Peering around the room, Lizzie turned back to the first dull-eyed boy. "Ah'll give yer a penny to do somethin fer me."

He nodded eagerly.

"See that big bloke in uniform," she said, pointing to Jonas Crowther who was sitting with his feet stretched out under a table.

The boy nodded again.

"Go crawl under that table and tie his boot laces together."

"What happens if I get caught, miss?" he asked, seeming only slightly worried.

"You won't, do it quickly though."

Thinking only of his reward, the boy moved nervously forward. Glancing back at Lizzie and seeing the penny she held invitingly between her fingers, he swiftly disappeared under the table. Quon stifled a giggle as the boy reappeared a short while later, flushed but with a look of triumph on his face. Grabbing the penny, he dashed away as if the devil himself were chasing him.

Fifteen minutes went by without Crowther noticing anything amiss. Then the liquor began to take its effect on the three men and an argument erupted. Lizzie grinned at Quon and they waited by the door for the inevitable. The conflict quickly became more heated and Crowther began making threats to his companions. Finally, he leapt to his feet, lurching violently and losing his balance. Grabbing for the table to steady himself, he spilled the remaining contents of his companion's tankards. Many nearby patrons quickly left their seats to escape his flailing arms.

"Drunken fool," someone yelled amongst the confusion. "Throw him out!"

Hurling abuse at everyone, Crowther picked up his three-cornered hat and staggered outside, aided by the two burly barmen. His fancy cane, thrown out onto the cobblestone yard by one of the onlookers, landed nearby.

"Damn you, Jones, I will have no more association with the likes of you!" Crowther yelled, finally realizing he had been the brunt of a joke.

Sir David had begun to follow Crowther but, noticing that the admiral was having difficulty breathing, he quickly helped him to a seat out in the fresh air. His cheeks were bright red and his large, bulbous nose wobbled violently as he spoke.

"The man's a menace," Jones gasped at Sir David. "I want him off the Admiralty Board immediately!"

Unnoticed amongst the crowd outside, Lizzie and Quon smiled, moving closer to better hear the men's conversation.

"... and give Davis his job back. I was suspicious of Crowther's motives from the outset," Admiral Jones declared.

Lizzie felt Quon's fingers grip her arm.

"But it's official," Sir David objected.

"Then we'll rescind the bloody order," the older man hissed.

"Profitable morning, dumplin!" Lizzie whispered, her arm sliding through Quon's as they moved away. "I think we've achieved enough here!"

Finding their way back to the familiar streets of dockland, Lizzie's mind turned to Gabriel Flood and the meeting with his father in Oxford.

ଓଓଓ

Arriving at his family home, Gabriel had patiently withstood the accusations of mistrust from his father and insinuations of foul play by his brother. Always the peacemaker, his mother stepped into the fray and rescued him from the tangle of family bitterness. She promised to meet with Lady Sutton and the mystery girl, Lizzie Short, at the earliest opportunity. Arguing that he couldn't wait that long, he finally gained their confidence although losing precious time in the process.

With his saddlebag stuffed with gold, he rode fast and recklessly taking the shortest route through the Buckinghamshire countryside, praying he would arrive in time and meet with no folly on the way.

ଓଓଓ

"I trust him, dumplin," muttered Lizzie.

Quon cocked an eyebrow but offered no comment, his sharp ears having caught the faint sound of a familiar voice in the background.

Lizzie suddenly stopped and held her hand to her ear. Looking back at Quon, she realized they were listening to the same sound.

"Are yer hungry, are yer hungry," the voice rang melodiously and strong. "Av got bread for sale, cooked by me mother."

Smiling at each other, they picked up their pace.

"Billy's got strong voice," Quon chuckled.

Rounding the corner, they had a good view of the new bake shop. Billy was standing on his barrel, yelling to a milling throng, occasionally adding meat and candle wares to his humorous chatter.

"Let's eat, Wizzy," he suggested, tugging on her sleeve.

Shaking loose, Lizzie led the way around the crowd and joined the queue being served by the butcher's wife.

"Two meat pies and a large helping of tripe," she said, fishing into her pocket when her turn came.

Placing the pies on the counter, Missus Sweeney stared hard at the young people for a moment before slicing their tripe.

"Yer Lizzie Short ain't yer, lass?"

"Yes ma'am, but how do you know?"

"Billy's Uncle Johann described yer."

"Uncle who?" Lizzie asked, a surprised note in her voice as she handed the lady a tiny, silver threepenny piece.

"Can yer come back later, luv?" the woman asked, shaking her money bag to find the ha'penny change and slipping it into the girl's hand. "We'd like to have a talk with you."

"Not today, lady," Lizzie frowned. "Who was that uncle who told you about me?"

"Uncle Johann, he's in the bake shop. Next please."

Standing back by the butcher's shop window, eating their meal, they watched Billy work the crowd remaining unseen by their friend. When finished, they sauntered over to the bake shop doorway. There, behind the counter, serving customers was Captain Davis.

"I don't believe it," snickered Lizzie, watching her partner's hands. "I know, I know!" she said. "He's had his beard trimmed and he's even wearing a baker's apron."

Sneaking away, Lizzie smiled to herself. *Oh my, I wonder what will happen when he finds out the Falcon is his again?*

"Will Captain Davis go back to sea, Wizzy?" Quon asked, as if reading her thoughts.

"For awhile, I think," she replied.

Suddenly, a voice shouted from across the street at the *Swans* ale house. "Miss Lizzie! Miss Lizzie!" They saw One-Eyed Jack coming toward them across the street. "Be it true, missy? Is me old mate Ben Thorn takin over command of *Falcon?*"

"Only rumours, lad, don't you believe it."

Adjusting the patch over his missing eye, Jack frowned. "But he ain't been near the *Falcon* for days."

"He's relying on you to keep everything ship shape," Lizzie replied, wagging a finger at her old friend. "Now don't you dare let him down."

Turning red under his tan, Jack backed away stammering an apology. Returning to his table he began to give orders, "Back to the *Falcon*, lads. Captain Davis ain't finished yet!"

Grinning with satisfaction, the youngsters turned away heading back in the direction of the new printing shop. They noticed a soldier standing near the corner by the shop lighting his pipe. Seeing his amused expression, they followed his gaze.

It was a scene of confusion that lay before them as out on the cobbles and spreading into the street, stood all the office furniture—worktables, chairs and other sundry items—strewn all over the curb causing people to walk on the street. Cuthbert was cleaning windows from atop a wobbly ladder that was missing one rung while from the open doorway, clouds of black dust billowed forth in such profusion it was hard to see who was behind it. Then, as if answering their question, the sound of coughing and grumbling could be heard telling them it was Fred—he had arrived for work as ordered.

"Not quite the right time for a visit, dumplin!" Lizzie chuckled, moving forward, despite Quon's enthusiastic tugging on her sleeve.

Fred saw them outside watching and he stopped to mop his sweat-stained brow. "I've seen dust before," he complained loudly, showing his frustration, "but never in such a quantity!" Blowing a cobweb away from his face, his sweeping seemed to gain a new determined urgency as his broom sent litter and dust flying into the street.

"I think Cuthbert's going to have to redo that window," she laughed.

"We come back tomorrow," Quon coughed, pulling her away.

Chapter 19

Two days later, the young partners stood in the rain waving as Captain Thorn took his now-famous grain ship out into the fast running tide. His sailors were dropping the slack topsail balanced precariously like monkeys in the rigging.

"That's him gone for three weeks," said Charley to no one in particular before whistling for the Grim brothers.

Moving up Water Lane, Lizzie and Quon called at the tailor's shop, slowly opening the door when they heard familiar voices inside. There stood Ada and Martha talking to Clara while a sour-faced Abe worked at his table cutting cloth and mumbling about chattering women.

"Hello, doy!" Martha greeted them. "Av got yer new dresses, Lizzie, and some trousers for you too, Quon Lee!" she said, waving the package in the air.

"Did you pay for them?" Lizzie asked.

"No, I didn't."

"I will," Ada called from the back where Clara was measuring her. "I'm buying a new dress. Don't you tell Mick, I want to surprise him."

Turning to go, the youngsters came face to face with two brawny strangers who had quietly entered and now barred their exit.

"Lizzie Short!" one of the men rasped. "Mister Crowther wants a word with you ...now!

He reached out for the girl's arm but was roughly blocked by Quon Lee as he stepped between them. Abe and the women watched in stunned silence. Avoiding the second man's grasping hands Quon turned quickly and kicked one of the men in the shins.

"No touch my Wizzy," he hissed, though clenched teeth pushing his partner toward Martha who grabbed her protectively.

Resisting valiantly, Quon held them at bay until, outnumbering him, they flung him violently aside. Flying over a sewing table he landed with a thud at Ada's feet. Dazed, he shook his head and the women noticed a trickle of blood running down his face. He struggled to his knees, wild hatred on his face.

Lizzie's eyes darted about the room noticing a broom a few feet away. Inching backwards, her fingers found the handle as she saw one of the men coming at her from her left. Turning quickly, she took hold of it swinging as hard as she could and hit the man in the chest. Wincing loudly, he recovered and grabbed the broom from her as she was about to hit him again. Delivering a punch to her face, she screamed in pain as she went careening into one of Abe's displays.

Ada also screamed, causing Martha to go into action. Seeing a flashback of the exhilarating encounter she had with the pirates a few years ago in this same shop, Martha charged wildly toward the men.

"Martha!" screamed Ada, as Lizzie got dazedly to her feet.

However, the human battering ram had already gone into action heedless of anything in her path. Mannequins and bolts of cloth went flying in all directions as she ran toward the nearest ruffian. Seeing this determined vision careening toward them, the two men ran for the door.

"Lock the door!" Abe called from his hiding place.

"No! Find a gypsy, Quon," Lizzie called, but hearing footsteps again, she froze and a look of panic came onto her face. "Too late, are they coming back?"

"You all right, Miss Lizzie?" called Dan, as he and Wick entered.

"Did you see those men?" she called. "I want 'em!"

The door closed and the sound of running feet and whistles were heard. Ada and Clara hurried over to help Martha, but she was already cleaning up the mess she had created.

"Martha, you amaze me!" declared Ada, rolling her eyes.

"Oh dumplin! That was too close ... you should see your head," Lizzie exclaimed. "We were lucky you were here, Martha!"

"Ohh, my head hurts!" Quon exclaimed, gingerly touching a bloody spot on his crown then looking at his bloody finger. "Wizzy got black eye!" he cried, forgetting his own problem as he looked at her face. They began to giggle nervously at first then collapsed laughing into each other's arms.

Martha and Ada finished tidying up the mess while Clara made them all tea, encouraging Abe to come out of hiding and sit down. Concerned for the youngsters, Ada asked Clara where Mister Kratze kept his clean rags and soon had a cold compress ready for each of them.

Not much later, the sound of loud voices was heard outside and the door flew open again. Wick and Dan led the two ruffians into the shop where they stood silently, looking down at the floor. Their toughness gone they had already been warned by the gypsies that Miss Lizzie would have no mercy now that the tables were turned.

"Who sent yer?" she demanded, as hands on hips she stood glaring at them.

Two soldiers had also entered, curiosity getting the better of them after overhearing the gypsies' conversation about this person named Miss Lizzie. Nathan had spoken to them, informing them to stand by as they would be needed to remove the scoundrels when Miss Lizzie had completed her questioning. This they wanted to see.

"Tell me or dammit ah'll hang yer right now!" the girl was saying as they entered. "Bring me that rope, Quon!"

This demand brought a look of confusion and fear on the prisoners' faces but the soldiers couldn't imagine how she was going to accomplish the threat. However, within the next few minutes, the ruffians had willingly spilled their information and Lizzie, with a look of triumph, turned to the soldiers.

"We can take them now, miss," said the first soldier, snickering.

"They won't trouble you anymore, Miss Lizzie," said the other, still shaking his head in disbelief.

After the four men had departed, Clara went over to the girl. "Oh, Miss Lizzie," she declared, "you are a sight! Look at yer nice new dress. You've got it all dirty and there's a tear at the back. Stand still and I'll fix it for you right now while you drink your peppermint tea and let's cool those cloths down again for you."

"By gum, lass, I believe yer goin to have a mighty black eye, you are," clucked Martha, as Nathan walked in.

"Thank goodness you were nearby, Mister Goldman," said Lizzie, trying to see him through the swelling.

"I had some business to attend to," he replied, concern on his face. "I have orders for Abraham. I needed to fix my commission."

"Money grabber!" Lizzie hissed. "He's your cousin, don't you ever do anything for free, Mister Goldman?"

The tailor grinned. He had taught Lizzie well and it particularly pleased him when she used her skills to his benefit.

"A man has to earn a living," pouted Nathan.

"You really don't understand women, do you Mister Goldman?" Lizzie sighed. "If you do the ladies a service their husbands will be most grateful and look on you with favour when they write up your orders. If I were you, Mister Kratze," she smiled coyly, "I'd tell him to go elsewhere with his orders."

Shuffling uneasily, Abe glared at his cousin. "No commission, cousin," he whispered nervously, glancing at his advisor.

"Blast you, Lizzie Short," the trader whined. "Once again you've cost me a commission."

Quon reached for his partner's elbow, his fingers hidden as he tapped out a message on her arm. Glancing over her shoulder, she winked impishly at him before addressing Nathan again.

"Have you sold all the surplus grain from the *Queen*?"

"Indeed, yes, yes!" he replied, excitedly, thinking of his commissions. "There is a shortage in London, young lady."

Lizzie walked to the door and reached for the door latch.

Suddenly realizing where the girl had led him, he tried to hide his nervous chuckle. "I know, I know," he moaned.

Lizzie winked at the embarrassed trader and stepped outside. The door closed and Nathan handed the orders to Abe.

"Beaten again, cousin!" the tailor sorely reminded him.

"You're both devoted to that girl, aren't you?" Clara whispered to the women as she took Ada's payment for the new clothes.

"Aye, we are lass," Martha chuckled. "She's a ray of sunshine is our Lizzie."

"But there's much more to that girl than what you have seen today," added Ada. "We know men who would follow her to hell and back without blinking an eye." She paused for her words to sink in. "And she's quite a business woman, too. Our Lizzie owns a big piece of this part of dockland," she exaggerated and, motioning to Martha, they left without a backward glance.

Up the street, Lizzie and Quon were surprised when Nathan's buggy pulled into the curb beside them.

"Gabriel's not back yet," Nathan announced, leaning from the window. "Shall I act for you at the government auction?"

"That won't be necessary."

"But it's only two days away and we should be making plans." Receiving only a nod in reply, he tapped his cane in frustration and urged his driver to move on.

Nearing the cottage, Lizzie and Quon watched as a bareback rider came galloping down Drovers Lane toward them. Reining in the horse just ahead of them, he called, "Miss Lizzie, Jeb says to tell yer, yer leavin on Monday mornin. Oh my!" he exclaimed, noticing the girl's black eye, but he turned his horse and rode off.

Quon's arms were moving like two windmills in a gale, he was so excited. At last they were going to see the children.

Turning into the rag yard, they could hear Willie's happy squeals. Looking around, they saw a stableman wheeling a straw-filled wheelbarrow in which young Willie sat hanging on for dear life. They came across the yard and he gently tipped Willie out at Mick's feet. Turning the child around, Mick pointed out the figures waving from the gate. Willie wriggled out of his arms and raced toward them.

"WE'LL TAKE HIM HOME," called Lizzie, gathering the boy into her arms and trying to hide her eye under her hair.

Leaving quickly to avoid any questions, they retraced their steps into the lane with Willie bouncing along between them, holding tightly to their hands. She felt the boy's tiny fingers, sending a surge of longing coursing through her.

It seemed so long ago since they had spirited those children away, fiercely protecting them behind a curtain of secrecy. As tortured thoughts of that night raged through her mind, Lizzie clutched Willie's hand and held back her tears.

Seeing her distress, Quon led her to the grassy bank where she sat holding Willie, rocking him gently. But the lad wanted to play and squirmed out of her arms. She wiped her eyes and tried to smile, realizing she was worrying Willie. Coming to her feet, she grasped the boy's hand.

"Let's go see what Martha is making for dinner, young Willie!"

That night Lizzie's black eye was the centre of attention as Ada and Martha described their afternoon's excitement in graphic detail. Angus had brought John Watson along at Joe's invitation and they sat without comment, fearing an outburst from Mick as his fingers drummed the tabletop with agitated energy.

"Ah feared this would happen, lass," Joe growled. "You've upset a lot of dockland folk over the past few years."

"It's time we gave *her* a gypsy bodyguard," said Mick, thumping the table with his hand.

"No, you won't," she retorted. "We're leaving on Monday!"

The words obviously came as a surprise to everyone as they looked from one to the other. Joe's head swung in her direction almost dropping his pipe. Quon began to tap urgently on the table.

"Leavin?" asked Mick. "Where yer off to m'darlin?"

"Yes, yes, I'm going to tell them," she assured her partner, rolling her eyes. "We're going to the farm to see the children."

"Yes, we've been expecting that to happen," Ada sighed. "It's been a long time, love. They'll be so pleased to see you again."

John looked over at Angus and the Scotsman cleared his throat. "Weel lassie, if we could give ourr rreport noow, we'll just be headin back tae the brrewery," Angus announced. "We have some work to finish beforre this evening is over." Receiving a nod from both Joe and the girl, they complimented Charley on his new invention. Then they quickly reported on their progress with the new warehouses and, murmuring their thanks to Martha, said goodnight to the others.

"I've had a chance to look over the Crowther vessel," said Charley, changing the subject as the door closed. "It needs some amount of work," he said. "She's leaking from her planking, but we can fix it, lass, without a lot of expense."

With business out of the way the mood relaxed and Charley and Mick ended the evening by exchanging some comical stories.

"How long will you be gone, Lizzie?" Ada asked, putting on her coat and going to pick up her sleeping son from Joe's lap.

"Three weeks or a bit longer; you can manage can't you?"

"Yes, love," Ada sighed, "but we'll be glad when you're back."

At the Johnson bakery the next day, they caught up with Olivera just before he left the yard with his loaded pony cart. He looked a bit forlorn when he told them Captain Davis had been called back to the *Falcon*. He looked at Lizzie curiously and she knew he wanted to ask about her eye, but he clucked at his pony and continued on his way.

"Did yon lad tell yer his news, didn't seem to know w'ther it be happy or sad," said the big Yorkshireman, wiping his hands. He picked up a still-hot pie and came over to join them. He was obviously excited and looked like he had something to say, but the sight of Lizzie's swollen black eye, now grabbed his attention. "It's true isn't it, an ah thought it were a rumour!"

"Cut the pie, Bill," Lizzie urged, "and stop yer moanin."

"They've arrested Crowther yer know," Bill muttered, cutting the pie into quarters. "Ther'll be a court case 'an them magistrates don't give a damn abart us workin folks."

"Stop worrying, old friend. We'll face it when we have to."

A noise at the gate brought a swift end to their conversation.

"MISS LIZZIE," panted the young gypsy, running up to her. "Jeb says to tell yer Mister Flood is waitin for yer at Sutton House."

"He's back!" Lizzie exclaimed, sending a shower of pie crumbs across the table.

Ducking through the last of the fences, the beautiful green expanse of almost flat common land now stretched out before them. They stopped briefly to eat the sandwich Martha had packed for them and then continued on their way toward the Sutton's. It wasn't long before they could see the smoke from theirs and neighbouring chimneys, swirling upward in the turbulent air.

Popping up from nowhere, a gypsy patrolling the grounds grinned as he murmured a greeting. Opening the garden gate for the twosome, he sent a shrill whistle of warning to the others.

The butler, alerted of the arriving visitors, came quickly to the door showing them into the lounge where Lady Sutton, Margaret and Gabriel were waiting. Beaming a welcome, Gabriel leapt to his feet. Lizzie noticed he was looking very haggard from his long and hurried journey. His glance strayed to her black eye but she ignored it.

"Were you successful?" she asked, eagerly. "Did you get it?"

"I did ... all fifty thousand of it!"

"We were getting worried you wouldn't get back in time," exclaimed Lizzie. "The auction is tomorrow you know."

"To be truthful, I was also," he said quietly, looking askance at her eye again.

Although she knew they were almost more curious about her black eye than the auction, she still offered no explanation. Ignoring the subject of the money, she began to lay out her plans.

Gabriel already knew from their previous conversation that he would be bidding on behalf of Lady Sutton, so he listened carefully to his final instructions.

Margaret, fidgeting with excitement, suddenly giggled. "Isn't this exciting, Mother?"

Lady Sutton's withering glance stopped her further chatter as Lizzie smiled patiently, waiting to continue. Her voice quickened in the now quiet room as she detailed Nathan's role telling them he would be merely acting as a distraction. He would be representing TLS, as would be expected, but his bids would be low to give the impression of disinterest.

"But how will that help?" asked Lady Sutton.

"Because they will think you are a fool, madam!" Lizzie smiled ruefully at the look of surprise on the high-born lady's face. "Especially when Gabriel continues to bid."

"They won't fall for that ruse," Gabriel whispered, his voice barely audible.

"Oh yes, they will," Lizzie assured him. "These are powerful men but they are not used to dealing with the mind of a woman in business!"

"She's right," agreed Lady Sutton, "but to make the picture complete, we must be very conspicuous, Gabriel. You will dress in your best foppish frills and I shall wear my most outlandish feathers!" She chuckled at her mind's picture. "Indeed, you can rest assured I will make every effort to be noticed."

Confirming the time and place of the auction, Lizzie appeared to be getting ready to leave.

"Don't you want to know about the money?" asked Gabriel.

Fascinated by their strange conversations, Margaret watched as Quon's hands spoke to his partner.

"What did he say?" she asked.

"He says I'm to tell you about the printer's shop we bought last week."

"You found a print shop?" Gabriel asked in surprise. "Where?"

"In dockland. It will take much work to learn the business and make it pay but Fred Monk is familiar with the press and will be an eager teacher." She looked over at the banker's son. "Now tell me about the money ... or shall I tell you?"

Lady Sutton was barely able to stifle the gasp that rose in her throat.

Gabriel's mouth dropped open. "Tell me," he said, quickly closing his mouth, hoping Lizzie hadn't noticed.

"You were greeted with suspicion weren't you?" she began. "That's why I sent you, the banker's son. I told you they wouldn't trust a woman but they couldn't throw you out very easily, now could they!" she laughed. "Quite probably, your mother came to your assistance."

Lady Sutton saw Gabriel's startled expression and began to laugh. He had already told them the whole story before Lizzie and Quon had arrived. Lizzie had merely proven just how accurate her intuition could be.

Grasping Lizzie's elbow, Quon indicated it was time to go.

"We'll show you the print shop after the auction," she said, as Quon pulled her toward the door.

Watching them leave from the window, Margaret turned to her mother. "Are you really going to make a spectacle of yourself at the auction?"

"Dearest daughter, that young woman is going to be our salvation. She's a born leader and a clever thinker who's unafraid to share her trust. My answer is yes, love. I shall follow her orders exactly." Slipping an arm around her daughter's slim waist, together they turned to face Gabriel who sat back in his chair staring at the ceiling.

Lady Sutton stood for a moment watching the captain of the Lancers. "Gabriel Flood?" she exclaimed loudly, trying to sound like a commanding officer. "Will you follow Lizzie Short?"

Jerked from his deep thoughts, Gabriel leapt respectfully to his feet. "You're darned right I will, madam," he boomed, trying not to smile. "I shall resign my commission in the army and follow the only general I trust, Lizzie Short!"

The door suddenly burst open and the butler raced into the room. "You need me, m'lady?" he asked, his face flushed with alarm as his eyes swept the room for some problem.

"No Jasper, everything is all right. Go away. I'm a woman released from bondage having a moment of joy!"

As Lizzie and Quon walked into the gypsy camp on their way

home from the Sutton's, their coming was well announced by the yapping dogs. Sitting at the fire Jeb saw them first, his dark eyes flashing under the wide brim of his hat. He said something in Romany to the woman attending the fire, and she scurried away. He indicated several empty seats and they joined him enjoying the warmth of the fire.

"We leave on Monday for the farm, Liz," he said and they both nodded, looking at each other as a big grin lit up their faces.

Just then the woman returned, carrying a bundle in her arms. they heard a whimpering sound and Jeb pointed at Lizzie.

"Take him, lass, that's your godson," he urged.

Gently cradling the child in her arms, Quon wonderingly eased back the covers. Blinking, the tiny form stared up at the strange faces.

"He's beautiful!" Lizzie gasped, settling slowly onto her knees in the grass.

Quon's hands began to move but when Lizzie noticed, she stopped him. "Say it out loud, Quon, he needs to hear you say it."

"You my godson, too, little baby!" he said, softly. "Quon Lee always your friend."

Jeb smiled. "Yer talking almost as good as a gypsy, Quon!"

Lizzie rocked the tiny bundle, humming softly until it let out a sharp cry. She kissed it on the forehead and handed it back to the old woman. "I think he's hungry!"

Walking back to the cottage in silence, Lizzie's mind turned to the auction and Nathan. A smile crossed her face when she thought of Lady Sutton in feathers and Gabriel dressed like a dandy. She had confidence in the trader—he was a born actor and would play his part well. *We'll find him in the morning to give him his instructions.*

A long shrill whistle from Goat Hill solved the problem as the trader's buggy appeared. Inside sat Joe with Nathan.

"I found your dad walking home," said the trader. "We need to talk about the auction, my girl."

"Come inside," Joe invited him, as the youngsters took his arms and guided him up the garden path.

"I don't have the time," he replied, impatiently.

"Then make time!" Lizzie purred, watching the trader out of the corner of her eye.

191

Reluctantly, he banged his cane on the carriage door and Wick jumped to the ground again and opened the door. Nathan stepped out and followed them into the house. Lizzie looked back and caught Wick's salute.

Joe went straight to his chair and Quon followed, dropping on his knees in front of him. With the help of little Willie, they removed Joe's heavy boots.

Pouting, the trader took a seat, grumbling quietly about the time he was wasting. "I shall simply outbid them at the auction," he stated, as Lizzie hung her coat up behind the door.

"Nathan, sit down!" Lizzie's voice cut through the chatter like a knife. Ada and Mick, just coming through the door, stopped in mid-stride.

"Misbehavin again, lad!" Mick taunted.

Ada's eyebrows raised but she remained silent. Slipping her coat off she picked up her son giving him a big noisy kiss.

"*You* won't buy anything!" said Lizzie, fiercely. "Lady Sutton and Gabriel will be buying the ship ...."

"No, no that won't do! You distinctly said at the Sutton's last week ...."

"I know what I said, I said you were the brains of the operation, and you are ... if you'll only listen!"

The cottage had grown silent except for Ada's 'sh-sh's' to Willie who was trying to tell her something. Every eye in the room rested on Nathan who was now quite red-faced.

"Your role is the most important one in this charade, Nathan," Lizzie began, speaking in a soothing tone. "Lady Sutton and Gabriel will be playing the role of fools with more money than brains. I don't want you to be surprised by anything they do!" Dropping her voice, she added, "Do your job well, my friend, and Gabriel will be able to buy the ship for a mere pittance!"

"But, but these will all be knowledgeable buyers," he reminded her.

"You've a reputation for inside information, Mister Goldman. Take advantage of that reputation and help me make fools out of the lot of them!"

Ada chuckled silently to herself. She watched as Nathan excitedly began tapping his cane on the floor then, muttering to himself, he turned for the door. He knew Lizzie's unusually simple logic could very well succeed … it had before and he had an idea.

Next morning, they joined Abe on his doorstep.

"Two of your ships left this morning m'dear," he announced, but his eyes suddenly swung past them.

"Inside young man, it's breakfast time!" Clara snapped with unfamiliar harshness.

Abe reacted immediately, shuffling off inside the store muttering away to himself as the dressmaker strode past them.

"I took a lesson from you, luv," she whispered. "You've got to be firm with the men!"

"Don't forget to be gentle, too, Missus Spencer," Lizzie grinned. "We love that old man."

Chapter 20

Quon's hands made it plain he wanted to visit the printer's shop, adding he would also like a piece of pie.

"No time for pie!" admonished Lizzie. "Print shop first, then it's to the auction."

As they walked along Chandler, they heard a loud crash and cursing as two large drays became wedged together as they tried to pass in the narrowest of spaces. Horses screamed as they tried unsuccessfully to pull immovable objects and a crowd was quickly gathering.

Bypassing the commotion, they slipped down an alleyway, emerging near the print shop. The open door gave them an opportunity to see inside before they were seen by Cuthbert or Fred. They noticed a new sign in the sparkling clean window. It read: PRINTING DONE TO ORDER.

"Looks like Fred's made some headway."

Moving cautiously forward, they could see the floor was clean though still stained with big, black splodges of ink. The walls, once dark with grime, had been white-washed and the shelves painted and filled with new supplies. In the middle of the floor stood the printing press.

"Gosh what a difference!" she whispered.

"Come in," Fred called. "I seen yer."

Cuthbert twitched with embarrassment.

"We already did one job," Fred told them excitedly, "though he said TLS would pay for it. It was Mister Goldman. I recognized him from up at the office. I hope we did right, miss."

"The little devil," Lizzie laughed. "Yes, you did right. What was the order for, Fred?"

"A large sign. I did it by hand, Miss Lizzie."

"What did it say?"

"It said: WOOD ROT INSPECTORS. He said he wanted it for a handcart."

Quon's arms went wild but Lizzie merely shrugged her shoulders.

"Tell them about that Portuguese lad," Cuthbert cackled, "the little one with the pony cart."

"Oh aye," Fred muttered thoughtfully, "that's Oly; we used to have that pony in the rag yard."

"What did he want?"

"Two signs and a hundred handouts advertising a bake shop, a butcher and a candle maker."

The partners exchanged glances.

"Did you make them yet?" Lizzie asked, eagerly.

"No," he sighed. "They're only youngsters and I didn't think they'd have any money."

"Make 'em!" she ordered. "Those bread lads are important to you."

Fred scratched his head.

Feeling Quon grip her elbow, she explained, "They're your contact between Ada and Mick at our office, Charley at the docks and our dad at the brewery," she said rather fiercely. "They're the eyes and ears of dockland!"

Surprised by the girl's outburst, Fred was rendered speechless and the youngsters disappeared out the door.

"Cuthbert, my friend," said Fred. "We're printers and we don't know a darned thing about business." Scratching his head, he moved back to his bench. "You make those handouts and I'll do the signs for the lads."

Lizzie and Quon hurried on toward the government dock knowing the auction was to begin shortly. They were only a few minutes away when Nathan's buggy pulled up beside them. Wick leapt down to open the door.

"Come," said the trader, smiling craftily. "We should be seen arriving together."

Many heads turned as the grey, came trotting along the dock past the large group of ship owners and company representatives waiting near the Crowther vessel.

"Stay close to me now," Nathan whispered, tapping his driver to stop. Climbing out of the buggy, they set off down the cobblestone dock. Looking very businesslike, Nathan nodded to his competitors and they marched through the top-hatted group.

"There," he said quietly, pointed his cane at a handcart loaded with peculiar equipment. "That's where we are going."

Quon's hand grabbed Lizzie's wrist, his fingers talking silently as his eyes fastened on the sign above the handcart.

"Hush dumplin, I can see it."

There on the cart, manned by four dirty-looking workmen, was the sign Fred had made. The numerous, well-dressed buyers stared as the trader made his way toward the handcart. Removing his flat cap, one of the workmen from the cart stepped out to meet him. After a brief, whispered conversation, money changed hands and the handcart trundled away through the crowd.

A buzz of excitement ran through the people gathered on the dock as fingers first pointed at the disappearing cart, and then at the trader. Lizzie and Quon had a hard time controlling their amusement.

"Listen to them," Nathan whispered. "That should set them thinking."

"Well, Goldman," one of the owners said, coming closer and scowling at the trader. "Is the vessel sound?"

"TLS won't be bidding, Sir Basil," Nathan growled. "We don't need to buy trouble."

Turning away, the ship owner rubbed his bearded chin and returned to his friends. They carried on a whispered discussion as others strained to hear the conversation. In no time, the rumour had quickly spread through the crowd.

Strutting along the dock, Nathan stopped to look at the Crowther vessel, very sure every eye in the crowd was upon him as he slowly shook his head.

What a performance, thought Lizzie, stifling a giggle.

Working their way to the back of the crowd, they climbed up onto a stack of bales for a better view and were just in time to see the Sutton carriage arrive.

A sudden silence settled over the buyers as Gabriel emerged from the carriage dressed in frills and tight breeches. Sniggering openly, the businessmen watched as Lady Sutton and then her daughter, also stepped onto the dock, looking ridiculously foolish for a ship auction in feathered hats, outrageously fancy dresses and frilled parasols.

The sour-faced auctioneer climbed up to his podium shaking his head in disbelief. He banged his gavel to begin the proceedings.

Describing the vessel in outrageously glowing terms, he glowered over the buyers, looking down at Lady Sutton.

"Are you a buyer, madam?" he asked harshly.

"Yes we are, sir, but we ask that you allow us to bid from the deck of the ship," Lady Sutton called out loudly, waving her garishly decorated parasol flamboyantly in the direction of the vessel.

"She's a fool!" Lizzie and Quon heard a voice nearby snicker.

Lizzie's eyes swept the scene taking in every detail. The ruse was working and Lady Sutton's intrusion was now turning the auction into a shambles.

First banging his gavel and then berating the crowd for their inattention, the auctioneer's voice thundered over the dockside. In a voice filled with frustration, he asked for a bid on the Crowther vessel.

"TEN THOUSAND GUINEAS I BID FOR THE HONORABLE LADY SUTTON," Gabriel's voice called from the deck of the ship.

Repeating the amount once ... then twice, the auctioneer searched the crowd for more bids ... his frustration becoming more and more obvious. Suddenly a buyer's cane waved and a voice yelled, "FIFTEEN THOUSAND."

"SIXTEEN," came Gabriel's immediate reply.

The auctioneer looked back at the second bidder, but the man cast his eyes on the ground.

After shouting himself hoarse, the auctioneer threatened to call the whole thing off if more bids were not forthcoming.

"OH NO, YOU WON'T, MY GOOD MAN!" Lady Sutton shouted. "THE LAW SAYS THREE BIDS MAKE IT A LEGAL AUCTION, SIR. SO BANG YOUR HAMMER, THAT SHIP IS MINE!"

Lizzie and Quon chuckled to themselves as they watched the mood of the crowd change, apparently taking an evil delight in watching a foolish old woman make such a disastrous purchase.

"Bang the hammer, bang the hammer!" they chanted, laughing at the auctioneer's discomfort.

Throwing up his arms in tormented frustration and his voice drowned out by the chanting, the auctioneer banged his gavel three times and pointed at Lady Sutton.

Slipping down from their vantage point, Lizzie and Quon

wandered through the crowd listening to snippets of conversation.

"I kept a close watch on that devilish sneaky Nathan Goldman," one buyer growled haughtily at his companions. "He certainly wasn't going to bid on that damned leaking hulk. Serves Lady Sutton right, she should have asked one of us for help. We're much more knowledgeable about these matters than she."

"We fooled them again, dumplin," Lizzie whispered to Quon as they watched Nathan strut along the dock, cane twirling happily as he beamed at Gabriel and the Suttons.

"Go pay the auctioneer, boy," he ordered Gabriel curtly. "And you, my dear," he continued, turning to Lizzie who had joined them, "owe me a shilling. That's what the men and the handcart cost me."

"Boy!" Gabriel mumbled under his breath. As he walked over to the auctioneer's carriage, he strained to keep his temper in check.

Reaching into her pocket Lizzie jingled some coins, pulling out a shilling and a penny.

"Here you are," she sighed, dropping the coins into his outstretched hand. "No doubt you'll want a profit."

The effect on the trader was dramatic as his face turned red and he stammered for words. "B-b-but Miss Lizzie," he pleaded. "I'm just naturally exuberant."

"You are just naturally an ass, Mister Goldman," the girl snapped. "Now go tell Charley to get this vessel around to our dock."

Farther up the jetty, a group of buyers watched the Suttons conferring with the young people and the trader.

"Hey, Goldman!" one of them called out as the trader walked toward them. "That foolish old woman doesn't need your services, and who's that pretty young lady with them?"

By now Nathan's pride had suffered enough. He walked up to the group of men, his eyes cold and hard. Pointing his walking stick under their noses and with a shaking voice, he retorted, "You stupid idiots! That's not a foolish old lady, that's Lady Sutton and her daughter," he snarled. "And that pretty young lady ...," he paused, grinning wickedly at his competition, "is Lizzie Short the most lethal woman you'll ever meet, gentlemen. I warn you, you would do best not to get on the wrong side of that one!" With regained composure he strutted toward his waiting carriage.

"Everything is legal," Gabriel chuckled, peering around as he returned to Lady Sutton and the others. "Where is that little turd?"

Quon pointed up the dock.

"He'll regret talking to me that way," he fumed.

"Oh leave it, Gabriel, it's not worth getting agitated about, my dear," said Lady Sutton. "He means well."

Rolling her eyes, Lizzie nodded in agreement, then led the way toward their carriage. Suddenly, a man stepped out from the group of buyers, barring their way.

"So, you are Lizzie Short are you?" he asked, belligerently.

Quon leapt forward startling the man who staggered backwards in surprise, bumping into his friends and raising his cane aggressively. Gabriel blinked at Quon's speed as the young man snatched the cane out of the man's hand.

"No, dumplin," Lizzie whispered in warning.

As if frozen in time, Quon suddenly stopped walking but his eyes burned with obvious hatred at the group of men.

"Dammit woman," one of the men snarled. "Who are you?"

Clucking her tongue, Lady Sutton moved forward jabbing at the group with her parasol.

"Mother!" Margaret gasped.

Lizzie glanced over at Quon. She winked at him as her fingers touched her shoulder sending a silent message for him to return to her side.

"Indeed, who is she ...you dare to ask?" Lady Sutton cried. Then in a totally controlled voice, she continued. "Why sir, this young woman is your worst nightmare come true, the ghost of all your tomorrows ... she's a woman with a brain!"

Shrinking away, the would-be buyers hurriedly left the dock muttering amongst themselves and glancing back at the obviously mad, parasol-waving woman.

Even before the men had left the area, Gabriel was climbing into the carriage, quickly closing the door and pulling down the blinds.

"Now what's he up to?" Lizzie asked, turning to Margaret.

"Changing from those silly clothes," she laughed. "He loathes them and its got so warm today he must be suffocating!"

As soon as he emerged, dressed more comfortably and looking quite relieved, Lady Sutton took her turn in the makeshift changing room. Discarding her feathers, she slipped into a plain black dress as her mind re-created the auction sending ripples of laughter through her body. The thrill of winning had been an enormously gratifying experience, thanks to Lizzie's plan. Once she had stashed her cast-off clothes in their box, she opened the door.

"There! That's much better, but I admit it was certainly worth the effort ... and the fun!" she giggled.

Standing beside the carriage, Lizzie quietly instructed the driver to take them to the printer's shop.

"That handcart was a brilliant piece of deception," said Gabriel as the Sutton carriage took them through the heavy traffic.

"Don't give me the credit for that," Lizzie admitted. "Nathan thought that up himself."

"Do people really live in this godforsaken place?" Margaret asked with a sigh, gazing out at the smoke-blackened buildings and shabbily dressed people.

"Yes, they do," Lizzie replied reprovingly, as the carriage turned up one of the backstreets and bounced along the uneven cobblestones. "These are my people."

The printers looked up from their work when the three well-dressed strangers entered the shop. Moving to the counter, Fred turned to Gabriel. "Yes sir, is there something we can do for you?"

Lizzie and Quon followed them in.

"Fred, we'd like you to meet your new boss, Lady Sutton," Lizzie began, noting the slight raising of his eyebrows before he smiled at the older of the two women. "And this is her daughter, Margaret, who will be assisting. The gentleman is their friend, Mister Flood.

"Pleasure, madam, he said respectfully, nodding to the others and holding up his ink-stained hands. "Forgive me for not shaking your hands but printing is dirty work."

"No need to explain, young man. Now, will you please show me around," she asked, moving toward the office area.

Lizzie and Quon looked at each other and grinned, standing back as the women moved about the room. Fred found himself answering a barrage of questions that Lady Sutton threw at him. Margaret looked around poking delicately at trays of typesetting material, removing her gloves, she carefully folded them and put them away in her little purse. Gabriel's eyes lit up when Fred moved to the printing press and explained how it worked.

"Quon and I have to leave now," Lizzie interrupted. "I know you'll be will be able to make this into a successful business, Lady Sutton, especially if you grow to enjoy it."

Determination showed on the highborn lady's face as she turned to her benefactors.

"With Fred's help, we certainly shall," she grinned. "Look, here comes a customer now."

Exiting quickly, Quon held the door for a timid young man who was waiting to enter.

"Do you print letterheads?" they heard him ask.

"Of course we do, my boy. Step inside ... step inside," came Lady Sutton's firm reply.

Quon grinned. "They do awight, Wizzy."

"Yes, I think they will, dumplin."

Just then the air began to vibrate with the sudden sound of rolling thunder. Gabriel's horses pawed the ground, as they whinnied in alarm, but Gabriel quickly appeared and soon had the matter in hand. He waved to the youngsters as they ran off trying to escape the large raindrops that had begun to fall.

Lightning cracked overhead as they hurried up Pump Street to Slaughter Lane. By the time they arrived at the cottage they were dripping wet.

"Is dad home yet?" Lizzie called to Martha from the doorway, as they began to remove their shoes and coats.

"Not yet, luv. Look at you two bedraggled souls!" she exclaimed. "Your dad is goin ta get wet tonight. Get those wet clothes off and dry off in front of the fire."

"Not yet, mum. Get the oilskin," she said to Quon, sending him back outside and racing for the garden shed.

When he returned, she joined him outside and pulling the waterproof cover over their heads they set out to meet Joe. Halfway down Goat Hill, they spotted him contentedly puffing on his pipe while sheltering in a doorway.

"Came to rescue yer old dad, did yer young'uns!" he exclaimed, pleased to see them as they got him under the oilskin with them. "At least I wouldn't have frozen today."

"But you might dwown, Glanpop," retorted Quon, causing them

all to laugh. They huddled together as they walked slowly up the road, stepping carefully over the river of water that had begun to flow down the hill.

All weekend it poured turning the slaughterhouse roads into a mud bath and sending a torrent of water rushing down the open street gutters toward the river. Mick organized dray-loads of sand and rock, struggling to keep the well-used lane passable using whatever labour he could find.

Soaking wet, almost before they left the cottage, Lizzie and Quon called at the bake shop and marveled at the boys' ingenuity with their oilskin canopy which stretched out beyond the shop front to keep their customers dry. Even Olivera's pony cart had a waterproof covering.

"They think good," Quon chuckled, as they jumped over the puddles.

Staring mournfully at the sky, Sid Sweeney greeted them with a wave from the doorway of his butcher shop. He stepped back to allow them to enter.

"Bloody weather," he grumbled, glancing over at his neighbour's makeshift shelter. "That Billy's a darned smart kid. Do you know what he told me last week?"

Lizzie's senses became instantly alert.

"He said we should advertise and get more customers. Maybe he's right. He said he would arrange it fer a small fee."

The handout is at the printer, said Quon's fingers on her shoulder.

"Are you going to do it?" Lizzie asked, cocking her head coyly.

"Fer sixpence a hundred, aye lass, I'm goin to try it."

"Billy wants to talk to yer, Miss Lizzie," shouted Tom, limping past the doorway.

Lizzie and Quon moved back outside. Their eyes met as they followed Tom over to the bake shop, watching his every movement.

"Your leg hurting again, Tom?" she asked.

"It's the rain, miss. Makes it ache somethin fierce."

Exchanging glances, they silently resolved to send Tom some of their special ointment.

Billy was serving a customer when they entered, an older woman who adjusted her hat and seemed to be enjoying his chatter, not wanting to venture back out in the rain. She listened intently when he told her of Sidney Sweeney's quality meat shop and of the couple who made candles at the shop on the other side.

It quickly became evident to Lizzie that this young lad had the silver tongue of a true salesman. He was brighter than most and had already realized that by promoting the shops around him, more customers would land in his own store.

Dallying no longer, the lady gathered up her parcels and went outside looking strangely at Quon who held the door open for her.

"You wanted me, Billy?" asked Lizzie.

"Ah need yer elp, miss," the young salesman pleaded. Receiving a raised eyebrow from the girl, released a torrent of words explaining his idea of producing an advertising handout for the stores.

"Slow down, Billy. I'm listening."

"Won't cost us nothin," he assured her eagerly. "Printing cost is paid by the butcher and the candle maker. We do the distribution."

"So why don't you do it?"

"Printer won't take me order."

At that moment, the door opened and a well-dressed woman entered the store. Shaking the water from the hood of her cape she pushed it back and turned to face them.

"Margaret!"

"Lizzie!" Margaret exclaimed, extracting a package wrapped in brown paper from under her cape. Setting it on the counter, she pulled back the folds to reveal a stack of printed sheets. She handed one to Billy. "Hello, Liz," she giggled, turning to face her. "I didn't expect to find you here."

"Let me see one of those," asked Lizzie, ignoring her friend's comment.

Taking one of the printed sheets, Lizzie and Quon's eyes flashed over the text. Quon's brow furrowed as his fingers began drumming out his thoughts on the counter.

Yes, I can see it," she said.

"See what?" Margaret whispered in alarm.

"We see that you've added TLS Shipping Company and included your own name at the bottom. I like the name you came up with."

"Yes, *The Print Shop*, that was mother's idea."

Lizzie's eyes narrowed and she glanced at Quon with a faraway look in her eyes. She was thinking of the conversation they had had only minutes before. Smiling, she now knew that her instincts had been right ... this was the way of the future.

"It's a superb idea," she whispered, and then introducing Margaret to Billy, she continued. "You'd be wise to talk to young Billy, Margaret, he's full of ideas."

Leaving Billy and Margaret talking enthusiastically across the counter, Lizzie and Quon said their goodbyes and set off into the rain. As they went up the street, they jumped into doorways for protection whenever possible, at the same time discussing their trip to the farm the next day. By the time they arrived at the gypsy camp they were soaking wet again but the rain had finally stopped.

The dogs barked from their dry beds under the covered wagons and a fiddler played lively songs for the children under the shelter by the unlit fire.

"Change out of those wet clothes," Jeb ordered gruffly, as they stepped under the canopy. "I ain't takin no sickly passengers!"

"We're going home anyway," Lizzie retorted.

"The rain's stopped, you change now," Jeb commanded. "You'll be travelling as gypsies tomorrow."

Led away to different tents, they quickly removed wet clothes and were helped into gypsy attire. Arriving back at the fire, carrying their bundles of wet clothes, they stared at each other.

"You look different, dumplin," Lizzie chuckled.

"You too, Wizzy ... we are twins!" he laughed, seeing his idol dressed as a gypsy boy.

"Go home and have a good sleep. We leave at seven in the morning," said Jeb.

All eyes swung to the door, staring in disbelief at the strangely attired pair.

"Ready for your journey, I venture," surmised Ada. Feeling some of the turmoil coursing through Lizzie's mind, she reached for her husband's hand.

Mick watched his wife in silence as she gazed at the former street waif and felt the same deep sense of loyalty and admiration for the girl. He gently squeezed his wife's hand before Martha moved in between them placing steaming bowls of food on the table.

Only intermittent conversation passed between them as they ate that evening, with apparently no pressing business issues on their minds. No one seemed to want to discuss Lizzie and Quon's trip and only furtive glances were exchanged between the older folk until the plates were cleared.

Charlie eased the silence by giving them all an overview of the dock operation, grinning when he announced that the Crowther vessel would soon be shipping grain ... all it needed was a little caulking and paint.

"I shall miss you, love," he whispered, giving Lizzie a quick hug before leaving with the Grim boys, "go and have a nice holiday."

Mick helped Ada with her coat, shook Quon's hand and gave Lizzie an affectionate hug. Ada gave Lizzie a hug and a peck on the cheek, extracting Willie who had wriggled away from his father and now clung fiercely to the girl's neck.

"My Wizzy, my Wizzy," he giggled as his mother took him in her arms, and they left hurriedly.

Soon afterwards, Quon began to yawn and announced he was going to bed.

"We'd better get packed first, dumplin. There won't be time in the morning," reminded Lizzie as she helped Martha finish the dishes.

"I packed yer trunks this afternoon an sent 'em up to the gypsy camp," announced the housekeeper.

"Oh, that's great, thanks Martha," said Lizzie stifling her own yawn. She gave Quon a quick hug and moved toward the fire. "I'll just sit with dad for a few minutes then I'm off to bed, too."

Removing his pipe and setting it on the hearth, Joe opened his arms and Lizzie slipped onto the old man's knee. Folding his arms tightly around her, he kissed her forehead and closed his eyes.

Chapter 21

The sunrise was just beginning to filter across the cottage garden as the youngsters said hurried goodbyes to Joe and Martha and departed for the gypsy camp. Jeb was directing last-minute preparations. Ten minutes later, the cavalcade of four wagons and six horsemen moved onto the rutted track leading north.

With their driver pointing out nearby villages, they passed the hamlet of Church End later in the afternoon and, at mid-day, stopped only long enough to give the horses a drink at the river and eat a quick meal of fresh baked bread and goat's cheese. Continuing until dark, they were well past Hadley Wood when the wagons finally pulled off into what appeared to be a well-used campground on the edge of Waltham Forest. A quickly built fire soon burst into life casting eerie shadows into the never-ending darkness.

Stretching their cramped legs, they attempted to make themselves useful searching for dry branches in the dim light. The men, looking quite adept at the task, suspended a cauldron over the fire and a meal was made ready.

The day had been one of new discoveries, as each trip tended to be for these young people who were so eager to learn. This time it was the newness of spring that intrigued them, and the hundreds of baby animals in pastures everywhere they went. Passing endless farmlands, orchards and old buildings, they listened enthusiastically to their guide who told them of the history and landmarks of the area, often catching glimpses of great houses and churches in the distance. Several coaches thundered past taking passengers to or from London and beyond.

After dinner, although they were terribly tired, sleep didn't come easy to the young city dwellers. Comfortably accommodated inside their wagon, the sounds of animals and men's voices kept them awake and talking for a long time. Finally, the men dispersed to their sleeping quarters either underneath the wagons or in the shelter of the trees, and the camp grew quiet.

The next morning, the sound of light rain on the canvas mingled with the noises of men and animals readying for the journey. Awhile later, looking outside, Lizzie was greeted by a marvelous vision of sun-kissed clouds as light crept across the horizon spreading its fingers of rosy light across the mottled sky. Their breakfast was a piece of cold chicken served on a metal plate with a hunk of bread and a frothy glass of fresh goat's milk, provided by the accompanying animals.

Breaking camp quickly, they set off into the shadows, huddled together for warmth beside the driver. Clouds rolled in obliterating any thought of a sunny morning but the wagon's canopy protected them reasonably well from the intermittent rain.

Continuing northward, they bumped along the rough track of the flatlands and, by noon, the sun had almost bitten through the clouds. A small village appeared and Jeb cantered ahead to arrange a meal and a change of horses at the coaching inn. As they ate, a coach driver recognized Jeb and came over to inform him that a bridge was down at Waltham Cross and he deemed it wise to make a detour before reaching The Abbey Church.

Pinching his dark eyes tightly, the gypsy leader frowned, merely nodding as the man walked away.

"Will that cause a problem?" asked Lizzie.

"No, we weren't going that way anyhow," said Jeb, offering no further explanation.

They finished their meal and climbed back into their wagon as fresh horses were being coupled. Rolling onward through the tranquil countryside, the driver pointed out a place called Epping Green to the west. Then, shielding his eyes as the sun came through the clouds, he pointed slightly to the north informing them they would pass within sight of the town of Hertford ... the home of a great castle that had once been a favourite to the kings and queens of England and Scotland.

"If the weather co-operated, you might be able to see it," he said, but pointing off into the hazy distance, he shook his head. Clucking his tongue, he added, "Not today, miss, looks like rain went that way. Perhaps we'll come near enough on our return."

In the early evening, they found themselves on the banks of the

Ash River and Lizzie suddenly understood Jeb's earlier curtness. Quon gripped her arm and she held her breath as the wagon drove straight into the fast-running, mud-stained water.

"Quon don't wike this," he muttered, gripping tightly to the seat as he peered over the side of the wagon and watched the angry water swirling about the horse's legs.

"I don't either, dumplin, but they must have been this way before," she whispered, grasping the seat so hard her fingers ached.

Mere minutes seemed an eternity and when they reached the other bank they were relieved when the wagons stopped briefly to allow the horses a rest. Jumping down, they took the opportunity to stretch their legs while those not tending the wagons got together a light meal. Too soon Jeb gave the signal that they still had several miles to travel before dark ... and they pushed onward.

On the third day out of London, Jeb suddenly rode up the line of wagons shouting something loudly in Romany. Lizzie thought he seemed quite agitated but, as it was growing dark, she anticipated they would be stopping for the night soon and she would question him then. Shrugging off her feeling of foreboding, she looked down at Quon, dozing on her shoulder and tried to put her concerns aside.

Half an hour later, they pulled into a stand of trees and the men unhitched the horses leading them to a stream nearby. She woke Quon and they joined several of the young men looking for dry firewood. Later, eating in the semi-darkness, Lizzie noticed that two saddle horses were now tied behind their wagon and Jeb was still acting strangely, often sending furtive glances toward the inky blackness beyond the fire.

You expecting someone, Jeb?" she asked, feeling a new tension in the camp.

Jeb's black eyes sparkled in the firelight, his teeth shining even and white. "Don't you worry none. They've been out there now for nearly two days but I'll fix them tomorrow!"

"Who's been out there and how are you going to fix them?"

"Never you mind, girl. You won't be here!"

Quon's cold fingers found Lizzie's hand in the darkness.

"Hush, dumplin. I'm thinking," she whispered into his ear.

"Take this and go to your wagon," Jeb instructed, handing Quon a lantern. "Put on your warm clothes and get yer coats, then leave the lantern on the ground and wait inside the wagon. Someone will come for you. Follow their instructions and no talking!"

The lantern glowed dimly lighting their path. Climbing up into the wagon, she found their coats and extra jumpers. In the near darkness, her mind went over Jeb's words and she felt her heart rate quicken. *There is something very wrong here. Jeb is very worried.*

Quon put the lantern down on the ground and climbed up beside her. They put on their warm clothes and sat very still huddled in the dark, waiting silently ... and wondering.

Ten minutes went by and finally they heard their names being whispered as one of Jeb's men came to the doorway of the wagon.

"Climb out the back ... now!" he quietly hissed.

Moving quickly, they went through to the back of the wagon and descended the short ladder to the ground.

"Over here," came the voice which led them into the trees. After a dozen or so strides, he stopped them and they heard the unmistakable snorting of horses.

"Jeb says yer to go with Edward. The horses are ready and yer leavin right now. Mount up, but leave the reins, Eddie will lead. No noise!" their guide ordered softly.

It was so dark Lizzie could only see the slightest outline of the men, but she could hear Edward's excited breathing as he assisted her into the saddle. Looking back, she noticed something shining brightly through the trees to her left and realized it was the campfire. Then the horse jerked under her and she grabbed for the saddle horn.

She looked again, positive it was Jeb sitting at the fire with two other people. If she hadn't known better, she would have thought those figures were her and Quon. The feeling of foreboding returned and she wished she could talk to her partner. Jeb was worried for their safety and this deception was meant to fool someone ... who?

Moving silently off into the night, all feeling of tiredness quickly disappeared as she fought to stay on her swaying beast. Riding was one of the activities she had often thought she should do more of ... suddenly wishing she had.

Knowing she had to warn Quon of the possible danger, she reached out toward him. Her groping fingers brushed his arm and he quickly caught hold of her hand. He began to tap a message, but she silenced him. Tapping her own message, she communicated her fears.

She heard his sudden intake of breath. Then the horses picked up speed moving them apart. Thankfully, their path was now lit intermittently by a half-moon as it peeked out from behind its curtain of clouds. Being able to see each other's silhouette from time to time gave them each a small measure of comfort.

After an hour or so, Lizzie became tired of peering through the darkness and dozed fitfully. Although she had grown more used to the rolling motion, she held tightly to the saddle horn.

As the first rays of morning began to creep across the sky, Lizzie noticed the change in the land. There were now fewer trees; and the air even smelled differently. When Edward noticed her sniffing the air, he drew back beside them explaining they were well away from London and almost into Hertfordshire. What they smelled was the clean country air away from the smoky city.

They were now travelling through very low rolling hills with forest on both sides. It was still quite dark but they stopped briefly, stretched their legs and ate a meal of bread and goat's cheese washed down by a drink of fresh river water.

By the time the sun was fully over the horizon they came upon a farmyard and found the farmer already at work in a large garden patch. Edward dismounted and went to speak with him. After a short conversation, they heard the familiar clink of coins as the gypsy removed some money from a small bag inside his coat. The farmer lay down his hoe and set off toward the house.

Edward came back and as he helped them dismount, he explained they would be staying here long enough to have a sleep and a good meal. Lizzie looked over at Quon and saw that he was as relieved at this news as she was. They hadn't eaten much since dinner the day before and they were not only hungry but very sore and tired.

The couple came to the door to greet them, then the farmer went silently back to his garden. She invited them inside, indicating several heavy wooden chairs around a large table.

"I'm Missus Anderson, you have come a long way and you are tired," she said, in an unfamiliar dialect, "but first have something warm to eat." She poured them some hot tea and, in a few minutes, they all had bowls of porridge in front of them.

As she ate, Lizzie introduced themselves to the kindly woman explaining they were going to visit family some distance away. When they finished eating, Edward went outside and Missus Anderson showed them to their rooms. She gave them each a towel so they could wash, indicating a large white bowl and pitcher on the dresser.

"I'll wake you in time for tea," she announced before leaving.

They were so tired they dropped asleep almost instantly. Awakened by Missus Anderson some hours later, they felt quite refreshed. When they entered the kitchen they discovered Mister Anderson sitting at the table. A steaming bowl of stew was placed in front of each of them and then Missus Anderson sat down without saying a word and bowed her head. Quon began to reach for his spoon but Lizzie gently touched his hand. They bowed their heads and Missus Anderson said a short grace then looking up, she indicated they could begin.

"We've heard much about you from the gypsy, my dear," she said, turning to Lizzie, "but you are so young."

"I grew up quickly on the streets of dockland," replied Lizzie, feeling quite uncomfortable with her questioning.

Quon tapped out a message on the table.

"Does thee lad talk?" asked Mister Anderson.

A knock on the door and Edward poked his head inside. "Time to go, Miss Lizzie."

They finished up quickly and their hosts walked outside with them. After helping Lizzie into the saddle, Edward also mounted. Then they realized Quon was still standing with the farmer and his wife.

"Come on, Quon," Lizzie urged.

Quon reached out his hand to the farmer. "Thank you, sir, for your hospitawity," he said, slowly and deliberately. "My Wizzy and I won't forget."

"My gracious, he does talk!" exclaimed Missus Anderson, watching Quon swing smoothly up onto his horse.

As Edward pulled into the lead, Lizzie and Quon realized they now had complete control of their own horses. They set their mounts into motion, with Lizzie positioned between them, and waved goodbye to the gentle couple.

Feeling rested and more comfortable on the horses, the ride now became much easier. Traveling at a quicker pace, they avoided any villages, changing horses and seeking rest and refreshment at coaching houses. When darkness prevailed they stopped at another small farmhouse like the Andersons.

Then, late in the afternoon on the second day with Edward, they crested a small hill and he pointed out several smoking chimneys in the distance.

"Blackrock Moor," he announced, "we're almost there."

Many miles to the south, the gypsy wagons slowly moved northward—two desperately weary prisoners walked behind. Their hands were tied to a long rope attached to the back of the first wagon.

The night before, Jeb's ploy had worked well on the men who he knew to be following them. After Lizzie and Quon had safely escaped in the dark, he had deployed his men bidding them to hide amongst the trees. Before sun-up, he and a handful of men broke camp taking all but one of the wagons. Darkness would make it impossible to see how many men accompanied them while the rest remained hidden in the wood.

Going only a half mile down the road, they waited until the sun was rising and quickly returned, making a frightful amount of noise as they neared the wood. Intended to confuse the suspected enemy they were not disappointed as the men in the lead caught sight of a pair of approaching horsemen just before they escaped into the trees. Alas, Jeb's men were waiting,

Jeb remained on his horse listening to the shouts and commotion, smiling ruthlessly when the two young men were dragged into the clearing and thrown at his feet.

"WHO SENT YER?" he yelled. "GET THE ROPES READY!" he ordered his men, not waiting for an answer.

Wide-eyed with terror, the men watched as ropes were made secure to stout branches of nearby trees.

"Yer first," Jeb snarled at the older of the two, a man of about 30-years-old "Blindfold them!" he ordered fiercely. With the blindfolds in place, he spoke in Romany telling his men to gag and remove the older man.

Trembling uncontrollably, the younger man, a lad of no more than 18, strained to hear the hanging. Two of the gypsies pulled on the rope just enough to cause the branch to creak and groan, while another let out a hair-raising choking sound.

"Bloody hell, what have yer done? Spare me," he wailed. "I'll tell yer everythin, please stop!"

"WHO SENT YER?" Jeb's voice thundered.

"W-W-Wallace Dawson."

"Who the hell is Wallace Dawson?"

"G-grain merchant, sir. Please don't hang me!"

"WHAT'S YOUR MISSION, LAD? SPEAK UP OR IT WILL BE THE LAST BREATH YOU TAKE!" the gypsy roared, swinging his leg over his horse and landing on the ground.

"We was supposed t-to kidnap L-Lizzie Short and that Chinaman of hers!" he stammered.

Silence struck the clearing and Jeb swallowed hard. He had been right. Her competitors were foolish men and really did fear this young woman. His face twisting into contortions of fury, he stepped forward, grabbing the rope out of his man's hand. In an instant, he had it flipped over the prisoner's head and the blindfolded man dropped to his knees moaning in terror.

"You were going to hurt her, weren't you?" the gypsy leader snarled in his face, grabbing the prisoner by the shoulders.

"No, no sir! We was to hold her 'til Dawson got the machine."

"What machine?"

"That new steam machine that unloads grain from the ships."

"What is yer name?

"H-H-Harry Stubbs."

"Stubbs, if Dawson told you to kill 'em, would you have?" Jeb demanded, but this time he was calm and he circled around behind the prisoner. Winding the rope tightly in his hand, he waited for an answer. When none came, he gave the rope a quick jerk with just the right amount of pressure. Stubbs mercifully fainted, falling face first into the dirt, and Jeb let the rope fall.

"Get 'em on ther feet and tie 'em to the back of the wagon, ther walkin!"

Unaware of events taking place behind them, Lizzie felt a tingle of excitement run through her body. She let Quon catch up then reached out for his hand. The children were so close, she could feel them. Quon felt it too and silently took her hand, squeezing it reassuringly.

"I wish they knew we were coming," she said. "It will be bedtime soon."

"It's only a mile," said Edward, reining in beside them. "I'll go ahead and you take your time. They'll be waitin when you arrive." Before they could object, he had galloped off.

A quarter of a mile away, three men were observing the scene with a great deal of interest. Hidden in a thick copse of trees, they passed a small spyglass between them.

"Who the hell are they, Patch?" asked Joel Ridley, the highwayman.

"Gypsies," replied the one named Patch.

"No, they ain't," said a third voice. "The one that left were, but one of 'em is a girl."

"A girl ain't any use to us," replied Ridley.

Cantering slowly toward the copse of trees enjoying the spring sunshine, Lizzie's thoughts were on the children and how each of them would look. Reining in her horse, she removed her head scarf. Shaking her hair free, her long auburn tresses caught the wind and blew about her face in the light breeze. She looked up at the blue sky with its fluffy white clouds and began to hum a tune.

"Wizzy happy," observed Quon.

"You should be too, dumplin. I wonder how much they've all grown. I can't wait to see them. Each time we go away, I miss them more and more, Quon. I wonder why that is?"

"Yer both idiots," hissed the third highwayman, "don't yer see. She's that girl from dockland ... Lizzie Short they call her. That other one's her Chinese partner. Ain't ya heard 'a them? There'll be people in London who would like to see that one dead and buried ... maybe both of 'em!"

"Are you sure?" asked Ridley.

"Indeed I am," his brother sneered. "I spied out for Captain Stroud a few years back before his whole crew mysteriously disappeared and him with 'em! Even his boat vanished into thin air. Talk was she had some part in it," he said, reaching for the reins of his horse. "But no one could ever prove it. Let's take 'em, Joel. Joe Todd will pay plenty to get 'em back."

"Who's Joe Todd?"

"It's said he's ther adopted dad and ther like gold to him. Let's go get 'em!"

"Wait, you half-wits!" Ridley snarled. "Let 'em come closer."

Patch Morse and Joel Ridley were wanted men, roughs of the worst kind looking for easy pickings as they made their way back to London. Already identified as the perpetrators of many northern stagecoach robberies, they were doomed to a life of running from the law. Slink, the younger Ridley, idolized his brother and would have done anything to prove himself worthy of joining them.

"If Todd'll pay to get her back, maybe those high and mighty merchants will pay even more!" hissed Joel, mounting up. As his bloodshot eyes followed the approaching riders, he knew this was an opportunity not to be missed.

"All right, let's take her!" grunted Patch, adjusting his eye patch. Mounting quickly, he urged his horse forward. The others followed.

Bursting out of the thicket, the riders startled Lizzie and Quon as they waved pistols menacingly in the air. Quon's protective instinct rushed to the surface and throwing caution to the wind, he dug in his heels, careening his mount toward the closest highwayman.

"RUN, WIZZY, RUN!" he screamed.

Violently pulling her mount around, her horse lost its balance momentarily. Wrapping her arms around its neck, as she had seen other riders do, she dug her heels into its flank and set off at a gallop.

"BANG!" cracked Patch's pistol.

Lizzie held on for dear life, petrified they were firing at her but worried for Quon. She heard him scream and looked back just in time to see him fall to the ground in a lifeless heap. Now frantic, her first thought was to go to him but she knew it would be useless. She couldn't help him—not yet. She dug in her heels again and headed for the trees.

Ignoring the wounded lad, the three highwaymen came after her gaining quickly. Suddenly, her tired horse stumbled. Unable to recover this time, they crashed to the ground. Tossed into the air, the next thing she knew was darkness.

Chapter 22

A shiver ran through Lizzie's body as she realized she was lying on ground that was cold and damp. Attempting to get her bearings, she tried to remember ... those awful men ... her horse had fallen. It must be their voices she could hear. When she tried to move, she realized her hands were bound behind her. She tried to open her eyes, but her vision blurred and her head ached. *I can't have been unconscious for long*, she thought. *It's still light.* Her brain screamed as a jumble of thoughts went through it. She tried to move, but a searing pain shot up the side of her head taking her breath away.

Hearing the voices again, she tried to focus her eyes ... to clear her brain, so she could think properly. They were very close, what was it they were saying? She tried to move her hands tugging on the restraining bonds, but it was no use; each time she moved the pain struck again. She moaned in frustration, then stopped, fearful they might hear her. Feigning unconsciousness, she decided to keep her eyes closed. Running her tongue over dry lips, she realized her bottom lip was swollen and bleeding.

Who are these men and what do they want? Suddenly, she remembered the gun shot and the vision of Quon lying in the dirt and she groaned quietly in desperation. *Where is Quon? Is he still lying out there? My poor dumplin! Edward ... surely he'll come looking for us. Yes, he'll be here soon,* she thought in desperation.

The men's voices grew louder and she realized they were arguing. She was shocked to hear Joe's name mentioned.

"Get her on a horse and let's get out of here!" Patch growled. "That shot may have been heard."

Nudged by the toe of a boot in the ribs, Lizzie groaned softly. Rough hands pulled her upright but she refused to co-operate and kept her eyes closed.

Saddle leather creaked as the other two men mounted and a moving horse brushed against her.

"Put her up here with me," the man on the horse ordered.

The hands holding her upright moved her forward and Joel Ridley leaned from his saddle grasping her shoulders. Her hand touched the round belly of the horse. Sagging against it her nimble fingers sought the buckle on the cinch strap. Pulling it as hard as she dared she could only hope they hadn't noticed. Her deft fingers had once been good at jobs like this. Then she felt herself being pulled upward and another searing pain shot through the top of her skull. She groaned uncontrollably.

Large hands adjusted her position astride the horse and she felt something tighten around her chest. *They've lashed us together!* she thought as panic engulfed her momentarily. The strong scent of male sweat hit her nostrils and she wasn't sure which was worse, the smell or the pain in her head. As the horse began to move, she realized her only hope was to stay calm and hope they met up with Jeb on the way to London.

Surely Edward has found Quon by now. Oh dumplin, I'm sorry. I've failed you. You were so brave. Groaning softly, as the movement made her head pound, she leaned against Joel and thoughts whirled about her head. *I had better be prepared*, she thought, remembering the cinch buckle and wondering what she would do if her plan succeeded.

Edward had just arrived at the farm and was walking toward the house when he heard the sudden sound in the distance. A chill raced up his spine.

"Was that gunfire?" he called to the two farm workers nearby. "Holy hell ... Miss Lizzie! Quon!" he gasped and, turning quickly ran back to his horse, yelling something unrecognizable as he bolted onto its back.

But it was enough to alert the two men. They raced to the barn, shouting to others as they quickly pulled bridles over their horses' heads and mounted. Riding bareback, they galloped after their friend who was already well ahead, pushing his tired horse unrelentingly.

Looking out across the flatlands in the gathering twilight, they could see nothing to indicate a problem, yet Edward was in a state of panic. All they knew was that it was something to do with Lizzie. They looked back and saw three more riders behind them.

As his anxiety increased, Edward urged his horse even harder. He knew he had failed to protect his young charges and he could only pray that the gunshot did not bespeak his worst fears. Searching the road, he could see nothing so he headed for the woods. *They can't have gone far, but where are they?* he thought, searching the empty horizon that would soon be dark.

Slink Ridley shouted a warning to his companions as they readied their horses. "THER COMIN!"

"NO MATTER," Patch snarled, throwing his comments into the wind. "IT'S ALMOST DARK AND WE'LL LOSE 'EM WHEN THEY STOP TO PICK UP THAT KID'S BODY."

Body? Quon is dead? Lizzie's brain screamed in silent pain, her eyes wide open now as she listened to the shouted conversation even though she could only see blurred images.

Seeing the body of Quon face-down on the road, Edward alerted the men then reined in his horse jumping to the ground as it still moved. Gasping Romany prayers, he gently turned the boy over wincing at the sight of his blood-stained shirt. When a moan escaped the lad's lips, Edward's relief was instant, although short-lived.

Quon's eyes fluttered open. "Hehp ... Wizzy ... pwease," he whispered almost inaudibly, then slipped into unconsciousness as the first two riders galloped up.

"Zack, take Quon to the house quickly. He's been shot in the chest and Miss Lizzie has been kidnapped!" cried Edward excitedly. "Send for the Chinese doctors. Rob, help him get Quon onto the horse." With the arrival of the other three men, he added, "Check for tracks. They must have gone into the woods, we don't have much time. We don't want to lose them in the dark."

Turning their horses, the three men fanned out searching the area as they moved toward the trees. Rob helped Edward get Quon's limp body into the saddle in front of Zack then watched as they moved off in the direction of the farm. A shout from the others drew their attention to the edge of the wooded area.

"Looks like a horse fell in this hole, probably the girl's," called Danny, studying the ground. He pointed to another spot. "Here's tracks of three more horses, they dismounted and picked her up. They went into the woods, here."

"SEARCH THE WOODS, MEN. QUICKLY, IT'S GETTING DARK. THEY MAY HAVE LEFT HER," cried Edward, fearing what they might find and hoping desperately he was wrong.

The forest was small and in less than ten minutes the men met in the clearing where the highwaymen had been earlier. Rob returned holding the reins of a limping horse.

"Found him grazing. No sign of anyone else, but they were here all right."

"That's Lizzie's horse. They've taken her," said Edward, shaking his head in disbelief. "What a disaster! How could I have been so stupid! Uncle Jeb will never forgive me!" he muttered, knowing that darkness would soon remove all chance of finding Lizzie and her captors until daylight. "Tie the horse to a tree, we'll find it later. Mount up, men, this night has only begun. Danny, Rob, come with me," he ordered his younger brother and the other young gypsy. "We're going to check Blackrock Inn. The rest of you head toward London, they won't have made many miles in the dark with Lizzie sharing a horse. Maybe they've crossed paths with Jeb already. God, I hope so! If we don't return within the hour, we need you at Blackrock." With that, Edward motioned to the other two and turning their horses westward, galloped off into the twilight.

Five minutes later the outline of Blackrock hostelry and two twinkling lights came into view. Moving more slowly, they split up carefully skirting the area listening for anything unusual. Hearing nothing suspicious, Edward rode for the inn finding the others had arrived ahead of him.

"They ain't been 'ere, lad," said the old stableman, shaking his head. "Yer friends have told me the story. Be careful, lads, it's mor'n likely it's those highwaymen agin. Ther ruffians of the worst sort, they are."

Deep disappointment filled Edward's mind as they cantered away. Pulling up a short distance from the Inn, he detailed Rob to stay behind and keep watch while he and Danny continued after the others.

Looking up at the dark, starless sky, Edward cursed their luck as they moved slowly along the southerly track. Remembering how Lizzie's horse had fallen, he was reminded of how treacherous travel could be in the dark.

Stopping often, they reined in their horses and listened carefully for any sound that might indicate their prey was nearby. Half an hour later, they caught up with the others but no one had seen or heard anything of the kidnappers. It had been two hours since the shot was fired and Edward feared the worst.

❧❧❧

It was almost midnight when the highwaymen heard the gypsy horses coming. Noticing that a few stars were now visible through the clouds, Joel Ridley feared detection for the first time since grabbing the girl. Pulling into a small stand of trees, they waited quietly ... listening.

❧❧❧

Seeing the faint outline of trees ahead, Edward and his men pulled up and listened. Edward sniffed the air, his keen sense of smell picking up the faint aroma of horse sweat.

"Ther close," he whispered to the man nearest him, signaling them to keep moving. "Danny," he commanded, softly.

Understanding perfectly, the others rode off in a different direction and Edward and Danny slipped from their horses tying them to a bush. Creeping noiselessly through the grass and heather, they followed the telltale aroma.

❧❧❧

Gagged, but still tied to Joel Ridley, Lizzie couldn't believe her luck as she heard the horsemen approach. But in the silence of the dark thicket, the welcome sound dissipated as the riders continued past. Her heart skipped a beat and a feeling of utter hopelessness seized her for the first time in her life. Desperation kicked in as she realized if she didn't do something now, they might lose their opportunity to find her before the highwaymen escaped in the dark. Her agile mind, already prepared for this moment, screamed out it's warning and summoning every ounce of strength she could muster, she flung her body sideways.

Joel's arms hastily encircled her and, for a split second, her heart stopped beating. *Will the cinch hold?* she thought, then, as if in slow motion, she found herself looking up at the stars just before they crashed to the ground.

"Oomph," Joel groaned, as they hit the ground. "Damn you, girl!" he hissed, fighting to free himself of the ropes and the girl.

Lizzie gasped for breath behind her gag. Feeling him pull on the cumbersome ropes, she wondered what he was going to do next. She tried to dislodge her gag by using her shoulder but realized it was hopeless. She could only hope that the gypsies had heard them.

Edward had heard them and whistled for the others. Unaware of Joel's trouble, Patch and Slink now dismounted a short distance away. Hearing the whistle, the highwaymen's riderless horses bolted, shooting out of the thicket almost trampling the highwaymen in their wild frenzy. Picking themselves up, Patch and Slink ran desperately after their mounts falling over roots and bushes as they fumbled about in the dark.

On the ground, struggling furiously to loosen the ropes, Joel freed himself at last and pushing Lizzie aside, took off after his own horse. Seeing the moving shadow, Edward and two of his men took up the chase. Edward reached him first. Leaping into the air ... they crashed to the ground but in the darkness the highwayman got away from him and escaped into the trees.

"LEAVE HIM, EDDIE," Danny called from the murky blackness. "I'VE FOUND MISS LIZZIE, SHE'S OVER HERE!" Following her muffled sounds, he had almost tripped over her. He quickly removed her gag and was untying her hands as the others joined them.

"Did you find Quon? Is he alive?" she asked apprehensively, fearing his answer but grateful to be rescued.

"Yes, he's alive," he reassured her, "but he's hurt bad. Zack's taken him to the farm and they'll send for the Chinese doctors. Get some torches men, we need to get Miss Lizzie to the house."

Dry grass and twigs were found and gypsy torches soon brought light to the copse. They were shocked with the girl's appearance and Edward pulled out a handkerchief to wipe away the trickle of blood running down the side of her face.

"Can you walk?" asked Edward, as he helped her unsteadily to her feet. "Danny, I want you and the men to stay here. I need those men found at first light. How many were there, Miss Lizzie?"

"There were three and they knew who we were."

At the farm, oil lamps burned all night as they took turns watching Quon. Riders had already been dispatched to London with orders to watch for Jeb and do whatever was necessary to find the Chinese doctors. Quon lay barely conscious on a cot, attended by Jessy and one of the gypsy women.

It was Jessy Jones who had taken charge of the nursing, gently cleaning the angry-looking wound in Quon's chest. Probing delicately with her fingers she could feel the lead ball but it was too deep. This was a job for a real doctor, but could they find one in time?

Groaning, Quon's eyes flicked open briefly and he tried to speak. Leaning closer, Jessy could barely hear his words.

"Find my Wizzy."

"They will find her, Quon," she assured him. "Please rest, you need your strength." Taking his limp hand in her own she stroked it gently. All night long Jessy sat beside her friend's bed watching his pale face, unsure what to do or say. She whispered a silent prayer hoping with every fibre of her being that he would survive. Even before the first streaks of dawn brought light to the land, she was awakened by one of the gypsy women.

"A rider is comin in, Miss Jessy," Erma announced, shaking her awake.

Leaving Quon's side, she hurried to the door as the lone horse thundered into the yard. Excited voices directed Edward and Lizzie to the schoolroom but Jenny reached them first, hugging her friend tearfully.

"Is he alive, Jessy?" she asked, desperation in her voice.

"Yes, he's alive ... come," she said, taking her arm.

Entering the schoolroom, she was stunned to see Quon lying so pale and helpless. She stumbled to his side and dropped onto her knees. "Oh, Quon dumplin," she cried, stroking his cheek. "You're not going to die. I won't let you!" Seeing no movement, she seemed to suddenly lose her own strength and her head dropped onto the sheets beside him.

Jessie saw it first.

Quon raised his hand and touched Lizzie's hair. "Hold ... me ... Wizzy," he whispered.

Lizzie raised her head in surprise and looked at him, disbelieving at first. Shaking her head as if to clear it, she placed her arm gently across his chest. Seeing him wince, she looked helplessly up at Jessy.

Jessy moved Lizzie's arm until it was over his waist. She patted Lizzie's hand reassuringly and stepped back. Lizzie leaned over her friend tenderly kissing his cheeks and forehead. She motioned Jessy to leave the room with her.

"He'll live!" she said, fiercely. "He has to, Jess, I need him."

Jessy clasped Lizzie's hand as the girls both tried desperately to control their tears. "It's almost time to wake the children. Jeb's not arrived with your trunk so I'll bring you a change of clothes. You'll feel better when you've washed and seen the children, Liz. Quon is strong and I know he's going to be all right, I just know it."

Lizzie nodded feebly and went to her room removing her dirty clothes. From a pitcher she poured water into the washbowl and washed the dust from her face and hair as best she could. Erma brought her a change of clothes and left her alone again. Lizzie slowly began to dress but suddenly realized how tired she was. She tried to brush her hair but her legs began to buckle under her.

"I must be strong for the children," she said softly, sitting on the edge of the bed and breathing deeply.

Ten minutes later, dressed in a brightly coloured gypsy dress, Lizzie made her way across the grass toward the little cottage the gypsies had built for the children and Jessy. She heard their chattering laughter and as her hand paused on the door latch, she noticed her heart was pounding with wild anticipation. She knocked, then lifted the latch and stepped inside.

For a moment there was absolute quiet ... then suddenly bedlam as many of the nine youngsters raced to her side.

"Mommy, mommy!" they cried, hugging her so hard she almost lost her balance.

Jessy's hands flew to her mouth as she watched the once-mistreated waifs rush forward, totally convinced Lizzie was their mother.

"Where's Quon," one of them asked.

The youngest girl clung to her hand as they all moved toward the oversized table. Lizzie sat down and tried to explain that Quon was sick and wouldn't be able to visit them for awhile. They all had so many questions but Jessy clapped her hands bringing instant silence to the room, announcing it was time to say their prayers.

Each child went to stand behind their chair. They linked hands and solemnly bowed their heads. As they began to recite their morning prayer, Lizzie glanced around at their happy faces. When they came to the last line, she caught her breath in surprise.

"... and God bless mommy and Quon."

She felt a tear run down her cheek and quickly wiped it away as they said their *Amens.*

Jessy began to serve breakfast with the older ones willingly helping. Looking over at Lizzie she was relieved to see the more relaxed look on her friend's face as she proudly watched.

My secret angels, Lizzie told herself, masking her worried thoughts of Quon with warm smiles as she listened to their happy chatter. Leaving them, as Jessy called for the morning classes to begin, she promised to come back at dinner.

"But aren't we going to the schoolroom, Miss Jessy?" a tiny voice asked as Lizzie closed the door quietly behind her.

Hurrying back to the schoolroom, she found the women fussing around Quon who lay motionless with his eyes only slightly open.

As she bent to kiss his forehead Lizzie realized he was trying to say something. She bent closer to hear.

"Take it out Wizzy."

"I-I can't, dumplin," she said in dismay. "I can't."

"You must Wizzy ... you must ...," he whispered haltingly.

A hopeless feeling enveloped her and she sagged to her knees. She was his last hope and his faith in her still rode high, even though he knew his life was slowly slipping away.

It was almost noon and Lizzie was still at Quon's side when she heard the wild thundering hooves of galloping horses and a door bang shut. Jeb, haggard and dirty rushed into the room with Edward. He quickly washed in the basin breathlessly barking out his orders.

"I need boiling water, a sharp pointed knife and the Chinese medicine water," he hissed fiercely, sending the gypsy women scurrying off to obey his orders. "Out of the way, girl," he snapped at

Lizzie, as Edward helped him move Quon onto a large table.

Sitting outside the door of the schoolroom being comforted by the two women, she waited for what seemed an eternity until suddenly she heard Quon scream loudly in pain. Then, there was complete silence as the world seemed to hold its breath.

"Here you be, girl!" Jeb's voice startled her, as he came to the door. "He'll get better now, you hold onto this." He dropped the tiny, pitted lead ball into her hand.

The Chinese doctors arrived the next day, nodding their approval at the gypsy leader's decisive surgery. They stayed overnight at the farm, checking a few minor illnesses of the residents, re-filled the healing water jugs, and moved off into the mist as quietly as they had come.

In the week that followed, Lizzie played her duel rolls to perfection, exuding the happiness of a mother with her children at the same time, coaxing Quon Lee back to health. She learned from Edward that the three highwaymen had been captured and, along with their other two prisoners, had been handed over to an army detachment, travelling as escort to a local magistrate.

Rapidly gaining strength, Quon was once more at Lizzie's side, wherever she went. They were enjoying the children immensely taking them on dray rides through the nearby village and picnics out on the grassy moor in the warmth of the afternoon sun.

The oldest, by Jessy's estimation, was an 11-year-old freckled-faced lad with a shock of red hair, named Abel. He liked to spend a lot of his time with little Jane, the tiniest girl who was now about 7. Tommy and David, the 10-year-old twins, were often found together giggling at David's left eye as it rolled into the corner. The three girls, Sarah, Meg, and Penny, all about 8-years-of-age, were always together holding hands, it seemed; and Hettie and Martha, the sisters who looked about 8, were probably closer to 10 years-of-age. Thankfully, their sickly little bodies had grown tall and strong in the sweet country air.

Sitting on the grass one warm afternoon, Lizzie's eyes roamed down the line of the nine children, taking note of the affectionate way they acted toward each other. Tears welled in her eyes and Quon's fingers gripped tightly on her arm.

Jessy clapped her hands. "What is your surname, children?

"Short!" they all shouted in unison.

"And who is your mother?" she asked.

Nine fingers pointed at Lizzie and the girls rushed over to sit beside her.

She felt the pain of motherhood when Jane came to hug her for no apparent reason, begging her to stay with them. There were moments when memories were stamped indelibly on Lizzie's mind. Sarah's missing tooth and Penny's beautiful blue eyes, Jane's long blonde hair streaming in the wind as she ran across the heather, and Meg's gentle, loving nature. Jessy had taught the boys well ... to be everprotective of their sisters ... these wonderful happy youngsters were a family and truly Lizzie's angels.

Five weeks passed quickly as May slipped away in the idyllic setting. The longing for home and the hubbub of London's dockland, began to disturb Lizzie's thoughts and ruin her sleep.

"Time to go home, dumplin," she whispered to Quon one evening at dinner, the decision to be parted from the children hanging heavy on her mind.

The next day they began to make the necessary arrangements for their journey back to London. Over the next couple of days they said their goodbyes around the village and found themselves trying to explain to the younger children why they had to leave again. Jeb made it plain he was taking no chances this time, saying they would be guarded continually and nights would be spent at coaching inns.

The day of departure, Jess stood at the gate her arms around Jane and Meg who looked as though they would burst into tears at any moment. Quickly hugging them all, Lizzie and Quon climbed onto their horses for the first time in over five weeks. Waving quickly, they turned their mounts southward.

Chapter 23

Four days later, the hazy, smoke-filled air of London hung like a cloud on the horizon.

"Home," Lizzie whispered, feeling a pang of relief in her heart.

Darkness had not yet begun to settle over dockland as they rode wearily into the gypsy camp and the familiar stink of the slaughterhouse filled their nostrils. They could see the smoke curling lazily from the cottage chimney and when they reached the gate, Quon quietly opened it.

Martha's eyes swung to the doorway as the floorboards creaked under their weight. Her mouth drooped in surprise as the youngsters stepped into the room. Joe's pipe wobbled precariously as he struggled for words and young Willie scrambled from his knee, rushing over to meet them.

"Welcome home, you two," Ada sang cheerily, leaping from her seat to hug them. "We have missed you both so much."

"Ah sure Charlie will be mighty glad to see yer," said Mick, giving Lizzie a hug. "Yer lookin grand, m'lad. We heard about yer trouble, but we'd like the whole story sometime when yer feelin like telling it." He took Quon's hand but shook it very gingerly.

My, how you've grown, Willie," exclaimed Lizzie, not wanting to get onto the subject of their troubles just yet. She joyfully hugged the boy then turned and noticed that Joe was not leaving his chair. She went over to kneel beside him.

Joe's lip trembled and his eyes misted over as she hugged him gently. "Ah missed yer, luv," he whispered, grasping her as if he didn't want to let go.

"I know, Dad. We missed you sorely, too."

Quon joined them, giving the old man a hug from behind. "It good to be home, Glanpop," he exclaimed, and everyone laughed because it was so good to hear him talk.

While eating, they relaxed the rules and allowed Lizzie to relate their adventures, including her kidnapping and Quon's attempt at rescuing her. She told of Jeb's surgery, putting her arm around Quon and hugging him at the same time.

After many exclamations of horror and then relief, Martha asked, "What about Jessy and the children?"

"They're happy and well," Lizzie assured her. "She's doing a wonderful job with the children. Those little angels are marvelous and not so little anymore!"

"I think that's enough for one day, these young'uns need their rest," Joe interrupted, tapping his pipe on the table.

Soon afterwards, they excused themselves and took to their beds. It wasn't long before familiar surroundings and especially the cozy comfort of their own feather mattresses, brought sleep quickly to the weary travellers.

Getting back into their routine the next morning, the first person they visited was old Abe. He told them Charley's machine had been silent for days and rumours were circulating that it was a failure and would never run again.

"That's what Mick meant last night," said Lizzie, frowning.

A door banged across the street and Clara Spencer's voice called a shrill good morning as she hurried into the shop with Abe's breakfast. The partners watched in awe as he sat down and began to eat without so much as a word from Clara who winked at them, welcoming them home.

Continuing down Water Lane, they could see Charley was just arriving at the TLS dock. They waited on the curb across from *The Robin* while an early morning stagecoach thundered around the corner into the hostelry yard. Passengers and baggage were quickly unloaded and one of the gentlemen passengers dropped his newspaper into the dirt, cursing violently and leaving it where it lay.

"Get it, dumplin!" Lizzie hissed.

Crossing the street, Quon picked up the dirty newspaper and slipped it into his pocket, rejoining his partner as she ran toward the busy intersection.

News that Lizzie was back had already travelled quickly that morning and Charley was waiting for them near the now-silent steam engine. Walking around it, they could see no visible evidence of damage and she looked inquiringly at the dockmaster.

"Sabotage," Charley growled, "but I can't figure out what they've done."

Quon's hands burst into life and Lizzie raised an eyebrow.

"Who's Wallace Dawson, Charley?" she asked.

"Biggest grain shipper in London."

"Where's he at?"

"Queen Anne dock ...," the dockmaster's voice trailed off as he shot a suspicious glance at the young partners. "He wouldn't have done this, he's a member of the local council," he said in a faltering voice.

"You could be right, lad," Lizzie replied, flippantly. "Looks like we need that Da Vinci fella!"

"Not possible, love," Charley laughed, "he's been dead three hundred years!"

Quon grinned mischievously when the partners turned away, leaving the dockmaster staring after them as they quickly disappeared back toward the street. Hearing Tom Legg's voice nearby, she felt the security of Quon's hand on her elbow, guiding her through the traffic as they followed the familiar laugh.

Surprise showed on Tom's face when he saw the partners and he banged his shepherd's crook excitedly on the cobblestones. "Heave to lass, drop yer anchor and buy old Tom a drink."

"Do you know the Queen Anne dock?" she asked.

"Dawson's dock ... ther grain shippers."

"Have you seen any of their men around here lately?"

"All the time ... they been watchin the TLS dock very closely since that devilish machine began runnin," the old mariner growled, "and they still are."

"They're here right now?" Lizzie snapped back. "Where?"

The mariner grinned, showing blackened teeth, then drained his tankard. "Missy, 'am ever so thirsty!

Coins rattled in the girl's pocket and she flipped a penny to Quon who sent it spinning through the air. Deftly caught by the old man, he dropped his shepherd's crook and yelled for more drink.

Waiting impatiently, she watched as Tom slurped the froth from his fresh tankard, flushing a little as her temper began to rise. Quon retrieved the shepherd's crook from the ground and stepped closer to his partner. Tom read the signs ... he'd gone too far. He raised his tankard and his eyes toward the rooftop garret room of the coaching house and winked at her.

Without being obvious, she averted her eyes—two men stood in the upper window looking toward the dock. One of them had a spyglass. Thanking Tom, they moved across the yard and in behind a nearby coach. Keeping hidden, they watched the spies for a few minutes making a mental note of their features.

"Let's go, dumplin," she murmured.

"Hello you two. I hear you had some trouble so I'm awful glad to see yer lookin so well," called Bill, from the doorway of the bakery. "You just missed Oly and he would have been very happy to see you. He asks about you every day. Come, have some apple pie and tell me about your trip."

He listened enthralled while they told him of their adventure, his eyes misting over as Lizzie told him about the children.

"Where's Clem?" she asked.

Bill burst out laughing as he pointed to the outhouse set back in the corner. "Oh, here he comes now!"

"Miss Lizzie, Quon," Clem called when he saw the young people, "nice to see yer both again." Coming closer, he continued, "It's been mighty quiet without yer visits! We heard my old steam engine broke down again."

"Know anybody who can fix it, Clem?"

"No ah don't, luv, that devilish contraption drove me to drink with its constant breakdowns. I'm glad to be rid of it."

Finishing his second helping of pie, Quon wiped his mouth on the back of his hand, grinning at his partner as his fingers began talking on her arm.

"What's he saying?" the baker's helper asked, totally mystified by their sign language.

"Just rubbish," Lizzie laughed. "He said we should ask a printer."

"A printer?" Bill gasped, "whatever for?"

Without offering further explanation the young partners left the yard. Shouting their thanks for the food they closed the gate behind themselves.

On the long walk to the printing shop, they noticed a strange sight … printed leaflets nailed everywhere to posts and doors. They were obviously Billy's, advertising the butcher, candle maker and bake shop. In bold, black letters at the bottom was the proclamation that *The Print Shop* was open for business.

"Young Billy, good businessman," Quon chuckled as they heard the church clock booming lunch time.

"But these poor folks can't read," Lizzie exclaimed, watching a group of people gathered around one of the posters. "Let's go see."

"What does it say," an old lady dressed in dirty rags was asking as they joined the group.

Painstakingly a young sailor sounded out the words in a voice loud enough for all to hear. A carriage pulled up to the curb and a well-dressed man pushed his way to the front and looked at the sheet.

"I TOLD YOU, FATHER," he shouted back to the figure inside the conveyance. "THERE'S A PRINT SHOP CLOSE BY."

"Then ask one of those rascals where it is, you fool!" a harsh voice thundered from inside the dark carriage. "We don't have all day."

"I know where it is, sir," Lizzie volunteered, in a timid voice.

Frowning the man turned and, parting the crowd with his cane, he followed the voice until it was pointing at Lizzie. Quon moved quickly, stepping in front of his partner and snatching the cane from the startled man's hand. Several of the crowd gasped and moved back even farther as the stranger reeled.

"Enough," Lizzie whispered.

Taking the cane from Quon Lee's hand, she calmly handed it back to the cowering man. He accepted it, relaxing slightly but his eyes remained on the girl.

"Do I know you?" he asked.

"You certainly will if you don't alter your ways, sir. This is dock-land, these people are poor, but we're not animals."

"That's Lizzie Short ... she's back!" a female voice called out.

"Dammit Simon, get back here!" the man in the coach ordered irritably.

"Who are you, sir?" asked Lizzie, blocking his path.

The stranger shuffled nervously with indecision. "My name is Simon Cambourne," he mumbled, as the crowd moved closer again. "My father owns a newspaper and wants to buy a print shop."

Stepping to one side, Lizzie allowed the stranger to walk back to his coach. As he climbed inside she also moved forward, holding the door so it could not be closed. Leaning inside, she looked directly at the red-faced old man glowering at her from the back seat. "The printer's shop is by Brown's Yard down Chandler," she purred.

Closing the door quickly, she grabbed Quon's arm and they began to run. They arrived at *The Print Shop* just ahead of the Cambourne coach. When it pulled up at the door, Simon stepped out first, holding the door for his father.

Rich and pompous, Josiah Cambourne was used to getting what he wanted, often resorting to bully tactics as he crushed all opposition to his printing empire. Having learned of the posters and handbills suddenly circulating the district from *The Print Shop*, he was determined to close it forever.

His eyes in this part of dockland were supplied by his friend Wallace Dawson, the grain merchant, who saw all the business licences as a member of the local council. It was he who had alerted the Cambournes to the threat the new owners of Dunbar's print shop presented when one of their advertising handbills found its way into his hand.

Banging the open door loudly with his cane, Josiah pushed his way into the shop allowing his son to follow. Puffing vigorously on his cigar, he went to stand at the counter loudly tapping the ivory top of his cane on the counter.

The partners ducked silently into the back of the shop totally unnoticed by the visitors. Lady Sutton and Margaret, dressed in work-stained smocks, looked up from the layout table with surprise at the ill-mannered, yet well-dressed, visitors' entrance. Lizzie chuckled inwardly when she read the fire in Lady Sutton's manner as she strode toward the counter.

"You great noisy oaf," she cried, snatching the smoking cigar from the man's lips and crushing it under her heel.

Cambourne recoiled, spitting the torn-off stub of his cigar from his mouth. "DAMN YOU, PEASANT," he roared. "I was going to buy you out, now I'm going to ruin you!"

"Out!" Lady Sutton yelled, defiantly.

Leaving obediently, he almost bowled over his son who stood behind him. The elder Cambourne swung a vicious kick at his son's rear end and laughter erupted inside the shop. The visitors hurriedly climbed back into their coach and it thundered away.

"Mother, you were magnificent," Margaret laughed, hugging her.

From their hiding place, Lizzie and Quon now came forward. Lizzie was wiping tears of laughter from her eyes.

"Margaret, Charley's steam engine needs your expertise it seems. Can you come to dinner tonight?"

"How long have you two been there?" asked Lady Sutton. "It's wonderful to have you back ... and safe!"

"Yes, thank you," said Lizzie. "We followed them here. Can you come, Margaret?"

"Indeed, Gabriel managed to obtain a copy of the Da Vinci drawings for us and I wanted to show them to Charley anyway."

"Who the devil was that pompous ass?" Gabriel interrupted, wiping his dirty hands on his apron.

"That was Josiah Cambourne," replied Lady Sutton before Lizzie could speak. "He's a newspaper owner who has always sought to squeeze small printers out of business. He's been at it for years!"

Quon's fingers gripped Lizzie's arm and her eyes pinched tightly in deep thought.

"You know him?"

"Yes and no."

"Tell me about him."

"He came to our home several times when we gave dinner parties while Lord Sutton was alive," said Lady Sutton, reaching back in her memory. "He's a braggart and a bully, likes nothing better than to hurt people." She paused. "I'm afraid he's going to be trouble."

"Maybe this time he's bitten off more than he can chew," Lizzie offered, her voice having an ominous tone.

Lady Sutton moved back to the worktable. "He's powerful and well-connected politically. His best friend used to be Councillor Wallace Dawson, perhaps still is."

Quon's fingers tightened on his partner's arm.

The clip-clop of small hooves brought a smile back to Lizzie's face as she peered through the window to see Oly outside.

"He's coming for more handouts," Margaret laughed.

"Miss Lizzie!" the boy yelped, rushing over to hug her. "More *Number 3* handbills, please, Mister Monk." Then wasting no time, he took the bundle Fred handed him and was gone again.

Quon made a quick hand sign.

"I don't know," said Lizzie, shrugging her shoulders. "Ask Margaret."

Watching them, Margaret had correctly surmised the question and lay three handbills on the counter.

"Here you are, Mister Quon," she said, proudly. "They're all slightly different and go to different areas of dockland."

Lizzie's eyes scanned the printed sheets as Quon's finger pointed silently to the differences on each handbill.

"That's very clever," she admitted. "I'll bet this was Billy's idea."

"Not all of it," Margaret chuckled, "mother and Gabriel helped him work it out."

"That's right," Lady Sutton called out from the worktable, "but Billy's a very smart lad."

"And we're getting lots of business as a result!" Gabriel called above the noise of the printing press."

Lizzie watched her partner's hands tap out a message on the counter. Grinning broadly, she nodded vigorously. "So, we'll see you at dinner tonight then?" As she waited for Margaret's reply she reached out and turned the handbills face down on the counter.

Lady Sutton and Gabriel were watching.

"What are you doing?" Gabriel asked, staring at the blank side of the three handbills.

"She's telling us to use both sides," said Lady Sutton.

"Can't do it," he growled. "Our machine only prints one side."

"Yes, we can," Fred interrupted, grunting with effort as he pulled on the printer's big lever. "But we have to wait until the first print is dry."

"Two sides of advertising, Lizzie?" asked Lady Sutton.

Lizzie shook her head and smiled one of her wicked smiles. "Power!" she said softly.

The printing press stopped its squeaking as Fred's hands dropped from the big lever in surprise. He had read Lizzie's lips and glanced in alarm at Cuthbert. Moving instinctively, both men joined their employers at the counter.

"Power, how so?" asked Gabriel. "They're only sheets of paper."

All eyes were draw to Quon's hands which were moving quickly as his fingers tapped out a message on the counter.

"Yes, my friends, power!" Lizzie's voice cracked with energy. "Power to influence people we've never met, power to inform dockland of the bullies who roam its streets … and power to give Wallace sleepless nights!"

"Yes, yes!" Lady Sutton squealed as the idea took hold. "We can use it as a newssheet, perhaps one day it will be a real newspaper!"

"Now you've got it," Lizzie laughed, backing toward the door.

In the absence of their young advisors, conversation grew fast and furious as ideas flashed with urgent enthusiasm between the friends.

Cuthbert Dunbar, meanwhile, wandered aimlessly around the shop, his mind in turmoil. *Power from a newssheet in his dockland? What was the world coming to?*

Chapter 24

It was late afternoon when the partners called again at the tailor's shop. Standing for a moment on the step, Lizzie looked down the street at the busy activity of the docks, her thoughts on Charley's steam engine.

Peering over his spectacles, the old tailor laid his sewing down on the table and waited. His half-closed eyes, followed their every move.

"You have need of me girl?"

"Where's Clara?"

"Doing a delivery."

Lizzie sat down facing the tailor and looked intently into his face. Abe fidgeted uncomfortably.

"Wallace Dawson," she said, pronouncing each word precisely. She could feel the gentle pressure of Quon's hand on her shoulder as she watched the tailor's reaction, which was instantaneous.

"Bad one! Bad one!" he ranted, jumping out of his chair. Then, as he often did when excited, his mouth dribbled spittle as he hissed his angry warning. "You steer clear of that one, girl."

"Tell me about him."

"Councillor Dawson," Abe hissed, mocking his longtime enemy as he paced back and forth, again wiping the spittle away with the back of his hand. "He's false, deceitful, and cruel but he has most of the landowners fooled." The old tailor's bony hands began their wringing motion as frustration drove him to exhaustion. His knuckles turned white and he collapsed back into his chair. "Oh, I could tell you stories about that one," he moaned.

"Could he have ordered his men to wreck Charley's steam engine?"

"Aye ... and worse," Abe whined. "You be careful, lass."

Yes, Mister Kratze, we're well-aware," said Lizzie, exchanging glances with Quon. They remembered Jeb's warning about the prisoners his gypsies had taken on that fateful trip to the farm, and their admission to being hired by Dawson.

"It's the first of June," called Martha, as they came through the door.

"Yes?" Lizzie frowned, noticing Charley and Margaret talking intently at the table with some papers and a slate in front of them.

"It's yer birthday next week, luv," Joe chuckled, releasing young Willie from his knee, "you'll be 18, and a woman."

"Never mind, luv," she purred, kneeling at the side of Joe's chair, "ah'll always be yer little girl!"

Margaret sighed loudly, grasping Charley's hand. Watching a tear run down the old man's face, Lizzie gently kissed his forehead and gave him a hug. It seemed for a moment like time was standing still in the little cottage.

Willie's scream broke the silence when he heard his mother's footsteps outside. Wriggling out of Quon's arms, he dashed to the open door.

"Come on, you lot," the housekeeper called. "Clear that table, dinner's ready."

After dinner the discussion naturally centred on Charley's steam engine and blank faces listened to the intelligent way Margaret questioned the engineer. Suddenly, she raised her finger.

"That shaft has a shearing pin through the drive wheel," she said, pointing to the chalkboard drawing she'd made. "Did you check it?"

"No," Charley mumbled, self-consciously. "I didn't know it was there."

"Then you'd better check it tomorrow, m'lad," said Ada.

"Tonight," said Lizzie, "when there's no prying eyes watching."

"What prying eyes?" Charley's and Mick's voices asked in unison.

"Dawson's men … in the garret windows at *The Robin*."

Charley and Mick stared at her, but neither had time to speak before the sound of heavy footsteps sounded outside. A hard knock followed by several agitated, 'Come in's' revealed Captain Davis.

"Docked late," he growled, finding an empty chair.

"Have you eaten?" Joe asked, through the smoky haze.

"Not much since yesterday morning on Sheppey," he said, with a wry smile at Martha.

"You better feed the poor lad, Martha," said Ada.

Martha was already dishing up a plate of her stew and you could almost see the captain salivating as she brought it to the table. With the urgency of hunger gnawing at his belly, Captain Davis shoveled it down. His eyes never once leaving the plate until it was empty, he listened to the conversation around him.

"Where the devil are we going to get men and lanterns at this time of night," Charley grumbled.

"And yer will need a blacksmith," Mick added.

The captain put down his spoon, wiped his mouth on the back of his sleeve and sat back in his chair. With black eyes burning like hot coals under his bushy brows, he said casually, "I got men and lanterns."

"All right, we'll get right to it as soon as we've finished eating," Lizzie snapped. "I want that steam engine lit up like daylight ... and you go get Dan Duffy, Mick. He's a blacksmith and a good man."

One hour later, the TLS dock rang with the sound of hammer blows on steel as the sweat-dripping men toiled to remove the large drive wheel of the steam engine. Success and failure swung on Dan Duffy's expertise as he heated the casing with a shovelful of glowing hot coals. Inch by inch it moved, until with one mighty blow, the heavy steel-driving wheel slipped into the arms of the waiting sailors who groaned under the weight as they lowered it to the ground.

"There!" Margaret cried excitedly, pointing to the smooth ends of the shearing pin. "Da Vinci was right!"

Dan Duffy peered closely at the machine. Skilled at making horseshoes, iron gates, anchors, hooks and balls, he'd never seen a shearing pin before. Charley quickly worked out its function as the blacksmith's hammer and punch sent the offending pin clanging onto the cobblestones.

For the next half hour everyone waited as Duffy worked to produce a duplicate of the pin. Finally with his heavy, blackened tongs, he held it up for all to see and the men got back into position. Sometime later, after many oaths of pain from sailors' whose fingers were burnt on hot metal, all heaved a sigh as their effort was turned into success and the drive wheel slipped back onto its shaft. A look of satisfaction flooded across Duffy's face as his newly-fashioned shearing pin was driven into place.

"OPEN THE VALVE," Charley shouted. "LET'S SEE THE DAMNED THING RUNNING!"

Grinning in triumph, Lizzie and Quon watched from their vantage point on the stack of grain sacks. Margaret was still standing beside Charley and it hadn't gone unnoticed that they were holding hands in shared anticipation. When the drive wheel shuddered and slowly began to turn, everyone cheered.

Charley, wobbling precariously, turned to face the young woman at his side. Grabbing her fiercely, he hugged her with wild abandon. "DAMMIT, I LOVE YOU, MARGARET SUTTON," he proclaimed over the noise.

"Woops," Quon chortled. "Charley in trouble now!"

"Quiet you, little turd," said Lizzie, clasping her hand over his mouth.

"Forgive me, Margaret," Charley spluttered, dropping her hand. Blushing furiously, he desperately tried to regain his composure.

"Don't be sorry, love," Margaret said softly. "You're entitled to be happy. You've got brains and drive and the courage of ten men and I admire you greatly."

"Lordy girl, I'm a cripple," Charley moaned.

"Tut tut, that doesn't matter. Like it or not lad, I am going to be your friend."

"CLEAN UP AND LET'S GET FINISHED HERE!" the voice of Captain Davis thundered from the edge of the darkness, his imposing figure outlined only by the faint glow of a lantern behind him.

It was almost midnight as Dan Duffy walked wearily off the dock, his workbag of tools weighing heavy on tired arms. The Grim brothers appeared like magic from the pitch black night and helped Charlie onto his cart.

As Mick escorted Margaret and the others to a dray he had standing by for the ride back up the hill, Lizzie looked back and felt a surge of pride for the men who had answered her call for help that night. She smiled when she heard Captain Davis' voice, detailing his night guards ... his last task before ending his own long day.

Quietly opening the cottage door, Lizzie showed Margaret inside. Martha, dozing in her chair, stirred and her eyes fluttered open.

"Are you hungry, luvs," she asked the three young people, shaking herself awake and watching them all nod their heads. "Then off to bed wi the lot of ye, this day's already gone on far too long."

Margaret awoke early to the sounds of Martha's pans and the good-natured banter of early morning callers. Light was just beginning to come through the window but she didn't mind. She loved the rough, good humour and simple life that she experienced at Joe's cottage. Following a hearty breakfast, she went with Lizzie and Quon down Water Lane enjoying the freshness of the cool morning air as the early June sun began its long climb in the sky. Fingers of light sparkled and danced off the waters of the Thames and a thrill went up Margaret's spine. *What a wonderful way to start the day!*

Abe eyed them suspiciously as they passed, his hands constantly rubbing together as he gruffly wished them a good morning. Like many others, he had already heard the renewed hiss and rattle emanating from the direction of the TLS dock.

Stopping across from *The Robin*, Lizzie and Quon cautiously centred their attention on the top floor garret window, hoping to see the spies. Margaret's eyes, however, were on the wharf searching for Charley. Suddenly, Quon nudged Lizzie. The men had come to the window but gesturing frantically they quickly turned away again.

"Go!" she hissed and Quon took off across the street and disappeared into the stableyard.

"What's happening?" asked Margaret.

Lizzie hardly heard her but a grin spread across her face and she began to chuckle as Quon came back into sight carrying a dirty sack. He was holding it in such a manner that it appeared he was trying not to get his clothes dirty as he walked toward the side door.

Soon after, the two spies appeared in the doorway arguing loudly. Quon flung the sack at them then darted away into the crowd.

The two men cried out then stood rooted to the spot, arms outstretched in horror. The crowd turned to look moving forward to see what was happening. However, this was short lived as they quickly moved away holding their noses when they realized the men were covered in a horrible, smelly brown slime.

"Those men don't look very happy, what was in that sack ?" asked Margaret, as her eyes searched for Quon Lee. "Where has he gone?"

A shrill whistle was heard from down the street and Lizzie began to walk nonchalantly back up Water Lane, leaving Margaret standing alone.

"Oh please, let's wait for Quon," she pleaded, running to catch up with Lizzie and grabbing her arm.

"Look," said Lizzie, pointing up the street. There, at the next corner leaning on the wall was a figure reading a newspaper. Lizzie giggled. "Our Quon's not the one with the problem, Margaret!"

Leaving the area, Lizzie and Quon now led Margaret through a winding maze of litter-strewn back alleys wanting to show her their dockland. Used to travelling in their enclosed coach or walking only short distances as she made deliveries for *The Print Shop*, it was as if she were seeing London for the first time. With fresh eyes, she saw the streets with their soot-blackened buildings and began to better understand the people who lived in such filth and misery. She especially noticed the children who peered through dirty and often broken windows as they passed. Looking into their sad eyes, she at last had a better understanding of their hopelessness. Margaret was getting her first real glimpse of poverty and she was overwhelmed.

She noticed Quon making signs to Lizzie who dug into her pocket handing him some coins. Passing several doorways, he pressed the coins into the grubby, outstretched hands of the street urchins huddled there.

They never forget their previous life, she thought, in wonder. *These are Lizzie's streets of hope and she is determined to do all in her power to help these people.*

As dockland awoke, they found themselves dodging an increasing amount of traffic and Margaret not being used to the danger was surprised at the speed they travelled. As they crossed the busy intersection at Water and Chandler, Quon, realizing she wasn't paying attention, found himself roughly pulling her out of harm's way when a coach came barreling around the corner.

When they reached the printing shop, he opened the door and it banged shut startling Lady Sutton and Gabriel who looked up from the worktable.

"We could use one of those fancy London newspapers," Fred greeted them. "We need a sample of how to set this up."

Quon held up his hand and diving into his pocket surprised them by producing the newspaper he had been carrying around since the day before. He lay it out on the counter and Lady Sutton came eagerly over to look at it. Seeing how dirty it was, she recoiled slightly at first, then using only two fingers of each hand she delicately lifted it and with a look of utter disdain took it over to the worktable. She dropped it in front of Gabriel as the young people giggled at their discomfort.

"What we need is some interesting local news. Do you have any suggestions how we might get it?" asked Gabriel, looking at each of the smirking youngsters with an expression of extreme seriousness.

Quon's arms whirled about with a not-often-seen excitement and everyone watched in puzzled amusement.

"What did he say?" asked Margaret.

"He says it's time we went on the attack!"

ଧଠ୍ଠଃ

Half a mile away in the offices of Wallace Dawson, the two men Quon had splattered with wet horse dung hung their heads with embarrassment. The office workers were reeling from the stench, and inside Dawson's private office, their boss was hurling a torrent of vicious abuse at the men.

"Everything's going wrong," Dawson screamed in rage. "Two men caught by the law and now this! Can't two grown men look after themselves? GET OUT OF MY SIGHT!"

Banging his office door behind them, his staff were still able to hear him as he paced back and forth cursing the four walls. Then a scraping sound was heard and finally a loud bang which sounded like a chair hitting the wall with great force. Soon after, the door opened.

"Damn that infernal machine ... and that woman! GET ME MY COACH!"

Within minutes he was on his way deep into the city intending to inform Josiah Cambourne of the new developments.

ଧଠ୍ଠଃ

Unaware of Dawson's panic, Quon's words had sparked a plan in Lizzie's mind and she looked up at Margaret Sutton.

"You could write about the men Quon splattered with horse dung.

That should give folks a laugh," she suggested, watching their horrified expressions.

"Wonderful idea, I volunteer for the job!" offered Margaret, almost too eagerly. "I saw it, too. Rest assured I'll mention they were Dawson's men!"

"You were at the coaching house?" asked her mother, cocking a shocked eyebrow.

"No, Mother! I was watching from across the street."

Quon's fingers tugged on his partner's sleeve pulling her toward the door. The others were too deep in conversation to notice.

"We find Dawson office," he announced, outside.

"Why?"

"Find out who work there. Might be useful."

"That could take days," Lizzie snorted.

They had only gone a block and a half toward the waterfront when Nathan's buggy drew up beside them.

"Needing a ride somewhere, my dear?" he inquired, and Dan scrambled down to open the door.

"Matter of fact, yes," she grinned. "Take us to Dawson's office."

"Wallace Dawson's office!" exclaimed Nathan, his voice ringing with surprise as his cane tapped nervously on the floor. He'd crossed paths with Dawson once before while acting as agent for one of the local millers. He had felt the bite of this man's quick anger and couldn't imagine what Lizzie would want with the man. "He virtually runs the council. You want to stay away from that man, my dear," he moaned, pointing his cane at city hall as they now moved through the eastern border of dockland.

"It's all right, Mister Goldman, we're only looking," she assured him, watching their route so they could find their way back later.

Two blocks farther, the coach came to a halt in front of a smoke-blackened building across from the Queen Anne Dock. "That's Dawson's building," he announced. "Be careful!"

Silently, Lizzie and Quon alighted and moved quickly to the other side of the street standing in the shadow made by a tall stone gateway as Nathan's buggy disappeared.

"Now, dumplin," she murmured, "you show me how we find out who works here."

"You wait. You watch," he whispered, a knife appearing in his hand.

Crossing the street, he went to a planter box in front of the neighbouring building. Carving out a square of root-matted soil, he disappeared down the snicket which ran between the buildings. Quickly finding the stairway to the roof, he carefully carried the soil over the parapet wall and cautiously began to climb up the slates.

Lizzie smiled gleefully, having now realized what devilment her partner was up to. Laying the soil over Dawson's smoking chimney pot, Quon quickly scrambled out of sight again. Her eyes now moved to the front door. Soon enough, their question would be answered.

Five more minutes passed before Quon returned to her side. Suddenly, the front door was flung open and five men and a woman clamoured outside amidst a cloud of dense black smoke. Collapsing onto the curb, they coughed and chocked, gasping for air.

"FIRE!" shouted a passerby.

Helped by the gathering crowd, the occupants were moved well away from the building as several men went to investigate. Lizzie's attention was drawn to two workers in particular. They were reasonably well-dressed but it was unusual to see a woman working in an office and she was far too old. Noticing the gentle concern the young man was paying the distraught woman, Lizzie moved closer to hear their conversation.

"It will be all right, Mother. Please don't fret, uncle can't blame us for the fire," he was saying in a soothing tone.

The word *uncle* seared Lizzie's brain and she glanced at Quon realizing he had heard it too.

Moving quickly toward the couple, Lizzie offered the woman her arm and coaxed them to follow. She led them across the street to a low wall where they could sit and watch.

"You'll be safe here, ma'am," she said, gently. "Whose office is on fire?" she asked, even though she already knew the answer.

"My uncle's," groaned the young man.

"You're Wallace Dawson's nephew?"

"Yes, my mother is Wallace Dawson's sister."

Quon's reaction was instant, his fingers quickly sending a silent message onto his partner's arm. Their eyes met for one fleeting moment. She nodded and Quon left them, running up the street.

"Were you visiting your brother?" she asked, taking the distraught woman's hand.

Again the son answered, this time his voice had a definite ring of animosity. "No, we work here!" he said sharply. "Uncle reluctantly gave us a job when we were unable to pay our rent recently.

Quon returned with a small jug of brandy and two small glasses. He offered a drink to the Harris' and they accepted gratefully.

As she relaxed, the old lady looked wonderingly at Quon. "You're a gentleman, sir," she whispered. "Thank you."

"Mother," said the young man, rising to his feet, "we haven't properly introduced ourselves to these kind people.

"Oh yes, forgive us, please," she murmured, then fell silent again.

"My mother is Minnie Harris, wife of Tom, a naval man lost at sea many years ago. I am Alexander, their only son," a wry smile twisted his lips and his voice became a mere whisper. "We're the only living relatives of Wallace Dawson."

Lizzie's pulse quickened as Quon flashed her a wink. *What a stroke of luck.* She introduced herself and Quon as being the adopted children of Joe Todd and made an offer to help them get home.

"No, no," Alexander replied. "Uncle Wallace would be dreadfully upset if we didn't stay the regular hours. Then, as if realizing for the first time that the building was on fire, a look of panic came onto his face. "My goodness, I had better go see what I can do to help. We have some buckets in the building," he mumbled, obviously beginning to panic as he ran across the street. A small crowd had now congregated and many of them carried buckets although no one seemed to know where to find water.

"THERE IS NO FIRE. IT WAS A PRANK!" a man's voice shouted from across the street as he pointed toward the roof. A young man was cautiously removing Quon's obstruction from the chimney.

Realizing the smoke had almost dissipated, Minnie Harris, looking visibly relieved, turned to Lizzie. "You could call and visit us at our home, if it pleases you, dear. We live on Brook Lane, up behind the cemetery. We don't have many friends."

Bidding their new friends good day, Alexander tucked his mother's arm in his and they hurried off.

Chapter 25

On the long walk back to Mast Lane, Lizzie and Quon watched the hurrying, vibrant life of dockland. They momentarily felt the undercurrent of intrigue as a top-hated gentleman talked guardedly with two local ruffians. Coins changed hands and they hurriedly parted company leaving the partners to wonder if some illicit deed had been arranged.

They noticed familiar handbills nailed on doorposts and smiled at people's reactions as they gathered round and someone read it aloud. About half an hour later, they were close enough to the TLS dock to hear the familiar sound of Charley's steam engine. Crossing the street to look, they saw the white vapour shooting high into the air as its piston and drivewheels kept up their repetitive clanking.

Moving back across the street and passing *The Robin*, Quon glanced up Mast Lane, sniffing the air for the scent of new bread. Lizzie grinned, flicking him playfully across the ear as she headed for Abe's door.

Sitting alone at his worktable, Abe peered over his spectacles at the late visitors, laying the garment he was sewing to one side. His lips twitched nervously when he noted the grim expression on Lizzie's face.

"Who's Minnie Harris, Mister Kratze?" she asked, settling into the chair facing him.

Abe's head jerked up, eyes narrowing. "How did you find her?"

Expressionless, Lizzie waited. Quon's fingers tightened on her shoulder in warning.

"I'd almost forgotten about Minnie," Abe mused, a fleeting smile brushing his face. "She's Dawson's sister but he never forgave her for marrying Tom Harris." The old man's eyes closed as he turned back the pages of his mind. "Minnie was a sweet girl, always loyal to that rogue of a brother, although he didn't deserve it."

"She would never go against him?"

"No," said Abe, leaning toward her and lowering his voice, "but her son would, I'm told."

Lizzie refrained from commenting. Suddenly, her partner's stomach rumblings shattered the silence. Her eyes flicked up to Abe's old casement clock in the corner—five o'clock it said, and she patted his hand.

Rising to leave, Abe held his hand out to stop her. Lizzie waited as his bony hands shuffled through some papers on the table before producing the handbill Tom Day had left with his bread order.

"I want to be on this," he growled, pointing a long finger at the names on the bottom, "and so does Benny at the saddler's."

"And what about the lady's emporium?" said Lizzie, smiling mischievously and watching her old teacher's expression.

Embarrassed, Abe fumbled for words. "I don't talk of such things. Go away, girl, and arrange it."

Relief from the girl's teasing came in the form of Nathan, noisily entering the shop and shouting excitedly to his cousin. "HE'S DEAD … DEAD I TELL YOU, DEAD!"

"Who's dead?" Abe snapped, irritably.

"Wallace Dawson … killed in front of Josiah Cambourne's office not two hours ago," Nathan gasped. "Run over by one of his own drays. He's dead, ah tell you … dead as a doornail!"

"Easy there, Nathan," soothed Lizzie, "don't you go making wild assumptions."

"I saw him myself," the trader's voice rose again. "Believe me, lass, it's true."

Doubt raged through her mind as they hurried up the hill toward home. They found Joe at the gate, quietly puffing on his pipe as he waited for them."

"Problems, lass?"

"Not really …," she began as they walked to the door.

"Granddad!" Willie called from the doorway, barring their way by stretching his arms between the door posts. "We're going to have a baby!" he announced.

Dropping on her knees, Lizzie hugged the little boy and his arms wrapped around her neck grasping her tightly.

"My word," Joe cried. "Ada's havin a baby!"

Entering the cottage, they found Ada talking to Martha who was standing statue-like, holding a hot pan of fried potatoes in her hand.

"Then it be true. That bairn's been sayin that all day."

"Yes, it's true," admitted Ada, smiling happily but blushing self-consciously. "We'll talk about it at dinner when we are all together."

Charley and Captain Davis arrived soon after and they sat down so Martha could begin serving. She kept chuckling to herself as she handed the steaming plates of food around. Once the plates were emptied and pushed away, everyone's eyes lit up when she produced a large gooseberry pie. Smiling contentedly at their sighs, she topped each dish with spoonfuls of sweet yellow custard.

"Dammit you're a wonder, Martha," Davis exclaimed loudly, wiping the excess custard from his beard with a rag from his pocket. "I've a bit of news for you, Charley, and the rest of you."

Spoons stopped rattling as the engineer glanced over at Davis. Joe retired to his chair and Lizzie looked at her partner and winked.

"Tom Day says," Davis began, slowly measuring his words, "he saw Wallace Dawson knocked down and killed by one of his own drays this afternoon."

"Nathan told us that, too," Lizzie concurred.

"Sure hoy heard our drivers talkin, too," Mick agreed, "but hoy thought it were only a rumour."

"Oh my, poor man," the housekeeper whispered sympathetically.

Charley, nor any of the others, made any comment, but as they looked from one to the other their expression spoke volumes.

Joe tapped his pipe on the fire grate and, grinning foolishly, stuffed his pipe with fresh tobacco. "Ada lass, I believe yer have somethin to tell us."

The bookkeeper's face went quite pink and she reached for Mick's hand under the table.

"I'm, that is, we're having a baby," she admitted, "it's due around Christmas."

"By gum lass 'am thrilled for yer," Martha exclaimed, never having been married but always wishing she could have had children of her own. "Willie must be too, the way he's been talkin about it all day!" She hesitated as her eyes worriedly searched the room. "Where is Willie?"

"He's here," said Joe, "fast asleep with his head on my boot."

Ada's finger's tightened on Mick's hand as they watched Martha lift Willie from the floor and lay him on Joe's lap.

Captain Davis suddenly turned his chair to face Charley, chuckling loudly as he slapped him on the back.

"Well done, lad, well done!"

"Hold on a minute," Charley objected, amidst the laughter. "Ain't me that's done it!"

"No lad, but not everyone can be an uncle," Davis added for clarification.

"We happy too, Ada," added Quon. We wuv children, don't we Wizzy?"

Ada and Martha giggled and Lizzie hid her smile behind her hand.

Then Lizzie locked eyes with Ada across the table. "He's right you know. How I envy you, Ada."

"One day it will be your turn, love. In the meanwhile, we're happy to be able to share our family with yours. I love this unusual family of ours and I wouldn't change a thing," said Ada, thoughtfully, "even for King George's crown jewels. Now, take us home please, Mick."

Davis, too, was preparing to leave but hesitated as he stood up and turned to Lizzie. "I'll be at sea on your birthday, lass," he said. Then holding out his hand, she realized he was giving her something. She held out hers and he put a small package into it. "You're no longer the cheeky young brat I first knew. Perhaps you'll do me the honour of wearing this one day."

"What is it?" Martha murmured, straining to see.

Lizzie looked down at the tiny parcel in the palm of her hand. It was a very small box wrapped in gold cloth and tied haphazardly with a thin red ribbon. As they all peered at the gift, they hadn't noticed Davis leave and they now heard the door quietly close and the sound of the captain's feet fade into the quiet of the dockland evening.

Quon craned his neck to see over Lizzie's shoulder, Martha looked on from the sink and Joe watched in curiosity. Lizzie slowly unwrapped the parcel extracting a fine gold chain to which was attached a simple round gold locket.

"What is it, luv?" Martha repeated, coming closer as she dried her hands on the towel she was holding.

Lizzie put the box on the table and held up the chain for all to see.

"It's a locket, but why has Captain Davis given it to me?"

"I think you should open it, dear," Martha advised, softly.

Snapping the catch, it sprang open revealing the painted face of a beautiful lady. Lizzie gasped. Quon reached out and moved her thumb revealing another picture on the opposite side of the open locket.

"Oh look! The little painting looks like me!" cried Lizzie, showing it to each of them in turn.

"He's given yer his mother's locket," said Martha in a respectful whisper, "and had your picture added to it, Lizzie."

"But why?"

"Yer 18th birthday, luv. That's a very special keepsake. I believe our Captain Davis considers you a very special girl."

ဆေါက

Rumours of Wallace Dawson's death made their way quickly around dockland. Groups of pipe-smoking men stood talking loudly on the corners of alleyways, their conversations easily overheard as Lizzie and Quon made their way to *The Print Shop*.

As they passed each group, Quon's fingers tapped rapidly on Lizzie's arm. It was the same comment time after time. It seemed that everyone was happy to hear of the sudden demise of a tyrant.

Arriving at *The Print Shop*, they found frenzied activity as Frederick and Cuthbert worked the levers churning out sheet after sheet of the first issue of their newssheet. Lady Sutton and Margaret looked weary as their eyes checked each sheet as it printed.

Gabriel saw them first, waving an ink-stained hand in greeting. "STOP, that's enough," he shouted to the men.

Reaching for one of the printed sheets, Lizzie's eyes scanned the text. FATE PLUCKS TYRANT FROM DOCKLAND it said, in big bold letters across the top of the sheet. Below the headline followed the gruesome, detailed description of the accident. The rest of the handbill was filled with snippets of local news no doubt gleaned from the delivery lads. Across the bottom, in smaller bold letters were the words: DOCKLAND OBSERVER VOLUME ONE – HALFPENNY A COPY.

"Well, what's your verdict?" asked Lady Sutton, brushing several wisps of hair from her face.

"It's great," Lizzie answered, "but I think you should put the name of your newspaper on the top. That's a good price … two farthings… you must think halfpenny sounds better?"

"Yes, half of anything sounds less than two, but the name was my mistake," Margaret sighed. "I was tired, we've worked all night at it."

Quon's hands and arms began moving and they all waited for Lizzie's translation.

"He says next comes the hard part. Now you have to sell them!"

"Wrong, young lady!" came a familiar voice, startling them as he entered the shop. "I already have orders for a 100 and Billy needs 50 at the bake shop," explained Nathan.

"How did you get here so quietly—we saw your horse at the blacksmith's only a few minutes ago," Lizzie asked, suspiciously.

"I walked," retorted Nathan, strutting toward them, "but I intend to take the ladies home tonight. My horse will be ready by the time we leave here."

Gabriel cocked a weary eyebrow at the trader as Fred and Cuthbert got the press in motion again and the last of the handbills was spit out. "That's it, boys," he said, with a sigh. "Now it's quitting time for all of us."

"No, no," Nathan exclaimed, "you can't stop now, we need more."

"Please leave it, Mister Goldman," Lady Sutton murmured wearily, taking her coat off the hook. "It's been a long day already. We'll be back at midnight."

Raising an eyebrow, the trader stomped up to the machine circling it as he tapped it with the metal tip of his cane. Grinning mischievously, Gabriel stepped in front of him blocking his path, a bucket of ink swinging ominously in his hand.

"Take the ladies home or have a bath, the choice is yours, sir!" he said, pretending to lift the bucket.

A tinkle of laughter inadvertently escaped Lizzie's lips, when Nathan jumped backward retreating to the doorway.

"Come along, ladies, I have no time to waste here!"

Lizzie and Quon also left the shop continuing down Chandler, stopping once in awhile to eavesdrop on conversations. At the *Swan's* ale house, they saw a group of workman conversing with the innkeeper at the outside tables. They also were talking about Dawson and seemed to be in some doubt that the grain shipping company would survive without it's tyrant owner.

"I wonder who will take his place on council?" asked the innkeeper.

"Won't matter," a drayman growled despondently, spitting on the cobblestones. "They don't give a damn about us poor folks."

"Let's ask Abe," Lizzie whispered to her partner in answer to his silent question.

Moving on, they were soon able to hear Billy's voice in the next block. As they got closer, they realized he was already announcing the new *Observer*'s news story about Dawson's death.

"IT'S ALL HERE!" he yelled, waving a copy of the newspaper. "Come on, folks. Only two farthins … read all about it."

Quon's hand suddenly gripped Lizzie's elbow, pointing urgently to the two men in brown Johnny hats pushing through the crowd.

"They're after Billy," she hissed, following Quon as he moved through the shoppers to intercept the danger.

Looky here, folks," Billy yelled from his barrel-top perch. "These two bully boys must want to hear the news, too!" He pointed an accusing finger at the young men snatching handbills from the frightened shoppers as they forcefully pushed their way toward him. Billy continued to taunt the men, his voice ringing with fearless confidence. Then he put his fingers to his mouth and sent a high-pitched whistle bouncing off the buildings.

Screaming wild threats at the boy, the bullies soon found they had someone else to contend with as Lizzie and Quon placed themselves in front of the taunting lad.

"Who the hell are you?" Lizzie snarled at the aggressors, stalling for time as her eyes searched the crowd for help.

Cursing viciously the men began to advance again, waving the newssheets wildly and threatening the shoppers with raised cudgels.

"That's far enough, you dogs!" the familiar voice of Captain Davis called, emerging from the bake shop doorway. Removing his apron, he flicked it to a startled shopper as he stepped in beside Lizzie.

Grinning broadly, butcher Sid Sweeney also stepped into view, his bloody meat axe resting on his shoulder. "Now lads, trouble is it yer seekin?"

Fear and indecision flashed across the bullies' faces and their eyes searched for an escape route but the crowd was pressing in around them.

"J-just jesting, sir," one of the young men stammered.

"Give those people their newssheets back," demanded the butcher, easing the meat axe from his shoulder.

The bullies quickly, but reluctantly, returned the handbills to the shoppers, some of whom were snickering openly.

Billy's voice shouted a pertinent question. "Who sent yer here?"

Davis swung around to face the boy on the barrel, wagging his finger sternly and motioning him to come down. Lizzie watched as the captain's eyes turned soft and gentle when Billy landed beside him, laying a protective hand on his shoulder.

"Well man, answer the lad," Davis exclaimed.

Suddenly silent, the crowd also waited for the answer, watching as the bullies stuttered and stammered looking for an escape route.

Sid menacingly shuffled forward half a pace.

"C-Cambourne, sir ... Simon Cambourne," one of the men whined.

"LOUDER MAN, LOUDER," the captain's voice thundered.

"SIMON CAMBOURNE," the terror-stricken bullies bleated together.

"What do you want us to do with 'em Miss Lizzie," Davis growled.

"Throw 'em in the river," an old pipe-smoking woman in black bonnet and tattered shawl began chanting, between cackles of humourless laughter. The crowd pressed forward until the captain's voice stopped them.

He strode up to the petrified young men and demanded their belts. "Now you can throw them in the river!" he chuckled.

Quon's fingers tapped a nervous message on his partner's arm, as they watched a large contingent from the laughing crowd push the bullies down the street toward the river while they clutched at their pants.

"They can't hold pants and swim at same time," Quon said sadly, his mind not quite grasping the humour of the situation.

"Dumplin, yer priceless," Lizzie gasped. "Yes, they're going to be the laughing stock of dockland when they come out of the water!"

Things quickly settled back to normal and soon Tom and Oly

arrived with their fully loaded cart.

Time to go, Quon's fingers told her, and slipping quietly away they headed toward Abe's. It was a lovely, warm day and so they found his door propped open. Cautiously they stepped inside. Pausing between stitches, Clara glanced up and smiled. Abe, unaware of their presence, stood at his worktable cutting out a garment with a huge pair of scissors. Walking quietly up behind the old man Lizzie tapped him on the shoulder.

"La-ah-zazell," the old man spluttered, scissors leaping from his hand as he slumped into a nearby chair. "Don't do that, girl!"

Quon Lee moved quickly to aid the old tailor, gently patting his arm. Clara handed him his cup of tea and watched in fascinated silence as Quon rounded on his partner, arms and hands flying about in wild gyrations.

"All right, all right, I'm sorry," Lizzie snapped, slipping an arm over Abe's shoulder to comfort him.

Clara was unable to contain her curiosity. "What did he say?"

"I can't repeat it, luv," she replied, curtly. "He was cursing me!"

Her cheeks, going beet-root red, the dressmaker neatly folded her apron and quickly bid them good night.

Abe had recovered by now and waited for Lizzie to explain the reason for their visit. Spectacles balanced precariously on his long, thin nose, his eyes peered through bushy eyebrows. His hands slowly folded and unfolded.

"How is the local council formed?" she asked, taking him by surprise.

"Property," he muttered, stroking his wispy beard. "Only property owners may vote."

"Could I be a councillor?"

"Certainly not! You're not 21, and yer a woman!" He winced when he saw the flash of anger in Lizzie's eyes and noticed Quon's hands grip her shoulders more tightly. *I've done it now!*

"Why not a woman?" she asked, definitely agitated as she banged the table with her hand.

Abe flinched. "Never been done before," he retorted, nervously. "There are no women landowners."

"Well there are now, lad!"

The old tailor looked steadily at his star pupil, his mind turning over as he tried to make some sense of the conversation. *What is she planning now? Hashem, help that local council!*

Abe became aware that Quon's fingers were tapping on her shoulder. The trace of a smile came on her lips and she nodded slightly.

"Wallace Dawson was the biggest landowner in the district," he growled. "Can't see how you could match that kind of holding even if all of us threw in with you."

"You mean you'd back me?" she asked, reaching for the old man's hand, which he quickly withdrew.

"I would for Joe Todd, if you asked me."

The spontaneous outburst of laughter from the youngsters startled the tailor.

"Not Joe, Mister Kratze. It's a woman I want on council!"

"Won't happen," Abe retorted, standing up and beginning to pace between his stove and worktable. "A woman? No, no, no, that will never happen! Now be off with you, you're wasting my time."

Chapter 26

Dinner was already on the table when they arrived home and Martha's frown took their attention immediately. Taking their places, Lizzie noticed Ada was picking at her food.

"Is something wrong?" she asked.

"Morning sickness," the bookkeeper whispered, smiling weakly as she looked around at the men who all had their eyes on their plates. "It happens to some women when they are expecting."

"But it's not morning," Lizzie pointed out, having no knowledge of such matters.

"It starts in the morning and she's felt poorly all day," said Martha.

"Will it last long?"

"Oh my, I hope not," Ada sighed, as Mick came in and threw her a questioning look. "Please, just eat without me," she begged, looking from Lizzie to Mick.

They realized she didn't want to talk about it anymore and the men looked quite relieved.

Quon's fingers sent a sharp message on Lizzie's arm, his eyes searching the room.

"Where's Willie?" she translated.

"With the gypsies," replied Martha, through a mouthful. "Jeb took him up to the camp this afternoon to see the baby and play with the children."

After dinner, Mick, with concern for his wife showing in his eyes, announced he was taking her home.

"Don't you worry none about Willie, he'll be pleased as punch to stay the night with us," Martha assured them.

No sooner had they left when Jeb returned with Willie and Martha went to find his nightshirt.

Suddenly, Captain Davis began to chuckle to himself, which

slowly turned into raucous laughter.

"Whatever's gotten inta him?" asked Martha, struggling to undress the boy because Willie was mimicking him.

When the captain's laughter diminished, he related the events of the afternoon for Joe and Martha's benefit, giving a graphic description of the two bullies floating in the river trying to swim while clutching at their pants.

"That'd be quite difficult, I dare say," Martha tittered.

"That's not all of it though," Davis continued. "I called at the printer's and saw Margaret Sutton. She said they would be printing it in their second issue."

"I bet that'll make Josiah Cambourne a happy man!" Lizzie commented sarcastically as the rattle of Charley's transport was heard outside.

Morning brought a cool wind coupled with a heavy mist that swirled around the streets of dockland giving the buildings an eerie appearance in the early light as Lizzie and Quon started on their rounds. Noses twitching at the slaughterhouse stink being blown their way, their shadowy figures melted in and out of the gloom as they walked toward the Thames.

Abe stood on his doorstep, his shoulders draped in an old woolen shawl as he strained to see through the mist. "A bloody nuisance," he grouched, puffing hard on his pipe totally unaware that Lizzie and Quon had come up behind him. "Can't see a blasted thing."

Lizzie was about to reach out and touch him when Quon grabbed her hand. Without noticing them, Abe clutched the shawl tighter around his thin body and shuffled back inside his store.

"We go see Bill," Quon muttered, pulling on his partner's sleeve.

Nearing the baker's yard, they heard the voices of Tom and Oly, followed by their loud laughter which always traveled farther through the quietness of a fog.

"NOW WHAT'S ALL THIS NOISE ABOUT?" Lizzie shouted, trying to make her voice sound like a man's.

"It's Miss Lizzie!" Oly cried, dumping an armful of bread on the cart as the partners stepped out of the mist.

"Av yer seen it yet, lass?" Bill asked, chuckling softly.

"Seen what?"

"T'Observer."

"Whatever is a tob-server, Bill?"

"He means the Dockland Observer, miss," laughed Clem.

"Oh yes, they've come out with their second volume haven't they? Let's see it, Bill," she said, blatantly curious.

Bill nodded. Then he began to laugh and his rotund figure wobbled even more as he walked toward her offering her his copy.

Lizzie read it quickly and when she reached the bottom she stared in disbelief at the picture drawn in freehand. She too, burst into laughter at the picture which clearly showed two men swimming in the river with their pants around their ankles as several ducks pecked at their bare bottoms. The caption beneath read: DOCKLAND JUSTICE AT WORK.

Laughing, Quon's arms flailed about wildly.

"I agree," Lizzie giggled. "It's brilliant, is it Fred's work?"

"Margaret said Fred did it, Miss Lizzie," said Tom, indicating to Oly it was time to go. "Mister Nathan already delivered 200 before we left the bake shop." His voice trailed off as he followed Oly out of the yard.

They stayed for awhile to talk with Bill, mentioning the council seat that Dawson's death had left vacant.

"I wonder who might be filling it now?" he mused.

"Would you back us if I put somebody up for it, Bill?"

"Careful lass," the baker began in a serious tone, "ah'll back you anytime … but only if yer get that pie-eating fiend outa here!"

"Oh, you keep him. I'm off!" she called, moving off quickly toward the gate.

The baker grinned as Quon Lee looked up in surprise and scrambled off after her, pie in hand.

"What's yer hurry, dumplin?" Bill heard Lizzie say as she linked arms with him.

ଞଔଔ

They stood watching as Charley directed the loading of Lady Sutton's new ship. Renamed *Restitution*, she had undergone some extensive renovations along with the necessary minor repairs, by the skilled TLS shipwrights. Lizzie's eyes came to rest on the steam engine now sitting on an empty dock. She stared thoughtfully at the empty space and the ghost of an idea crept into her brain.

Quon's fingers sent a swift message through her hand and she gazed down the street where several groups of merchant traders had congregated. She heard loud laughter and realized they were reading the Dockland Observer pinned to a nearby pole.

"Dawson's office," she muttered determinedly, pulling him along by his coat sleeve.

As they walked, they noticed other groups reading copies of the newssheet and their enthusiastic laughter told the story of their enjoyment. Fred's new cartoon was a huge success.

Warm sunshine had begun to penetrate the mist and by the time the dark, foreboding exterior of Dawson's building came into view, they were feeling quite warm.

Confidently opening the door, they stepped inside.

"What the hell do you want?" the man sitting behind the desk in the outer office rasped.

"Missus Harris ... or Alexander, if you please, sir."

"Nobody here by that name, begone!"

A woman's distressed voice drifted out through a slightly open door and the low voice of Alexander Harris consoling his mother was heard in the outer office.

"Don't recognize those names, sir?" the girl exclaimed, smiling coldly as she moved toward the open door.

Quon's eyes narrowed and he stepped in behind Lizzie just as the clerk leapt to his feet, sending his stool crashing to the floor. Not bothering to pick it up, he tried to reach the door first but Quon barred his way. The noise brought Alexander to the door which he flung open, coming face to face with Lizzie.

"Gordon Piggot," he shouted, "that is quite enough!"

Sneering, the clerk faced Alexander, hatred burned in his eyes. "Yer nothing but a clerk! I run this firm. IT'S MINE NOW!" he screamed, his voice rising as he got more and more agitated.

Alexander came toward them, looking helplessly at his emotional staff member as Quon moved hurriedly outside. A long, shrill whistle sounded and Lizzie knew he had signaled for help.

A red-faced Minnie Harris appeared to stand beside her son. "Please, Gordon, be reasonable," she whispered, tearfully.

"Damn you all, madam, it's mine ...," the clerk insisted, banging his fist violently on the desk, his face contorted in anger. "Wallace always said ...."

Suddenly, the outside door burst open and Piggot's face turned ashen as Nathan Goldman's two large gypsies ran into the room, cudgels in hand.

"Yer need us, Miss Lizzie?" Dan asked, as they flanked the young people.

"Throw that one out," Lizzie commanded, pointing at the clerk. "He's not needed here."

"Oh my," Minnie wailed. "What are we to do?"

"Hush, mum, it's all right," Alexander whispered, slipping an arm around the older woman and gently coaxing her back into the owner's office.

Piggot, eyes wide as the gypsies advanced on him, made a wild dash for the door aided by a firm gypsy boot landing solidly on his posterior. Nathan, waiting just outside the door, jumped backwards when the man stumbled past him.

"Is it safe to come in now?" he asked, poking his head tentatively inside. Receiving no answer, he timidly stepped inside, eyes darting around the office. "Lizzie," he bleated, finding no one there except his own two men.

"In here."

Hearing her voice, he squared his shoulders, removed his hat and marched confidently into the room he knew to be the owner's office. His footsteps faltered, but only for an instant, when he saw Minnie and her son behind the desk.

"Nathan Goldman, ma'am, at your service," he said, recovering from his surprise and bowing slightly.

"Stop crying, Missus Harris," Lizzie was saying. "We want to help you, so please listen for a moment."

Minnie Harris dried her eyes and looked up at the young woman who of late had seemed to always appear when they were in trouble.

"We are from the TLS shipping company ... your competitors, Missus Harris," Lizzie began. "You're going to have trouble running this grain business now that we have the unloading machine working again."

"You're going to ruin us, aren't you?" Alexander interrupted, his fingers tightening on his mother's shoulder. "Uncle said you would."

Eyes flashing, Lizzie turned to the young man.

"Can you run this company?" she snapped, watching him shake his head. "Then don't make stupid assumptions."

Nathan chuckled quietly. *That was your first mistake, m'lad. You'd better not assume anything about this young lady.*

Careful, said Quon's fingers gently gripping her elbow, his stone-faced expression giving nothing away.

"Hush Alex," his mother gently scolded. "Let her speak."

"Missus Harris," Lizzie began again, her eyes locking on Minnie's across the desk. "Alexander will be able to manage this business if he gets some help from Charley Mason."

"Who is Charley Mason?" she asked.

"Our dockmaster," Lizzie replied. "We will unload your ships at our dock with our steam engine … for a fee of course!"

Minnie's eyes jerked up to look at her son. He ruefully smiled down at her, patting her on the shoulder as he nodded his approval, knowing they had no choice.

Scratching his chin, Nathan tried to find the key to Lizzie's reasoning, biting hard on his lip in frustration when he found none.

"That's very decent of you," Alexander was saying.

"There's more to it yet, lad. I want your mother's backing for a new member on council … someone to take the place of your uncle."

I should have known, thought Nathan.

Minnie Harris stared at the lovely, yet brash, young woman whom she hardly knew. Unsure why she should trust a competitor and a stranger to help them, she considered her options. *There really aren't any,* she thought, her eyes misting over again. *No, I have a good feeling about this girl.* She felt Alex's hand tighten slightly on her shoulder and she looked up at the girl and nodded her head. "Josiah will not like this one bit," she murmured.

"Who the hell cares!" Lizzie retorted, moving closer and leaning across the desk. "We don't like his methods either!"

Stifling his urge to laugh, Nathan tapped the floor with his cane and strutted over to the desk. "Madam, Nathan Goldman at your service, would you like me to take care of the funeral arrangements for your dear, departed brother?"

Missus Harris' lip trembled a little. "Oh, Mister Goldman, such a lot has happened in the last two days." She looked up at her son who nodded. "We would be most grateful."

"Leave the arrangements to Mister Goldman, luv," said Lizzie, "we'll come back in a few days."

"No, no, please don't go yet," the older woman pleaded, hearing the sound of movement in the outer office.

"WHAT THE HELL'S GOING ON HERE?" demanded a man's loud voice.

Dan appeared at the door. "We have a sea captain out here, Miss Lizzie, says he wants to see Mister Dawson."

"Elijah Harmon!" Minnie groaned.

Lizzie noticed the colour drain from Alexander's face and glanced inquiringly at her partner as his fingers sent an urgent message down her arm. However, before he could finish, the hulking figure of Captain Elijah Harmon stomped into the room.

"I WANT DAWSON!" he demanded, his voice seeming to make the pictures rattle on the wall. He looked menacingly around the room. "Where is Dawson?" he repeated.

"He-he died!" said Alexander, haltingly. "I-I'm in charge now."

"Like hell you are, lad. I'll not be taking orders from a pup!" he cried and turning on his heel, Harmon moved toward the door, scowling at the gypsy blocking his exit.

Lizzie's voice cut through the tension. "Let him go, Dan. He's too stupid to see the prospects of making good money."

Elijah Harmon stopped and slowly turned to face the girl who dared to taunt him. Scowling, his eyes raked the figure of the nubile young woman who stood calmly waiting for his reaction. He looked about the room and noticed that the young Chinaman who had been at her side since he entered had now stepped slightly between them, a movement which screamed caution to the wily captain. *Could this be the red-headed girl he'd heard so much about ... Lizzie Short? Yes, that was her name. It had been tossed about by many a sailor and merchant in recent months, and not all of it was favourable.*

"You're Lizzie Short," he hissed, through clenched teeth.

"Yes, I am, and like it or not you're going to listen, Captain Harmon."

Over the next half hour Lizzie turned Elijah Harmon into a believer as she explained the increase in bonus that was possible for him to earn under her system. The figures she threw at him regarding tonnage of grain delivered, and off-loaded at dockside, finally brought a smile to his weather-beaten old face. He didn't much relish the thought of sailing his ship into the TLS dock to be unloaded ... after all they were Dawson's competitors, but he was certainly not stupid as she had at first intimated.

Minnie Harris watched silently as Lizzie skillfully turned Elijah's thinking around. Competition or not, this girl had a grasp on business matters few men could lay claim to; the way she controlled the conversation and tamed the wild captain had been easy for this confident young woman. Glancing up at her son, Minnie resolved to give Lizzie Short her total support—she liked this girl!

Captain Harmon was a happier man as he strode up Dock Street to his favourite ale house, waving to Nathan as his coach trotted by. He felt strangely good, despite discovering that his friend had died, wondering briefly what had happened, deciding it didn't really matter anyway. Dawson had made money for them ... lots of money, but he would never call him a friend. His fortunes were changing again and he could deal with a girl much easier than that bombastic Dawson. Doubt, however, still lingered deep in his mind. Who was this Lizzie Short? He planned to keep a close eye on her from now on.

As Lizzie and Quon left Dawson's office, Lizzie lapsed into silence as she weighed her options in the naming of a person to council. Engrossed in her thoughts, she hardly noticed the passers-by. In sight of the *Swans*, Quon grabbed her elbow and pointed across the street to a fruit vendor whose mobile barrow was stacked high with apples for sale. They watched as three street urchins plied their tricks as they tried to steal apples from the man. One ragged little boy fell to the ground groaning in pain as the vendor moved to investigate. Behind his back, two more dirty urchins quickly filled their pockets.

Lizzie gasped when she saw the danger lurking, wanting to warn them, but alas, it was too late as two men came forward and quickly seized the lads. Throwing caution to the wind, she grabbed Quon's arm and raced across the street. The vendor, now holding tight to the sobbing decoy, violently berated the frightened young lads, as a voice from the gathering crowd yelled for the law. Quick decisions had to be made and Lizzie knew it. Her fingers swiftly checked the coins in her pocket, as she pushed through the crowd.

"How much for yer cart full of apples?" she called to the vendor.

"Two shillings," he lied, but his look of innocence quickly turned to surprise when Lizzie slammed two silver shillings in his hand.

"FREE APPLES, 'ELP YERSELVES FOLKS!" she yelled.

Suddenly, there was a wild scramble with people pushing and shoving and the young urchins were totally forgotten.

Quon disappeared as Lizzie grabbed the young lad from the startled vendor's grasp, moving quickly into the crowd. Dragging the boy behind her, she ducked down a snicket, racing through familiar alleyways to emerge at the back of the *Swans*. Red-faced and panting, she pulled the confused urchin to a halt and pointed to the darkened corner. There on a barrel sat Quon holding onto the lad's two partners.

"Dammit, that was too close, lads" she said, winking at Quon Lee.

"Thank yer, miss. Can we go now please, miss?" begged one of the older boys, edging away from the group.

"Come back here, lad. We're not going to hurt yer," she assured them. "We can catch you again, if we have to."

Only the noise of ale house laughter broke the stillness of the yard as the boy weighed his chances of escape, his eyes measuring the distance to freedom. Slowly, he came back to her side.

"Yer wouldn't have made it, lad," she said, slipping her arm over his shoulder.

Talking quietly to the three petrified boys loosened the tension and Lizzie began to explain the risks the boys were taking, and the consequences if they were caught.

"But we were hungry, miss," the young decoy interrupted.

Lizzie felt a lump form in her throat as memories of her dear friends, Willie, Kate and the Smith boys crossed her mind. It seemed like only yesterday when they had been caught and she could still see that dreadful scene as they were hauled off to jail. She could still hear Kate screaming. Then the heart-wrenching court scene when the judge passed their sentence of deportation. She heard they had gone to Australia and had never seen them again.

"Tell yer what, lads," she whispered, her voice hoarse. "If you ask anybody at the slaughterhouse for food, they'll feed you, and then ther's Billy at the bake shop on the corner—he's usually got a spare loaf or two." Lizzie knew her advice would go unheeded. This was a way of life for the hundreds of dockland urchins and they only trusted their own.

"We wate again," Quon muttered.

"Yes lad, we're late again," Lizzie sighed as she flicked her hand and the three young lads disappeared amongst London's labyrinth of alleyways. "Let's go home, dumplin."

Going past the *Swans,* they noted it was filled to capacity spilling patrons out onto a cobblestoned area where they used upturned barrels as tables. They were a mismatched group of rough sailors and merchants in their fancy beaver-skin top hats. Skirting the crowd, Quon pointed to Tom Legg, moving about precariously as he balanced a drink in his free hand with its conspicuous missing fingers.

"Ignore him, dumplin," Lizzie muttered, "he's drunk, we'll get no sense out of him today."

Tom's loud voice still echoed in the background as they turned up Pump Street.

₧₧

"Is Willie with the gypsies again, Martha," asked Lizzie, joining the others at the dinner table.

"Aye lass, he loves it up there and asked to stay the night. He's been home twice through the day," the housekeeper chuckled. "Had ta see his granddad at lunch time for somethin, then he brought a bunch of gypsy young'uns in the middle of the afternoon an they et all my fresh-backed scones."

"Good for him," Joe grunted, not lifting his eyes as he rocked gently in his chair and stuffed tobacco into his old smoke-blackened pipe. "That's what grandma's are for, ain't they?"

There was no reply from the housekeeper who found a long sliver of wood to light the old man's pipe. Poking it into the flames, she watched it catch fire, then held the flame to his pipe.

"Careful woman," Joe growled, before sucking deeply on the shortened stem. "Yer going to set me nose on fire!" A ripple of laughter went around the room.

"Didn't you get the new pipe I sent you, Joe?" Ada asked. "I gave it to Mick this morning." Turning to her husband, she raised her eyebrows questioningly.

"Ah sure hoy gave it ta Martha, hoy did!" retorted Mick, a hurt look on his face.

"Aye lass, he gave it ta me alright," said the housekeeper, as she flicked the burning splinter into the fire. "But that old softy gave it ta Willie at lunchtime!"

"He needed it!" Joe grunted softly.

"Needed it for what?" asked Lizzie, watching his eyes flicker and shut.

Joe ignored them letting out a contented sigh, but a little smile bent his lips and as he continued to draw on his pipe. Waiting for Martha to answer, he let the blue smoke trickle from the corners of his mouth as he pretended to be asleep.

"Fer blowing soap bubbles!" the housekeeper exclaimed, shaking her head. "Not many granddads would allow that!"

Chapter 27

"So, young lady," Ada asked purposefully turning to Lizzie after dinner had been cleared away. "Talk around dockland says TLS is taking over Dawson shipping. Have you got something to tell us?"

Quon noticed Charley's instant reaction and his hand disappeared under the table. Lizzie leveled her eyes on the bookkeeper, slowly shaking her head. Paying close attention, Charley's gaze swung from one woman to the other while, unseen Quon's fingers screamed, 'Nathan, Nathan' on Lizzie's arm.

"Nathan told you, didn't he? Well, as usual, he got it all wrong."

Charley's shoulders sagged with relief.

"We made a deal though," Lizzie continued. "We're going to unload their grain ships with your steam engine."

"Their men and drays?" asked the dockmaster. "I haven't any men to spare."

"Yes lad, their men, their drays, our steam engine and operator and we get a fee." She noticed Ada's eyes brighten. "This way, Missus Harris will be able to keep Dawson's going, men will keep their jobs, and more hungry children won't end up on the streets begging for food."

Under the table, her fingers searched frantically for Quon's as long-ago memories returned.

"You can't change the world, love," Ada whispered.

"You ain't heard it all yet," Lizzie's face twisted into a smile. "Minnie Harris has agreed to back my choice for council."

"Now who would that be, darlin?" Mick asked. "Not yer dad, hoy'll be bound, nor me or Charley!" he laughed. "Could it be yer plannin to turn Captain Davis loose on them high-and-mighty gents?"

As the laughter died, Ada looked over at Lizzie. A feeling of trepidation had crept up her spine knowing in her heart Lizzie fully intended to shake dockland with her new machine, and her future plans, whatever they might be.

"Who do you want?" the bookkeeper whispered. "And how will you get him nominated? He'll have to be a property owner."

Charley heard his transport arrive but showed no sign of moving.

"I'm going to get a woman accepted onto council," she retorted.

The words struck like a thunderbolt.

"Yer not old enough," Joe growled, his eyes flicking suddenly open. "Yer only 18, and that's not 'till Friday."

"Not me, Dad."

"Then who?" Ada persisted.

Quon's hand jumped onto the table tapping wildly.

"Lady Sutton," Lizzie stated, grinning mischievously as she added, "but she doesn't know it yet!"

Gasping, Ada shook her head. "You haven't told her?"

"No!"

Joe's pipe rattling on the fire grate rescued Lizzie from further questions. "Bedtime folks!" he exclaimed, rising to poke at the few remaining embers on the hearth.

Shuffling painfully toward the door, Charley stopped for a moment behind Lizzie's chair. He placed a hand on her shoulder and proclaimed softly, "You lead little captain, and I'll follow." Helped out by the Grim boys, they soon heard his transport rattle off.

Still shaking her head in confusion, Ada allowed Mick to lead her out the door and down the stairs. After banging the gate behind them, Mick pulled her close and they walked home with arms around each other.

"What the devil is she up to now?" she whispered, looking up at him.

"Opportunity, m'darlin," Mick answered, squeezing her closer, "she's plannin somethin, that's for sure."

Joe, now fully awake, took a seat at the table and indicated two chairs to his young partners. Adjusting his pipe, he wheezed a little then cleared his throat.

"There'll be trouble lass, council men won't take kindly to a woman."

"I know."

"Then you'd better make sure you can swim before you jump into that water, it's not a bunch of drunken sailors yer dealing with this time."

"Do you know any of them, Dad?"

"Aye lass, and so do the both of you."

"We do!" she whispered, looking over at Quon. "Who?"

"Well, first off, the local minister always has a seat on council."

Lizzie and Quon's eyes flashed at each other and Quon reached for the slateboard behind him. Oh yes, they knew the minister all right, they'd often seen the man and watched his cruel intimidation of the old gravedigger.

Joe scratched his whiskered chin. "Ther's also Admiral Jones from the Navy and Jonas Crowther who owns several corn mills." He added quickly, "Yer already familiar with that nasty one. On the other hand, there's Richard Byrd, a timber merchant. He's a good old fella is Dick." The old man paused, puffing blue smoke as he tried to remember the others. "Dawson's dead," he said under his breath. "Oh yes, there's Judge Harvey, he's the one who sent yer friends to Australia, lass ... the bastard. And there's two representatives from local tradesmen, but ah can't recall their names."

"Got all that?" Lizzie muttered, looking at Quon who was writing furiously.

"Did!" he answered.

Martha sighed as she watched Lizzie and Quon help Joe to his room a few minutes later. She turned the oil lamps out one by one and the cottage fell into darkness.

Hurrying, the two partners made their way down Water Lane, hoping to catch Abe. There were questions Lizzie needed to ask the old tailor and Abe always seemed to know the answers.

"Good morning, my dears," he murmured pleasantly.

"Why are you so happy?" Lizzie inquired, suspiciously.

"Heard a rumour," he chuckled. "Come in. Come in. Have a peppermint tea with old Abe."

Shrugging their shoulders, they followed him into his shop. Abe's mood had them baffled, his usually grumpy attitude was missing. He was even humming a little tune as he poured the hot water onto the peppermint syrup and pushed two tankards toward them.

Taking up their usual positions, she shot a question at the old man.

"So what's the rumour you heard?"

"Heard TLS had taken over Dawson shipping."

"Well yer wrong, we haven't."

"Don't lie to me, girl," Abe snapped, his humour disappearing, "I saw one of Dawson's ships pulling into your dock."

"We're unloading for them using Charley's steam engine."

The tailor thumped the table. "Dammit girl you're creating your own competition. Dawson's are finished, Minnie Harris is a nobody," he said, angry that she could make such a business blunder.

Quon's fingers tightened on Lizzie's shoulder, but too late. He saw her fingers ball into fists and she leapt to her feet, eyes blazing. Unnoticed, Clara Spencer had entered with the tailor's breakfast. With hands shaking, she put down the tray and, stood quietly.

"Shut your mouth," Lizzie cried. "Minnie Harris is a woman, a human being who needs help."

Abe cowered in his chair, his nervous twitching fingers upsetting his almost empty teacup. His spectacles slipped down his nose as his eyes followed the liquid dripping through a crack in the table.

Clara's knees threatened to give way as she listened to Lizzie's barrage. This girl had gumption there was no doubt about that.

"I'm going to help her," continued the girl, settling back on her chair. She was now in complete control. Her voice had become softer but her intensity hadn't wavered. "You say we are creating our own competition, well I say we're controlling it!"

A sudden silence settled over the store as the tailor shuffled uncomfortably under Lizzie's eyes. Inwardly, he was stunned by the subtle logic of his pupil. Perhaps he was wrong this time.

"Your breakfast, sir," Clara said timidly, taking the opportunity to come forward with his tray.

"Leave it there, luv," said Lizzie, indicating the worktable, but her eyes had not left the tailor who was obviously feeling quite uncomfortable. Clara left quickly, and the door banged shut behind her. "Now, tell me about the council."

Abe's head jerked up. "The council?"

"Yes, what happens now Dawson is dead?"

"I already told you, the landowners pick a new man."

"Or woman," Lizzie whispered, leaning toward him.

"No, no lass, no women … all men."

"And what do the rules say about that?"

"The rules," Abe muttered to himself, tapping a bony finger on the tabletop. "The rules give the seat to the man with the most support from landowners on the tax rolls. He must be a landowner, also."

"Or she ...," Lizzie corrected, smiling disarmingly.

Brow furrowed, the tailor stared at the girl, quaking a little as he adjusted hid wire-framed spectacles. *What the devil is she up to?*

"Dawson's the biggest landowner in this borough," he muttered, "then William Crowther, Admiral Jones, Richard Byrd, the Suttons, and some of the nobility."

Eyebrows raised, he waited for the next question. He suspiciously glanced at Quon as his fingers made a sudden movement on Lizzie's shoulder.

"Well, then old friend," she chuckled, "if I get Dawson, Sutton and TLS to agree, I could put on someone of my choice."

The tailor nodded thoughtfully. "You need a nominator, someone who owns land, but you'll never get Dawson or James Sutton to agree."

"Dawson's dead!" the girl reminded him. "Minnie Harris owns Dawson land now and Lady Sutton is rid of James, permanently!" She paused, watching his expression become one of panic as he tried to work out what she meant. "And yer my nominator!"

Abe spread out his hands on the table and he glared at her across the table. "Yer not old enough, lass."

There was absolute silence in the room as he waited for her reply.

"Not me, silly, Lady Sutton!" she laughed.

Abe's face showed some relief but he was sweating profusely by now. "I must ask one question," he said, although it was most apparent that he feared the answer.

"Ask!"

"What happened to James Sutton, is-is he d-dead?"

"No, he's on a ship bound for Australia. He's earning his keep as an indentured sailor, a fitting ...."

"Enough! Don't say anymore," he retorted, wiping the sweat from his brow.

Lizzie winked at Quon and she began her negotiations. In less than two minutes, a gold sovereign had changed hands and the old tailor assured her of his complete co-operation. Lizzie poured him a fresh cup of peppermint tea and told him to relax and eat some breakfast. "Everything is going to work out fine, Mister Kratze. Remember, you taught me!"

The distinctive smell of new bread met their nostrils and the sounds of Oly's pony cart wheels filled the air as the partners turned into the wide alley leading to the bakery.

"Apple pie time, Mister Bill!" Quon shouted punching the air and eagerly dashing ahead of his partner to join the men who were busy reading something on the table. The men began to laugh uncontrollably and the partners hurried over to see what it was all about. On the table was the freshly printed Dockland Observer and Fred's latest cartoon.

"Over here, Mister Quon," Oly yelled, his squeaky young voice cutting through the laughter.

Coming closer, Bill handed Lizzie the paper.

"By gum," Bill spluttered, "that lad has a rare sense of humour."

Fred's drawing was of an angel beating the living daylight out of a strange likeness to Wallace Dawson. A tiny cross hovered over his outstretched hand which held a gold sovereign. Bold letters formed the caption: JUST DESSERTS? The question mark was hugely exaggerated.

When Oly had left with his loaded cart, Lizzie explained her proposition to the baker between mouthfuls of apple pie. Bill frowned a little at the strange situation of supporting the very first woman councillor of dockland.

Listening from the bake house doorway, Connie Johnson joined the discussion, loudly voicing her own strong opinions on the role she thought women should play in local government. Lizzie grinned at way the lady berated her husband and vowed their support, winking at the girl as she turned away knowing she'd completely convinced her husband.

"Are you trying to start a revolution where women think ther equal to us men, Miss Lizzie?" Clem chuckled.

"What did you say, Clem?" demanded Connie, storming back out of the bake house, eyes blazing and finger raised as she headed toward their assistant. Picking up a loaf out of the stale-bread barrel, she raised it into the air. Running for cover behind the barrels, Clem screamed in mock terror as the hard loaf bounced off his head.

"You turd!" she yelled, standing hands on hips in the middle of the yard, "so yer think yer Lizzie Short's equal do ya lad? Well think about it. Who owns yer damned steam engine now?" She paused to smile coyly as she adjusted the little white bonnet on her head, then she glowered at Clem again. "Yer think yer equal to Ada at the TLS offices, Lady Sutton at the printers, or Minnie Harris down at Dawson's shipyard? I think not lad! And then there's me," she hissed. "Tell me lad, do you pay me ... or do I pay you?"

By now Clem had his hands raised in surrender and his face was beet-root red. Connie, obviously satisfied with herself, brushed her hands over her apron and stomped back into the bake house.

"So now tha knows," said Bill, grinning at his helper who was looking rather dazed.

"Oven's ready, Clem," Connie's voice rang across the yard, and he scurried off.

Quon grinned through his mouthful as his partner joined him at the table.

"You greedy little pig." she wailed, staring at the small portion of pie he'd left her. Suddenly, she reached over and seized Quon's cap from his head, flinging it into a nearby rain barrel.

But Quon had seen his chance and, snatching the last of the pie, raced for the lane.

"Would you believe it, he's pinching me pie ... me that's looked after him all these years!"

"God bless him, lass," the baker muttered, thinking how lucky they all were that Quon protected her so well. "That lad would die for ye."

"Aye, and damn nearly did," she replied, leaning across the table.

"Ah'll get yer sum pie, lass," Bill growled, laying his hand on her shoulder, "then you tell me what yer want me to do."

With a fresh pie in front of them and Quon nowhere in sight, she and Bill began quietly discussing strategy. When Quon returned he crept over to the table, sat down, and listened.

"I can control that seat on council with the Sutton, Dawson and TLS land, but if we get a hundred small landowners like yerself to back us, they'll not be able to stop me."

"You've come a long way from the days when you used to deliver bread from a basket, luv."

"Long way to go yet, lad," she chuckled, as she stood up. Scooping Quon's soggy cap from the rain barrel, she threw it at him.

Over at the printing shop, Margaret and her mother were pouring over the growing list of advertisers. Behind them Fred and Cuthbert grunted with exertion as they printed the backside of the handouts.

Outside, the two partners watched from across the lane as Gabriel handed out parcels of ten sheets into the eager hands of street urchins who scampered off in different directions.

"What they doing?" Quon asked, watching the parade of street lads.

His question remained unanswered as Lizzie tugged on his sleeve and pointed at the coach coming slowly up Chandler. The driver's eyes were searching every opening before slowly stopping at the entrance to Brown's yard.

Pointing at *The Print Shop* the driver opened the door and a tall, foreboding figure stepped out onto the cobblestones.

"That's Judge Harvey," Lizzie whispered, a trace of fear in her voice.

Walking stick waving wildly, Judge Harvey snarled abuse at the line up of street urchins waiting outside the door. His stick slashing the handouts from one of the youngster's hands caused the rest of the lads to shrink back in fear.

Lady Sutton, hearing the commotion, came to the door and called loudly. "Aurelius Harvey, stop that immediately!"

Eyebrows raised, the partners looked at each other. Here was an interesting twist of fate. Lady Sutton obviously knew the judge.

"Penelope Sutton!" London's most notorious judge growled in disbelief as his long clay pipe dropped from his hand to smash on the cobbles.

They had known each other all their lives—each from noble families when their fathers had been friends. She knew of his brutish, bullying ways and remembered the time her father had threatened to whip him for the hurt he'd caused her as a child. There were no friendly feelings in Lady Sutton's heart for this man, only hate and loathing lingered there.

Gathering new courage, thanks to Lizzie's tutelage and armed with the knowledge that she'd been blatantly cheated by a man, the once-demure Penelope Sutton was no more. Now, she feared no one.

"Out of my way, woman," Judge Harvey snarled. "I'll speak with the owner."

"I am the owner."

Shocked by her answer, he reeled a little, his eyes quick to notice the black-aproned figure of Gabriel Flood moving protectively to her side. But he failed to see the wink of devilment the old lady shot across the lane at Lizzie and Quon.

Backing away, Judge Harvey shouted one last threat. "My council will close you down, Penny Cross."

"Who's Penny Cross?" Quon whispered.

Lizzie shrugged her shoulders and they watched as the coach departed and Penelope Sutton returned to her work. She stood by her worktable, pleased with herself as she blew at a wisp of hair that had fallen across her face. Her eyes danced with excitement as they landed on Lizzie coming through the door.

"Thanks for giving me courage, love," she murmured. "I'm really enjoying myself!"

"You were magnificent, but who's Penny Cross?"

"Me! Cross was my maiden name. Daddy was Sir William Cross."

"So you're ready for a fight, are you?" Lizzie whispered.

Quon clutched at her sleeve to get her attention. She watched his arms whirling and nodded.

"What did he say?" Margaret giggled.

"He says I have to tell your mother."

"Tell me what?"

Lady Sutton's question brought a sudden quietness to the shop.

"You are going to sit on the borough council, Lady Sutton," announced Lizzie.

There was absolute quiet in the room for a moment as they all looked at her in amazement.

"Have you gone crazy, girl?" Gabriel asked, taking Cuthbert's place at the press. "They're no more than a bunch of rogues, those old men. They'll tear her to pieces."

"No, they won't," Penelope said defiantly, "but they won't take kindly to it."

"Yer not afraid?" Lizzie asked.

"Don't need to be, when my husband was alive, we entertained four of them at Sutton House, on separate occasions. I could tell you stories of those four gentlemen that would make your hair curl. They are gentlemen though and would treat me fairly, I truly believe."

Lizzie and Quon's eyes clashed as similar thoughts flashed thought their minds.

Treat you fairly, like a snowball in hell they would! was Lizzie's fearful belief. "Will you write me those stories, Lady Sutton?"

"Of course I will love, you shall have every sordid detail!"

Before leaving the shop, Quon's fingers reminded Lizzie to ask about the street lads running off with bundles of handouts.

"Oh, that was Billy's idea," Gabriel laughed, his eyes swinging momentarily away from the printing machine.

"DAMMIT IT, pay attention, Gabe," Fred yelped in pain, as his finger was trapped under the heavy print bed.

"Better go," Margaret whispered, ushering them outside, "why don't you walk with me to see Billy at the bake shop?"

Chatting together, the three young people walked along Chandler and Lizzie continued her education of Margaret. She pointed out barefooted children playing in the rubbish-littered alleyways and women dressed in rags standing forlornly in the doorways. They cut down backstreets, through a well-know snicket, and smelled the stink of outhouses. They even watched as two drunken sailors brawled loudly in a dusty yard, before emerging back onto Chandler and hearing Billy's voice calling his wares.

"Well, Miss News Gatherer," Lizzie chuckled, "now you've seen the real dockland."

"Golly Liz, I don't even notice half of that stuff when you're not with me," admitted Margaret.

"Wizzy," called Quon, coming back and taking his partner's arm, he pointed to his ear. "Wisten."

The girls understood. Billy was shouting something different today. Moving closer, they could see him quite plainly above the shoppers. His new top hat with the wide red, white and blue band bobbing precariously on his head, as he yelled his lungs out.

"HALF PRICE FOR NEXT TEN MINUTES, JUST FER POOR FOLK!" he screamed at the eager shoppers. "Not you, Mister Moneybags!" Billy pointed at a man in a beaver-skin hat. "Let that lady through!"

"The cheeky brat," Lizzie laughed, "how does he get away with it?"

"Because he's Billy," Margaret giggled, hurrying toward him.

"What is it, dumplin?" Lizzie asked impatiently as her partner again tugged on her arm. While she was trying to decide what he was pointing at, she saw Mister Sweeney intercept the man with the beaver-skin hat before he could get to Billy. Still watching, her eyes followed Quon's arm as it swung to the bake shop doorway where a huge bearded sailor filled the opening.

"Him smart, got protection," Quon grinned. "Davis gone *Falcon*."

Notepad resting on the now vacant barrel, Margaret wrote furiously as Billy whispered tidbits of dockland news in her ear. Once again he'd demonstrated his business brilliance. He had arranged with Lady Sutton and Gabriel to allow the street urchins to spread the Observer newssheets into every corner of dockland. Half the money they kept for themselves … money which they promptly spent on food from the bake shop, as they told their news.

"Miss Lizzie, I heard a rumour," he said, his face turning serious. "Jonas Crowther has a new man for council."

Margaret's face turned ashen. "That spells trouble."

"Not if you do what I tell you, lass," Lizzie grinned, wickedly. "Get those stories from your mother, and quickly!"

Chapter 28

Looking up at the local council office building standing starkly majestic and fearsome in the square, a shudder ran up Lizzie's spine as she remembered the courtroom inside. Terrible memories came rushing into her mind and she looked from the tall stone columns to the huge double doors closed up tight. Suddenly, the door opened and a charwoman not much older than she was stepped out.

"Come on," Lizzie murmured, grabbing Quon's hand.

Hearing running footsteps behind her, the startled cleaning lady pressed her body against the door in fear and tried to work the heavy latch to reopen the door, but it wouldn't budge. Turning at last, she realized her mistake as the two young people stood at the bottom of the steps and looked up at her.

"Sorry, miss, we're closed on Sunday," she announced, tremulously.

"Could we just take a little look inside," Lizzie purred, as they slowly came up the stairs and offered the girl a shiny new penny.

"Well, 'am not supposed to let yer in, but ...," she hesitated, her eyes fastened on the penny. "But ah will if you promise to leave in ten minutes," she added, snatching the penny from the girl's hand.

Brooms, buckets and mops littered the wide hallway as the partners stepped inside. "The courtroom's through there," she said, pointing to a huge door. "Council chamber's across the hall."

Dark panelling, a very high ceiling and a dimly-lit staircase rising to the upper floors, gave the place an eerie feeling as their every footstep echoed through the building.

Lizzie turned toward the courtroom.

"No, Wizzy!" Quon begged, grasping her arm and pulling her back.

Relieved that he'd stopped her, she swung to face the council chambers and pulled the heavy door open. Together they sniffed the stale air, grimacing at the odours of wig powder, sweat and pipe smoke. Slim shafts of sunlight knifing through partly opened drapes gave the room a medieval feeling. A portrait of King George hung on the marble chimney breast illuminated by a ghostly light. Outlined in the low light were eight chairs and the longest table they had ever seen.

She felt Quon's fingers again tighten on her arm. Her eyes roamed about the room, *So this is where the fight will begin.*

Then, as their eyes adjusted to the light, they noticed the neat piles of papers on the table. Straining to see, she read the heading: COUNCIL MEETING SCHEDULES. Snatching up one of the small piles, she pushed them toward Quon.

"Hide them in your shirt," she hissed.

Returning to the main hallway, the charwoman met them and ushered them back outside. Relieved to be outside once again, they felt the warmth of the sun on their heads as they made their way back along the river road.

Marveling at the array of different company and country flags flying from tall masts, they stopped on Dock Street to peer over the railing at the TLS wharf. There seemed to be some frantic activity going on as the *Restitution* was unloading grain.

Shading her eyes, Lizzie checked to see who was standing beside the figure of Charley as he sat on his cart watching the steam engine. She smiled to herself when she recognized Margaret, whose hand lay on the engineer's shoulder.

Quon's fingers instinctively felt for the papers in his shirt as they set off again.

Ignoring the shouts of Tom Legg at the coaching house, they hurried on, noticing a group of soldiers hassling an old sailor on crutches. He may have been crippled but he was plenty defiant as he cursed his tormentors, his courage not yet beaten by his cruel injuries.

"Hey," Lizzie shouted, "leave him alone."

Glancing in the direction of her voice, the uniformed young men looked surprised to see it was a girl but decided to disperse and quickly moved off, unsure of themselves as Lizzie stood her ground.

"Thanks, missy," the old man muttered, wobbling off toward the tavern.

Abe peered over his spectacles as the latch on his door rattled its noisy warning. "Been expecting you, young lady," he said, reaching for the small pile of papers sitting on the corner of his table.

Lizzie took her place at the table while Abe hunted through the papers, grunting sourly as he located the ones he sought.

"Nomination paper," he began, and one by one he identified the documents, grumbling to himself as he handed them across the table. Lizzie held each one so Quon could read over her shoulder. Finally, smoothing the last one with his hands, his eyes narrowed behind his wire-framed spectacles. "This document is to list the landowners represented and has to be signed by each one of them."

Lizzie scanned the sheet and nodded in answer to Quon's silent question. From his shirtfront, he produced the council papers and handed them to Abe. Seeing the heading, his spectacles dropped from his nose dangling from their chain.

"Where on earth did you get these from?" he asked, his hands beginning to shake as he flipped through the pages. "These are items to be discussed at the next council meeting."

"We borrowed them, didn't we, dumplin?" Lizzie giggled. "Read them and give us your opinion."

Shoulders hunched, a tiny drip of excited spittle balanced on his lip, the old man became totally engrossed in the documents, hardly noticing his visitors leaving.

Quon closed the creaking old door and glanced up at his partner. Their eyes met for a moment, each deep in thought, before setting off toward home.

ৠᐧᗱ

Somewhere in Waltham Forest, Jeb grinned as he surveyed the subjects of his happy errand. Jessy and the three older children— Abel and the two inseparable twins, Tommy and David—rode ahead behind their gypsy guide, mounted on their own sure-footed ponies. The rest of the children rode pillion, each strapped tightly in front of six gypsy riders. Their laughter and singing rang through the forest as the strange cavalcade made its way toward London.

ৠᐧᗱ

"Have you heard the news, lass?" Joe called as he walked in. "The *Golden Lady's* on her way in."

"Is Patrick with 'em?" she asked expectantly, eyes sparkling.

"Ah sure hoy would be thinkin he would be now," Mick answered, "it's yer birthday, ain't it?" Mick winced as his wife's foot kicked him sharply under the table. "Moyt not be headin here though," he added sheepishly.

"Come on you lot, dinner's ready," called Martha, interrupting Mick when she realized his mistake and rattling the plates loudly in an effort to save the situation.

A smile began to spread across Lizzie's face. Glancing quickly at Quon's moving fingers, she whispered, "They're up to something, dumplin." She heard Ada and Martha talking about Willie staying over at the gypsy camp again. "When is he coming home?"

"Friday...."

Ada's answer was interrupted by the sounds of laughter and the rattle of Charley's transport. Sighing, Martha rose from her seat to dish up another plate as Charley stepped through the door, grinning sheepishly as Margaret followed him.

"Yer stayin for dinner, luv?" Martha addressed the girl.

"If I may?" she replied, blushing a little as she assisted Charley to his seat, then sat down beside him as the housekeeper slid a meal in front of each of them.

"Ah, ye've not finished unloadin that vessel, av yer now?" Mick asked.

Nodding between mouthfuls, the engineer glanced over at Margaret. Laying down her cutlery, she daintily wiped her mouth with her napkin. Her eyes fairly shone with admiration as she looked at the young man who was becoming such a special part of her life.

"He's a genius," she said, her hand reaching for his arm. "It's amazing, a revolution in the art of unloading grain. I stayed all afternoon watching."

Under the table, Quon's fingers were beating out a message and Lizzie saw the humour in his twinkling eyes.

"Stop that, you little monster," she grinned, nudging his shoulder.

Ada giggled, almost choking on her food.

"What did he say?" asked Margaret.

"Stuff he shouldn't be thinking!" Lizzie replied.

"Let 'em eat!" Joe growled, tapping his pipe on the fire grate.

Iron shod hooves were again heard in the lane, the garden gate banged and a tired, 'hello' floated through the open doorway.

"Mother!" called Margaret, leaping from her seat.

They hugged briefly before Lady Sutton moved to the chair that Mick had vacated, sitting down with a sigh.

"Mug of cool cider, m'lady," Martha gently coaxed.

Nodding, Lady Sutton smiled gratefully, her eyes flashing suddenly to the door as they heard Nathan's voice nearby.

"Bring them in lads, bring them in," he called to his drivers, who each carried several small, but obviously heavy bags in their arms. They went over to Lady Sutton and piled the bags on the table in front of her. The table creaked under the weight.

"Is it money, Mister Goldman?" asked Margaret.

"Not mere money, lass, they're gold sovereigns, every last one of them!" the trader declared, waving his cane at the table, "That's a measure of my efficiency, Lady Sutton. Your vessel has been docked, off-loaded and all the cargo sold for cash. Just one last account to be collected and I shall be back in one hour to take you home." Tipping his hat, he turned for the door feeling his importance growing. "And don't forget my ten percent commission, young lady!" he added, looking over at Lizzie.

"Nathan!" Lizzie's voice cut into the silence with a quiet insistence. "Yer doing it again."

"All right, all right," the trader growled, his shoulders sagging a little as Ada chuckled quietly in the background. "Five percent!"

"Nathan," Lizzie whispered, "one percent, or nothing."

"Damn it, yer a hard woman, Lizzie Short," he mumbled, stomping off down the stairs.

"Well, we had better get this money put away," suggested Ada.

"Mick help me. We put away, Wizzie," said Quon, picking up two of the bags and moving toward the back of the house.

"We'll have to sit down and work this out, but now isn't a good time," said Lizzie, looking at Lady Sutton, who was grinning giddily.

Toes tingling with excitement, Penny Sutton's blood raced through her veins as she watched her share of the money being put safely away. She felt young again, her life full of purpose. Glancing around the room she saw contentment in their faces—Joe's drooping eyelids as Martha slipped the smoking pipe from his hand, Ada and Mick quietly holding hands, Quon Lee's fingers tapping messages on

Lizzie's arm and her daughter looking adoringly at Charley. *This old cottage*, she thought to herself, *is a wonderful place.*

"Stop that!" Charley whispered to Margaret, pushing her hand away from his arm.

"Margaret are you annoying that man?" asked Lady Sutton, trying to look stern as everyone's eyes focused on the blushing engineer.

"Tell her Mick," Charley pleaded. "I'm a cripple, only half a man."

Quon's fingers went wild on the table, pounding out urgent thoughts to his partner, whose eyes flashed in Mick's direction.

"Sure and begorra yer more man than me, lad," the Irishman growled. "Ye've overcome every obstacle and yer the best dammed dockmaster on the Thames. What more do yer want?"

"To walk again," Charley said quietly.

"It doesn't really matter you know Charley," Lizzie whispered. "Sometimes the one you most respect is different." She turned to face Quon, affectionately wrapping her arm around his neck. "He might be short, fat and ugly like my dumplin ...." A ripple of laughter ran around the room as she lightly kissed his cheek. "He might talk with his hands and steal yer apple pie, but he's always there when you need him, and just maybe, Charley, Margaret wants to be that someone for you."

Quon's eyes never left Lizzie's face and making a fist, he punched it slowly into the air. "My Wizzy," he mumbled, his voice cracking with emotion.

Charley looked up at Margaret and saw the tears in her smiling eyes. He slowly reached out his hand. She took it, bringing it slowly to her lips and kissing it lightly. Charley went red as a beet-root but allowed Margaret to lower his hand until it was under the table. Looking at each other shyly, they squeezed and let go.

Sighing, Martha turned back to the fireplace, glancing at Joe fast asleep in his chair. Ada's chair screeched as she pushed it away from the table, announcing it was time they went home.

"Would you like me to tell you about the councilmen, Lizzie?" Lady Sutton quickly interjected.

"Yes, I really would," she replied. "Hold on a minute, I need pen and paper."

"I'll write it down, Lizzie," called Ada, hesitating at the doorway.

"I'd like to hear this, too, if I may, Lady Sutton."

"Sure and begorra, me also!" piped up Mick. Seeing her nod, they came back into the room. Mick made his way quickly over to their sleeping host. "Joe, you better wake up. I don't think you'll want to miss this!" he said, touching the old man on the shoulder, rousing him.

"First of all, I think it's time you all called me Penny," Lady Sutton announced with a chuckle, standing up and moving so everyone could see her. "In case you don't know, Lizzie has told me today that she wants me to run for the empty council seat. However, she voiced some concern that there would be great disapproval from the present, male members of the council. I have known these men for many years and what I am going to tell you now, should dispel these concerns!" She stopped and looked around the room briefly. "So, I'll begin with that brute Aurelius, you know him as Judge Harvey. Well, would you believe it, that pillar of society fought with the rebel Irish army against his own countrymen many years ago."

"Can you prove that?" murmured Lizzie. "When?"

"Forty years ago, he was twenty. His sister was so ashamed she gave me his papers to burn."

"And did you?" Lizzie whispered, already knowing the answer.

"Of course not, I was no fool, even at that young age," she grinned. "I kept them safely locked away, just in case!"

"Holy hell," exclaimed Ada, her hand flying to her mouth when she realized what she had said.

"You could ruin him," Charley added.

"Or control him!" Lizzie giggled wickedly.

"If you think that's bad," Penny continued, "just listen to what the admiral told my husband in a drunken moment."

"Which admiral?" asked Joe, now wide awake.

"William Thomas Jones, sir."

"Ahoy!" Joe grunted. "Yer mean keel-hauling Billy Tom?"

"Did you know that as a First Officer of the Royal Navy, he killed three young sailors," said Penny, her voice trembling slightly.

"Ah wor there, lass," the old mariner whispered, spitting into the fire in disgust as his memories flooded back. The fire crackled, sending a shower of sparks out onto the floor. "My back has felt the bite of that rogues lashes!"

Stunned by Joe's admission, everyone in the room stopped breathing as they looked from Joe to each other. Several hushed comments were exchanged and Lizzie went over to give him a hug.

"But did you know he did some pirating, also?" Penny continued.

"That was allowed on Spanish vessels," Joe muttered.

"But he attacked English merchant ships in the Americas!"

"Ye've no proof of that!" he retorted.

"Oh yes, I have!" Penelope Sutton purred. "Lord Walton and his ship disappeared, and that man wears Lord Walton's gold watch on his chain. He showed it to my husband."

"Damn him," Ada snapped venomously, as thoughts of her deceased first husband passed through her mind. Her pen scratched the paper fiercely. "He should be hung!"

"Not yet," said Lizzie in an ominous tone. "He might wish he were dead before I've done with him, though!"

"Why, what will you do?" Margaret's voice trembled.

Reaching for her hand, Charley smiled at her wryly mouthing the words, "You'll never know."

Margaret blinked, looking at him in dismay.

Lady Sutton smiled. She admired this girl from the streets of dockland who'd made her mark in this cruel world of deceit. London's waterfront was no place for the timid. She alone was responsible for turning Penny Sutton's life around—for teaching her that she could trust the dark-skinned gypsies and call working-class people her friends. Who would have thought it possible that Lady Sutton, daughter of Lord William Cross would ever, ever allow herself to work as a labourer. *And look at me now*, she thought, looking down at her stained hands.

Every day was a thrill in this newfound freedom. Penelope had at last become a real person, a woman with strong opinions, unafraid to express them. She'd seen the change in her daughter from the high and mighty rich girl, to one who cared for the welfare of others and enjoyed mixing with the fascinating people surrounding Lizzie and the TLS enterprises. She turned again to Lizzie as a thought flashed through her mind. "Daisy tells me it's your birthday on Friday."

The room went strangely quiet for a moment. Lizzie nodded, glancing at the old man who fidgeted nervously. A slow smile eased across her lips as Joe sat bolt upright in his chair puffing hard on his pipe. Martha stifled a gasp. Quon watched their faces, senses alert, his talking fingers hovering over his partner's hand.

Quick to react to this unexpected situation, Ada's nimble brain swept into action. *Only two more days to go*, she thought desperately looking over at her husband for help.

"Ah sure, you'll both be joinin us, Lady Sutton," said Mick. "We'll be wishing our Colleen a happy birthday around this table."

"A party?" Margaret squealed enthusiastically.

"No," Ada replied with a frown, "just a little cake Martha's making." Sighing, she dipped her pen in the ink pot. "Let's get on with this, I'm tired."

Penny apologized for the diversion and continued. "You may know of Arthur Miller. He ships wool to France and Spain."

"Holland," Charley corrected her, "same port Richard Byrd's timber goes and Patrick Sandilands' paper."

"Think again, young man," Penny chuckled. "They are escorted into the Mediterranean by French or Spanish gunboats and off-loaded at Estapona."

"Doesn't sound right to me," Charley mumbled. "Who told you that?"

"They both bragged about it to my husband on his deathbed, not realizing I was listening."

Voices sounded outside and one of Nathan's drivers appeared at the door.

Beggin yer pardon," said Wick, looking slightly embarrassed and snatching his cap from his head, "is her ladyship ready for home?

"You go ahead, Lady ... Penny, we'll talk to you tomorrow," said Lizzie. "Thanks for sharing your stories."

Saying their goodnights, the Suttons left but the room remained quiet as each seemed to have their own thoughts. Mick joined Ada at the table. With like minds, they looked across at Charley.

"Come on, lad," Ada whispered, "we know you don't believe Lady Sutton's story ... why?"

Scratching his head, Charley frowned. "Just isn't possible," he muttered, "they're not away long enough, although there's definitely something strange going on. Their ships ride very low in the water which has puzzled me. Must be damned heavy wool Miller's ships are carrying."

"Now would yer be thinkin that ther runnin liquor back to the Thames, lad?" asked Mick, watching the dockmaster shake his head.

"I don't think so. Davis checked 'em out, they come back empty."

Lizzie's eyes narrowed. She looked over at Quon and they locked eyes. The only sound in the room was the crackle of the fire. Ada noticed Quon's fingers gently touch Lizzie's hand and the almost imperceptible nod that passed between them.

Shrieking in alarm, Martha broke the silence as a log slipped from the fire sending a shower of sparks around her feet. Mick leapt to her rescue, kicking the log back into the fireplace before stomping out the burning embers on the mat.

"You tryin to burn the place down, lass!" Joe grunted, sleepily.

"Ee," she clucked, "it just slipped out."

A smile flashed across Lizzie's face, her fingers tapping the table in excitement. "Wait a tick, I've got it!"

"Got what?" asked Ada.

"I know what they're doing," replied Lizzie, her eyes turning cold and calculating. "They're exporting something. I'll get Tom Legg to watch 'em."

"Good idea, lass. Now, I'm going to bed ... I don't care about the rest of ye," Joe grumbled tiredly.

A glorious June sunset was settling over dockland as Ada, Mick and Charley stepped outside. The quiet of the evening was broken only by the lowing of cattle nearby and the distant sounds of a soothing gypsy fiddle. Saying goodnight to Charley, Mick and Ada clasped hands and started up Slaughter Lane.

"I miss Willie something fierce, Ada. When's he comin home?"

"Another day, love. I know, I miss him too, but he's having so much fun up at the gypsy camp it's like a holiday for him. It's so good for him to be with the other children and we see him often during the day." Then changing the subject quickly, she asked, "Do you think Lizzie guessed about our surprise party?"

"No, luv," Mick sighed, hopefully, "her mind's full up with these council matters."

Chapter 29

Sleep didn't come easily to Lizzie that night. Her mind twisted and turned thinking about future council meetings and the difficulties Lady Sutton would face. *I hope we're not getting her into something we can't handle,* she thought, turning over for the last time.

Waking to Martha's usual noises and early morning sunlight streaming through her window, Lizzie's nose picked up a vile aroma creeping in through her window. *Hog day at slaughterhouse!* she thought to herself, jumping out of bed and closing the window.

After breakfast, Lizzie and Quon were just leaving the house when Nathan's high-stepping grey pulled up at the cottage gate. Smiling broadly, he greeted them as Dan opened the buggy door.

"Get in, young lady," he ordered, unceremoniously.

She cocked an eyebrow, an unspoken question in her eyes as she stared at the trader.

"Dammit woman, get in," he growled, irritably. "I have things to show you."

Quon's hand gently urged her forward, his fingers sending a message on her back. As they settled into the soft leather seat, the buggy lurched forward.

The city was already awake as early shoppers went about their business, urchins scrambled hungrily through garbage, and sad faces stared out from behind curtained windows as they drove down Goat Hill.

Nathan tapped the driver's seat with his stick, a pre-arranged signal for the gypsy to turn into the labyrinth of alleyways, slowing to avoid the barefooted children who lived there.

"Why have you brought me here?" she asked, fiercely.

"You're going to see that Lady Sutton gets a council seat, aren't you? Well, this is what she's facing, my girl," Nathan snapped, waving his cane about as the buggy rumbled on even more slowly. "You're using her so you can try to help these people and she's going to get hurt."

Lizzie's back snapped up straight. Quon's fingers tightened on her arm. Lips quivering with an unspoken comment, she stared at the trader for a moment before answering. "So, Mister Goldman, you really care about Lady Sutton," she whispered sarcastically, "but you don't give a damn about these poor folk."

Nathan's shoulders sagged. Yesterday, Cousin Abe had extracted a promise from him to never tell her what he had found in the municipal rules of government. Apparently, it was landholdings that counted; there was no mention of age. It had been assumed that only men of substance and power would hold the seats—the law had never considered there would be a woman like Lizzie Short to emerge in dockland.

I have to tell her, he thought to himself. *There's not much time. The candidate and landholder's proxies have to be registered by the twelfth. Abe is worried sick that if Lizzie finds out, she'll want to take the seat herself.*

Face flushing, the trader shuffled uncomfortably in his seat. He had a decision to make and protecting Lady Sutton meant he had to break the promise to Abe. The buggy stopped at Dock Street, slowly merging into heavier traffic. It had become very warm and sweat was beginning to bead on his brow even before he noticed her staring at him.

"All right, all right!" he said aloud, gathering his wits. "Y-you can t-take the seat yourself," he said, falteringly.

"I CAN WHAT!" she gasped in astonishment, turning to face him. "Who told you that?"

"Cousin Abe found the loophole in the municipal documents. I promised not to tell you," he said guiltily.

The buggy rounded a corner, lurching violently. Not holding on, Lizzie slid forward and was thrown across the coach, landing on the surprised trader's lap. As Nathan's hat flew off, she flung her arms around his neck planting a kiss on the embarrassed man's forehead.

"Wizzy!" Quon gasped, his fingers going wild on her arm, as he helped her back into her seat.

"Hush," she whispered, then more loudly. "I'm going to face those bastards myself—we'll see how they like my brand of justice."

Unsure of himself, Nathan stared at the floor of the buggy for a moment. He'd broken his promise to cousin Abe, but then he'd done that many times before and they'd always remained friends. He shrugged his shoulders, smiling weakly and his moment of guilt and embarrassment quickly passed.

Dan moved the grey expertly through the heavy midday traffic, pulling into the curb opposite the busy Lancaster dock.

"Look, look," Nathan said urgently, pointing with his cane. "Millers are loading that vessel."

Following Nathan's direction, their eyes raked the dock where bales of raw wool were being hoisted aboard a dockside vessel. Two men were carrying the bales from a dray to the loading hoist. Lizzie glanced at Quon who shrugged his shoulders.

"What is it, Nathan?" she asked, suddenly growing more interested.

"Just watch, watch!"

Three more bales were loaded when a handcart was brought around to the side of the dray and eight men struggled to lift the bale it carried.

Quon's hand grabbed Lizzie's arm. "Wizzy, that bale too heavy."

Nathan's head jerked around in surprise when he heard Quon speak, but Quon had his hand on the door and before Nathan could say a word, the door was open and they were out on the street and running.

Watching them go out of view, Nathan realized they had seen it, too. He had achieved his intent. Tapping Dan with his cane, the buggy moved off.

Moving toward the quay, they used the skills remembered from earlier days on the streets, easily avoiding the posted guards, and eventually found themselves behind the warehouse by the Miller vessel. From their hiding place, they could see a heavy-loaded dray half hidden amongst the bales. Moving closer, they read the nameplate, *Benson's Foundry Products*. It meant nothing to them.

It was almost two in the afternoon when they finally headed back along the waterfront. Hunger gnawed at their stomachs, but their minds were too full to notice. One-Eyed Jack yelled at them from the government dock, giving Lizzie an idea. He was waving for them to come over.

"Is he in?" she asked the mariner.

"Aye lass, and mad as a tick on a dog's back," Jack grimaced. "He hates goin and leavin those lads now."

"What the hell do you want, woman?" Davis snarled from the rail above.

Lizzie ignored him and ran up the gangway. They found him standing by the cabin door, arms across his chest and scowling. His great bushy eyebrows almost covered his eyes as he glared at them. He turned away and stomped into his cabin.

"I should be back on the weekend, can't it wait?" he growled.

Ignoring him, she settled into her usual chair with Quon behind her. "What does Benson's Foundry make?" she asked.

"Cast iron, mainly cannon barrels. Why?"

Lizzie frowned. He watched the girl intently as she pulled at her bottom lip. He saw Quon's fingers move on her shoulder. He loved it when Lizzie got excited about something. You never knew what she was going to do next.

"What has he said?" he demanded.

"Have you ever searched Miller's wool ships?"

"Of course, many times!" Davis growled, leaping from his chair and stamping around the cabin.

"When they're on their way *out*?" she grinned, looking at him coyly.

Davis stopped in mid-stride and turned on her, his face twisting fiercely as he tugged on his beard. Slowly, he settled back in his chair, his eyes burning as he stared intensely at the young woman.

"Now that's a thought!" he hissed savagely, leaning toward her. "What do *you* want from this?" he asked suspiciously.

"The arrest papers ...."

"WHAT!" Davis bellowed, banging the table with his fist almost before the words left her lips. "You want me to give you the arrest papers?

"Yes, and scare 'em to death with yer ranting!" she added.

Davis was about to say something but he knew she was right. His respect for this girl knew no bounds but he didn't often show it. Drumming the desk with thick fingers, he stared at her. "If I find a hidden cannon, m'girl, I'll hang 'em."

"Hang 'em later. Hold 'em at Sheppey for now."

Mumbling under his breath, Davis stood up again and began to stomp around the cabin. *What the devil is she scheming?* he screamed silently at the wall before turning to glower at the girl again. "GO!" he roared.

"Ye've upset him again, lass!" Jack chided, as they went past him.

After dinner, Ada gently broached the subject of council. "Guess what I found out today," she said. "Richard Byrd and Arthur Miller are married to the Benson sisters, daughters of the big foundry owner. They are brothers-in-law!" She watched the girl's face as a wide grin appeared. "I thought that might help," she whispered.

"Help, luv?" Lizzie laughed. "It gets rid of two birds with one stone!"

Joe banged his pipe noisily on the fire grate.

"'Am not sure Penny Sutton can handle them rascals on the council, luv," he grunted, "I think ye'd be better off sendin a man."

Leaving her chair, Lizzie walked around the table, perching on the arm of his chair. They had been through a lot in the seven or more years since she had come to live with him. She knew what she was going to tell him would have a profound effect on him and she dearly wanted to soften the blow.

She slipped her arm around his shoulders and kissed the bald spot on top of his head. Everyone watched with bated breath.

"Yer right, Dad. I've changed my mind."

The bookkeeper's eyes jerked alert as a sinking feeling hit her still-sensitive stomach.

"I'm sorry Dad, but I'm going to take the seat myself."

Joe's pipe fell from his mouth shattering on the stones of the hearth. He turned to look up at her, a helpless expression on his suddenly pale, wrinkled face. "You can't, luv … yer-yer too young!"

Ada glanced across the table at Quon who was obviously hiding a grin behind his hands. "You little devils have found something out," she said, coming to her feet.

"Yes, we have," said Lizzie, her chuckle giving herself away. "And that's all we're saying about it for now."

The room erupted with noisy questions as everyone talked at once. Lizzie calmly got up and left the room.

Ada rounded on Quon as he moved to follow her. "Well, young man?" her voice pleaded.

Quon stopped and turned to face the family; stretching his short frame upwards, he seemed to grow taller. There was an air of confidence in his eyes as he grinned at them.

"My Wizzy is right. Quon will keep her safe. Don't worry, Glanpop, or Ada."

Stunned into silence, they watched as he also went to his room.

"He'd follow that lass to hell and back," Joe whispered as Martha handed him a new clay pipe already charged with tobacco. She lit a splinter and held it to the bowl as he drew in his breath.

"She's serious," Ada sighed, as troubled thoughts bounced around her head.

"An you lot might as well get used to it," Martha chuckled, "cos dockland is about to wake up. Them councillors have never faced anything like our Lizzie."

Lizzie lay wide awake watching the shadows creep across her bedroom wall. With the darkness came, at last, a calmness that enveloped her tired body and mind. She felt content with her decision and actually quite ready to take on the old male establishment.

The bellowing of cattle in the holding pens floated through her open window, mingling with the familiar stench of the slaughterhouse. *This is going to be fun,* she thought as sleep rescued her from her devilish thoughts.

Edward, her gypsy friend, stood watching that very cottage window. His pipe glowed in the twilight as he talked in undertones to the two men sitting on their heels in the grass.

"Watch her carefully boys," he muttered. "I got that awful gut feeling something's about to happen again."

When Joe and Mick appeared for breakfast, they found Martha singing an off-key rendition of the Yorkshire song, O*n Ilkley Moor Baht' At.*

"Can yer sing that in English, lass?" Joe grimaced sarcastically, as Quon brought his boots over to his chair.

"Ah sure, don't yer be listenin to him, me darlin," Mick grinned, "it be like angels singin." He paused to whisper behind his hand.

"Aye, angels with a toothache!" Seeing it coming, he hastily reached out and caught the piece of crusty bread Martha threw at him, scuttling around the table out of reach when she playfully came at him brandishing her wooden spoon.

"Ah'll give yer a toothache, yer cheeky Irish pimple," she grumbled, chasing him out of the house.

The upbeat mood continued through breakfast then Lizzie and Quon hurried down the street to the tailor's. Getting thirsty, they ran over to *The Robin's* water trough and got a drink. Hearing the wonderful rattle of Charley's steam engine a block away, they looked at each other and grinned.

Drays passed by with their grumpy, cursing drivers urging their horses into more effort as they struggled up the hill. Lizzie had to smile. *This is home*, she thought, grabbing Quon's arm.

Shading his eyes, Abe stared at the bustling docks puzzled why the *Falcon* had so hurriedly left on the early tide.

"Strange, mighty strange," he kept repeating to himself.

"What's strange?" Lizzie asked, coming up beside him.

"You are! Come inside, I need to talk to you. I need to visit the council offices and register that Sutton woman's claim to a seat," Abe growled, picking up a piece of official-looking paper and reaching for the inkpot and pen. "Full name of claimant," he read, his head lifting as he waited for an answer.

"Miss Lizzie Short," she replied, glancing over at Clara.

Abe's head jerked up violently, his spectacles falling off his nose and his pen falling to the table. "B-but," he stammered, "you can't!"

"Yes, I can and I will!"

Lizzie's voice held that familiar ring of determination he'd heard so many times before and he already knew it was fruitless to argue. He clenched his hands so hard to stop them shaking that his knuckles turned white. He recovered the pen and mopped up the splattered ink on the table.

Clara had also heard and her needle stopped in mid-stitch—the cold hand of fear grasping the back of her neck. *Council is a man's world*, she thought, daring not to speak. *They'll never allow it.*

Quon sent a message to her shoulder. She nodded gratefully and reached up to pat his hand. Abe followed the movement, glancing furtively at the stony-faced young man who served Lizzie so capably.

"Quon wants to know if you want us to do anything to help."

"Just go," Abe wailed, supporting his head in his hands. "Meet me at the council offices at two tomorrow."

"Abe very worried," said Quon as the door banged shut behind them. But Lizzie wasn't listening as she hurried ahead leaving him to catch up. *Me worried, too!* he decided, silently.

Even before they reached *The Robin* they could hear Tom Legg's voice above the laughter.

"COME ABOARD ME HEARTIES," his voice boomed when he saw them approaching, his tankard of ale sloshing foamy liquid as he held it high. A look of dismay spread across his face when Quon took the tankard from his hand and set it down on the next table.

Hands on hips, Lizzie glared at him. "You want to earn a penny ... or two?"

Nodding his head vigorously, Tom tried to focus on the girl.

"Lancaster Dock ... I want Arthur Miller watched," she said quietly, then seeing the stupid way he looked at her, she threw her arms up in frustration. "Oh forget it, yer drunk!"

Angry strides took her quickly away through the milling traffic with Quon again hastening to catch up. A few blocks later, she stopped at *The Print Shop* gasping for breath.

"The *Falcon* left this morning," Margaret informed Lizzie.

"How do you know?"

"Street boys told me."

Glancing over at Lady Sutton, Lizzie noticed for the first time the lines of worry and tiredness on her friend's face. The jump from being a lady to a working woman was taking its toll on this courageous woman ... and Lizzie knew something else, too. Walking across the room, she took Penny's hand.

"Stop worrying, luv," she whispered. "You don't have to face those rascals on council, I can do it myself."

"No, you can't," declared Gabriel, "you're only seventeen."

"I'm eighteen tomorrow."

"You're still too young. They won't allow it."

"I have Aurelius's letter," Penny sighed, reaching into her bag, "and remember the admiral's watch."

"I remember," Lizzie replied calmly, watching the letter slide onto the table.

Gabriel's hand reached for it.

"Leave it!" she snapped and Gabriel's eyes flashed with annoyance. Ignoring him, Lizzie continued thoughtfully. "Keep it for now. I don't want to take it today."

"Easy lad," soothed Fred quietly, seeing Gabriel was still smarting. Then he added, "Show Miss Lizzie our new edition."

Smiles soon replaced frowns as Gabriel laid the newspaper in front of the partners and the others watched the youngster's expressions. Gabriel had deliberately turned the page to Fred's latest cartoon, a caricature of life in dockland. Lizzie giggled at the picture, showing the council members huddled in a corner and a group of prosperous business men lined up carrying signs saying *Pick Me*. Over to one side stood a shabbily dressed woman with two young children hanging onto her torn skirt. She held a sign which read, *Sorry, it's my turn.*

"You've a wicked sense of humour, Fred," Lizzie giggled, but there was a tone of admiration in her voice.

"That might have been the cause for my undoing at the monastery," the printer admitted with a chuckle.

"It was our gain, lad," she said softly.

Quon moved closer to Lizzie and whispered, "Time to eat, Wizzy."

"Yes, I think it must be lunch time. I'm hungry, too."

Leaving them, they found Margaret outside chatting with the street urchins who were their delivery boys. Lined up and waiting quietly, they each accepted the small bundle of newspapers she presented to them. Tipping their hats, they hurried away to their designated area.

"Margaret teach boys very good manners," said Quon.

"She's trained them well," Lizzie agreed, slipping an arm over his shoulder. "That's how she gets her information ... just like we do!"

Up ahead they could hear Billy's voice as it bounced off the buildings. Across the street Quon noticed two ragged, young urchins intentionally bump into a top-hatted older man. He grabbed her arm to get her attention and they watched the flurry of action. Darting away, the youngsters, whom they had never seen before, easily avoided the man's swinging cane as they raced into an alley followed by the man's bellowed curses.

"There's no way out of there," Lizzie whispered, "we gor 'em cornered."

Walking to the entrance of the alley, they listened but could hear no sound nor see anyone in the shadows. Quon's eyes narrowed as he moved slightly forward. He knew every nook and cranny in these alleyways. The boxes, barrels and piles of garbage fell swiftly under his gaze. Then, moving with the speed of a striking snake, he leapt into one of the piles of stinking garbage. When he emerged, he was holding the squealing urchins by their collars and grinning.

"Drop 'em," Lizzie ordered.

Released, the two boys scrambled backwards, their eyes searching for an escape route. Knowing there was none, they stood close together and began to whimper.

"Right lads, hand it over," said Lizzie, holding out her hat.

Shaking with fright, they produced a purse, watch and chain, two silk handkerchiefs and a thimble. Smiling, Lizzie backed away with her booty-filled hat, leaving the menacing figure of her partner to guard the young pickpockets. She understood their plight and felt the pangs of hunger gnawing at her own belly. There was nowhere to turn for help—the street urchins were alone, fending for themselves. Society bore no responsibility for the youngsters and the law dealt cruelly with offenders when they landed in Judge Harvey's court.

Cold fingers of pain grabbed Lizzie's heart for the youngsters' plight as her eyes ran over their ragged clothes, pleading eyes and trembling thin bodies. Sighing, she decided to offer them a glimmer of hope, if they would accept it.

"Bring them along, Quon," she whispered, "we'll feed them first, then find them a job."

Nervous, suspicious glances passed between the two young pickpockets as they moved out of the alley, Quon's strong hands holding tight to their collars. Walking down the sidewalk toward the bake shop, Lizzie glanced at the booty in her hat ... purse, watch and handkerchiefs were normal, but what the devil was a thimble doing in a dandy's pocket.

Heading over to the lad's bake shop, the young miscreants were quickly fed and put to work sweeping the stable. When Billy and the two partners sat down to eat, Lizzie emptied the contents of her hat onto the top of the small barrel they were using as a table. There were coins in the purse and a gold ring with the engraved initials of A.P.

Billy grinned when he saw the same initials on the silk handkerchiefs. "They belong to Albert Potter," he laughed. "He's an artist ... paints pictures. He lives up there," he said, pointing to a rooftop garret across the street.

"The councillor?" Lizzie whispered in disbelief, her eyes following his hand.

"Yer want to meet him?" asked Billy, leaping to his feet, "cos here he comes!"

Striding across the cobblestone lane, Albert Potter cursed fluently to himself as he pushed through the shoppers. "BILLY!" he yelled, his goatee and waxed moustache twitching violently. "Who the hell's got my purse?"

"Cover that stuff up," Billy whispered. "He thinks I know everything."

Grinning, Quon sat down on the barrel.

Albert's short, slightly built frame moved pompously toward them. When he stopped, he flung open his black cape revealing a delicately embroidered waistcoat and white silk cravat. Standing with hands on hips, he glowered at the boy as shoppers watched.

Councillor Potter knew the bake shop lads well. He was hardly a stranger to their capabilities. Having asked them for help several times, he was often startled by their speed at locating his missing belongings when he absentmindedly left them on the waterfront.

His eyes strayed to the unfamiliar girl standing beside the Chinese lad. She was quite beautiful ... her arm resting affectionately over the boy's shoulder. *Quite unusual!* he thought. *Too young to be lovers surely ... but she would make an interesting subject.*

"Can I paint you, young lady?" he asked, his temper evaporating as he stepped closer.

Leaping from the barrel, Quon jumped between them, his eyes mere slits screaming a silent warning to the artist.

"Better keep yer distance, mister," Lizzie grinned, at the artist's startled expression. "Is this what yer looking for?" Her lithe young body stepped aside to reveal Albert's watch, purse and handkerchiefs.

Eyes wide with surprise, he examined the goods. "The thimble is gone," he said in a trembling voice.

In her pocket Lizzie's finger gently toyed with the missing object.

Opportunist streetwise instincts had told her the tiny object had great significance to the councillor.

"Was it valuable?" she murmured.

"Irreplaceable," he said sadly, "it brought me luck. It belonged to my grandmother." Shoulders sagging, he scooped up his possessions but his brash confidence had disappeared. Stumbling as he turned to go, he muttered, "I am a dead man!"

"I know, I know," Lizzie mouthed as Quon's fingers tapped on her hand as he went out the door. "Mister Potter is very superstitious!"

Glancing at his watch, Quon tugged on Lizzie's arm alerting her to the time ... two o'clock. She nodded, waving to Tom through the shop window before they disappeared into the crowd. Billy's voice slowly faded amongst the street noises.

ಬಗಿ

Standing with his back to the great oak door of the council offices, Abe watched as they appeared through the traffic. His knuckles turned white as his grip on the cloth bag containing his papers increased.

"Damned young fools," he moaned to himself, as they darted between drays.

Quon pushed on the heavy door and, hinges creaking, it opened into a spacious hallway. Two soldiers standing near the mutton-chop-whiskered clerk, glanced suspiciously at them.

"What do you want?" asked William Toppit, the clerk, sneering at the tailor.

"A moment of your time, sir," Abe replied, "to register a claim to the vacant council seat."

Silence struck the clerk and his jaw dropped. He could hardly believe his ears. His eyes twitched nervously as they studied the old man and his two companions. He'd worked for many years at this job and was deemed an expert on the rules. Landholdings were the criteria for members of council and a vote of acceptance from sitting members was absolutely necessary. There would be hell to pay from Judge Harvey and Admiral Jones if this application were to qualify; they would move heaven and earth to block the approval of a new member who was not to their liking. He knew tempers would flare if their personal selection was to be ignored.

The clerk quaked inwardly. This was his worst nightmare come true. Hands shaking, he checked the papers Abe offered. The land-holdings and proxies were legally signed, there was no way this applicant could be denied a seat on council with the holdings of Lady Sutton, Minnie Harris and the TLS company backing her ... *her*, yes it was definitely a her ... Lizzie Short, it read.

Who is this upstart who dares to make this claim? he thought to himself. A rush of air escaped his lips and his long bony finger shook uncontrollably when he pointed at Lizzie's name on the application. "Th-this is a w-woman's name," he stammered, sweat beading on his forehead. His spectacles slipped from his nose, clattering noisily onto the desk. William Toppit was speechless, a state of affairs which did not often happen to this particularly outspoken clerk.

"Get on with it, sir," pressed the tailor, skillfully using his advantage.

A grin passed between the two soldiers as they hurried to the door. This would make quite a story.

Pen shaking, Mister Toppit signed the documents, whispering almost inaudibly. "The meeting is on Monday the twenty-ninth of June ... sir."

Chapter 30

Docklands' jumbled street noises greeted Abe and the young partners as they stepped out onto the curb outside the Council Building. The heavy oak door banged shut behind them in an act of finality. Clutching the cloth bag to his chest, the tailor, muttering to himself, shuffled off without a backward glance.

Eyes narrowing, her jaw set grimly, Lizzie watched the frail old man disappear amongst a group of inhabitants. The first step in her plan was complete and her fight had now begun.

Quon's silent fingers touched her elbow, their eyes met for a moment and her arm slipped into his.

"We'll win, dumplin, we'll win," she muttered, a trace of a smile bending her lips as she pulled him playfully along.

Heavy traffic lined Dock Street in the afternoon sunshine and drivers yelled impatiently at snorting horses trapped in the throng. Crossing the street, they were stood watching a three-masted schooner manoeuver slowly into its berth at the TLS dock when Nathan Goldman's buggy pulled up beside them.

"So young lady," he frowned, "it's all over dockland."

"What is?"

"A wicked rumour."

"What rumour?"

"That you've registered your claim to a council seat," Nathan grinned. "Causing quite a stir amongst the gentry, it is."

"It ain't finished yet, lad," she said, with a shrewd grin, her eyes watching Quon's hands.

Shouting was heard from across the street and Lefty drew their attention. "Hey there, Mister Goldman," he yelled, shuffling through the traffic. "Missus Mick wants yer in the office."

"Missus Mick!" Nathan chuckled. "I'd better be off then."

A clock began striking three as the partners hurried up Baker Lane. Up ahead they saw Oly walking wearily ahead of his pony, as they turned into the yard.

"Miss Lizzie coming!" the boy yelled at the baker.

"Damn!" Clem Radcliff muttered, racing to hide the giant fruitcake while Bill rolled one of the big doors shut. "We nearly got caught, Billy boy!"

"Only one day to go," the baker groaned, as he watched Lizzie and Quon stroll into the yard. "Yer ready for Bill's apple pie are yer, lad?" he called.

The dark eyes of the young Portuguese lad glowed with pride as they rested on his idol. He knew the secret that was waiting for her on her birthday and he hugged her tightly.

"Them council men will never give their approval," Bill said worriedly.

Connie Johnson came over and sat watching them eat, noticing the sly glances that passed between them. *Those young'uns have got a plan*, she thought to herself. *God help them council men.*

Walking home up Goat Hill, Lizzie's thoughts were racing. *There has to be a way to help them*, she puzzled silently, as her eyes caught sight of three battle-scarred old mariners sat in the grime-blackened doorway of a disused warehouse talking to a group of neighbourhood children.

Quon's hand caught her arm as they stood and listened to a grey-bearded sailor as he told tales of adventure in foreign lands and rousing battles at sea. He respectfully touched his cap with his pipe stem as Lizzie passed and she noticed the hook he had in place of a left hand. Walking away, her partner's hands began twirling furiously. Reaching out, she stopped him.

"Talk to me, luv," she said, quietly.

He stopped. "That could solve big problem in dockland."

"The old and the young enjoying each other's company?" Lizzie mused quietly. As they crossed Slaughter Lane to the cottage, she stopped. "Now that would be a new idea, dumplin."

At the dinner table, subdued chatter and furtive glances passed between Ada and Joe. Quon's spoon rattled noisily onto his plate and his eyes met Lizzie's.

"So what are you lot up to?" she asked, glancing around.

Ada's head jerked up. She needed an excuse and quickly. Fortunately, luck provided a diversion with a light tap on the door and the entrance of Nathan.

"I have a message for you, Mister O'Rourke," he said, strutting over to stand behind Lizzie's chair. "There's a vessel just entering the Thames. The captain wants to meet you at three o'clock tomorrow in the rag yard."

"You'll need Lizzie there?" Ada interceded quickly.

Nodding, Lizzie pushed her chair away from the table. "I'll be there," she muttered, pulling on Quon's arm as he followed her out of the room.

That was brilliant, Nathan," Ada whispered. "I was wondering how we were going to manage it."

Eyes wide, the trader stared innocently around the room.

"But it's true," he said softly.

"Ee by gum," Martha bleated, "will that spoil everythin'?"

"Not if his name is Patrick Sandilands," Nathan laughed, softly. "We have her fooled all right; she's totally absorbed in planning some nasty surprises for our councilmen."

By the time the cottage lapsed into darkness, the gypsies had already taken up their positions outside. The smoke from their pipes wafted gently into Lizzie's open window. Her eyes flicked open as her nose picked up the strong aroma of gypsy tobacco.

"There are gypsies close by," she thought to herself, *"but why?"*

A streak of moonlight hit her window and her senses leapt into action. Her bedroom door creaked slightly as if being opened.

"Wizzy? You awake?" a voice softly hissed. "Gypsies outside."

"I know," she whispered back, as Quon's shapeless figure draped in his long white nightshirt was illuminated in the doorway. "Go back to bed, dumplin'."

Calls of 'happy birthday' greeted her as she entered the kitchen for breakfast the next morning.

Joe winked at her then pulled her onto his knee, his arms wrapping tightly around her tiny waist. "Lordy, you've gone and growed up on your old dad, lass."

Ada and Mick arrived. He was carrying a red rose he'd just picked in the garden. He blushed a little, tussling Lizzie's hair affectionately, with a work-hardened hand, as he self-consciously presented it to her.

The noisy meal went quickly and as if on cue everyone began leaving for work as the Grims arrived for Charlie.

Ada stopped to give Lizzie a hug at the gate. "Rag yard at three o'clock, my girl, now don't you get too busy and forget!"

Lizzie nodded, hugging her back. Joe waved before disappearing down Goat Hill and they set off toward the tailors.

"Anything new happening?" she asked, finding Abe on the curb gazing intently down the street.

"That dammed machine on your dock," Abe growled, "it never stops. Doesn't it ever need feeding?"

"Feeding?" Lizzie echoed, glancing at her partner who had begun to snicker.

Scowling angrily, Abe stared at the girl. Being from a different era, he had no concept of the effect these steam engines were going to have on dockland. As far as he was concerned they were noisy, vile-smelling beasts. His attention was suddenly averted by Clara's voice calling to him as she trotted across the street with his breakfast tray.

"Don't forget we need Miss Lizzie at two, sir," she whispered, as she squeezed past the tailor into the shop.

"Yes, yes," he agreed, "we need you at two this afternoon."

"Why?" asked Lizzie.

Ignoring the girl's question, Abe turned and disappeared into the store, banging the door behind him. Lizzie and Quon stared at the door for a moment. She shook her head and began to laugh.

"Come dumplin, we'll let him eat in peace. Let's go see Lady ... I mean, Penny and Margaret."

They had only travelled a block when a white-aproned shopkeeper stepped from his store, blocking their path, Quon moved ahead protectively, his eyes blazing fire at the man.

"Easy lad," said the man. "I'm a friend. I've given you my proxy lass, but I'll bet they never let you sit on council."

"Let her pass, you oaf," a loud voice snarled from the window of the shiny black coach that had pulled up beside them. She noticed the large "M" emblazoned on the door just before the coachman's whip cracked an inch from the storekeeper's nose, totally unnerving the poor man who leapt to one side. The door swung open and a big barrel of a man dressed in top hat and a black cape over a fancy suit, eased himself from the coach.

"I'm Arthur Miller, Miss Short," he sneered, doffing his hat with a flourish. "I'm one of the councillors who will be voting you off council!" Feet astride and hands on hips his eyes darted over her entire body examining her from head to toe ... obviously relishing his part. "Wallace Dawson would not have stood for this!" he said contemptuously.

Quon jerked to attention, his hand touching the scar on his chest from the highwayman's ball. Glancing at his partner, Lizzie saw the revengeful look cloud his eyes.

"Not yet," she hissed in a whispered voice, gripping his arm.

"Perhaps I might vote you in," his strong voice thundered sarcastically, "if you strapped me to a cannon!"

"That could be arranged, sir," Lizzie replied coyly, looking him square in the eye.

Colour draining from his face, Arthur Miller backed away, a cold chill running up his spine. This lovely young woman was anything but ordinary and she frightened him, although he would never admit it. He had heard stories about Lizzie Short for some time and now he felt firsthand the power that others had merely spoken of. Turning, he climbed quickly back into the coach, his hand shaking as he sat down and removed his hat, before slamming the door.

The wool merchant's fears were justified ... his nightmare had only just begun.

Miller's ship, *My Belle*, that so innocently sailed from the Lancaster dock the night before, had been seized and impounded only hours before and was on its way back to the government wharf with Davis' crew in control.

Captain Davis had done his work well in the wild waters of the English Channel, surprising *My Belle*'s crew even before the sun broke the horizon. Grinning wolfishly, he trained the *Falcon*'s guns on the Miller vessel, boarding and searching her under protest of its officers.

When First Mate, One-Eyed Jack, reported the discovery of two cannons hidden amongst the wool cargo, his face contorted with such rage and contempt he frightened his own crew. But this time, he relished his part, screaming treason in the faces of *My Belle*'s crew.

Underway again and heading for home, Davis stood at the helm and a feeling of national pride swept over him. He had not often had the opportunity to be involved in this great war but as he looked out across the sea toward France where Napoleon was continuing his lengthy battle against the world, he hoped this small effort might make the war a bit shorter.

His face set in a fierce scowl, he patted the chest pocket of his greatcoat. Safely nestled inside that deep pocket were the arrest papers and the confession of the *My Belle* captain. He was deeply aware that his next actions held the key to the future of two very powerful people.

Meanwhile, unaware of Captain Davis' quick success and early return, Lizzie and Quon made their way to *The Print Shop*, a plan forming in their minds.

They were all having a lunch of cider and sandwiches as Lizzie and Quon arrived. Invited to join them, they accepted a small drink and began to explain the plan they had been discussing.

"Could I have that letter now, Penny?" she asked.

"Can you copy it, Fred?" she asked, when Penny handed it to her.

Fred laid his sandwich aside and, with dancing eyes, reached for the letter. First, he rubbed the paper slowly between his fingers then, bringing it to his nose, he sniffed tentatively. They all gathered around to watch in fascinated expectation. Vigorously shaking the inkpot, Fred grinned up at them, then drew a knife and prepared a fresh quill. First, sweeping his arm across the table, he cleared it of any offending dust then, he selected a piece of paper from his shelf and lay it on the table smoothing it out. Looking totally relaxed and enjoying himself, he began to write a perfect duplicate of Judge Harvey's signature. Sitting back, he carefully blotted any excess and applied dusting powder, blowing it gently away when he was absolutely sure it was dry. Turning both sheets so everyone could see, they looked at the two signatures. It was a perfect match!

"Now do the whole letter, Fred," Lizzie urged, excitedly.

He was halfway through the task when the clock on the wall chimed a quarter to the hour and Quon tapped Lizzie's arm to remind her of their appointment at Abe's. An anxious expression crossed her face.

"Don't worry," Penny assured her, "we'll take care of the letter."

Ten minutes later, they walked into Abe's shop.

"Come in, my dears," a noticeably more pleasant Abe called to them when he heard the bell jingle and saw Quon peering around the door frame.

Going inside, they saw four tailors' mannequins standing stiffly at attention by the side of the worktable. Lizzie's eyes sparkled and a smile lit up her face when she saw the dresses. Fashionably cut and beautifully tailored, their deep rich colours made her gasp.

"Ther you are, lovey," sang Clara, coming out from behind the screen. "All finished!"

"Who are they for?" Lizzie murmured in envy.

"They're yours, of course," Abe growled, "I will not have you dressed as a pauper at those council meetings."

Squealing with delight, Lizzie moved closer and caressed the high-quality cloth. Clara took her by the arm and led her behind the screen where Lizzie saw more clothes. She began to undress and Clara helped her into a new petticoat, holding one of the new dresses ready. She indicated the highly polished black boots and matching cape and helped Lizzie into them. Turning to walk out from behind the screen, Clara grabbed her arm.

"The hat, don't forget the hat!" hissed the seamstress, fussing with the felt, feather and lace creation she had made. "Now let's go to the mirror, shall we?" she said excitedly, giving Lizzie a little push.

This was not the first time Abe and Quon had witnessed Lizzie's transformation, but it had been several years ago and this metamorphosis left them completely speechless.

Walking over to Abe's full-length mirror, even Lizzie couldn't find the words. She stared at the image in front of her turning this way and that. Her face lighting up with more pleasure at each turn. Finally, she turned to face them.

Suddenly, the familiar sound of Dan's voice rang through the air as carriage wheels rattled to a stop outside. They heard Nathan's voice almost at the same instant as he entered the shop.

Lizzie saw the movement of Quon's hands and quickly turned her back to the door as he hid behind one of the mannequins. The dressmaker noticed their antics but had no time to question them as Nathan strode toward them.

"Have you seen Lizzie, cousin? Ada said she was intending to pay you a visit." His voice tapered off to a whisper when he saw he had interrupted one of his cousin's high-class female clients.

"Sorry madam," he whispered humbly, taking a step backwards, his eyes still flitting about the room. "I can wait."

Abe grinned through blackened teeth and a stifled chuckle rose in the dressmaker's throat.

"Meet my new Wizzy, Naten!" Quon laughed, stepping from his hiding place.

Mouth drooping with surprise, the trader watched the figure slowly turn to face him. "My goodness, is it really our Lizzie? Y-you are beautiful ... absolutely stunning, my dear."

"You were looking for me?" she purred, beaming broadly.

Yes, that familiar look of impish devilment was in her eyes, yet this was no longer their Lizzie. This was a seductive and confident young woman who had no idea why they were looking at her with such amazement.

Blinking, Nathan shook himself free from her spell. "Ada needs you in the rag yard immediately and I am going that direction," he said, glancing at his watch.

Even though she was beginning to swelter, she asked, "Can I keep the dress on?"

"No, certainly not!" replied the tailor, "they're for council meetings, not rag yards."

Pouting, the girl quickly changed back to her other clothes. Casting one last impish glance at the frowning tailor, she winked at Abe and Clara then followed her partner out of the store.

"Who did you say we were meeting?" she asked, as the buggy moved off into traffic. A twinge of suspicion crept into her brain as she glanced at her partner who was surprisingly quiet. Nathan merely looked out the window, ignoring her.

Passing the TLS offices, they swung into the rag yard, strangely empty and quiet. Puzzled, Lizzie glanced at Quon. He shrugged his shoulders. The buggy suddenly picked up speed and tore into Drover's Lane, bouncing on past the stable buildings to the gypsy camp. Glancing again at her partner, she noticed he was holding on tightly but he had a rather puzzled expression on his face.

੪੭੪੪

Watching the arrival of Nathan's carriage from their makeshift seats in the centre of the camp, Joe felt a large lump form in his throat and his heart began to pound. Behind him stood several of the men who had been instrumental in shaping Lizzie's life. Mick, the jovial Irishman, Jeb, the gypsy leader, and Patrick Sandilands, the giant, red-bearded Scot. Gathered around them were the smiling faces of dockland characters whose lives had been altered by his adopted daughter. Joe could barely contain himself. He was so proud of her and yet deep down he didn't want her to ever grow up.

The giant cake Clem and Bill had baked and Connie had beautifully decorated, rested on the top of a huge barrel guarded from the many playing children by Connie and Ada.

A group of fiddlers burst into a rousing tune as the buggy slowed to a stop. Patrick stepped forward and with a rather large flourish opened the buggy door as everyone screamed 'Happy Birthday'.

Lizzie squealed and, seeing Patrick, jumped into his waiting arms as the others surged forward.

There were crippled sailors employed in the rag sheds, dockworkers, and brewery men, along with Angus and John Watson and, Lady Sutton waving happily from under her colourful parasol, while holding tightly to Gabriel's arm.

"Happy birthday, lassie," Patrick murmured, kissing her cheeks.

"Cut the cake first, luvy," Connie Johnson urged, taking her arm and leading her through the crowd. "The lads are hungry!"

"Just a little cake, is it!" she said coyly, winking at Ada as she looked down at the huge cake. Connie handed Lizzie a large knife and the girl reached for Quon's hand, pulling him closer.

"I think Quon should celebrate his birthday today, too," Lizzie announced. "It's about time he had a party even though no one knows when his birthday is!"

The cheer that rose told them everyone agreed. With both of their hands on the knife, they cut the first slice together. Leaving the rest of the cutting to the women, Lizzie and Quon made their way over to Joe, greeting friends and workers as they moved through the crowd.

Joe wiped his eyes and loudly blew his nose. Then she was standing in front of him looking radiant, and so grown up. Joyfully he wrapped his arms around her. *Our little dockland princess has come of age*, he thought. "Get Quon to take you home, luv," he said softly, swallowing hard. "There's another surprise for you there."

"Now?" she asked, looking at him inquisitively, suddenly thinking that he was looking very old today.

He nodded, trying to smile as he waved his hand to dismiss them. Quon took her arm and eased her away.

At the gate, they stopped and looked at each other. Without a word, they began to run. Nearing the cottage, they stopped momentarily noticing several gypsies standing outside the yard. Then they heard high-pitched laughter and saw Margaret and Jessy coming from the garden.

"They're here, dumplin!" she cried, gathering up her skirt and breaking into a run again.

Throwing open the gate, she was about to turn toward the house when Jane saw her from the garden.

"Mummy, Quon!" she squealed, leaping to her feet and running toward them. Sweeping the still-small girl into her arms, Lizzie surveyed the scene as several more of the children came to hug her, wishing her a happy birthday.

"Oh my, just look at you all dressed up! What a wonderful surprise you have brought me, children. I think some of you have even grown since we last saw you," she exclaimed, swallowing hard to keep back the tears. She flopped down onto the grass amongst them and was immediately swamped as eager young bodies smothered her with love.

Margaret sighed and looked over at Jessy, a puzzled expression on her face.

"Don't even ask," Jessy whispered, "just believe. Those children belong to Lizzie Short."